The Adventures of
NATHANIEL SWUBBLE

"We name our fondlings in alphabetical order. The last was S, -- Swubble, I named him. This was a T, -- Twist, I named him."

When I first saw this proud boast of Mr Bumble's in print, I was jealous that Mr Charles Dickens had written a whole book about Oliver, but had mentioned me, Nathaniel Swubble, only once.

Then, over the years, people asked me the same questions over and over again. How, when he was brought up in such degrading surroundings, did Oliver speak and act like a young gentleman? Why were such harsh conditions in force when Oliver was nine years old, when the New Poor Law of 1834 could only have come into force when he was a little older? Who was the man in the white waistcoat and how did he die? What induced Oliver to ask for more?

Realising that I knew many things which Mr Dickens, and even Oliver, did not, I determined to write my own story, from may abandonment at the workhouse gate to the age of thirteen or so.

Here is that story. It answers all those questions about Oliver and more, but, above all, it is the story of my own childhood, of the early lives of my friends, Felicity Fidget, Georgina King, Paul Quince, Virtue Verily and Tom Wilkins, and the inhabitants of the town and workhouse of Myddlington.

Other books by the same author

To be published later in 2007

The Other Side of the Coin

A story of life in a country village
in the years after the Napoleonic Wars

ISBN 978-0-9555497-0-0

Printed and bound in Great Britain by Heronsgate Print Ltd, Basildon, Essex.

HOUSE
PUBLICATIONS

Published by InHouse Publications
Rose Farm, Top Road, Wingfield, Diss, Norfolk. IP21 5QT

www.swubble.co.uk

THE ADVENTURES OF

NATHANIEL SWUBBLE

LILIAN SPENCER

HOUSE
PUBLICATIONS

CHAPTER ONE

While George the Fourth, bloated and richly clothed, sat on the throne in London, some seventy miles away I, Nathaniel Swubble, lay hungry and covered in a sack at the gate of the workhouse in Myddlington. Surprisingly, George, at the apex of society, and I, at the base of the pyramid, shared one thing in common – those in-between resented our claim to support from the public purse.

The date was January, Eighteen hundred and twenty-four and the weather, thank God, was clear, with the first weak rays of the rising winter sun falling upon me. Complaints against the charge my arrival placed on the parish rates were voiced immediately by the man who discovered me.

"Porter! Porter!" Mr Bumble yelled at the top of his voice, at a volume which would have done credit to a town crier. For a few seconds he paused in his shouting to smash his staff several times against the railings. Then, worried that this might damage the cane, which he saw, along with his staff, as on a par with Black Rod's staff, a bishop's crozier or a field marshal's baton, he resumed shouting even more loudly.

"Jack Star, if you value your job, open this gate at once!"

Later, Jack Star always claimed that, when he did open the gate, the beadle, whose ample girth reflected his ample diet, stood there, red in the face, stamping his surprisingly small foot.

The porter, in contrast, was tall and lean, with a pale complexion which belied his years at sea. He limped forward, touching his cap with a flourish, which, while pleasing Bumble, indicated to any old soldier or sailor in the gathering crowd that he was saluting out of respect for the office and contempt for the man.

"You're always early, sir, but this is a full two hours before your usual time." Again, while the porter pacified the beadle, he indicated to those around that Bumble invariably postponed the start of the day until he had consumed a hearty breakfast.

"It's not me, man, has wanted to come in. I was hurrying by to the farm for half a dozen newly laid eggs and a can of fresh milk when I happened to glance down and see this bundle here."

"It's a baby, sir!" Jack exclaimed in amazement.

"Even a bachelor can recognise a baby. Pick it up, man." Frustrated at

1

the delay in obtaining his breakfast, Bumble shook his head to confirm to the crowd that, in his opinion, the porter was not only slow, but also stupid.

Quite a crowd had gathered in minutes, proving that, in local affairs, the telegraph still cannot spread news as fast as the beadle's shouting, neighbours knocking on each others doors and windows or the sound of feet scurrying to a mysterious commotion.

As Jack Star picked me up, Bumble sniffed fastidiously and delicately touched the edge of the sack to reveal my face. Mr Sowerberry, the undertaker, who had pushed his way through to make a business-like examination, reluctantly announced that I was alive, but hung about just in case the situation changed.

From the crowd there were mutterings.

"Poor little mite!"

"'Oo could do such a wicked thing?"

"It's a miracle 'e's still alive!"

"'E'll need more than a miracle to survive in there!"

The sack Jack Star threw down to replace with his warm scarf was examined minutely and even smelt and turned inside out for any clues identifying its last owner.

"It's a boy!" the porter announced. Those around who badly wanted their own baby boy to carry on the family name and trade expressed surprise that anyone should abandon a male child. Girls were a different matter.

Bumble, as usual, had the answer. "Of course it's a boy. Ain't they always the most troublesome?" Remembering the many snow balls, rotten apples and the conkers which had struck his cocked hat and threatened his dignity by knocking it forward over his face, he added, "All boys is bad 'uns."

After a brief pause, he asked, "Ain't there no message saying, 'Feed and clothe this little parasite at public expense until he's old enough to go orf and enjoy hisself?'"

"Nothing like that, Mr Bumble."

"Course there ain't," Bumble agreed, as usual changing his argument in mid-stream to be on the winning side. "Don't want to leave no address to send him back, do they?"

Mistaking the concerned looks on the face of the people around as pity, rather than resentment, the beadle smiled encouragingly and asked, "Ain't

2

there no Christian lady or gent has could give the little mite a warm gown?" It would always be possible for Mrs Corney to sell it later and share the profits with him.

The wife of a prosperous tradesman gave her daughter instructions to hurry off home and bring the old shawl, which she no longer needed and had put aside for the poor. Mr Sowerberry tutted in disapproval and there were angry murmurings in the crowd.

One woman, in well worn clothes, held up her own baby for all to see. "'Ere's my child with 'ardly a stitch on 'is back and 'is father works from dawn to dusk to keep us in food and clothing and keep a roof over our 'eads."

Her sister, equally poorly dressed and with a baby in her arms joined in. "It comes to something when honest folk is passed over." Pushing her way through, she shouted, "'Ere, let me leave this one at the poorhouse gate to get 'im fed and clothed on the parish."

When the girl ran up with the warm shawl, it was immediately snatched and replaced with a thinner one and so on through the crowd until I was left with a grubby, tattered and threadbare piece of blanket, which no one else wanted.

"Mr Bumble," the porter said, "We need to get this child into the warm."

The beadle looked less convinced, but gave his approval. Seeing Bumble would not take me and, in any case, not being the sort of man who would place a child in the beadle's care, Jack Star held me firmly in one arm and shut the gates with the other hand. They closed on mutterings of how the feckless always seemed to come off better than the honest, hardworking poor.

"It'll need feeding." As he so often did, Bumble stated the obvious. He acted as though he had to feed me from his own pocket. In a low voice, to convey that all these female matters were distasteful to him, he added. "There must be a woman in the workhouse who can wet nurse him. It'll cost seven pence a week to farm him out to Mrs Mann."

Whispering, "Now you know what to expect," in my ear, the porter carried me into the workhouse and up the stairs towards the infirmary. He was met at every turning of the stairs and every landing by women gathered from the far corners of the workhouse. They pressed around me, their skirts hitched and their sleeves rolled up. Their wrinkled hands, and the knives, coarse soap and brooms they held in them, told of the kitchens, steaming coppers, dolly tubs, laundries and floors they had deserted to come and

3

witness my arrival.

"Make way there, you women," Mrs Corney, the workhouse mistress ordered, using her elbows to good effect.

Simultaneously, Old Sally achieved the same end silently and unnoticed. "'Oo's 'e look like?" the old nurse demanded, voicing the curiosity of all, including Mrs Corney.

"'Ow can 'e look like anyone at a few hours old?" Jack Star mocked. "'E's more like a skinned rabbit than a 'uman."

Shaking their heads and smiling at the ignorance of a mere man, the women pressed round, noting my eyes, nose, ears and mouth and comparing them with this loose woman or that man with a roving eye. Only reluctantly, they gave up.

"You need the Ma and Pa next to it to be sure who it favours," Mrs Corney decided. "Where's that useless beadle? Has he checked on all the women about to have babies? No, he wouldn't have thought of that, would he?"

Strangely, the beadle was doing just that, having been provided with a list by his mother, whom he had rushed home to tell. While Mrs Bumble seldom left the house, gossips came to her like wasps round jam.

"'E's 'ungry." Old Sal pronounced at last.

"Ain't I been saying just that?" the porter demanded, exasperated by the delay.

"Give it here," the workhouse mistress demanded. "You, Jack Star, get yourself back to your post. Never has been any place for a man in the women's infirmary."

Without more ado, Mrs Corney marched with me upstairs and pushed open the infirmary door. The only occupants of the long, gloomy room were an old lady, almost blind and deaf, and the young woman – hardly more than a girl – she was comforting in a rough kind of way.

"There, there, my love. Gawd knows best. 'E took 'im and we don't 'ave no choice in the matter." Sensing Mrs Corney's presence, the old woman added, "I'm just telling 'er, ma'am, as 'ow this won't be the last time she'll cry for a little 'un."

"Take that one away. Enough to make anyone morbid clinging on to a dead body. She'll see it was for the best in a day or two. Her unmarried and only seventeen. She should be on her knees thanking the Almighty for His kindness." Tearing the dead child from its mother, she went on. "Gawd in

His mercy's sent you another little brat to look after."

I was forced into the young woman's arms and, nature taking its course, I immediately tried to suckle at her breast. Mrs Corney's large hands held me there until the girl's weeping and protests turned to mute indifference.

"That's better" Mrs Corney told her. "This way you can earn your keep, my gal. This ain't an inn, where you're paying good money for your board and lodging. This is how you pay the taxpayer back over the next few month, so the sooner you get used to it the better for all of us."

"Tidy this place up," the workhouse mistress went on. "We don't want Mr Sowerberry telling everyone we don't keep a respectable house. He'll be up here for the dead one any minute. Sally, you dress this live one. Bumble'll give him some stupid name or other, you wait and see. Where's he got to in his alphabet? S ain't it? "

"'Ow about calling the little beggar after me?" Sally laughed.

"Have you bin at the daffy already?" Mrs Corney demanded.

"The girl didn't want it, did she? I offered it. What more could a body do? She pushed it away. I were afraid she'd waste the lot."

"There ain't bin a drop of daffy wasted in your time here," Mrs Corney stated with no fear of denial. "Get that child dressed, if you can see where his arms are meant to go."

"If I can see?" the old nurse muttered. "I done this more times than I've 'ad 'ot dinners, that's for sure. I could do it with me eyes tight closed."

Without more ado, I was dressed in the yellowed calico gown passed down like any heirloom from pauper baby to pauper baby from time immemorial. Before the week was out, I had been taken to church to be christened Nathaniel Swubble and that very gown had been passed on to Oliver Twist.

CHAPTER TWO

Mary Abbott, the young girl at whose breast I was placed on my first day of life, continued to care for me until I was about two years of age. That was the age by which, being able to walk and talk, it was thought I was old enough to take orders and keep out of everyone's way–the two basic requirements for life in the workhouse. Sally, the old inmate who acted as nurse for other inmates of the workhouse, used to tell me what happened after Mary had left.

"You're that little 'un young Mary took to, ain't you?" she would ask every time she saw me. When I agreed, she would laugh, showing great gaps in her teeth. "You wasn't 'arf a cry baby when she were gawn. Tottering around on your little pins looking for 'er you was. When you couldn't find 'er, you'd roll around on the floor yelling your 'ead orf. Mrs Corney said she'd slap them tantrums out of you, but it did no good. Then she tried to quieten you with daffy, but you spat it in 'er face. Mary never would let you be knocked out with daffy. You 'ad't got the 'abit, you see." Laughing, she would add, "I know what you're thinking. Old Sal's got the 'abit, ain't she? Never 'ad it til me old man died."

I would wait in silence for her to go on. Sally never needed prompting. "Then I'd try cuddling you and rocking you, but you paid no 'eed to me. Then you just sat doing nothing. Like a stuffed dummy you was, staring at the door. Then you give up looking for 'er and just curled up in a corner. Thought you was dead sometimes. Jack come in to see you. That cheered you up, but 'e never did 'ave much time from 'is duties on the gate."

When I was a little older, to learn more, I would join Jack Star at the gate. I would make him repeat the same stories. Although I knew every detail of each by heart, it was I who prompted him with my questions to repeat them again. With no parents or grandparents or, indeed, any relations that I knew of, I seemed to need some anchor to the past and to the wider world. As he spoke, the porter would look around in case he was needed or would walk away to check anyone wanting to leave or enter. Sometimes, when I saw he was busy, I walked away and finished telling the well known story to myself. At others, I would wait patiently for the story to be continued.

"Tell me about Mary Abbott," I would prompt.

"I've told you many times, Nat. Young Mary, she were no more than seventeen 'erself. She took you in place of 'er own baby what was born dead. 'Ow she loved you, Nat! Fed you regular and carried you close to 'er tied with a shawl around 'er shoulders. You fitted in so snug. You was a lovely baby, Nat – not like you is now." Here Jack would give me a playful shove and pause for me to laugh at his teasing. "And she 'ad the old wicker basket they used in the laundry. She carried that about and placed you in it wherever she were working."

As I grew older, occasionally, a new question would occur to me. "'Ow did she stay 'ere so long, Mr Star? Why didn't they shove 'er out after 'er baby were born?"

Jack always smiled at my quick understanding of the workhouse system. "She 'ad to look after you, didn't she? That saved sevenp'nce ha'penny they'd 'ave 'ad to pay to that thieving Mrs Mann at the baby farm. – Forget that, Nat. – Didn't mean to let that slip out. You forget that, or I'll be for the chop."

I'd swear eternal silence before he'd go on.

"Then, well, Mary ,'ad been a lady's maid, 'ad't she? Not what you'd call a proper one, mind, but she were being trained up to be one for the young lady of the 'ouse where she worked." Here the porter would pause to walk to the gate and gaze along the street for a few minutes, just as he must have stared out to sea many times.

Returning, Jack would continue, "Well, Mrs Corney 'ad always fancied 'erself...."

"Still does," I'd put in.

"And I'll forget you said that, young man. As I were saying, before some cheeky boy interrupted me, she always fancied 'erself as a real lady and what do real ladies need?"

"A real ladies' maid," I answered promptly.

"So Mary worked for 'er. She had Mary running 'ere, there and every where. It were 'Yes, Ma'am, this,' and 'No, Ma'am, that,' until the poor girl didn't know whether she were coming nor going."

"And what about me, Mr Star? Did she get paid enough to keep me?"

"That's what she wanted, Mary did – to make a 'ome for you and 'er. No, Mrs Corney never paid 'er a penny. Fiddled the books to keep 'er, I shouldn't wonder. Cross that out, too, Nat. Shouldn't 'ave said that. No, Mary stuck it out to be in the workhouse with you. She 'ad you with 'er all the time as long as she could, but you would insist on growing, running about and getting inter everything. And then talking – my Gawd, you could talk the 'ind leg orf a donkey by the time you was eighteen or twenty months.

"Is that good, Mr Star?" I would ask, seeking confirmation of my precocity.

"Is that good? What about them three year olds what ain't even started talking yet? Mind you, that's Mrs Mann's doing. Thinks a baby farm is just like any other farm where you lets the animals just grow. 'Uman babies need training and learning, Nat. She dumps them young 'uns on the floor and 'ardly lets 'em move. Anything to stop 'er 'aving to bother with 'em. That girl what 'elps 'er talks to 'em, but Mrs Corney tells 'er to get on with it 'cos she ain't got all day." He sighed. "Now they're keeping on young Oliver Twist to 'elp and 'e's only a little wisp of a thing 'issell."

"Did I get a wet nurse just before Oliver?" I liked to ask, referring to my one and only triumph in life so far. It had happened, quite by chance, that I had arrived at the workhouse just a day before Oliver was born there, but I liked to take credit for having had a wet nurse all of my own. Another day and Mary would have looked after Oliver instead of me.

"Yes, son. You was just in the nick of time, or it'd 'ave been the baby farm for you."

Always, I checked, in the early days hopefully and then, later dreaming of wealthy parents, less eagerly, "Are you my Pa, Mr Star?"

"No, boy, I ain't. Calling you 'son' is – well, it means I'm a sort of uncle to yer, that's all."

"Did she 'ave to leave me with the other little 'uns?"

"That she did, Nat. 'Ad to leave you in the care of the old ladies – old Sally, Martha and Alice. Wouldn't let 'em give you a drop of daffy, though. She'd come and check you whenever she could. Then, once that matron Mrs Mann 'ad set 'er free about eleven at night, she'd snuggle you up in bed until she was up again early next day running attendance on that woman again at 'alf past five."

"What 'appened in the end, sir?" I anticipated how the porter always began the final part of the story.

"In the end, Nat, there was 'ell to pay. Mary said she were taking you orf with 'er. She'd get work somewhere and 'ave you with 'er. Mrs Corney said like 'ell she would. She wouldn't stand for it and she'd make sure that soft Bumble wouldn't stand for it neither. That matron could always twist 'im round 'er little finger. Bumble said Mary was a wanton, no-good hussy and Mary said she'd tell 'ow Mrs Corney 'ad cooked the books to get 'erself a personal maid. In the end – well, Mary lost the battle. Them in authority always win, Nat. She did manage to get a recommendation out of the matron by threatening to tell and she went to work in a good 'ome some miles away where they didn't know 'er story. Swore she would earn enough to come back for you, Nat. Said she'd take you away with 'er."

"She weren't a wanton woman, were she, Mr Star?"

"No, it were the young son of the 'ouse. As usual, the old, old story."

It was not often that we had time to continue this story further. Usually, I just watched Jack Star caught up in conversation or hurrying off to help with a difficult inmate and I'd run off to play or to complete my own duties about the workhouse.

Only occasionally there was time for me to ask, "Did she come back for me, sir?"

"You know she did. Don't you remember when you was about four or five?"

Sometimes I think that I can remember those early days after Mary left, but, when I try to recall them, it is as though I am standing outside the picture, observing my younger self within it. Perhaps they are not my own memories, but things I have been told so often that I mistake them for my own recollections. Perhaps they are not even memories of myself, but my memories of all the young children I saw pass through the workhouse.

In my mind's eye, I see myself as a small child, ill-fitting clothes hanging on my thin frame, wandering across the grey stone floors between grey stone walls among women too busy to take much notice of me and I recall how it was.

In the corridors and wards, I would see women sweeping and scrubbing and, in the kitchen, washing pots, peeling potatoes and stirring great pots. Through the steam of the laundry I would watch them returning from the pumps with buckets of water hanging on yokes from their shoulders. I would see them heaving the water into giant coppers under which fires had been lit since before the sun was up. Sitting on the steps, I would see how they took boiling water from copper to tub and then how they energetically twisted and turned the dolly or vigorously rubbed the clothes against the scrubbing board. Their faces flushed, they would pause to wipe the sweat and steam from their eyes and to push damp strands of hair under their caps. Then, their bodies straining back, they would lift the clothes, heavy with water, from the tub, struggle to the mangle and, last of all, hang them on long lines stretched across the garden.

Whenever I saw my chance, I would slip my hand within any woman's hand within reach or scramble onto their laps as they took a rare, brief rest. I recall that I would smile, cry, fall over or do anything for attention. Sometimes I was rewarded with a squeeze of the hand, a smiling face looking down at me or a tickling, which would make me laugh and squirm and beg for more. Best of all, a woman would hold me and place a gentle kiss on my head.

But always, the women would end by saying , "Mind yerself, Nat," or "Down yer go, there's a good boy. Time for me to get on." When they were being hurried or harried by Mrs Corney, they had no time for me. Then it would be, "Out of the way. I'm up to me neck without you fussing around." Sometimes, I would be given a slap on the leg or a cuff on the ear. It was no more than they would have given their own children, but, for me, there was no cuddling and making up later.

It was Paul Quince, a few years my senior and Felicity Fidget, a few years older still, who took me in hand and cared for me. These fellow foundlings taught me when it was safe to approach grown-ups and when it was not and how to laugh off a slap when you got it wrong. Perhaps they had some inborn instinct to care for a younger child or perhaps they needed someone for whom they could care. Maybe they observed the families who passed through the workhouse and saw how ten-year old looked after eight and eight-year old looked after seven and so on down the line.

Whatever the cause, they looked after me well. In the boys' ward Paul dressed and undressed me, roused me in the morning and tucked me up at night. At meals, they protected me from raiding neighbours, patiently shovelling food into my mouth, telling me, "We know it's 'orrible, but it's all you're going to get."

So I came to the day, the day I do recall, when I was about four years old. As I played in the yard, a young woman approached me. From her clothes, free of all darns and patches, I knew she was not asking to enter the workhouse.

As she approached me, her face broke into a smile. "There, I'd know you anywhere Nat Sprat. Ain't you grown!"

Instinctively, I asked, "Are you Mary?"

Her face alight with pleasure, Mary turned to the young man who was reluctantly following her. He, too, was dressed in his best clothes, the very possession of which proclaimed him to be a prosperous tradesman.

"Look, Fred, he knows me."

"Don't look like it to me." His expression was surly and he made it clear he had been dragged into the workhouse against his will.

Reluctantly at first, I let the young woman hug and kiss me. Then I seemed surrounded by a familiar warmth and comforted by the familiar smell of her skin.

"He'll do for us, Fred, honest he will. Please, Fred, it'd make me so happy to bring him up as our own." Pushing me towards him, she willed me to win him over. It was no use. I did not like him.

"Looks a sullen little brat to me. 'E's best orf 'ere, among 'is own kind." Turning to go, he added, "I told you, Mary, 'ow this weren't a good idea. Me Ma told you, too, she don't want no work'ouse kid in 'er 'ome."

"Please, please, Fred. You don't know him like I do. He'd soon love you, like he loves me. He'd respect you and look up to you, I know he would."

"Look," the young man said firmly, "We don't want no reminders that you was once in the work'ouse. 'Ow you come to be there, I'll never understand. It's easy enough for any young girl to find work."

Mary was silent. There were things she was never planning to tell him.

"Come on," Fred urged, "if we can't 'ave any of our own, we'll take on one of me sister's tribe. Gawd knows, she's got enough. Blood is thicker than water." He turned to leave.

As Mary kissed me, I felt her tears on my cheek. "I'll keep trying," she promised. Then, drying her eyes, she ran after her companion and out of sight. I was left with a loneliness I had felt before.

An arm came around my shoulder. Paul had watched all this, edging himself forward, trying to tell Mary that he was my best friend and I never went anywhere without him. While he had been frightened I might be taken away, he had half hoped he might be taken along with me. He had smiled his most appealing smile, tossed his dark curls and clung to Mary's skirt as she held me in her arms.

Now, flopping down on the steps, he pulled me down to sit beside him. "You still got me, Nat. I ain't going to leave you." Born to look on the bright side, Paul continued, "It ain't too bad 'ere, is it? You should 'ave bin at the baby farm, like I were. Gawd, that weren't 'arf 'orrible."

CHAPTER THREE

You will have gathered that Jack Star kept an eye on us children. He warned us against every possible danger which might befall us, including getting our heads stuck in the railings. According to Jack, this was a mishap which could happen all too easily and would cause us pain on account both of its crushing our skulls and forcing the workhouse master to pay a blacksmith to cut us free. He said that he had known a boy stuck there, with the town boys throwing rubbish at his head, for three hours, while the master tried every free solution suggested by the assembled crowd.

Paul, always ready to go one better, swore he had heard of a boy stuck there for three days, with his neck stretching longer and longer as people tried to pull him out. In the end, the unfortunate child had to wear a wide leather collar, like those worn by rat catching dogs, to stop his head lolling backwards so that he had to look at the sky or forward so that he could see nothing but his own chest.

Usually, being a naturally cautious boy, I clutched the rail on each side with my small fists and rested my head on my knuckles to avoid its slipping through. Being a naturally curious child, I longed to walk out of the gate into the street. It may have been only the narrow High Street of Myddlington, but, to me, it was the world. Perhaps most importantly, it was on the other side of the railings where I had been left and where my parents must live. When Jack told me that, on the very next day, he would take me out through the gate, I danced with excitement. There was no sleep for me that night and, instead of sleeping in just my shirt, I kept my trousers on, too.

Seeing my eagerness to be off on this great adventure, Paul's last words to me that night were, "Don't you go running down in the morning without me to look after you."

I had already determined to ignore such advice. After all, I was four or five years old and old enough to go outside. I was going to show everyone that I was not a baby anymore.

At the sound of Sally's key in the door of the ward, I slid out of bed and straight into my boots, placed exactly where I would land. Then I grabbed my jacket and, as she rang her hand bell loud enough to wake boys, let alone the dead, I dashed past her and into the yard.

It was a winter morning and, if I had been with Paul, we would have waited in line leading to the buckets of water, and contented ourselves with polishing the spot upon which we stood with our feet to up-end any new boy, who did not know our tricks. Sliding across the frosty ground was forbidden. Broken bones took time to set and the less the master saw of the workhouse doctor, or, rather, the less the doctor saw of us, the better the master liked it. This day, full of joy, I ran into the yard, threw out my arms, and slid at speed to the pump, where some older boys were breaking the ice on buckets they had filled the day before. In one of these, I planned to cup my hands, fill them with water to satisfy anyone sent to supervise us, and then let the water seep out between my fingers so that as little as possible of the ice-cold liquid reached my face. That is what we usually did and, in the middle of a crowd, we got away with it. But I had rushed ahead and was in full view of the male inmate forced to stand in the cold and see we obeyed the rules. Suddenly, my hair was grabbed from behind and my whole head immersed in the icy water of the trough. I came out shaking my head like a drowning dog and gulping for breath.

"There, you lazy little urchin, take this soap." The man forced a bar of carbolic into my hand and gave me a kick when it slipped out and I had to pick it up. "Wash yourself properly, or I'll do it for you. Be'ind your ears and all." Tugging at one ear to inspect it closely, he observed, "You could grow a crop of onions on 'em. And tuck your collar in and scrub your neck. 'Ope for your sake Mrs Corney don't see that soaking wet shirt."

My face must have shown my resentment and hurt, for he laughed, but said quite kindly, "I'm telling you for your own good, lad. I know as 'ow you ain't got no Pa of your own."

That hurt more than the soaking or the kicking.

Within seconds, the thought of my treat uppermost in my mind, I was congratulating myself that I was first to arrive at the door of the hall. I stood up straight, proudly first in the line. Spotting Felicity amongst the girl preparing for our arrival, I called to her. Glancing around to make sure no one was watching her, she hurried over.

"What you doing, Nat? 'Urrying won't make the time go faster. Go back and wait for Paul."

Shaking off the guiding hand she had placed on my shoulder, I snapped, "I'm big enough to look after meself. I want to be first."

"You won't be for long," Felicity warned.

As always, she was right. I was pushed aside by older and bigger boys until the line sorted itself into biggest to smallest as efficiently as if we had all been put through a sieve. On my way to the end, Paul grabbed me.

"Ain't I always told you to wait for me? 'Ope you've learnt your lesson."

It would be more accurate to say that I had remembered one. Long ago I had learned that might was right in the workhouse.

Having waited to collect our bowl and spoon, we waited again to reach the huge copper and waited again for the large dollop of porridge to fall from the ladle, where it hung defying gravity, into the bowl. I had to admit to myself that I was glad Paul was there to protect me from the pushing and shoving, which would have sent the porridge to the floor and me into the corner with no breakfast.

My excitement at the thought of my outing now held firmly in check, I reverted to our everyday behaviour, first licking the tea running down the outside of the mug at my place at the table. The chance of burning my tongue was very slight. Then, keeping one eye sufficiently closed to fool the master and sufficiently open to warn off any marauding hands, I said grace in a sing-song chorus with the others. Having thanked God for his generosity in providing our food, I did my best to ensure that I consumed my rightful share by hunching over my bowl and shovelling the contents into my mouth with one hand, while I wrapped the other arm right around my bowl and mug. The last morsel eaten, I joined Paul in looking around at the other boys' bowls. While we had our principles and did not bully others into giving us theirs, we were all too ready to take slowness in eating as a sign that someone did not want his and would be only too happy for us to eat it up for him.

With no one having any to spare, I licked my lips to rid them of the remnants of clinging porridge and to show my enjoyment. Thick, congealed porridge, thin vegetable stews, chunks of bread with slivers of cheese or a spreading of treacle, thick, sticky delicious treacle, were all we knew for our three meals a day and all we expected. My stomach had adjusted to the far from ample quantities and my taste had been honed on mouldy cheese and the pieces of fat and gristle we fished out of our watery stews on our twice weekly meat days to save until last.

The budget for food was far from generous in the first place and was even further reduced by Mrs Corney's deals with the tradesmen of the town. While she expected to take her cut out of any financial transactions, the butcher, the baker and the candlestick maker, as well as the grocer, expected not only to make a profit, but, also, to recoup their handouts to officials and the taxes they paid as citizens of the parish. It was even rumoured that the fresh vegetables grown in the workhouse garden and intended for our plates, were exchanged for rotten ones from the greengrocer.

At last, on this particular day, it was time to thank God for what we had received and hurry to our chores. Already at five, I was an old hand at sweeping and scrubbing, polishing boots (Mr Bumble often asked for me by name to clean his) and lugging tinder logs and coal to the kitchens and laundry. As I groaned under the weight of a bucket, Geogina, her skirt hitched up and sleeves rolled back, stopped to tuck in a damp curl, which had escaped from her cap.

"Just thank Gawd you ain't a girl. We're couped up in this 'ot, steamy place hours on end. Look at me 'air 'anging down. Weren't worth putting me rags in last night."

I was unmoved. That was a girl's lot in life.

Seeing I did not care, she sought her own back. "What if Mr Star's sent on an errand. 'E won't be taking you out then, will 'e?"

"'E promised," I protested.

"Promises don't mean nothing around 'ere. If you get your orders, you 'ave to do what you're told. And what if you 'ave to run an errand? Even a boy with legs as skinny as yours can run an errand. You reminds me of a daddy-long-legs."

I walked away, knowing that Geogina, like Felicity, knew how things worked. It was true. Old Sal was always saying, "Just save me old legs, Nat," and Ben would tell us, "Best to wear out the young 'uns first." I had no choice but to hide. It wasn't likely any grown-ups would come looking for me with other errand boys closer at hand.

When, at last, the time came for my excursion, I ran up to Jack and he swung me onto his shoulders. At first, I was disappointed not to be running and jumping beside him along with Titan, his mastiff, but, as we dodged horses, in ones, twos and threes, pulling carts and waggons and carriages and jumped over their piles of dung, I knew my arms would have been pulled out of their sockets had I been holding Jack's hand. I hung on as tightly as I could, my arms around Jack's head.

On the other side of the street, Jack turned and I had my first view of the workhouse from the outside. It appeared like a long, high wall with, as

Dickens said of it, "Dismal windows frowning on the street." An arch in the outer wall framed wide gates and, pointing to the ironwork above them, Jack read, "Industry shall conquer poverty."

"Conker?" I inquired, puzzled.

"Means," Jack explained, "if you works 'ard and earns wages you won't never 'ave to enter a work'ouse." Reflecting on this for a moment, he added, "Must be up there to make the taxpayers 'appy. Ain't many paupers can read what it sez. They might think it sez, 'Welcome, one and all.'"

"Place don't look very big," I commented.

"Now," Jack explained patiently, "if you was that old pigeon sitting up there, you'd see it looked like an aitch, or a big, square number eight, with the courtyards as the 'oles. Some people," he went on, "is jealous of all what's given to the poor and calls them pauper palaces. That's from the outside. If the king see the great, empty grates and felt the draughts howling down the chimneys and had to walk on the cold stone floors, he wouldn't want to live there."

Naturally, I asked what a palace was, and when Jack had told me, he added, "But you've no need to be jealous of the king, you live in the biggest building in Myddlington and you've probably got more space to play in than 'e 'as."

We had plenty of space because, in those days, only the young, the old, the sick and those admitted temporarily remained to rattle about in the immense edifice. What I did not know then was that it had been built with the best of intentions. An Act of Parliament some years earlier had allowed parishes to build houses of industry to accommodate and confine all who sought poor relief. They were to be set to work to learn habits of industry and independence. Like most other good intentions concerning poor relief, enacted from the reign of Elizabeth to the present day, it had not worked. The articles produced in the workshops were shoddy and no one wanted to buy them. Before very long, the overseer and other officials fell back into the old way of giving outdoor relief, in the form of money or food, to those in need.

Turning out backs on the workhouse, Jack let me look over the high wall which surrounded the Yard opposite. I could see waggons and carts loading and unloading timber, grain and the wide variety of goods brought in and out of the canal basin by the boats which plied their trade from London and Birmingham. From the great notice outside, Jack read, "William

White and Son. Carriers. Boat Owners. Coal Merchants. Grain Merchants."
The list went on and on.

"You see, Nat. Myddlington is White's and White's is Myddlington." I
did not know then what he meant, but I was to learn in the years to come.

We turned and walked along the High Street. It has become the fashion in guide books to describe the main street of every provincial town as
rivalling Regent's Street in the grandeur of its buildings and the variety of
its shops. No one could have said that of Myddlington and kept a straight
face. The town was like other small towns of its time, with houses, shops
and public buildings of every age, shape and style crowded together. The
tour of the public buildings did not take long. The church was familiar to
me from the workhouse windows, but the number of chapels caught my
attention.

"Are they all the same, Mr Star?" I asked, not just to obey his instructions to ask him anything I wanted to know, but because I was five and full
of questions.

"Depends what you mean by 'the same'."

"They looks the same. They're all square."

"But see them numbers up there. Them's the dates when they was built.
That makes 'em a tiny bit different. And the difference between what one
or the other believes is about the same, if you ask me,"

"Where are all the waggons going, Mr Star?"

"In and out of White's Yard. You just see 'em."

"Why are they called 'White', Mr Star?"

"'Cos that's their name."

"White's a colour," I pointed out, making a rare statement amongst the
questions.

"So's green and black, Nat, but some people 'ave them names."

"Do you know a Mr Blue?"

"Can't say as 'ow I can recall one."

"Is Swubble a colour, Mr Star?"

"Not to my knowledge, Nat." Jack went on to explain that some people
had the names of tradesmen, probably because a relation long ago had
worked at that very trade.

"Did the first Mr White have a white face and the first Mr Black a black
one?"

"Well, it ain't lasted if they did. The old Mr White has a sort of grey heart, but the young Mr William White has a heart as black as coal."

"Where does Mr Bumble get our names from, Mr Star?"

"Orf the top of his 'ead, Nat."

"Why did Mr Bumble make up my name, Mr Star?"

"'Cos you didn't 'ave one, Nat."

Such reminders of my foundling status always made me sad, even on a day like this one. It was a comfort, when I returned and ran into the workhouse, to find that it was one of Sal's flea and nit hunts. Her attention had been drawn to Paul's scratching even more than usual. She had searched his clothes and, in spite of her failing eye-sight, had caught several. Years of experience had given her the art of trapping one between finger and thumb and then edging it between her thumb nails to crack it. Proud of her skill, she displayed each one to our gaze for us to marvel at the tiny black body and the red smudge on her nail."

"That's your blood there," she would say, making us as grateful as if she had plunged a stake through a vampire's heart.

After the reminder that my parents had abandoned me, I welcomed Sal's search for nits. She sat down, pulled me close and ran her hands gently and comfortingly through my hair, back, top and sides, turning me gently as she went. Ending up facing her again, I was allowed to kiss her wrinkled old face. It was the closest human contact we had.

CHAPTER FOUR

Life was not all work. We had huge rooms and wide grounds in which to play happily for hours. We had few toys, but what child needs toys to run, to jump, to turn cart wheels, to skip or to climb trees, play piggy-back and hide-and-seek? Without toys, we had pieces of wood, which, in a moment of magic, turned in our hands to flashing swords, soldiers' rifles and high-waymen's pistols. We rode invisible horses, which responded instantly to our commands and to the jerking of invisible reins and the swish of invisible whips. We fought battles against our ancient enemy, the French, by land and sea. Whether we wore our cocked hats from front to back, like Wellington, or side to side, like Nelson, we always triumphed.

There was hour upon hour when we forgot that we had been abandoned, but the memory was always there, a wound, which, just as you thought it was closing over and healing, burst open, sore and bleeding.

We all knew that we were foundlings and what that meant, almost from birth. We had been told it in words so many times and read it in people's reactions to us. We knew beyond doubt that being a foundling put you at the very bottom of the pile. We had learned long ago that children came and went in the workhouse. In the outside world these children and their parents were looked down upon by those who had never known abject poverty or who would rather have died than accepted poor relief, but, in the workhouse, they were at the top of the pile. Their mothers told them not to play with us, claiming that our parents were no good and we would follow in their footsteps. "Play with the orphans instead," they would say, "They can't 'elp being mother and fatherless."

The names given us by Bumble were marks of our inferiority. Orphans, after all, came with names, only foundlings did not. The names had nothing in common except for being allocated in alphabetical order. First in our foundling tribe was Felicity Fidget, but being seven years older than me, she was usually too busy in the workhouse to join in our games. Next came Georgina King. Bumble had hoped for a boy for K, but overcame his disappointment when his mother suggested Georgina instead of George. While she appreciated a royal connection, Georgina preferred to see herself as a duchess.

Next came Paul Quince, three years older than me and my friend and protector. He hated his name, saying that it was as bad as Paul Apple or Paul Pear. After me came Oliver Twist, half orphan on his mother's side and half foundling on his father's. It was not known at that time whether his father was dead or alive. After Twist came V, but before I tell you the full name, let me tell you how it came into being. When a newly born little girl was found in the church porch, Bumble had the idea to call it Vilkins. The vicar, feeling some proprietary right over a child found on church premises, was most annoyed.

"Vilkins, Mr Bumble! If I say Vilkins at the font, everyone will think that I am a common cockney who confuses V and W. There is a name Wilkins, Mr Bumble, which you may save for the next child. But Vilkins!" The man's face bore an expression as though he were experiencing an unpleasant taste or smell. "There is no name Vilkins, I can assure you of that."

To make sure he found a name which really did begin with a V and sounded like the vicar's V's, Bumble looked for a suitable book. The Bible, he decided, was just the one he needed. There could be no arguing with the Good Book, but names beginning with V were not to be found in abundance. At last he brightened. Here was a person whose name began with V and who, what was more, was frequently addressed by Jesus Over and over again, Bumble found, 'Verily, I say unto you'. To further please the vicar, on his mother's suggestion, Bumble gave the girl the name of Virtue Verily. The name Wilkins was kept for a little boy, Tom, found at the workhouse gate. Thus our tribe consisted of Felicity, Georgina, Paul, me, Virtue and, in time, Tom. What of all the missing letters and what of the name Unwin, which Bumble had long planned to use? It was not that Bumble's imagination or memory failed him. He even excelled with Bob Xtra. No, they were given to babies who died soon after they were found or after a while in Mrs Mann's tender care at the baby farm. "A waste of a good name," as Bumble said accusingly of any child dying in these circumstances.

What of Oliver Twist? As you know, there was no wet nurse for him in the workhouse and he was sent off to the baby farm. At around three or four years, he should have returned, but Mrs Mann and Bumble delayed his return on one pretext or another. As Bumble confided to Jack Star, "That boy's mother was a lady, if ever I see one, and where there's gentlefolk there's money. When his father turns up looking for him, they'll not think twice about paying Mrs Mann for his board and lodging since birth." Rubbing his hands, he added, "And they'll give a bit extra for keeping the boy out of the workhouse." Unfortunately for Oliver, as appeals and adver-tisements brought forth no relations and the possibility of financial gain receded, the boy was kept on as an obedient drudge.

Perhaps, knowing his family were gentlefolk, Oliver was better off than us foundlings, perhaps not. Knowing nothing of our families, we could let our imaginations soar, picking on this servant or that gentleman as our fathers and this cottage or that large house as our rightful home. Each of us built up a picture of a home to which we could escape in mind and spirit from the realities of life around us. Let me mention here how I came to find the home around which I built my dreams.

We, children were not kept prisoners in the workhouse in my early years and, when we had finished our chores, we were allowed to walk in the town. One day, having walked further than usual and reached the outskirts, where streets merged into fields, we wandered along a lane with farms and houses scattered randomly here and there along it. Almost at the end of the lane, I stopped, grabbed Felicity's hand with one of mine and pointed with the other.

"That's where I was born," I exclaimed. "In that 'ouse across the end of the lane."

"No one don't live there," Paul commented.

"It's empty," Geogina observed.

"It's deserted," Felicity said, her vocabulary being more extensive than ours. "Look, the bushes and flowers have spilled over into the path. No one is caring for it."

Just as I had once stared out of the workhouse railings to find my par-ents, now I stared in through those at the front of the house. "I were born 'ere, honest I were."

"Babies can't remember nothing," Geogina pointed out. Then she con-ceded, "It does have servant's rooms in the roof." She was the only one of us, she was sure, to be born to a mother who employed servants rather than working as one. "It's not as big as a mansion." In her dreams, Georgina knew she hafd been born in a grand house.

"'Ow did you come to be found outside the workhouse, Nat?" Paul asked. It was not an unreasonable question.

"The gypsies took me."

"I was surprised at Paul's agreeing, until he added, "Took a quick look at you and put you down as quick as they could. Bet you was a skinny little baby. Let's go in, Lissy." He pushed the gates open.

"No," Felicity told us firmly. "There'll be a caretaker about somewhere." She put her arm gently around my shoulder and turned me to face the way we had come.

"That's my 'ome," I protested, refusing to move in the direction in which she wanted me to go. "My family are away searching for me. They're searching the 'ole world."

Felicity gently pushed me in the right direction. "Well, now you 'ave a dream 'ome of your own, Nat," she said and I knew that she, somewhere, had one too.

CHAPTER FIVE

In telling of my discovery of the house at the end of the lane, I have jumped ahead a few months. So that you learn something of the town in which we lived, let me take you back to my first outing without Jack Star and with my friends. Jack did make sure it was a time when Felicity was free to take charge of me and he asked us to take along, Peter Pace, an orphan, who was a little older than me and had just been admitted to the workhouse. "'E needs 'is mind taking orf 'is troubles," the porter told us, before he ordered me to be a good boy and do what Felicity told me. Then, as he was about to give us our final instruction, we all chorused, "You don't want the bogey-man to get yer." It was what he always said.

Our first stop, at Paul's request, was at Mr Sowerberry's, the undertaker's. It seemed Paul had been in the habit of lying down outside, while Georgina called into the shop that someone had dropped dead outside. They enjoyed watching the speed at which Sowerberry emerged to claim a new customer. It had taken a while for them to realise that, after the first few times, the undertaker was using their game to his advantage to show how respectful and considerate he was and how he could tell the difference between a dead and a living body – a skill people valued in an undertaker.

Now Paul had taken to walking into the shop, turning and staggering out again, his limbs held stiffly by his sides, his eyes upward and his mouth open. Georgina, recoiling in horror, would then tell passersby, "We thought me brother were dead yesterday. Sowerberry were going to bury 'im today when we see 'im blink. 'E sat up and spoke to us."

"Just going to nail me down, 'e were," Paul would complain to the annoyance of the undertaker, who tried to laugh and share the joke with those who gathered outside.

We could make jokes at Sowerberry's expense. In daylight, death held no fear for us. We had seen too many children die of scarlet fever, measles, whooping cough, typhoid and other diseases, which carried children off in the twinkling of an eye. In the dead of night, with no parents to cling to, it was a different matter.

On this occasion, Felicity saw that Peter's lip was trembling as he thought of his parents' funeral. "Come on," she said, taking him and me by the hand. "Let's go to the shops where all the rich people go." She had been taken in by the claim, displayed prominently outside many shops, that they catered for 'the Nobility and Gentry of the County'. In fact, people of that rank preferred to shop in London, Bath or Brighton. They patronized the local shops only when they had overrun their credit in these places. When tradespeople knew that the sight of a member of the aristocracy or upper ranks of society alighting from a carriage and entering their premises would attract all those who had money to ape their betters, they were eager to extend credit indefinitely.

For the convenience of customers dismounting from carriages, the better class of shops nestled together, draper next to tailor, milliner next to shoemaker, clockmaker next to jeweller, gunmaker next to saddler and so on through all the trades catering to the needs or, rather, desires of those with the money to pay.

The girls wanted to look in the draper's, but the apprentices from that shop soon chased us off with brooms, which whipped our feet from under us in a second. We were not to impede the progress or sully the path of the customers. The apprentices and assistants put up with low wages, but reaped the reward of feeling superior to those workers who dirtied their hands. With long hours, they had the pale skins of all those confined within four walls, for days on end.

"Pasty faces," Paul called back at them.

"Are they pastry all over?" Peter asked. Feeling superior, we laughed. "Pasty, not pastry," Felicity corrected him.

"Oh," Peter said, "My mother used to make me a little pastry man with bits left over from the pie. She filled him with currants. They were that yellowy-white colour before they were cooked."

We did not feel superior any more. Peter knew about mothers and pastry and pies, which was far more than we did.

His remarks gave Paul an idea. "Go and bake your face," he called to the shop boy, happy to have had the last word.

With no money in our pockets, we gazed at all the goods on display, but when were children content to look without touching? While the activity did not appeal to Felicity, the rest of us tried to reach up to the claws of the birds hanging in the poulterer's window. We were half afraid they would suddenly scratch us and were glad we had no chance of reaching them. But we could, and did, test their plumpness and touched their skin, even dryer and rougher than Old Sal's. Paul dared me to put my finger in the biggest fowl's beak, so I had to do it.

At the butcher's, I marvelled that most of the cuts were red and oozing blood. In the short experience of my years on earth, I had seen nothing but yellow fat and grey gristle.

"Ma used to go to the back door," Peter told us, "and buy the odds and ends the butcher had cut off. She used to wash off the sawdust and make a stew."

'Oo'd want sawdust stew?" Georgina asked, pausing for a moment in admiring herself in a window.

"Why didn't she go in the front door?" I asked.

"You'll learn," Felicity answered.

My attention was drawn to a shop with a small crowd around the window. "What are all them people looking at?" was my next question.

Grabbing my hand, Paul ran towards them. "It's the print shop. They must 'ave got some new ones in. 'Ere, I'll lift you up to see."

I had never seen pictures before and here was row upon row from top to bottom of the bow window.

"Look! There's a work'ouse," I exclaimed, pointing to a print of a castle.

"Was I ever that stupid?" Paul asked.

"Yes," was Felicity's firm reply.

"Look at that picture of them 'orses," Paul marvelled.

"Look at them dresses!" Georgina marvelled in return.

In a few minutes, before we were pushed aside, I had learned that the king was very fat and ate enormous meals, that there was a Duke of Wellington with a great hooked nose and a hat like Bumble's and that Nelson, whom Jack Star often talked about, looked very pasty as he died on the deck of the Victory.

The shops, as we walked along, became gradually smaller and meaner as the population for which they catered became poorer and poorer. Some were just houses with a few knitted garments or other homemade items in the window, and some a hole of a shop with a few, broken pieces of furniture outside. Men and women poked about to find something they could use, or could mend and sell for a profit of a few pennies. The signs had changed. They were no longer painted in black and gold, but were scrawled on scraps of card and paper. Many said, "No credit." Felicity told us what credit was and explained how it was always denied to those who had need of it.

"Is that a church?" I asked, pointing to another building and half recalling one of Jack's lessons.

"No, it's a chapel," Felicity replied. Seeing my mouth about to open again, she added,"And don't ask me the difference."

I changed the question. "What's it for?"

"Praying, preaching and singing 'ymns," Paul declared, summing up the activities of the Primitive Methodists, who worshipped there. "And the steps," he added, "is for standing on and showing orf your Sunday best."

"We'll just go as far as the Circus," Felicity decided.

We were almost there and, turning back, my legs were aching. No doubt I began to snivel and drag my feet in the hope that someone would pick me up. I had never walked that far before. At last, Paul bent down and I scrambled onto his back. Staggering, he raised himself again and began to walk back towards the workhouse. Soon, I was smiling again and asking questions and receiving unsatisfactory answers as to why some huge houses had only a few people in and some smaller ones had dozens.

At last, exasperated beyond the bounds of patience, Paul demanded, "Why do cats me-ow and dogs go woof, woof?" Letting me drop to the ground, he continued in the same tone of voice, "It's bad enough 'umping a great sack of taters around, without 'aving to carry a sack of taters what keeps asking daft questions." I was left to force out a few tears before Felicity took her turn at giving me a piggy-back. Then Paul and Peter ran up and down the theatre steps and I wished I had stayed on my own two feet and joined in.

At last, Felicity, collapsing under my weight, put me down. She took my hand, but all her attention was on Peter, who was tellling how his family had been able to afford two rooms to live in before his father died. It was time to ask another question.

"Lissy," I asked, "Will Bogey Mann really come for us?"

Paul jeered, "Bogey Mann! 'E ain't old lady Mann's 'usband."

"Well, 'e's dead, ain't 'e?" I protested defensively, although beginning to realise that I had made some kind of silly mistake.

"Why d'yer ask?" Felicity inquired gently, leaning down to me. When I made no reply, she urged,"'Ow can I explain, if you don't tell me what you was thinking?"

"Bogey Mann!" Paul roared, "That's a good name for the old witch 'erself." Paul would never forget his time at the baby farm.

"Don't listen to 'im, Nat." Felicity sqeezed my hand in encouragement. "Go on, tell us. We won't laugh."

Putting his hand in front of his mouth, Paul mumbled, "I might." Then, removing his hand he smiled sweetly. "Go on, Nat. We're 'ere to 'elp yer."

"It's just…," I began slowly, "It's just that I'd like someone to come for me. I'd like someone to want me."

"Oh, Nat!" Lissy murmured, holding me to her side. "No one ain't coming for us." Always trying to look on the bright side, she added, "One day, Nat, we'll all find someone to marry, settle down and 'ave a family of our own at last like everyone else."

"Not me," Paul said firmly, spoiling Felicity's attempts to cheer me up. "I ain't never going to get married."

Realising that I had not understood Jack Star's exhortation to "Mind the bogeyman", Lissy explained patiently, "What Mr Star means is that wicked people can take you away. The bogeyman is something like the Devil, I suppose."

"What would 'e do to you?" I asked.

"Better you don't know," Paul said, having no idea himself.

Felicity had to think hard. She had heard from women's gossip vague ideas of what might happen to little girls, but she was not sure about boys.

"'Orrible things," Paul uttered in a hollow tone. Pulling a face he intended to be evil, he placed his hands on my throat. "Might murder you."

"Why?" I wanted to know. "I ain't done nothing to them."

Paul's ideas had run out and Georgina was busy smiling at a young apprentice, but Felicity tried her best.

"The women say there's wicked people what take children away to London and make slaves of them."

"Mrs Corney does that 'ere," Paul commented predictably.

"I've 'eard they train you to steal. Not," she went on, looking accusingly at Paul, "that some people need learning."

"I ain't done no thieving for months," Paul protested with a look of pure innocence on his face.

"You'd better not," Felicity told him. "You know what Mr Star said 'e'd do to you if you taught Nat bad 'abits. Any way," she continued, "they ain't taking you away for your own good, that's for certain."

"They buy some children from their parents," Paul said. "As we ain't got no parents they'd get us for nothing, so we got to be especially careful."

We went on in silence. I was worrying about how I would distinguish my parents, when they recalled they had left me and came to find me, from bogeymen.

CHAPTER SIX

Nowadays, whenever I hear of the huge schools set up outside towns in which orphan and foundling children are incarcerated for their young lives, I feel not only sympathy for them, but also anger that such a system can exist. It is claimed to have great advantages, isolating the young from evil influences, but it isolates them from their towns and from its inhabitants so that they belong nowhere. When they reach working age, they are expelled out into the world with no roots, no neighbourhood in which they are at home and no one to whom they can turn for advice and support.

In our case, we had no relations of any generation, but we were part of Myddlington We had roots in the neighbourhood. For this we had the old people in the workhouse to thank. I have mentioned them before. They were not, of course, a group of people who were all much of a muchness. Old people do not change their characters as they grow old. Some kept to themselves, as they always had, others stayed with the group of friends they had known from childhood. Some loved children and some hated them. Our old people were Sally, Alice, Martha, Ben, Digger and John. These linked us not only with their own pasts, but with their parents and grand-parents going back a century or more.

These old men and women had time on their hands to revisit their pasts, to deny, regret or explain all that had happened to them by the actions of others or of themselves. The passing years had not made them detached from these events. Instead, with time now to indulge their feelings, they would grow angry once again at the wrongs done to them, or glow with pleasure to recall the joys they had lived through. I am not saying that, listening to their stories over the years, we became, in line with the modern obsession for improvement, better people, but I am sure we became more human and more in touch with our fellow beings than children confined in a large orphanage, exposed only to moral tales and religious exhortations.

Old Sal we came to know well. It was no good Jack's telling us to have some respect for our elders and to call her Mrs 'Obbins. If we did, she would say that no one had called her by that name for years and she hardly remembered it was her full name. Perhaps, at ten or eleven, we became too full of ourselves to listen to others and convinced there was nothing we

29

could learn from older people, but, in those early years and in later years, we recognized her as our authority on life and the ways of the world. On the workhouse, Sally ruled everywhere. While Mrs Corney took the title, income and perks of matron, she left the day to day running of affairs to Sal. Forget the drunken old sot portrayed by Dickens. In those early days Sal liked a drink, but she was a woman who had enjoyed her youth, fought against all the hardships life had brought her and had, at last, found the scope to exercise her abilities as organizer and healer.

We had plenty of opportunities to listen to Sal's stories. She told them to young women having babies, to widows and deserted wives, giving them the strength to face up to the battle of life and win as she had done. Most of all, she chatted to Alice and Martha in the infirmary as they watched through the night for our fevers to subside. In keeping with Sal's theories, we were herded together through chickenpox, mumps and measles. "Get them all over while you're young," she'd tell us, as, one by one, we succumbed and were tucked up in bed. But, in scarlet fever and diphtheria, she kept us strictly segregated. "Knock you all out like nine pins they will," she would say so that the very names struck terror into our hearts.

When we were ill, as we slipped in and out of consciousness through a haze of fever, we would hear old Sally begin, "D'yer remember Martha when ......?" or, "Annie, didn't we laugh when....?" But as this is the story of my life, I shall condense the story of her life into a few paragraphs. She was born the daughter of a farm labourer and began work with the gangs working in the fields at five or six. She married at sixteen to the handsomest man in the area and they produced thirteen children. One of these, if the old women were to be believed, was born in the corner of the field where she had been working. "Produced me own little 'arvest, I did," as Sally always put it.

Although she had thirteen children in all, Sal never had thirteen together around her. Two were still born and two died within a few days of birth. "Then there was little Tom," Sally used to relate, looking into space as though still seeing him at play in the distance. "'E were always into mischief, 'e were. A real boy 'e were and 'andsome as 'is Pa." With a sigh to cover her tears, she went on, "Then there were Eliza, pretty as a picture and the soul of an angel to match. They died before they ever grew up, just like my precious little Betty. She were only two."

We never heard more of Betty. Perhaps she was precious beyond words.

After a while, pulling us to her, she would continue, "They said Jesus wanted them with 'Im in 'Eaven. They said it were God's will. But I'd begged 'Im not to take Betty." Pulling herself together and releasing her hold on us, she would finish. "Never said much to 'Im after she died."

While Sally and her husband had clung together in their misery, Samuel gradually began to drink more than he had before. Sally let him, something she regretted. "If I'd 'ave nagged 'im. If I 'ad sent one of the little ones to shame 'im out of the alehouse, it might never 'ave 'appened." Occasionally she would add, "If only 'e had looked what 'e were doing." But she seldom blamed her husband for his own death, whatever others may have concluded. Returning home from the alehouse, he had walked in the path of a carriage.

One by one, her other children had died until only Joseph remained. The heartless of the town described him as the runt of the litter, but Sally put his thin and twisted limbs down to his having been her thirteenth child. He was always in poor health and could not support himself, let alone his mother. He was in the workhouse.

"No mother could have been better," Joseph would tell us. "She's 'ad sorrow 'eaped upon sorrow. 'Ow she bears up, I don't know. Laying 'ere, I see everything. There's old men in and out of the work'ouse 'oo'd marry 'er in a trice. Wouldn't look at any of 'em. She loves me Pa to this day."

"Is it good 'aving a mother?" I would ask. Georgina had decided, seeing them stopping children from doing what they wanted, that parents were not altogether a blessing.

"There's mothers and mothers, Nat. My Ma is the best of 'em."

Of the other old people, there was John who said the least. He liked to sit quietly and read his Bible. We knew little of his life, except that he had tried to live by God's word as he and John Wesley interpreted it.

Ben had worked all his life in White's Yard and it had really been the whole of life to him. He still walked around it evey day to talk to old friends, among whom he included the horses he used to care for and drive. Paul would listen to him for hours telling tales of noble horses and exciting journeys. Left to choose the topic of conversation himself, Ben would always tell tales of the Yard and tell time and time again what a good master Mr White was.

Digger always answered, "Very good 'e must 'ave bin. That's why you worked all hours God sent."

"So did 'e," was Ben's reply.

"Aye, but 'e's rich and you're poor. 'E lives in a grand 'ouse and you live in the work'ouse," was Digger's set answer.

Without fail, Ben defended his master. "There's good masters and bad, and you can thank God if you gets a good 'un."

"Shouldn't be no masters and servants. We was all born equal." It was from remarks such as this that I learned that Digger was so called, not simply because he had been a gardener, but because he believed in the principles of the Diggers of Cromwell's time. He had thought the American fight for Independence and then the French Revolution would bring liberty, fraternity and equality, but had lived to be disappointed. The others, never having experienced these ideals, except to have had the liberty to practise fraternity and equality amongst themselves in their poverty, thought him harmless, but misguided.

Now and again, the others would tease him. "What's equality mean, then, Digger?" Martha would ask.

"Like what you and your wife 'ad, weren't it, Digger?" Sally would ask just as innocently. It never failed to get the same response.

"Women, what they got to do with anything?" Digger would demand. "And what's the 'ome got to do with it? We're talking about votes and government and doing a proper job for a living wage. In the 'ome the woman 'as charge of women's work. My Patsy was 'appy to get on with that and leave men's affairs to me."

The old women would just wink at each other and say nothing.

CHAPTER SEVEN

The country around Myddlington was our playground, but it was also our work place. There was a great demand for boys to scare birds or pull up weeds and farmers saw using our labour as taking back some of the taxes they paid to feed us. It was at such work, when I was about six, that I first met Oliver Twist at close enough quarters to talk to him.

The day started with a changing of shirts. Paul was just preening himself as proudly as any dandy when the breathless message was brought by a new boy, who had not yet learned that Bumble was a nobody, that we were summoned immediately to the beadle's presence. We took our time. Paul did this to impress the new boy and I did it because he did. After the usual prod and poke with the beadle's cane, we were told we had to go to work in the fields. I was to go scaring birds and Paul was to go weeding.

"I've just got a clean shirt," Paul protested. "Can I put me old one on again while I'm in the fields and save me clean one?" Seeing the sense of this, Bumble hesitated, but Mrs Corney was close by. "Just keep it clean, Quince, or I'll want to know the reason why."

I tell these minor details to illustrate that one hand in the workhouse never knew what the other hand was doing. Whatever laws governed poor-houses in the nation at large, it was the efficiency or inefficiency, the honesty or the corruption, the organisation or the bungling of the small men and women in charge of the workhouse who ruled our daily lives for good or ill.

As we approached the front gate, Jack Star leaned forward and screwed up his eyes, as though having difficulty identifying us. "Oh! It's you lot," he said at last. "Wondered 'ow a couple of gents and a lady was coming out, when I ain't let 'em in."

The lady was Felicity, who had just joined us. "I've just got a clean frock," she complained, "and now I've got to go weeding."

"'Itch it up," Paul advised. He thought himself an expert on just about everything.

Felicity eyed him with contempt. No boy she had ever met knew anything about hitching up frocks. The achievement of a perfect result required the nimble hands of a woman.

After we had been given a lift on a passing cart, Felicity went one way and Paul and I cut across a field, arriving at my workplace first. "'Ow do I scare birds?" I asked.

"Just look at 'em with that ugly face of yours," Paul advised, walking off to the farm along the lane. Over his shoulder he called, "What d'yer think you've been given a rattle for? You ain't meant to play with it like a baby. If there's anybody about, run around and rattle it. If there ain't, then sit down and 'ave a rest."

Not more than a minute later, Oliver walked along the path to join me. Even if Jack had not told me to be kind to him, Oliver looked so small and apprehensive that I would have shown him some consideration.

"'Ave a sit down," I said, seeing no one about.

"Yes, sir." He took this as an order.

"I ain't a sir, I'm Nathaniel Swubble."

At once, he realised that we shared at least one misfortune. Bumble had named both of us. He relaxed a little.

Have you been bird scaring before, Oliver?" I asked him.

"No, I ain't, Nat. I'll do me very best, honest I will."

This was an odd one, I thought. But who would not be flattered by such subservience?

"Come on. I'll show you," I told him, as though I knew myself. I flapped my arms and ran about like a huge bird, screaming and screeching. Oliver's laughter spurred me on and I hopped, jumped, dived and turned here, there and everywhere.

Slowly, Oliver joined in, at first silently and then more and more noisily and excitedly. I was a sparrowhawk scaring birds. Oliver was a small bird released from a cage. Together, we rushed around the fields, dashing madly at any sparrow which dared to settle. One bird took no notice and I bent down, picked up a stone and threw it. Oliver went very quiet. He made me feel ashamed of my action.

"You've got to show 'em 'oo's boss," I claimed defensively.

"'E chirps so beautiful," he said.

"'E ought to, the amount 'e's eating." Not wishing to be seen taking advice from him, I continued to throw stones, but made sure I missed the birds.

"Sit down 'ere," I ordered to reassert my authority.

Oliver sat and admired a wild flower growing near by. "God made the birds and flowers," he announced, solemnly. Such thoughts were not usually ones which occupied my mind. I turned to more earthly thoughts. "Where's your food?" I asked. "We'll be 'ere till the birds go 'ome to roost."

"Ain't got none," he answered, trying not to look enviously at my chunk of bread and cheese.

"Want a bit of mine?"

Oliver was human and hungry enough to transfer his thought from flowers to food. "Yes, please, Nat." Taking the piece I offered, Oliver broke it in half and placed half in his pocket.

"You don't 'ave to save any. I've got some more for later."

"I'll keep some for the toddlers at Mrs Mann's, if you don't mind, Nat."

"Don't you get bread at your place?" I asked.

"Not much," Oliver conceded, as though being more definite would show ingratitude to Mrs Mann.

When he had finished his bread, I handed Oliver my bottle of water. As he stretched out his hand, he said, in the high, precise tones of the vicar, "Thank you so much, my dear Mrs Mann. I think I might be persuaded to take just one small glass of sherry. Just the smallest glass, Mrs Mann, just the smallest." It was Mr Clack exactly.

We laughed and I asked Oliver if he could mimic anyone else. Flopping back on the ground, Oliver took off his cap and wiped his head with the rag he carried as a handkerchief.

"Me 'ead, Mrs Mann, is as 'ot as a hegg boiling in the pot." Bumble's rather hoarse voice was unmistakeable. Oliver mimicked other people and I guessed who they were, but, finally, there was one that I did not recognise.

"It's William White," Oliver told me.

"Don't sound much like 'im."

"The son. I weren't doing the father."

"I don't know 'im. Only know 'im by sight. 'Ow 'ave you come to 'ear 'im speak?"

"'E's Mrs Mann's nephew. 'E always wears a white waistcoat."

"Why?"

"'Cos of 'is name, I suppose."

It made sense.

Taking some crumbs from my pocket, I asked, "Shall we feed the birds?"

"Yes, we should share our feast with God's creatures."

I began to laugh, thinking he was mimicking Mr Clack again, but he was not. I thought to myself that he was a strange boy and no mistake.

We threw crumbs until sparrows, blackbirds and starlings were fighting for their share.

"'Ere, you work'ouse brats." The loud cry came across the field. We looked up to see a gang of boys, a few years older than us, hurrying towards us.

"Shall we run?" Oliver inquired, with more common sense than I would have credited him with.

"They can run faster than us."

The boys, looking immensely tall and strong, stood before us.

"You work'ouse brats is as lazy as your parents. Idle to the core. You needs to be taught a lesson."

"We just dropped a few crumbs from our dinner. We was trying to get all the birds 'ere so we could stone 'em." I lied with little hope that they would believe me. Grabbing at straws, I added, "I were just going to grab that big 'un when you scared 'im orf."

"Now I'm going to grab you, ain't I?"

It was clear that he was. Oliver moved towards me, or perhaps I moved towards him. We certainly sought support from each other. We felt like two little six year olds facing the world.

"'E ain't from the work'ouse," I told them, trying to save Oliver.

"Baby farm. Same thing," one of the giants decided. "What shall we do with 'em?"

There was no lack of blood-curdling suggestions. "String 'em up," was the most popular idea. They had no doubt heard it expressed by their fathers many times.

The largest giant looked round and smiled. "Grab 'em," he commanded, in the tones of one used to being obeyed. With our arms held firmly and painfully behind our backs, we were marched to the middle of the field, where a scarecrow was tied to a post. In minutes, we had taken his place, tied back to back and unable to move.

They surveyed their handiwork with deep satisfaction. "'E were better dressed than them," one laughed. The others joined in the mockery. As they finally gave up and disappeared across the field, one called back. "You'll be in trouble. You won't get paid and old Bumble'll give you a whacking."

I could hear Oliver sobbing and hoped that he could not hear me. We knew any passing school boys would come and tease us. The sun was not strong, but it blinded my eyes. As the final insult, I could feel birds walking up and down my outstretched arms, looking for choice shoots to steal. Some droppings landed on my head. We were hungry and thirsty and very tired.

"There's a big boy coming," Oliver sobbed. I could not see in his direction and braced myself for attack.

"Can't leave you alone for a minute, can I?" an approaching voice announced. "When I'm not around, you can't keep out of trouble."

I wept with relief. It was Paul. In seconds he had us untied.

Looking at him as though he were the angel Gabriel, Oliver whispered, "Thank you, sir. I shall never forget your kindness to us."

Paul gave him a strange look, but grinned with pleasure. "You get orf back to the baby farm. I nearly said, 'Get orf back 'ome,' but I used to live there and it ain't much like 'ome, is it?"

Oliver was off like a bolt from a bow.

Turning to me and putting his arm around my shoulder, Paul said, "Look at your shirt."

I looked. It was covered with mud and with the substance Mrs Corney condemned most of all – grass stains.

"Look at yours!" I exclaimed. Paul had obviously wiped his grubby hands on it.

We walked on, thinking of the caning to come. Then, trying to look on the bright side, I said, "Good job we don't wear white waistcoats like young Mr White does as 'e walks around the town." Then I wondered, did William White wear a white jacket because his name was White, or did he wear it to hide his black heart?

CHAPTER EIGHT

While I had come to know the main areas of Myddlington, Jack Star had forbidden us to go into the dingiest areas. Unusually, as she was so obedient, it was Felicity who disobeyed. Bumble christened her Felicity Fidget, but never had a baby been so wrongly named. Her hands, when not busy with day to day tasks, rested relaxed, and she radiated calmness and competency. Above all, Felicity possessed that rarest of qualities – common sense. She corrected our bad behaviour, but never confused small misdemeanours with sins. She followed principles, in which she firmly believed, yet knew that sticking to the letter of the law could distort its very spirit. When need be, she could stand her ground, but listened to others and acknowledged their right to stand theirs.

In appearance, at first sight, Felicity was quite plain, with straight hair, which, by nightly tying in rags, she tried to persuade to fall from her cap in ringlets. If she appeared to have succeeded for the first five minutes in the day, another five in the kitchen or laundry saw her hair fall back into its natural state. These great efforts with her hair suggested that, had there been a good fairy to grant wishes, Felicity would have asked to be beautiful, but she patiently settled for looking kind and having a smile which cheered even the lowest spirits.

Felicity had been born with a mother's instincts. With us, she was like a mother hen, clucking and protecting us from danger and chirping and leading us to the most enjoyable aspects of life. From the beginning, although I never saw her be cruel, she showed that instinct necessary for mothers of poor children who had to make their way in the world, of knowing how to be firm to be kind.

No doubt irritated by my snivelling and my frequent references to my own cruel abandonment, she took my hand one day and said she would show me what real misery meant. Paul came just for the company. Georgina came as she was at the stage of believing that walking made her cheeks rosy and had not yet reached the stage where she thought it lady-like to be pale and languid. Going without Jack's blessing and knowledge meant going without his dog, Titan, to protect us.

Purposefully, Felicity led us through back streets to the Hole in the Wall, the very place we had been forbidden to enter. I was torn between my goodie-goodie attitude of saying Mr Star had told us not to go there and my curiosity to see this forbidden scene.

Only a step or two into the passage-way between tall houses, with the sun blocked out and our eyes plunged in darkness, our noses were assailed by the most awful smell on earth. It was a mixture of open sewers and rubbish dumps, only much worse. Entering our nostrils, it filled our lungs until we could scarcely breathe. We pinched our noses, but the stench entered through our mouths, filling our stomachs and churning them until we felt sick.

I asked to go home, but Felicity dragged me on. Sooner than we expected, the passage opened out into a yard. There must have been an opening onto the sky, but it offered no exit for the smell or entrance for light and air. Houses surrounded the court. Perhaps, once, they had been tall and had stood proud and straight. Now, they leaned heavily upon each other for support, their wooden frames rotten with years of being exposed to wind and rain. In some cases, the walls were propped up with beams, which, in turn, had been propped up with other poles themselves.

I wanted to run back, but Felicity held me firmly by the hand. Her expression showed disgust, but also determination to see this through and teach me a lesson.

"Look at them, Nat," she insisted in as firm a voice as she could muster. "Take a good look at them, Nathaniel Swubble."

For the first time, I made out several children. The eldest was about Felicity's age and was nursing a filthy bundle, which I took to contain a baby. They sat or stood staring back at us, obviously as used to the pond of stinking, stagnant water with its islands of human waste and rotting matter, as we were to the clean, if stark, floors of the workhouse. It seemed that someone had collected together all the waste of the town, rotting vegetables, broken furniture, old rags, scraps of metal, which, having passed through all layers of society, could descend no lower. We spotted the source of the offensive smell. It was a pile of rotting animal remains at the back of an abattoir.

A boy approached me, a great deal of dirty skin showing through his tattered clothes. I realised he would find my patched ones highly desirable. I wanted to leave, but still Felicity held my hand tightly. I whimpered, "You're 'urting me 'and, Lissy."

Felicity, ignoring me, spoke to the girl with the baby. "Are you looking after it?" she asked.

"'Course I am. It's mine ain't it?" the girl answered grudgingly.

"'Ow old are you?"

"'Ow do I know?"

How would she know? There seemed no clear days or nights, summers or winters in this grim place. I looked at a child eating a crust of bread as filthy as she was. She stared back with dull, empty eyes.

From one of the doors, a woman emerged, her eyes half closed and streaming from some concoction she was cooking.

"What d'yer want? We don't want people pinching nothing what's ours."

"Nothing," I was quick to reply. "We ain't touched nothing, missus."

"Nothing, thank you, madam," Felicity answered, with more composure than she felt. With firm selfcontrol she turned and led us out.

Back in the road, we wanted to do nothing but stand breathing in the relatively fresh air outside. But my lesson was only half done.

"Where would you rather live, in there or in the work'ouse?"

"In the work'ouse." There was no doubt in my mind.

"'Oo would you rather be, that boy or yerself?"

"Meself," I answered, as though repeating the catachism.

"Then remember," Felicity told me, "that when you're worrying about being left outside the work'ouse gate, there's a good chance you could ave been worse orf."

I was silent for a moment to take in the point of this lesson. "D'yer mean that 'orrible woman could 'ave been me Ma?"

"No I don't," Felicity answered with feeling. "You're a born worrier, Nat Swubble. Give you an answer to one worry and you're orf on another."

Putting her arm around me, she hurried us on. She was beginning to think she had been too impulsive in bringing us. Even here, the streets were narrow and mean and we were some way from the workhouse. "I just brought you 'ere to show you that your Ma and Pa might 'ave been thinking what was best for you. What else can you do with a baby when you can't feed nor clothe it?"

Reluctantly, I nodded in agreement. Felicity was always right. Shut one line of thought to a worrier and another opens. Before, I had hated my parents for leaving me. Now I thought they might have been kind and caring and I worried in case I would never see them.

We began to walk along the road, when, from a door nearby, a man emerged. To us, in our frightened state, he appeared as the devil in man's form. His eyes, or I should say, one eye was dark and menacing. The other was half closed and surrounded by swollen purple flesh. Every feature of his face seemed mis-shapen, with a flat nose, missing teeth, bruised cheeks and twisted, swollen ears. As he staggered towards us, he mumbled something. The words were not intelligible and the tone was low. We were sure it was some terrible curse or threat he was uttering to us.

With one accord, we turned and ran. Had we known, we would have recognised him as a prize fighter, who had fought too many fights and was punch drunk. He was, in fact, quite harmless, but we were in a mood to see everything in this terrible area as threatening and harmful. To us, he was the devil incarnate or the bogeyman himself.

We did not stop running until we had left that wretched place. We stopped to get our breath. Here, the rows of houses and their inhabitants clung desperately to respectability, maintaining appearances by letting out clean, if sparsely furnished rooms, to lodgers who could pay the small amount charged for them. We stopped, already half ashamed of our fears.

"Did you see 'is eye?" Paul marvelled. "I bet it 'urt."

With increasing confidence, we began to laugh at his appearance and our fright.

"Just you see," Felicity advised Paul, "That you don't try to get rich that way."

"Me shoe come orf," Georgina laughed."I 'ad to grab it and 'op as fast as I could."

"And Paul's never 'eld me 'and so 'ard since 'e were four or five."

"I never." Paul denied Felicity's claim vehemently.

"Look at me 'and, then," Felicity ordered him. The white marks on her skin exactly matched the shape of a tightly clasping hand. Even Paul had to give in and half smile.

As we stood there, a man and woman passed and smiled at our laughter. Their worn, but clean and neatly mended, clothes proclaimed them as striving for respectability. We smiled back at them.

"Are you children lost?" the woman asked, in a kindly voice.

"Not now, thank you, ma'am," Felicity replied. "We know our way back from 'ere."

"On your way back!" the woman exclaimed. "Don't tell me you have been to the Hole in the Wall!" Looking at the two children who stared out of the window, she went on with great feeling, "I'd never let my children go anywhere near there."

"We ain't got no parents," Paul informed her. "We're orphans from the work'ouse."

"Then someone should be responsible for your welfare," the man stated sternly. "I'll come down there tomorrow and give them a piece of me mind."

"Children should not roam here, there and everywhere. There are dangers lurking," the woman added in a gentler, but equally serious voice. Seeing our worried faces, she put her hand on her husband's arm. "No, my dear, you mustn't tell the authorities or these sweet children will be in trouble. I'm sure they've learnt their lesson, haven't you, children?"

We assured her that we had and were greatly relieved to know they would not tell tales on us.

Smiling now, the woman changed the subject. "What pretty embroidery on your dress, my child," she told Georgina. "Don't tell me that they give you such pretty frocks in the workhouse."

"Felicity did it," Georgina said, turning round and round to reveal the full glory of her dress. "Old Sal cut it down from a lady's dress and showed Felicity 'ow to embroider it."

"You must be a quick learner, Felicity," the woman told the smiling girl. "I have tried and tried, but my fingers always seem to get in my way. Such nimble fingers at your age! I'd never have guessed that work was not done by a skilled woman."

Felicity was embarrassed, but delighted by such comments. "I've done simple things before," she explained, "but Sal said I were ready for something 'arder."

The woman smiled and was then struck by a bright idea. "How, Felicity, would you like to embroider my daughter's dress? I'd pay, of course. I can't afford much, but sixpence would buy you something in return."

"Oh!" Felicity protested. "I wouldn't want money. It would be a pleasure to do it for nothing, Mrs...."

"Mrs Brown, my dear, that's my name. Now we've introduced ourselves, would you come in and look at the material and tell me what silks to buy?"

Felicity hesitated. The woman noted this with a smile. "Just you, my dear. The youngsters can play outside with my boys." She turned to her husband. "Send the boys out, my dear, I know we don't usually let them out to play with other children and learn bad habits, but these two boys with

Felicity are so well behaved, I don't mind them being together for a few minutes."

Georgina was about to follow Felicity into the house, when Mrs Brown said, "You wait there my dear. Sit on the step and have a rest, if you're too big to play with the boys."

As Mrs Brown led Felicity into the house, the two boys came out. From experience, we were suspicious of other boys, but one of these carried a wooden cavalryman and the other the wooden horse on which he rode. Soon we were examining the toys and then vying with each other to play with them. Paul had the horse in his hand, when one of the boys snatched it and ran with it down the road. "Come on, slowcoaches," he called. "Let's go round the corner and then charge back."

Paul needed no more encouragement and dashed after him, intent on getting his hands on the cavalry man and his steed again.

Knowing I had no chance of having a go, I followed reluctantly, just behind the younger of the two boys. Once round the corner, we saw the others were far ahead. We trudged on until, tired of trailing behind Paul and his new friend, I stopped. "If we wait a minute," I suggested to the boy, "we can join in when they come running back." He just stood and stared at me. He was about my age, but thinner, with sad, large brown eyes. "Are you ill?" I inquired, putting my hand on his shoulder. "What's your name?"

I could scarcely hear his reply, "Matthew," and I noticed tears in his eyes.

"My name's Nat. Shall I 'elp you walk 'ome and tell your Ma you ain't well?" My mention of home seemed to upset him more, but then he sniffed, wiped his eyes with his sleeve and turned away.

Paul came flying back on his return journey. He had easily outrun the other boy. When he was playing horses, no one could catch him. I joined him, running as fast as I had ever run and leaving the unhappy boy behind me. Something was wrong, I knew it.

"Where's Gina?" I shouted breathlessly as I ran.

Paul stopped, without even bothering to rein in his horse. "She must 'ave gawn into the 'ouse"

We pounded on the door. "Lissy! Lissy! Is Gina there?"

In a second, Felicity was at the door, her face anxious and worried. "I left 'er with you two."

"She ain't 'ere now."

"There, there," Mrs Brown comforted Felicity. "She"ll be somewhere near by, you mark my word." Concerned and business-like, she ordered, "Felicity, you go that way with the boys. Me and my boys'll knock on the doors and ask if anyone's seen your pretty little friend. People know us and will tell us if they've caught sight of her."

Grabbing Paul and me by the hand so as not to lose us as well, Felicity did as she had been told.

I went, but became more and more uneasy. "Felicity," I suggested, "Do you think Mr and Mrs Brown 'ave got Georgie?"

For a moment, Felicity stopped and thought. "No, Nat, she is such a kind woman."

"That little boy was crying. 'E ain't theirs I'd swear."

For once, Felicity did not give me a lecture on swearing. Her hand went to her head. "I'm a fool," she moaned, "a stupid, conceited fool."

We looked back along the road. There was no sign of Mrs Brown and the boys knocking at doors. I think I was crying.

"They'll be orf out the back door," Paul announced. He seemed to have an instinctive understanding of how villains' minds worked.

Dashing off, he cut through an arch way between the houses into the next street. We could hear him shouting, "Stop! Stop! Kick 'im 'ard, Gina. Kick 'im as 'ard as you can."

We joined Paul and saw the Brown family hurrying away as fast as they could. Mrs Brown was carrying a bag of their belongings and dragging the youngest boy. Mr Brown was half carrying, half dragging Georgina. One hand was around her mouth to stop her screaming and attracting the attention of the people in their houses.

Paul ran even faster than before and Felicity, holding up her skirt, was only just behind. Exhausted, I stopped, took a couple of deep breaths and yelled, "Bite 'im, Georgie! For Gawd's sake bite 'is 'and."

That was exactly what Georgina had been trying to do, but Mr Brown, no doubt from practice, held his hand in such a way that she could not get her teeth into it. Inspired by my shouts, she grabbed his hand with her own, forced it closer to her mouth and bit it with all her might. Swearing and blaspheming, he let go with one hand. Georgina made the most of the opportunity to scream loud enough to wake the dead. People came to their windows and doors.

"Let 'er go. Let 'er go!" Mrs Brown pleaded. "Take them bags from the boys and let's get out of 'ere."

Flinging Georgina away from him, Mr Brown did as he was told. I swear the younger boy was going to run back to us, but Mr Brown grabbed his arm and ran with him, leaving his wife and the other child to follow. Which way they turned, we did not note. Paul and Felicity had reached the weeping Georgina and were hugging her and begging her forgiveness for letting her out of their sight. Georgina was begging theirs for accepting Mr Brown's offer of finding her a piece of cake while Mrs Brown and Felicity talked. Paul listed some terrible things he would do to Mr Brown, if he ever set eyes on him again. We were all delighted to see Mr Brown's blood on Georgina's teeth.

Somehow, it seemed in minutes, the story got back to the workhouse and we were in serious trouble. Mrs Corney said Felicity was not too old for a beating and gave her one. We were not allowed out for a few weeks and were forced to occupy our time completing the most unpleasant and dirtiest jobs in the workhouse. No one had any sympathy for us. Jack told us we should never have been there in the first place, let alone accept an invitation from strangers.

Immediately we had arrived back, Jack had waited just long enough to get a description of the Browns and had then gone with friends to find them. A startled occupier of the house into which Felicity had gone said his lodgers had seemed most respectable. They had left suddenly without paying the rent. Enquiries, around the town, led to the discovery that they had been begging, representing themselves as poor, but caring, parents, whose children were ill and in need of medicines and food. They were too proud, they had said, to make paupers of themselves and their children, but had thrown themselves on the charity of townspeople. With the pale faced little boy with large brown eyes, they had done very well. Clergymen, ministers and private charities had accepted their story on face value. With Georgina, they would have at least doubled their takings. One way or another, everyone had been as poor at spotting real bogeymen as we had been.

CHAPTER NINE

Gradually, as I was approaching seven years of age, I developed a passion as strong as Paul's passion for horses – I wanted to learn to read.

Most people, in my world at least, felt no need for book learning of any sort. They had no call for it. A labourer could spend his whole life without being asked to read or write. Even at marriage, the cleryman expected nothing more than that the parties should make their marks. I know many a tradesman or craftsman who looked for a wife to do the accounts and cope with any writing and reading which he required in his business. If any public notice were displayed in town, a small crowd would collect and one of its number would read to the rest.

It was while I was at the print shop window that my desire to read was started. When new prints arrived, whether making fun of or praising national figures or showing noble buildings and scenes, people would press around. Someone would urge, "Read it out, John," or "Read it to us then, Tom." Often, the reader was younger than the people around him, but the words he read out could make his audience laugh or disagree, but they always brought gratitude for the reader. How I longed for the day when they would say," Read it to us, Nat."

Whenever we passed by the bookseller's with volume upon volume piled up on the stall outside, I would pick up a book, not quite sure how reading worked, and hold it at arm's length and say whatever came into my head. Then, realising from Jack Star's reading of notices and papers and pamphlets that a stream of language fell into separate words and that each spoken word was represented by a separate word on the page, I looked along each line for a word I might recognise. It was a long, unproductive search.

Seeing boys coming home carrying their books, I realised that school was the place where the skill of reading was to be aquired, but they all, even dame schools which did little more than teach children their letters, charged at least a few pence a week. The fashion for charities which provided Sunday schools for the poor had not yet reached Myddlington. While the taxpayers provided a roof over our heads and food for our bellies and clothes for our backs, it did not even occur to them to provide anything for our minds.

With no financial support, I turned to people in the workhouse for help. Some of the old women could write their names and identify labels on a bottle, but that was not what I called reading and writing. Ben couldn't read. "Look at them what can read," he would say. "Most of 'em can't knock a nail in straight or mend a broken 'inge, let alone drive 'orses." Paul, all too readily, agreed with him.

Digger and John could read and I turned to them. "Read me a bit," I would say to Digger in my most weedling tone.

"Don't whine," he would tell me. "You ain't a girl and I ain't Sal or one of 'er cronies what spoil you children."

In my most masculine tone, I would repeat my request. "Just a few words, Digger."

"Ain't you forgotten something?"

"Please, sir."

"I wouldn't read from this book to a child if it were the last book on earth." He was reading the Bible.

"Why, please sir?"

"'Cos it were written to keep people in order. To make them obey them as, it's claimed, Gawd 'as set over 'em. It's meant to make men 'appy with their miserable lives on earth, in the 'ope that they get to 'eaven."

I hesitated to ask why, in that case, he read it himself.

Guessing my thoughts he said, "I'm glad you're not one of them cheeky boys what questions their elders and betters, so I'll tell you without you 'aving to ask." He duly told me. "I carry it about with me, 'cos there's some of them casuals what come in 'ere what'd steal your breath if you let 'em get close enough. That's one answer. The other is that it's all we're given to read in 'ere."

"That's true," John agreed.

"Oh, yes," Digger resumed, "You pays to come in 'ere. Not with money. You pays with your soul. You be'ave yourself and resist evil. And they believes it's about as evil as working men can get if they dares to think for theirselves. Words is powerful things."

It was getting a bit beyond my understanding, but it made me want to read all the more.

Luckily, John was only too happy to read to me from his Bible. He saw it as his Christian duty, but, in the past, he had found no child who wanted to listen.

"They like to catch you young," Digger grumbled.

"Don't listen to the grumpy old feller," John told me. "I'll read you the Sermon on the Mount. That ain't never done no one no 'arm."

I listened intently, my eyes on his lips, as though reading in every word as well as listening. I was preparing the ground for my next request. Trying not to sound weedling, I asked, "Would you teach me to read please, sir? It would be good for me to read the Bible, wouldn't it, sir?"

"Traitor," Digger said, walking away.

John laughed, "'Aven't you talked to that friend of yours, Jack Star lately?"

"'E's always too busy."

"Well, we've been 'aving a talk together, seeing 'ow you've set your 'eart on reading. Jack says we can all learn you to read when you're seven."

"Why 'ave I got to wait?" This time I did whine.

"Ask Jack. 'E seems to act as though 'e was your Pa."

As soon as I could, I did ask the porter.

"There's other things as important as reading." Jack told me. "One's growing up as fit and strong as you can. Don't want you sitting in when you could be out in the fresh air, walking and running and growing as strong as you can."

"Some children go to the dame school when they're only three or four," I complained.

"I ain't got nothing to do with that, 'ave I? Dame schools is mostly just to keep children from under their mother's feet and keep 'em out of mischief."

"Some can read," I persisted.

"There's reading and reading," Jack told me. "There's just barking at words and there's understanding what you're reading. There's a 'ole world of difference."

"But I'll get left be'ind."

"No you won't. When you're seven, you'll learn much faster. Before you're eight, you'll 'ave caught 'em all up. Now, stop pleading and weedling, Nat. I've made up me mind."

When I related these conversations to the others, Felicity and Georgina said that they would like to read, too. I suppose that Georgina realised that, even if a pretty face were enough for a duke, any dowager duchess would expect her daughter-in-law to read.

Predictably, Paul said, "I ain't bothered about reading."

Before Virtue and Tom could say what they thought, I told them firmly, "You're too young for reading."

Sal had her say. "You don't need books to read. There's words all over the place, ain't there? 'Ow d'yer think Digger and John come to read? They didn't go to no school. They taught theirselves." Pausing in her task of cutting large potatoes into small pieces, she went on, "Even I can read. Listen." She recited the name and type of every shop in the High Street in order.

I put her right. "That ain't reading. You 'ave to look at the words and then say them."

"Lor!" she retorted. "Is that so? 'Ere's me, seventy years old or more and I ain't never worked that out before." As she winked at them, the others laughed. "Must be luverly to be clever," she added.

I hated it when they teased me, but, when I thought it over, I decided there was something in what Sally said. There were words everywhere. Felicity and I set about learning them all. We worked out which were names and which were occupations in the signs over shops. We were delighted when we recognized, on a second shop, a word we had learned from a first. Often, we had to ask passers-by what notices and signs said and sometimes it was a long wait to find someone who could tell us. We discovered that there was, indeed, reading and reading. Most men could read, "Gin," but were not so good at, "Your sins will find you out." From the words we learned, we worked out our letters. S was for Sowerberry, for example. We had a little trouble working out what H stood for.

Eventually, we had exhausted the High Street and were repeating everything from memory. Then Felicity had one of her bright ideas. "There's the churchyard," she announced. "There's all those names on tombstones. If we can spot which is which, it means we can read."

The idea was so good that we did not even stop to argue about it. Off we went to the chuchyard. Not wishing to show how uneasy I felt in such a place by holding on to Felicity's hand, I made out that Tom needed help and held on to his. Any human contact was welcome in this place of spirits. "Don't let's go round the back of the church," I said.

Both Felicity and Paul guessed I was scared. "Ain't nobody there," Paul joked. "Just a ghost with no body, that's all."

As usual, Felicity was kinder. "We'll just read those here, by the gate. The sun's on them and they're easier ter read."

"Look, there's a Sowerberry." We looked first for those names we could recognize, and then worked out others. Very soon, we could read the names of all those families in the town who could afford tombstones, all the months of the year and some words such as 'daughter' and 'beloved'.

Our efforts, I thought, must win round Jack to helping me with my reading before I was seven. Then, I would be able to teach the others. But it was no use.

"I don't want you to turn into someone 'oo knows everything and does nothing. There's people in Parliament 'oo can read Latin and Greek and 'ave never raised a finger ter make people's lives easier. Listen to Digger and John – and there's many more like them – and 'ow they know 'ow to make heaven on earth. They're all words and no action. What I say – and there's none enjoys reading more than me – is that if you've always got your 'ead stuck in a book, you can't see a simple action what needs doing to 'elp a neighbour."

At last, my seventh birthday arrived on a bitterly cold and wet day. Fierce rain blew from the north west and I was soaked and shivering as I ran to the gate, where Jack stood taking his first look of the day along the street.

"Anymore babies there, Mr Star?" I joked.

"'Fraid not, Nat. Did you want a little brother or sister for your birthday? Well," he went on, "Let's 'ave a look at you."

Rain was running down our faces, but we were both laughing. "Best thing I ever did, finding you, Nat." He gave me a brief, embarrassed hug.

When I had run out to see Jack, all that had been on my mind was my birthday and reading, but I suddenly found myself asking, "Ain't you got no idea 'oo me parents are, Mr Star?"

Avoiding a direct answer, he replied, "Now don't start that again, Nat." Then, feeling in his pocket, he mumbled, "Now where 'as that baby's first reading book I got you gone to?"

My heart sank. With all the work Felicity and I had done, a first reading book would not last me five minutes. But I would have to smile and thank Jack and not let him see how disappointed I was.

He laughed. "No, I ain't got you nothing to read. 'Ere, Nat, 'ere's your present. It ain't new, but it's in perfect condition." The porter held out a clasp knife. "I got it at the pawnshop," he explained. "Suppose someone 'adn't the money to redeem a pledge."

"It's the best thing I've ever 'ad in me life," I exclaimed truthfully.

I went to throw my arms around him, but, as though embarrassed, Jack gently held me off. At that moment, we realised that Bumble was standing by.

"Don't get too friendly with the boys, Star, if you value your job," the beadle reminded him.

"I were just wishing the lad a 'appy birthday, Mr Bumble," Jack explained. I looked at Bumble, expecting him to add his good wishes. He snorted in reply and walked away.

"Don't let old sour face spoil your day," Jack told me. "Now, run and get your breakfast and come back straight away. I got another little treat in mind."

I flew off, eager to show my new treasure rather than to have breakfast.

"Why's 'e so good to you?" Paul inquired thoughtfully, stroking the knife as though it were a living pet.

"'E's good to everyone," Felicity said, gently nudging Paul to indicate that he was not to spoil my day by envying me.

"Would you like me to look after it for you?" Paul asked. "You can't trust no one around 'ere. Someone might thieve it from you."

"Don't think Nat's going to take 'is eyes orf it for a while." Felicity had never spoken a truer word.

"I suppose it's alright for a boy," Georgina decided. "They ain't very interested in their appearance. Me, I want ribbons for my birthday."

"That's a change from wanting diamonds," Felicity commented.

Later, we all set off to meet Jack, assuming that, if one were invited, we all were. He was waiting with Ben and, walking over to White's Yard, we had to walk slowly for the old man to keep up.

"It ain't no good going without me," Ben informed us. "It's me what's going to get you into the library." He looked at Jack, "Oh dear! I weren't meant to say that yet."

"The boy would 'ave found out soon enough," Jack said. "You see, Nat, Mr White 'as started a library for 'is men, including them as 'as retired like Ben. There's all sorts of books. Ben says as 'ow there's 'ard ones and easy ones."

"Can I join?" I asked.

"No you can't," Ben asserted, enjoying his priveleged position. "I can borrow the books and I'll let you read 'em, if you're good."

Ben was, indeed, our ticket into the little library, set up in an unused building in the Yard. It had been set up to encourage men to improve themselves instead of wasting time and money drinking or gambling.

We all looked along the volumes, Digger reading their titles and Georgina looking for pictures.

"Are there any romances?" Gina asked.

"This ain't a ladies' lending library," Ben told her.

"You know why they've done this, don't you?" Digger asked. Without waiting for a reply from anyone else, he provided his own answer. "Just so as working men'll read what their masters want 'em to read and won't read what they don't want 'em to see. There ain't no politics. There ain't nothing about democracy, nothing about...."

"Keep your opinions to yourself for once," Ben urged him. "I don't want to get thrown out." Turning to me, he said, "'Ere, boy. Choose what you want."

I was spoilt for choice. First I picked up one and then another.

"You better take one what ain't too 'ard to start with," Jack said. "I ain't discouraging you, but there ain't many books made up just of words like 'Sowerberry' and 'Ere lyeth'."

I still picked up one book after another. It was like finding buried treasure. Paul had disappeared to look at the horses and Georgina had gone with him to look at the stable boys.

"Stop drooling over 'em and get a move on," Ben ordered. "I can't stand 'ere on this leg much longer. It's giving me gip today."

Eventually, Jack chose for me. He chose a book of extracts from many authors and promised to read it with me.

As it was my birthday, I was allowed to carry it back. Imagine my disappointment when I was not allowed to read it first. Digger and John read it, while I went about my chores and neither was willing to surrender it. Birthday or no birthday, grownups came first. Giving up a book to a child would have been spoiling me and condemning me to Hell fire.

It was Paul, as usual, who helped me over my disappointment. "Come on, Nat, let them read their old books. I've got another treat for you. We'll creep out and go to your house at the bottom of the lane."

"Really?" I had never forgotten my dream house, but I had not realised Paul had remembered. We set out, running, jumping and skipping until we reached the lane. I slowed down. Would my house, where I had lived and played in my dreams, disappoint me when I set eyes on it once again? No, there it was with its neat low wall, topped by railings too close together to trap a child's head. I counted the bedroom windows. There were still four and three attic rooms.

"'Ow do you think you got to the work'ouse, then, Nat?" The question still puzzled Paul and he was more than willing to go along with my fantasies as long as I allowed him to pretend my knife was his.

"The gypsies stole me and they was just passing the work'ouse when they thought someone were after them. They put me down and ran off." Many times I had asked myself the same question and had the answer off pat.

Paul raised his hand to push at the gate, but dropped it quickly. We should have noticed that the shrubs and flowers had been cut back and tidied up. A family was moving in. The dog, which had made Paul decide not to enter, sniffed at us through the gate. He bared his teeth and growled.

"'E don't know you, Nat."

"'E were only a puppy when I were born. He were born the same day as me," I added to make my story sound more convincing.

"Be off with you," a gardener shouted. "Don't want no children around 'ere, especially work'ouse brats."

Our cut-down clothes and patches had given us away again.

"Come on, Nat. Let's go to our real 'ome. Looks like someone's moving in. Could be your parents 'ave come back. Can I keep your knife on the way 'ome to the work'ouse?"

CHAPTER TEN

That William White and Son ran the Yard opposite the workhouse and half of the town besides, I have already made clear. We saw the father quite often, but only occasionally caught sight of the son. As on other cases, our information about them came from the old people in the workhouse. It was one evening, when we were all huddled round the kitchen fire, that the name of William White was brought up.

"Which one?" someone asked.

"William John Bull White," Digger announced, in slow, solemn tones in keeping with such a grand name.

"'Oo?" all of us children chorused.

"'Oo you talking about?" Ben asked, putting his hand to his ear to hear the reply.

Digger could not resist announcing the son's name again, as though introducing a guest at an official function.

"'Oo give 'im that 'andle?" Paul inquired. "Bumble?"

"Don't you young 'uns make fun of things you don't understand," Ben warned him. "Them Frenchies nearly done for us in them wars. That Napoleon feller swept all before 'im until 'e come up against us Englishmen."

"What," demanded Paul, "were 'e frightened orf by a baby named John Bull?"

"John Bull's our figure 'ead. Mr White knew that when 'e named his son. Mr White is a true patriot."

"'Oo wouldn't be," Digger asked, "if they was making as much money as 'im out of the war?"

"Is that 'ow 'e come to make 'is money?" Felicity inquired. Some round the fire agreed with Digger and some denied it. Old Sal got to the root of the answer. "Married Emma Trumpshaw, didn't 'e? A lovely girl, but timid as a mouse. 'Er father 'ad the corn mill. William White knew what 'e were doing when 'e married an only child."

"It's only common sense to look for a good marriage," Georgina claimed.

As Sally paused for breath, Ben took his opportunity. "About that time they built our small canal to link up with the big one. All sorts of trade began passing through Myddlington then. 'E began trading in corn as well as milling it. Then 'e started dealing in coal."

"Then," someone put in," 'e started dealing in anything what couldn't move on its own legs and quite a few things what could."

"'E shifted anything what anyone wanted shifting as well as shifting all the stuff for 'isself," Ben continued, giving the man a withering look. 'E got carts and waggons and coaches..."

"And boats," a dull-witted boy announced, contributing his little piece of knowledge.

Ben was patient with him. "That's right, lad. And boats."

"And now 'e owns all them 'orses and stables," Paul marvelled.

"And the wharf and warehouses at the canal basin," Digger said. "They say as 'ow 'e could buy out 'alf the gentry in the county if 'e 'ad a mind to."

"And a few dukes as well," Ben added, with pride in his old master.

We children made the appropriate noises to convey our wonderment and our appreciation of all we were being told. After all, we didn't want to go to bed in the freezing cold.

Old Sal was not fooled. "Felicity," she ordered, "take that warming pan and put it in the little 'un's beds. Then it'll be your turn Paul Quince and Nathaniel Swubble."

Paul asked, as though absorbed by the conversation, "What's 'e like, old man White?"

"'E made 'is money by 'ard work," Ben stated, gazing at Digger, as though defying him to answer.

Digger could not resist having his say. "'E made 'is money by the 'ard work and sweat of 'alf the men in Myddlington, that's true."

Taking another line in defending his master, Ben argued, "'E put that money to good use, no spending it on 'igh living. 'E's built a big 'ouse for 'isself, I'll admit, but none of this buying 'is way into society."

Grudgingly, Digger had to admit this was true. William White had used his capital in new business and brought a measure of prosperity to the town.

"Is 'e a gent?" I asked.

"There's some as would say 'e is, and some as would say 'e ain't," Martha asserted.

"A gent," Ben said firmly. "To my mind a man's a gent if 'e behaves like one."

"To your mind, perhaps," Digger told him, unwilling to avoid any dispute, "but you ain't the one to decide 'oo is and 'oo ain't a gent. The real

55

gentry sez you ain't one of them unless you was born and bred one of them."

"Or," Martha said, "'ave the money to live like one." She had worked in great houses, even if in a very humble capacity, and saw herself as the foremost authority on the subject within the workhouse.

"And," Sal put in, "you ain't living like one if you're down the Yard every day getting your 'ands dirty alongside your men like Mr White does."

"To be a true gent," Digger explained, accepting the rules he claimed to despise, "first, you need to 'ave bin born to it. Then you need to 'ave parents with money, as well as breeding, 'oo can send you away to school with other little gentlemen, so as you can learn a lot of useless things like languages what only dead people speak. After that, you 'ave to go all round them foreign countries just staring at things."

"As though them foreigners 'ave got anything to teach us," Ben interrupted.

"I were speaking," Digger pointed out, staring aggressively at Ben. "I were saying that you 'ave to go to foreign places and bring back all sorts of pictures and statues what'd keep ordinary men in food for a life time." Taking a breath, Digger gazed at Ben daring him to interrupt. "Then you marry an heiress with money and settle down to waste it all on drinking, gambling and pretty women, while the workers on your estate slave away to make you some more."

"Don't sound too bad," Paul commented, nodding his approval.

"You only 'ope, if you wasn't born a gent, but 'ave money," John put in, almost timidly, but quite correctly, "is to buy land. A big estate goes a long way to making you a gentleman."

"William White's never done that," Ben declared. "I've 'eard 'im say putting money into land were like putting it into a big 'ole in the ground and watching it disappear."

I had been frowning at Paul for speaking and drawing attention to us, still up well past our bed-time. He had decided that the better tactic was to keep talking and encourage other people to do the same.

"William John Bull White looks like a gent." Paul threw out the comment as though it were a ball for someone to hold and then throw to someone else.

Digger never missed a catch. "'E were born when 'is Pa 'ad made a pretty penny. Sent 'im to a young gentlemen's school miles away."

Ben, seeing himself as the authority on this subject, was about to speak, when Sal contributed her share. "Didn't never want 'im turned into a gent, though. Said so, many a time."

Ben had to agree. "Yea, that's true. 'E never did. Said 'e wanted the lad to learn 'ow to talk to 'em on their own terms and run rings round 'em in business."

"That is what 'e said," Sal went on, "But it were only 'cos 'e wouldn't admit 'e wanted 'is son turned into a gent."

"You reading minds, now, are you?" Ben demanded.

"Always did," Sal claimed, winking at me.

"Then tell me why his Pa put 'im to the business so early." Ben demanded of her. "I remember Mr White bringing the lad to the Yard when 'e were no more than four or five. Made 'im learn every side of the business, 'e did. I were teaching 'im 'ow to 'arness 'orses one day, when Mr White sez, 'Let the apprentices do that. You got other work to do.'"

"Old miser won't waste a penny," Digger mumbled, keeping his voice low to annoy Ben, who was becoming hard of hearing.

Ben ignored him for once and continued his story. "Mr White believed as 'ow your men don't respect you if you ain't familiar with all branches of the business yourself."

"That boy never wanted to leave 'is 'ome," Sal claimed, resuming her strand of the tale. "Our young Sal worked for 'em and I can recall every word what she told me."

We had no need to encourage her to tell us what these words were.

"I'll tell you what she told me. She said that little lad come out one day to go with his Pa to the Yard as usual and 'is Pa sez, 'You're going to school today, son. Your bag's been put on the waggon. It must be a good school, the amount it's costing me. Climb up now. You're 'olding up the driver. 'E's got other deliveries to make."

"That's the Gospel truth," Ben agreed. "I were the driver and I 'eard it with me own ears, every word of it."

From Sal and Ben and anyone else who had a bit to contribute, we put the whole story together.

"Shall I be home before nightfall, Papa?" the boy had asked.

"No, son. You'll sleep there with all the other boys. I'll see you match them in everything....clothes, tuck, money in your pocket."

Seeing the tears in his mother's eyes, the child had become frightened. "Shall I be home tomorrow, Mama?"

"No, my darling," she had replied. "Your Papa wants you to stay with the other little boys." Trying to cheer him, she had added, "You will have so many playmates, you won't want to come home."

"But who's to go round the Yard with Papa?" he had asked.

Mr White had answered, "No one will take your place, son. When you get back, you can run the business alongside me."

"You mean I'll be in charge when I'm only seven?" the boy had asked, in surprise. He did not know that school lasted some years.

No one answered and he ran off and clambered up beside Ben.

"Remember," Mr White had called after him, "You're as good as them. You stand up to them, lad."

That was how young William White had come to arrive at his new school in a waggon bearing the message, "William White and Sons. Carriers, etc. Myddlington." "Carrier, etc," had been his name from the start.

True to his word, William White had showered his son with gifts for him to enjoy and to impress the other boys. Young William had not objected to the carts and waggons calling. Each arrival had been an opportunity for him to rush out, cling to the driver and plead, with tears streaming down his face, to be taken home.

After a while, Mr White had received a letter from the head master asking for the gifts to stop. It also suggested that young William should not go home at holidays until he had accepted the discipline the school demanded and "raised himself to the standard of the other young gentlemen in speech, moral fibre and character." None of this was passed on to Mrs White. She was told her son spent the holidays at the homes of his new friends. "Learning how the other half lives, that's what he's doing," her husband explained. "Do him as much good in dealing with 'em in business as any book learning."

Only reluctantly, did William White give in to his wife's pleading and agree to visit the child at school. On their first visit, the boy had cried a great deal, clung to his mother and asked her why she did not love him anymore.

"It's just as I've told you," Mr White had told his wife. "He's been too long tied to your apron strings. Stop them tears, boy, and live up to your name."

When he continued kicking and screaming, his father and the driver prised his fingers from his mother's skirts and handed him over to a school master.

On the return journey, Mrs White had dared to ask her husband what point there was in having a child whom they never saw and to whom they could show no affection.

"You women just don't understand," her husband had explained patiently. "It's not your fault," he had conceded, seeing how upset she was, "but only a man knows what he expects of a son. I might ask you what's the point of a whole life spent in building up a business, if there's no son trained up to take over when I'm dead and gone?"

"But you have always said, William, that you don't want to be a gentleman. Why should you want to turn our son into one?"

"You know my views, my dear," her husband explained patiently. "If we'd had only gentlemen to fight Napoleon, we'd all be talking French now and eating frogs' legs. Leaving aside Nelson, God rest his soul, and Wellington, they're a spineless bunch. It's men like me – men of the middling classes – who make this country great."

Mrs White opened her mouth to speak, but could not get a word in edgeways.

"You've never heard me say I want my boy to be a gentleman in anything else but honest dealing and keeping his word in a contract. I want him to understand their ways, talk on their terms with a spot of Latin or Greek thrown in here and there to impress. Given half' a chance, they try to run rings round us. Thanks to his education, my boy will be too clever for 'em."

Again, Mrs White tried, unsuccessfully, to have her say.

"Now don't oppose me, my dear. What I'm doing, I'm doing for the best." He patted his wife's hand. "Let's stop on the way and buy you a new gown. You're still a handsome woman, my dear, and do me proud."

Mrs White dried her tears. She did not want a new gown, but she saw it as her duty to support her husband in everything. Her pain over her son remained."

So the visits continued, year after year. The boy's violent sobbing gave way to silent weeping and then the tears ceased. He began to regain the weight he had lost and his eyes were no longer red and his face no longer marked by signs of sleepless nights and anxious days. He no longer clung to then, but neither did he reach out to them in any way.

Mrs White noticed that the boy's speech grew further from theirs and closer and closer to that of his school fellows. Even his enquiries as to their health were formal and as detached as all his conversations with them. Mrs White felt that she was losing her son. At around twelve, young William moved to another school, where he appeared to settle in quickly. On his visits home, the sons of his father's workers, who had once played with him in the Yard, looked at him in astonishment and grew tired of repeating everything they said until he could translate their rough speech into his own precise sounds. They doffed their caps and went on their way . Even the sons of his father's friends, educated in the local grammar school, found they no longer had anything in common with the boy they once liked. And there were no invitations from the gentlemen's sons of the locality for a boy whose father still worked in his own Yard, yet thought himself better than they were. As Sal put it, "The lad weren't fish nor fowl."

"Couldn't 'ave put it better meself," Digger agreed.

"And father and son never agree for two minutes on end," Ben put in, "I've 'eard 'em going at each other 'ammer and tongs in the Yard. That's when the boy troubles to go there."

"What's that about, then?" Martha asked, somehow having missed the gossip on this topic.

"Well," Ben began, taking his pipe from his mouth and preparing for a long speech.

"We ain't got all day," Digger cut in. "These children should 'ave been in bed 'alf 'our ago. I'll tell it in 'alf the time. Young White brought 'ome this Duke's son from school. Didn't like 'im, but already 'ad 'is eye on a seat in Parliament when 'e were a few years older. Mr White was disgusted with the Honourable's green striped pantaloons and 'is drunkenness. Sent 'im packing and made the boy leave school and come and work in the Yard."

"And," Ben was quick to resume the story, "'e 'ates it. Never goes there. Slips orf making speeches on this and that and anything that'll get 'im attention and catch the eye of someone with a seat in Parliament in his pocket." Smugly, the old man added, "Bet you a pound to a penny you don't know what 'is latest is?"

It was Sal who took the smile from his face. "'Eard it's to be sorting out work'ouses and such like. Ain't that the great moan of the day, 'ow them as works 'ard 'as to pay taxes to keep us lot in idleness?"

Martha asked, "And 'ow does 'e propose to do that?"

"Well," said Digger, who read the newspapers in the inn, "they plans to send a Commission all round the country to inquire on why the poor rate 'as risen sky 'igh and make up their minds what's being done and what needs doing. If young White can get their attention and put a plan before 'em, 'e could be a made man."

"'Ow's 'e plan to do that?" Paul asked in a last desperate effort to avoid having to go along long icy corridors to an icy ward and to bed.

"'E'll write a book or a pamphlet – that's like a little book – called something like "Ow to Run a Work'ouse on Tuppence a Day," Digger guessed.

"'E'll start on us, you mark my word," was Sal's last remark as she shepherded us to the door. "'E'll get this place running on a shoe string and then invite them 'missioners to come and clap their 'ands and slap 'im on the back."

"That would get 'im 'is seat in London," Ben agreed.

"Ain't a chance in 'Ell as 'ow Robert Campion'd let 'im," Digger claimed.

We all knew that Robert Campion was the old Mr White's life long friend and right hand man. We did not know that they had both been radicals in the heady days of the French Revolution. Then White had made his fortune and given up, as he said, 'his childish fancies', but Campion, or Radical Bob, had clung to his ideals and still argued for them when he could.

CHAPTER ELEVEN

All of this went on over our heads, especially after there was a new interest in our lives. One morning, I found myself, along with my companions, being assembled in the large, draughty hall where we ate our meals and being ordered by Mr Bumble to move the benches into rows in the centre of the room. He was even more bustling and officious than usual, a fact which could be put down to his trying to impress a man standing quietly by the door.

"Move, boy, move yourself," he ordered, jabbing me in the back with his cane. "Put it here, not there, you idiot. 'Ere, on that spot."

Paul whipped the other end of the bench round to drop it just next to Bumble's feet. Bumble grabbed him by the hair. "Take care, sir, of this one. Be vigilant over this young feller, sir." He displayed Paul, held with his feet almost off the ground, to the man, who was now walking further into the room. "This one does the Devil's work."

"What's your name, young man?" the stranger asked, indicating to Bumble that he should release his grasp on Paul's hair.

"Paul Quince, sir." Paul's face wore the expression we all displayed when we were asked our names and expected to have to bear any comments people cared to make on their quaintness. He clearly warmed to the man when there was no remark, offensive or jocular, from him.

"Now you are here, Paul, to do your own work. To learn to read and write and employ the gifts God gave you for good, rather than ill."

"Yes, sir," Paul answered meekly. Butter would not have melted in his mouth, but I knew that he was simply summing the man up.

Never slow to seek attention, I called out, "I can already read and write, sir."

"I am very pleased to hear that...." He waited for me to supply my name and then continued, "That is very good, Nathaniel Swubble, but there is always room for improvement."

"People call me Nat, sir."

"I shall call you Nathaniel. We shall do everything exactly right in my school. There will be no short cuts or dilatoriness. And," he added firmly, "there will be no calling out. If you wish to attract my attention, you will raise your hand and wait for me to give you permission to speak."

School, so that was what was happening. The wonderful truth sank in at last.

"I ain't sure," Bumble suggested, also liking to have attention paid to him, "that the vestry wants these here pauper urchins to be taught nothing more than to read the Bible and learn their manners."

"But we do not want pauper children to grow up to be pauper adults, do we, Mr Bumble? I am here to give them the tools to improve their lot in life."

"Improve their lot in life! Only within reason, sir. There's independent labourers' sons what ain't getting no schooling and God had them born above this lot and above them 'E hintended 'em to remain."

If Bumble thought he knew our place in society, the new teacher, clearly a gentleman in speech and dress, certainly knew his with regard to Bumble and was not going to argue with a beadle.

By this time we were excitedly running around and fighting for places. Bumble walked along the line, darting at one after another of us with his cane raised to little effect.

"Silence, children!" the man said. We all obeyed. We had been taught to be in awe of gentlefolk and he was so self-confident and sure that we would do as he said, that we did not think of disobeying him.

While we all had our eyes fixed on him, the gentleman turned towards the door. "Come in young man," he said, smiling at the thin, pale boy standing there. We watched Oliver Twist, nervously clutching his cap in his hand, walk hesitantly to sit on the end of the bench nearest the door. He seemed to wish that he could make himself invisible.

"Sit 'ere, Ollie," I called, pushing the others along to make room.

"Sit here, Oliver," the man said. He spoke gently to Oliver, but then looked sternly at me. "If you call out again, Nathaniel, I shall have to make an example of you and send you to stand with your face to the wall."

"That's better," Bumble commented, taking full credit upon himself for the silence which followed.

"Just call me if they misbehave again. A cuff on the ear's all some of 'em listen to."

"I won't put you to any trouble, Mr Bumble."

"Trouble comes my way, sir, whenever paupers is concerned. A beadle knows nothing but trouble."

Although the new teacher gave him a look to indicate he could leave,

Bumble settled himself to watch, ready to report to his mother and to the vicar on all that happened that day.

Impatiently, I waited for my chance to display my skill and to feel superior, while the other children, foundlings and orphans, learned their letters. I waited in vain. First, the gentleman told us that his name was Mr Lowe and that we were not to call him just 'Mister'.

Then, having told us we must shut our eyes firmly to concentrate our thoughts on God, he said a prayer and called a blessing on this new venture. We were made to repeat 'Amen' a few times, before he was convinced that everyone was joining in. Having told us he expected us to have the room ready, with benches in place, when he arrived, he taught us how to stand when he entered the room and how to reply to his greeting, "Good morning, children," with, "Good morning, Mr Lowe." After that, he explained to us, in the same clear and precise way, that we must wait for his permission to sit after this greeting and must do so without pushing and fighting for places. It was this last part of the procedure which caused such trouble that we had to practise it at least a dozen times. That we had not yet learned the discipline required of us was revealed when Mr Lowe told us that encouragement would take the place of punishment. We all looked at Bumble and cheered.

Now, I thought, it must be time for the lesson proper to start, but I was wrong yet again. We had other things to learn first. We had to learn to sit and stand up straight, pretending, Mr Lowe suggested, that we had an iron rod down our backs and another across our shoulders. This way, he assured us, we could breathe more deeply, feel wide awake and work much better than when we slouched. I was bursting to call out and tell him that Billy, with the hump-back, just could not sit straight, however hard he tried. It was Felicity who put up her hand and, when told to speak, informed Mr Lowe of Billy's difficulties. He said that Billy would be excused from pretending to have a rod in his back. In the days which followed, Mr Lowe often patted Billy gently on the back to encourage him and to show us that the hump was nothing to be frightened of. Some children said that, if you touched Billy, you would grow a hump yourself.

We were next called upon to demonstrate our newly aquired skill by standing, straight as posts and without fidgeting, waiting for Mr Lowe, or one of the big girls, to examine our hands, palm and reverse, our necks and behind our ears. Along with my friends, I had learned to read scrambling over muddy graves, but it seemed this was the wrong way to set about it. Mr Lowe explained that cleanliness was next to Godliness and had the added advantage of keeping dirty and greasy marks off our books and slates.

At last, Mr Lowe told us to sit down, which we managed to do without too much shoving and elbowing, to sit up straight and to listen. To my surprise, he obviously planned to read to us, rather than to ask us to read to him. He opened his book.

"Now listen carefully," he told us. "I shall read you small extracts – pieces, that is – from several books. One is about elephants, one about Africa, one about London and one from the Adventures of Robinson Crusoe. They will show you that, through reading, you can soar beyond the walls of the workhouse or beyond the trials and difficulties of your future lives into a magical world of facts and imagination.

When I have finished," he continued, "I shall ask you questions. If you answer correctly, I shall place a mark by your name on the chart on the wall." Here, he directed our attention to the chart, with a picture which provided a splash of colour on the grey wall. "At the end of the week, the boy or girl with the greatest number of marks will wear this sash." The red sash which Mr Lowe held up was another splash of colour in our grey world.

Putting up a hand to silence our gasps, he continued, "Here is a second sash for the boy or girl who makes the greatest progress by hard work and effort." More was to come. "The first Sunday in each month, my wife and I shall be happy to welcome the two winners into our home to join us for tea." Pausing, he was wise enough to loosen the rein on us to allow us to express our amazement at such an opportunity. A forest of hands was raised in the air. He let us ask our questions one by one.

"Will there be buns, sir?"

"And cups to drink out of?"

"Most certainly," Mr Lowe replied. "There will be ordinary bread and fruit loaf, both with butter and jam if you wish. Slices of fruit cake and slices of plain cake and a gingerbread man or two. Oh!" he added, as though having almost forgotten to tell us, "I think that my wife mentioned something about jelly and cream."

We were almost fainting, just with the thought of such a feast, but Mr Lowe recalled our attention to the book he was going to read. It was very seldom that we had been read to and never with us all together. We listened in absolute silence, but paying attention to every word was not easy. Written sentences were longer than the spoken ones we were used to and we were so used to blocking out the vicar's voice, the only gentleman's voice we had heard at length, that we sometimes found ourselves automatically blocking out Mr Lowe's. I am afraid that some children, and they were not all small ones, fell asleep.

At the end, Mr Lowe posed a question to each of us, with the easiest ones for the youngest and a few hints to the slowest. Everyone achieved a mark.

"I have read these pieces this morning," Mr Lowe explained, "to show you that both worlds – the world of the imagination and the world in which you live – are wonderful places, which you may visit through books. Reading allows you to travel the world, to visit jungles and mountains, continents and oceans. Reading introduces you to people of all races and all classes, wise men and famous men. And, of course," he noted, smiling at the girls, who smiled eagerly back,"wise women and famous women."

"Ain't none," Paul asserted with absolute certainty, only to be reminded that he must not call out.

"Mary, Mother of Jesus. Mary Magdalene. Martha and Mary."

"Only in the Bible," Paul conceded, before being sent to stand with his face to the wall.

Mr Lowe went on through the list. "Queen Elizabeth. Mary, Queen of Scots. Queen Anne. Our next monarch will be a queen, you know."

"Ain't never 'eard of any of 'em," I heard Paul mutter. Mr Lowe probably heard him, too, but chose to ignore it on this first day of school.

Finally, we stood for a prayer and to learn how to thank Mr Lowe for our lesson, while he thanked us for our attention. When I called for three cheers, "for Mr Lowe, our new teacher," everyone joined in enthusiastically, except Paul, who complained that I had called out and should be made to join him facing the wall.

The lesson over, we crowded round the chart to see the marks by our names. Most had never seen their names written down before. Then Bumble ordered us to place the benches ready for our meal. I spotted Oliver just about to leave and ran over to him.

"Did you 'ave to walk all the way over 'ere?" I asked. It was a three mile journey.

"Yes," Oliver replied. "It weren't.....I mean, it wasn't....'arf.....half a long way."

"Didn't you get a ride?" I really knew the answer before I asked. Oliver would have plodded along without the cheek to ask. "I'll come back with you. Show you 'ow to do it. Come and 'ave some food. No one will notice."

"I can't," Oliver protested, a worried expression on his face. "I don't live 'ere.....here."

"Look!" I said, pointing to old Sal and lying, "That lady runs the work'ouse. If she sez you can stay, will you stay?" Of course, with me giving her a wink behind Oliver's back, Sal was overcome with the prospect of entertaining Oliver to dinner. He was not a chatty companion and saved some of his food for the children at the farm.

When we had eaten, I took his hand and led Oliver out of the workhouse and across to the Yard. He came only reluctantly. I knew he would have preferred to go quietly on his way, but I somehow felt it my duty to teach this timid, innocent child the ways of the world.

When we entered the Yard, there was the usual apparent chaos, with carts and waggons criss-crossing in every direction. All around, there was the clatter of chains and harnesses and the clomp, clomp of the huge hooves of the giant Suffolks. Dodging the hooves and wheels and watching out for porters, who called, "Mind your backs, there," from right and left, gave us no time to talk. I just dragged him along from waggon to waggon, asking for a lift. Unusually, no one seemed willing to give us one.

"Tell you what, Ollie," I decided in the end, "Look as though you ain't bothered whether you get a lift or not. Then we'll wait outside and jump on the back of the first waggon to turn our way and 'ang on."

Turning paler than ever, Oliver's attempts at good grammar failed him. "I ain't very big, Nat. I might fall under the wheels."

"You'd be all squashed, like that dog what was run down last week," I said, jokingly.

"Please, Nat, let me just walk back."

"I'll get 'old of you round the waist," I assured him, "and lift you up."

Tears came into Oliver's eyes. "Please, please let me walk back."

"If you want," I agreed in the end. "Suppose you're not trained to it like us work'ouse boys are. Felicity and Georgina were good at it, until they got too big." Scrambling onto a pile of sacks, I told him, "We'll watch the 'orses for a bit."

"I don't like those huge, rough 'orses.....horses," Oliver protested.

"What makes you say everything twice, Ollie?" I inquired at last, not having wanted to draw attention to something which might have been a handicap he could not help.

"I'm trying to talk like a gentleman," Oliver answered with quiet dignity. That was Oliver's form of bravery. Nervous of horses, he would say things which brought derision from the rest of us.

"What for?" I demanded as though he had said that he wished to speak Chinese.

"My mother was a lady." Oliver explained. "Everyone who saw her agrees with that. And I'm sure my father is a gentleman. Mrs Mann always said that my relatives would come looking for me one day. They'll expect me to speak like a gentleman, don't you think?"

"Won't they want you, if you can't?" From Oliver's tears, I knew that I had said the wrong thing.

"Do you think they will leave me with Mrs Mann?"

"Gawd forbid," I uttered, as Oliver winced. Then I took the opportunity to ask a question which had puzzled us all. "'Ow is it you're still at Mrs Mann's? She only 'as babies. Not," I added hastily, "that you're a baby. You're the same age as me." As I spoke, I wondered whether always being with younger children accounted for Oliver's readiness to cry.

"Mrs Mann thought that my relations would be grateful that she had taken good care of me and kept me out of the work'ouse."

"Good care!" I sneered. "Look at you. Your elbows is out of your shirt and you're as thin as a rake. You'd be better orf in the work'ouse, any day."

"Mr Bumble says that I'm better off away from the influence of wicked, rough boys in the work'ouse. Or even of rough girls, he always says."

"Better than wicked and soft, like Bumble," I pointed out.

"I don't think they'll come for me, now," Oliver concluded, sadly." Mr Bumble and Mrs Mann don't think that they will. That's why they give me more and more work to do and treat me unkindly." Tears ran down his cheeks. He turned to me and spoke so sincerely, that I felt ashamed of myself for forcing him to accompany me to the Yard when he had not wanted to come. "I want my mother, in Heaven, to be proud of me, Nat. She would want me to be a gentleman, I am sure."

"Talk 'ow you like," I told him. "'Ere, give us your 'and and let's 'elp you down. I'll walk 'ome with you."

Although we were the same age, I led Oliver through the traffic until a boy came running after us and told us that the young Mr White wanted to see Oliver in his office. Oliver was terrified and I went with him. I was ready to tell Mr White that we had not been begging for a ride, but expected to work in the Yard to earn the trip, but Mr White ignored me.

Gazing at Oliver, the man said, "So you are Oliver Twist, the boy whom my aunt has in her care." The young William White spoke like a gentleman, if anyone did.

"Yes, if you please, sir," Oliver managed to say through trembling lips.

"'E's shy, sir," I explained. Again, I was ignored.

"Why are you so far from home, Oliver?"

"If you please, sir, I've been ter.....to school in the work'ouse."

"And have to waste an hour walking there and another hour walking back."

"I'll work 'arder when I get back, sir. I promise I will."

"My aunt tells me that your people were gentlefolk and might come for you one day."

Oliver perked up at this. "Yes, sir."

"Then you will need more than workhouse lessons, young man. You must speak like a gentleman, bear yourself like a gentleman and act like a gentleman."

Oliver's spirits fell again. How could he ever achieve this?

"How would you like me to teach you all of these things, Oliver?"

The child's eyes lit with pleasure. "Oh, please, sir. Yes, sir."

"First we must get rid of that hang-dog look. We must make a man of you."

Turning to the boy from the Yard, Mr White ordered him, "Find Oliver a ride to my aunt's. Then see that urchin off the premises and back to the workhouse, where he belongs."

Oliver stopped to thank me for looking after him and then skipped off back to Mrs Mann's and his promised lessons.

CHAPTER TWELVE

"'Ere 'e comes," Jack Star muttered. He gave a dramatic sigh to show that he was only joking. "Good job I can walk, keep watch, listen, think and talk all at one and the same time."

Since lessons began, I had been overwhelmed by facts, all new and amazing to me, and I shared them with the porter to help me digest them and, if I am honest, to show off this new knowledge of mine. Always, he seemed to sort out the confusion in my mind and add to my knowledge.

"Mr Star," I began.

"Yes, teacher," he replied, standing up very straight.

"You know the Earth....," I began again.

After careful consideration, he gave his answer. "Think I've 'eard it mentioned within my 'earing."

"Do you think that it's really round?"

"Not only think, I know. I've just about sailed all round it, ain't I?"

This took a little thought. The idea which I could still not take in was that people could live on the other side of the world and not fall off. It was hard to believe that they could stand up and see the land and the sky just as we did. If I asked, "And you didn't fall orf of it?" I knew that I would look silly, when I was trying to look clever.

Guessing my difficulty, Jack asked, "Didn't that teacher of yours tell you about the world rotating, spinning round at tremendous speed? It's like swinging a bucket of water in a circle very fast. If you're quick enough, nothing falls out."

"Yes, of cors 'e did." I was not going to accept the slightest suggestion that Mr Lowe was not the best teacher in the world. "But when it's in the air, the bucket and the water's upside down. People on the other side of the world's up the right way."

"They certainly seemed that way, when I saw 'em." I was afraid Jack was trying not to smile, but he continued seriously, "It's all about gravity. Didn't Mr Lowe tell you about that?"

"I can see that. I know about gravity," I declared, impatiently.

"I'm sure you do. You and Paul 'ave 'ad enough conkers and apples fall on your 'eads when you've been shaking 'em down."

We talked on for a while. It was easier to keep up with the porter, now that I could walk nearly as fast as him, when he was just strolling up and down.

"I know the name of just about every town in England," I claimed, exaggerating in my innocence.

"Think about how many workhouses that adds up to," the porter replied.

That thought had not struck me. The workhouse was, to me, my home and unique in the world. I stood still for a while, letting Jack stroll up and down without me.

"There are dozens of work'ouses like this, dozens of porters like me and, I suppose, thousands of children like you," he remarked, as he passed me.

So I was not one of a few unwanted children. There were thousands of us. The thought did not console me, but made me sad.

"Why do parents pray for children that they don't want?" At this time, I was accepting the official version that babies were sent by God to those who prayed for them. That seemed more likely than the version Paul gave me, even though women's swollen bellies supported his opinion. There were no grown-ups ready to tell us more, or even to answer our questions.

Walking a little faster, Jack mumbled over his shoulder, "Suppose God sends 'em to the wrong place. Or people change their minds."

I let it go, my mind on the discovery that there were workhouses all over the country. Ordinary houses varied, even within Myddlington, and I knew there were igloos in Canada and mud huts in Africa. I asked Jack whether workhouses were all the same.

The porter interpreted the question as going beyond mere architectural style. Coming to stand by me, he said, "It depends on 'ow big the parish is and 'oo's in charge. In London, there are great big ones. In the countryside, a village might just 'ave a few ordinary 'ouses for paupers to live in. Generally, where there's just a few paupers, they're treated pretty well. Where there's too many, them as pays for 'em all start complaining."

"Pays for 'em?" I asked in surprise.

"The boy 'oo thinks 'e's so clever! 'Oo d'yer think pays for your food and clothes? 'Oo d'yer think pays my wages?"

"Somebody 'oo can't afford much," I said, showing the patch in my shirt.

"Many a true word spoken in jest," Jack Star commented. "Or is it a case of 'out of the mouths of babes'?"

"What d'yer mean?"

"What you said was near the truth, Nat. Some of them what pays their rates to keep paupers are almost as 'ard up themselves. Rates is going up so 'igh and so fast some small farmers and craftsmen will all be in need of 'elp theirselves."

"There ain't that many of us in the work'ouse," I protested.

"True, young man. But you ain't the only ones what the ratepayers 'ave to support." Jack always took his duty of teaching me everything I should know as seriously as Mr Lowe took his. "Ever eard of outdoor relief?"

"No," I admitted grudgingly. I had set out to impress Jack Star and here he was, again, teaching me.

He continued, "Outdoor relief, means people 'oo can't support their-selves get 'elp in their own 'omes without going into the workhouse. They go to the overseer and gets a little money, some bread and cheese or a bottle of medicine. If they get very low wages, they might get a shilling now and again to 'elp them feed their families."

"Why's it called a work'ouse?" I inquired, as usual gobbling up all infor-mation like a pig at a trough.

"'Cos they can make you work. That way, you 'elps to keep yourself and get in the 'abit of working. Used to be like that 'ere, but it didn't work out. The stuff made was so shoddy, no one wanted to buy it." The porter con-tinued to explain matters to me, then concluded, "It's one of life's great problems, Nat. 'Ow d'yer 'elp them what really needs 'elp, without 'elping them what is just idle and lay about all day long. If you're generous to them what really needs 'elp, you give it to the idle as well. If you try to stop 'elp-ing the idle, the real needy suffer. Can't see anyone ever finding the answer to that one."

I must have looked puzzled, for the porter patted my head. "Don't worry, Nat. No one expects you to find the answer. There's a rumour that young Mr White thinks 'e can find the solution to that particular problem."

Relieved of the burden of solving this insoluble problem, I was struck by another thought. All our lessons on geography had made me have itchy feet. I longed to set out on my travels and see all the sights.

"I could travel all round the country," I said, "Staying at other work'ous-es."

"That's what I were saying," Jack pointed out. "Work'ouses ain't the same as inns and 'otels. If you set orf on your journey, you'd find you belong to the parish where you was born. Other parishes would only look after you if your own parish agreed to pay all your expenses. Others'll send you straight back to where you belongs. If you're taken ill in some places, they take you out of the parish, dump you on the parish boundary and wash their 'ands of you. You're lucky if you're still alive when you do get back to your own parish."

"I'll stay 'ere till I can pay my own way," I decided.

"You could do worse, Nat. You wouldn't get a teacher like Mr Lowe anywhere else. It ain't the ratepayers what pays for 'im, you know. It was Miss Aldbury what said she would pay 'is wages." Miss Aldbury was a wealthy woman, related to the local aristocracy, who did much good for the poor of Myddlington.

"And, what's more," Jack added, "though I sez it meself, you wouldn't get a charming and intelligent fellow like me as a porter anywhere else."

I smiled and ran off. Jack always seemed to guess what I was thinking and as he had always been so good to me, I felt guilty about letting him read my thoughts at the moment. Just lately, I had given up my long-standing hope that Jack was my father and replaced it with the hope that my father was just like Mr Lowe.

CHAPTER THIRTEEN

I must mention here an event concerning Old Sal, which I knew nothing of then, but was told about much later. It concerned her last surviving child, the invalid Joseph, and, as it adds to the events recorded by Dickens, it seems worth relating.

Joseph fell ill and, as the days passed, his usually pale face became greyer and his already weak frame became frailer. With her centuries-old knowledge of herbs and cures, passed down to her from mother to daughter over the generations, Sal administered her potions. In Joseph's presence, she was cheerful and smiling, but this outward confidence disappeared once she was out of his sight. For all her skills, she had lost twelve children and, in her heart, she knew that her son had not long to live.

In her heart, Sally knew, too, that no one could save him, but, in her desperation, she turned to every old wife, charlatan and quack in the district. At last, all other hopes having failed, she turned to Mr Jonathon Jupp, the latest physician to arrive in the town. In the eyes of many of those who considered themselves leaders of fashion and opinion, and in his own eyes, he was a miracle-worker. Sal persuaded Jack Star to go and beg him to visit her son.

Knowing such a doctor would refuse to see him, a humble workhouse porter, Jack arranged for one of the man's servants to let him in the back door. Then he persuaded the servant, for friendship's sake, to pretend that he thought the physician had agreed to see Jack. The servant showed Jack into the consulting room. The doctor looked him up and down and demanded, "Who is this fellow?"

"He's come about a patient, sir."

"The servants of my patients wear livery. For whom does he work?"

"He's the workhouse porter, sir."

"Good God!" the physician fumed, "Show him the door. Have the maids clean the room thoroughly. I shall be out on my visits." He turned to go never having addressed a word to Jack, muttering that he hoped those he visited that day would not find out that he had stood in the same room as the workhouse porter.

"Please, sir," Jack began, trying not to show the annoyance he felt at being talked about over his head. "I've come on be'alf of a poor old lady, 'oo's only son, 'er last living child, is dying."

"How does that concern me, my man?"

"Will you see 'im, sir, for charity's sake?"

"Charity's sake!" the physician exclaimed, as though all was suddenly plain to him. "It would indeed be charity. No doubt you wish me to see her without charge. For those in pecuniary difficulty, I have a special fee of one guinea. Has this old woman a guinea?"

"No, sir. She 'asn't twenty one pence, let alone twenty one shillings."

As though talking to a child, but imagining himself showing great patience, the doctor explained, "It is not greed, which makes me insist on a minimum fee of one guinea. Indeed, I am exercising charity in making my fee, in a few special cases, so low. I must set a fee, even if as low as one guinea, to protect my patients from the diseases harboured in the dirt and poverty of many areas of the town." As he spoke, Mr Jupp looked from the porter to his own clothes, apparently fearing that he might already have been contaminated. "It is not," he added sanctimoniously, "that I am not aware of Our Lord's exhortation to help the poor. I give to many charities and the poor have the workhouse apothecary to whom they may turn."

"The apothecary can do nothing, sir"

"What apothecary can?" the physician asked, under his breath.

Jack tried flattery. "You're our only 'ope, sir. People speak so 'ighly of you and of your skill and your kindness, Mr Jupp. That's why I 'ad the courage to come and beg for your 'elp, sir."

The doctor received this as his due. "All my patients acknowledge my skill and the ladies, in particular, appreciate my kindness and my charm. But none would ever consult me again were I to set one toe inside the work-house gate." Overcome by a sudden burst of generosity, he added," To show that I do not turn my back on those in need of my God-given skills, if you bring the sick man to the back door and pay your guinea, I will see him there. Now, my man, be off with you. There are many sick in this town, who are in urgent need of my help."

When Jack had left, the physician set about the servant with angry words. "Never, never let such a person over the threshold again."

"He came in the back door," was all the servant could think of to say in his defence.

"Back door! Side door! Window! Never let such a man in again." Mr Jupp shuddered. "What would happen were it to be known that I dealt with such people? I can tell you. No one of quality would enter this house again. And they would certainly not allow me to enter theirs."

When Jack arrived back at the workhouse, Sally was eagerly awaiting him.

"Sorry, Sal," the porter told her, as gently as he could, "There ain't a ounce of 'uman kindness in the man." To tell her honestly what the doctor had said, he went on, "'E'll see Joseph if we bring 'im to 'is back door. And then you 'ave to pay 'im one guinea. I tell you Sal, if I 'ad a guinea, I wouldn't give it to that quack. 'E's just a puffed-up nobody without 'alf the skill you 'ave, Sal."

Sally did not seem to be listening. She stood up, threw on her shawl and left the building.

Assuming that she had gone to plead with the man, Jack declared, "'E'll not come. 'E knows we ain't got a guinea between us."

"She's been sitting staring into the fire nearly all the time you been gawn, Jack," Martha told the porter. "Except she went up to the infirmary. Said as 'ow she wanted to be on 'er own. When she come down, I could 'ave sworn she were 'iding something in 'er pocket."

"She couldn't 'ave 'ad a guinea tucked away, surely," Jack commented. "Shouldn't think she's ever 'ad that much in 'er 'and in 'er 'ole life."

"Ain't likely, is it?" Martha snorted.

It was half an hour before Sally returned. "I've 'ad a word with 'im. 'E sez 'e'll see Joseph if we get 'im to the back door of 'is ouse".

Jack was amazed, but Sal clearly meant what she had said. As gently as he could, he pointed out, "I think Joseph 'as only a few hours to live."

"Then you must 'urry," Sal urged. "It's 'is only chance."

With blankets and pieces of wood, Jack and a few other men made a stretcher to carry Joseph to the physician's house.

When it was ready, Jack said, "You lead the way Sal and we'll follow close be'ind."

Sal did not move. "I ain't coming, Jack. I could see the look on that doctor's face when 'e smelt the beer on me breath and saw the patches on me clothes. 'E's a poor opinion of me, I could see that and it might turn 'im against Joseph. I want that man to treat my son like 'e'd treat any other patient."

"'E don't treat 'em at the back door," Jack thought, but he and the other men set off without Sal.

At his house, the physician came out into the garden and, looking around to see no neighbours were watching, gave Joseph a cursory examination, gingerly fingering his clothes and not touching his body.

"The man is dying," he announced. "He is passed any human help, even mine. Take him away with all speed." He waved them away. "It would be a disaster for my practice were a man to die in my garden."

"It's not a case, then," Jack commented bitterly, "of 'Take up your bed and walk'."

Already, the physician had disappeared into his house.

"Well," Jack addressed the servant,"at least it were free."

"Free!" the servant exclaimed in surprise. "Old Sal came here and gave me a guinea to take in to the master. It was only then that he came out and told her to have her son brought to the back door."

"'E charged 'er a guinea! 'E didn't even give 'er no medicine." Pushing the servant aside, Jack caught up with the doctor inside the house. "I'll 'ave the money back, please, sir. It's only fair, if you did nothing for 'im."

"I examined the man and gave my opinion. I used my knowledge, skill and experience. I have no qualms in charging the old woman." Ordering the servant to remove Jack from the premises, the doctor added, "I have no doubt the old woman had stolen the money and has no right to it whatsoever. No one should be allowed to benefit from illgotten gains." He walked away.

"'Ow can you work for 'im?" Jack asked the servant.

"Same reason as most people work for their masters. He pays my wages, Jack."

On the way back, Joseph reached out and touched Jack's hand, indicating that he wanted them to stop. Asking the other men to stand a little aside, Joseph spoke to Jack.

"Ma must 'ave stole it, Jack," he murmured, breathing as deeply between each word as his lungs would allow. "She done it for me. See she don't get into trouble and go to prison."

"Rest easy, Joe. On my honour, I'll see she comes to no 'arm," Jack promised. A minute or two later, he closed the dead man's eyes.

After Sowerberry had buried yet another pauper, Jack approached the grieving mother. "What you been up to, Sal?"

"Whatever you talking about, Jack Star?"

"That guinea what you give to the doctor, Sal." Jack hesitated to ask her straight out where it had come from.

"What guinea?" Sally demanded, playing for time. "'E said it were free, but I weren't to tell anyone or everyone would expect charity from 'im."

"Pull the other one, Sal. I ain't blaming you, whatever you did and I don't think God would, either, but I promised your Joseph that I'd 'elp you and 'elp you I shall."

For a while, Sal was silent. Then she wept. Jack waited, but she was not going to tell him the whole story.

"I know you mean well, Jack. You've always been a good friend to me and me family. But I must shoulder the burden of what I've done on me own. I can sort it out. Maybe, Jack, now and again, you can lend me a penny or two. But I'll give up drink and scrape enough together to manage without 'elp, if I can." Out of the blue, as it seemed to Jack, Sal urged, "Keep a eye on the lad, Oliver Twist, over at Mrs Mann's. There's something what I 'ave to tell 'im, when 'e's a little bit older."

Realising Sal had said as much as she was going to, Jack let the matter drop.

CHAPTER FOURTEEN

As William John Bull White rode the three miles from the town to the baby farm, the workmen he passed along the way were quick to step aside as well as to touch their caps in respect. This man, the man in the white waistcoat, showed little respect to others. Whatever his aim, and today it was simply to cover the distance in as short a time as possible, he set out to achieve it without thought for anyone in his way.

A little behind William White, rode his servant, a tall, heavily built young man, who accompanied him everywhere. The servant was deaf. His name was Martin Horsley, but, as his master never bothered to tell people his name and as he could not give it himself, people made one up for him. They called him 'Seize 'im', after the instruction most frequently given by a local gamekeeper to his huge dog. Rumour had it that, when William White had hired 'Seize 'im', the servant had been boxing at a fair. What people did not know, was that the reason he was hired lay in his master's determination never to be attacked or beaten again.

William White had come to his aunt, Mrs Mann, to ask her help in his latest venture. Having left 'Seize 'im' at the door, he approached the topic indirectly.

"You make a good living, then, aunt?"

"Not good, nephew. Just a modest living."

"But, considering your outlay and the work called for, there's a good profit to be made from each child."

"Always told your father there would be more in it for me if he became involved in local affairs and sent more children my way."

"Exactly, aunt. A little help and advice from you and I shall be in the position to increase your income."

Mrs Mann looked puzzled. "You want to be elected overseer, nephew? There's more work than profit in that. And it's the quickest way to have your neighbours turn against you."

"Overseer!" William exclaimed with contempt. "That's work for a tradesman, not a gentleman. But," he added, "whether I am popular with my neighbours is no concern of mine. However, if my plans work out, I would be very popular. I am going to cut the poor rate and save them a great deal of money."

"What is your plan, William?" Mrs Mann hoped it would be a plan involving a great deal of profit for everyone in the family.

"It is perfectly simple. The tax-payers will pay me to run all the poor relief in the parish. I shall charge much less than it costs them under the present scheme."

"But you'll make no profit, William." Mrs Mann could see no point in any action which did not lead to a profit.

"My aim is not to make a profit, but to show everyone that the cost of poor relief can be cut by a large margin."

"But how can you do it for less then the present cost?"

"By efficiency and economy."

With years of experience in cutting costs, Mrs Mann told her nephew, "That would mean gruel for every meal."

"Exactly, Aunt Mann. Exactly. But why should those who don't work expect to be fed better than the labourer who is independent and does not seek handouts?"

Mrs Mann was thrilled to see her nephew had turned out so well She had been afraid that a fancy school would have given him fancy ideas. "But why put yourself to all this trouble, if there's no profit in it for you?"

"My profit, aunt, will be a draw myself to the attention of those in government and obtain a seat in Parliament."

"There's profit to be made there, William." Mrs Mann rubbed her hands, as though feeling coins falling into them. "But is it legal? Is it allowed, this plan of yours?"

"Most certainly, aunt."

"It comes to me now. Wasn't there a man who did that for the work-house somewhere and he went bankrupt? The overseer sent every one wanting relief into the workhouse. They poured in."

"That is why, aunt, I shall contract to take over both the workhouse and outdoor relief. I plan to have a board to help me, but I shall hold the reins, make no mistake over that."

Mrs Mann said not another word. She was listening to see how she fitted in and how her profits would increase.

"First," her nephew instructed his aunt, "don't breathe a word to a soul. I do not want any opposition. Best spring it onto 'em. But, when I put the plan to the vestry, I want to have prepared the way. I want to have eliminated any possible source of opposition and have built up a core of support."

"You're your father's son, William."

In his own mind, William considered himself far superior to his father, but he knew that his aunt and father had been close and did not wish to offend her. "Father would want you to help me, I am sure, aunt."

"Just give me my instructions, William."

"Tell me where the opposition will come from, aunt."

"You needn't worry about people like Bumble, nor the workhouse master or Mrs Corney." Apparently unaware that she was no better than they were, she went on, "Promise of a little profit and you'll have them eating out of your hand."

"And who will oppose me in the parish?"

"Well, Radical Bob, for one."

"Robert Campion, my father's foreman? I have him down as a trouble-maker already. I dispise him. All talk of 'the people' and no talk of profit for those who risk their capital."

"He has quite a following, nephew. They mostly kept quiet during the wars, but they're all raising their heads again. He's all on the side of the poor. The idle, I call 'em. Them that ain't got the sense to look after theirselves." Mrs Mann frowned, concentrating on her task. "Digger might have been trouble once upon a time, but he's in the workhouse himself now."

Impatiently, her nephew said, "They are mere midges."

"Now," Mrs Mann asserted," I'll tell you who could be a problem for you. You won't have come across him yourself. That feller what runs the school at the workhouse. Richard Lowe's his name. He's a strange one. He's a gentleman, there's no doubt of that, but there he is teaching paupers."

"That makes three, then," William concluded. "No one I cannot deal with."

"Who's the third one?"

"The small farmers who pay low wages knowing their men can come begging for more from the taxpayer. There will be none of that, when I am in charge."

Mrs Mann smiled warmly at her nephew. "I could do with a few more children to care for, William. Wouldn't say no to another ten or a dozen."

"Well," her nephew laughed, "it would be one way of cutting the number of children dependent on the parish. Fewer come out of your tender care, aunt, than go in."

Mrs Mann was uncertain as to whether she was being praised or criticised. She was even more puzzled when he laughed again and asked, "Have you been reading Malthus, aunt?"

"Do I get time to read?" Mrs Mann mumbled, not wanting to reveal that she had no idea what her nephew was talking about. It seemed safest to change the subject. "Will there be a lesson for Oliver, today?"

"I told you last time, aunt," William White said, his tone and manner making it clear that he was displeased with the boy. "These pauper children are idle and ungrateful. They are too lazy to take an opportunity to improve themselves when it is offered."

"He is a wicked one," the aunt agreed. "Has to be hurried and harried to make him get all his work done helping me." She did not add that, unfeeling as she was towards Oliver, she did worry that her nephew's even more severe treatment of the child might rebound on her one day. As a mild warning, she did ask, "Are you sure his relations won't come for him one day?"

"After all these years and after all the attempts the authorities have made to find him?"

"But he might seek 'em out himself, when he's grown up."

"Where would he begin his search, aunt? There is not a single clue as to his parentage. Where is the young ruffian now?"

Mrs Mann was tempted to say the boy was away on an errand, but she was eager to keep in favour with her nephew now he had this new plan. "He's looking after the little 'uns."

With a show of reluctance, William White told her, "Fetch him, aunt. I know my duty. He shall learn to be a gentleman, however demanding the task is upon my time and my temper."

Oliver appeared. In trying not to tremble, he had become so tense that he trembled all the more.

"Look at you," William White taunted the child. "Think that you could ever be a gentleman? Gentlemen have spirit, Oliver Twist. That is something you will never have."

"I try my very best, sir."

"Try! You had better try harder, sir, or you will feel my cane." Sneering at his victim, the man went on, "You are filthy from head to foot. Is that the style of a gentleman? Stand there where I cannot smell you."

Oliver hesitated to say that he seldom had a chance to wash and was seldom given clean clothes. Such a remark would imply a criticism of Mrs

Mann and would be punished instantly.

"Stand up straight."

Oliver tried to stand straight and look his tormentor in the eye, but he knew he would be frightened by the hatred he saw there.

"Let me hear you say, 'Henry the Eighth had six wives.'"

Oliver's young heart sank. He could say it. He had said it to himself over and over again with not one mistake. He could do it and he must do it.

Taking a deep breath, Oliver made a run at it. "Henry the Eighth had six wives." There, it was done.

"Don't swallow your words, boy. Call yourself a gentleman. It's not the blood of gentlefolk which flows through your veins. What kind of woman your mother was, I can only imagine. Ladies do not struggle through hail and storm to find a workhouse in which to give birth to a child. She wore no wedding ring," White sneered. "Say it again."

Trembling with anger as much as frustration, Oliver attempted the sentence again. 'Enery the Heigth 'ad...'ad...had eight wives." Tears sprang into his eyes.

"Go and get on with your work," Mrs Mann told him. For once, she was being kind.

"No, no, Aunt," William White said, smiling to himself. "You go and leave me to deal with this snivelling boy."

Mrs Mann hesitated, but only for a second. Her nephew could provide her with money for her old age. Oliver had no power to do anything for her.

The child stood there, waiting for what was to come. He knew that, when he had left this place, he would never again let anyone insult his mother.

Mrs Mann hurried out of earshot. Rumours were circulating about her nephew's beating the boy. She had told Susan, the maid, to keep her mouth shut, but indiscretion was the stupid girl's middle name.

As he left, William White said, "We'll send that child to the workhouse. With only younger children around him, he fancies himself better than he is." If his plans worked out, he would have total control of Oliver's life. He would make that gentleness and openness disappear from the child's face by one means or another.

CHAPTER FIFTEEN

Every school morning, I was awake before the lark and, the second our door was unlocked, I was off to the courtyard and washing under the pump. Ears, neck and face were rubbed vigorously and, to wash my hands, I pushed my shirt sleeves up as far as they would go to include my arms as well. In my efforts to win attention and praise from Mr Lowe, I was determined to pass every inspection, which might be sprung upon us.

After breakfast, I was the first to arrange the benches and to stand ready to greet our teacher. With children of all ages, some fast and some slow at learning, Mr Lowe had divided the children into groups and appointed monitors to help him. We monitors - I was one, of course – had our lesson first and were then told what we had to drill into our groups in that day. While I enjoyed helping my group, most of all I enjoyed the lesson given just for the monitors at the beginning of each day. There was always some-thing new and challenging for us to learn.

The only stumbling blocks I had come across so far in my own progress were in spelling and speech. Jack had taught me to write, sounding out the letters. This worked some of the time, but I had fallen into the habit of spelling a word more or less anyway I worked it out at the time. Mr Lowe insisted that each word could be spelled in one, and only one, way, and we must consistently spell it correctly. In speech, for the first time, listening to Mr Lowe, I had become conscious of the errors I made. Attempts to correct them had led only to my speech sounding as odd as Oliver's had done, when he had first tried to improve. Paul fell about laughing and mimicked my attempts, but Jack told me to try to improve just one error at a time and not try to change over night. Jack could recognise the errors, but said that he had been too long among rough men on board ship to change his own speech now.

We were in the middle of the monitors' lesson one morning, when Bumble entered, looking smug. I had noticed that he had not been, as he usually was, already there to listen to every word Mr Lowe uttered.

The cause of Bumble's smugness was soon apparent. Mr Clack, the vicar, arrived and stood beside the beadle.

"There," Bumble almost exploded with indignation, "I told you they were learning writing!"

"Dear me," Mr Clack agreed, dithering, as usual. He knew Mr Lowe had been appointed at Miss Aldbury's insistence and that she was paying his wages. Mr Clack was, also, only too conscious of the contributions that lady made to church funds and of her connections with the best families in the area. What was more, Mr Clack was uncertain of the exact status of Mr Lowe. There was no doubt that Mr Lowe was a gentleman, even if he were, at present, occupying the ungentlemanly position of teacher to workhouse children. This contradiction, Mr Clack could only put down to the teacher's being one of those Christians, of whom the vicar had only heard, who felt a calling to help the poor in a practical, face-to-face way. For his own part, Mr Clack found that the noise, ignorance and smell of the lower classes confined his mind and spirit to Earthly things, when they should be free to soar Heavenwards. True spirituality and Christian devotion could, in the vicar's mind, be achieved only by those who, freed from the demand of daily labour, could cultivate their finer feelings. It was amongst such people, that he preferred to spend his time.

Rising and smiling a welcome, Mr Lowe signalled to us to rise and greet our visitor. We obeyed, as one, and waited for Mr Clack's reply. None came. Mr Clack was still struggling to find the correct approach to the situation. He would have preferred to have ignored the school altogether, but Bumble would insist on bringing it to his attention.

At last the vicar spoke. "Writing, Mr Lowe. I must say that I am surprised to see that you include writing in the curriculum."

"At the moment, Mr Clack, we are simply practising the letters of the alphabet and examples of the sounds each can represent in various words."

"Then this is simply to help their reading?" Mr Clack inquired hopefully. Never content with just one sentence, the vicar continued, "I assured Mr Bumble that you would be teaching only reading and that only for the purpose of reading religious and moral stories and tracts."

Bumble's girth visibly expanded with pride at hearing his name on the lips of a man of the cloth.

Mr Clack had not finished, "And, perhaps, Mr Lowe, you would be so good as to teach the children to write their names. Signatures look so much tidier in the parish register than mere marks. The poor make their crosses so rambling and spider-like that they often spread into the record of the next marriage.

At once, Mr Lowe told him, "I would not like to leave you with the wrong impression, Mr Clack. I have every intention of teaching writing to these children. And a little history, geography and science."

There was not a sound from us. We were all listening intently. We watched Mr Clack turn pale with shock.

"No! No, sir! I shall not allow it," Mr Clack asserted, forgetful, in his outrage, of Miss Aldbury's generosity. "For my part, I see no need for these children even to read. Religion and moral education is all that they require. Religion will teach them to live contentedly and industriously in the station of life in which God has placed them. It will teach them to respect their betters and obey their masters. Where religion is well established, sir, you will hear no talk of equality and democracy and other such nonsense." Even Mr Clack had to pause for breath, before concluding, "And religion alone is sufficient to ensure their salvation on the Day of Judgment."

"I cannot see," Mr Lowe replied patiently, "that raising these children from the ignorance, to which they had previously been condemned, will undermine society. Educating them can only benefit society at large. I shall share the benefits of my own education with them, in as far as they have the ability to learn."

"Ability!" the vicar mocked, as the beadle spluttered with amusement. "Shrewdness and native cunning are all they possess and they have these in abundance. Your teaching will be wasted."

"Then my efforts will not turn them to riot and rebellion, as you seem to suggest, Mr Clack. I shall at least have kept them out of mischief, wandering the streets and fields unsupervised." As Mr Clack sought a reply, Mr Lowe suggested, "Let us leave this discussion until later. The children are waiting."

Appalled that we children, whom he had hardly noticed, should be shown any consideration, Mr Clack left, with Bumble hurrying at his side and muttering, in a dozen different ways, "I told you so!"

Although I tried to concentrate on Mr Lowe's words after this, it was very difficult to do so. Mr Clack and Bumble had stopped just outside the door. Mr Clack was, apparently, trying to think what to do next, and Bumble was, as usual, making free with his opinions.

"Writing, sir," the beadle declared, "is for them what has pocket books." Here, we could imagine him producing his own leather one, of which he was so proud. "If you're in the station of life which requires a pocket book and can afford one, then, and only then, you have need of writing."

There was no reply from the vicar. He was either still working out his next step or puzzling over Bumble's reasoning.

The silence gave Bumble the opportunity to continue. "What have these paupers to write on, I ask you? They'll be writing on walls next, you mark my word."

"Be silent, Mr Bumble. I must have time to think," we heard Mr Clack say, but it was almost a plea, rather than an order.

As Bumble never spent much time on thinking, he gave Mr Clack only a few seconds of silence before continuing. "Counting, sir. He's learning 'em to count. I've seen it with me own heyes. Counting! There's nothing as likely to make paupers discontented as counting. They'll be counting each mouthful of food and swearing someone's had more than them." To add weight to the point he was making, he added, "Them Frenchies had learned to count, I'll be bound. What did they count? Heads! Chopped orf heads, that's what they counted! It'll be happening here soon, sir, if this goes on."

"Silence, Bumble! Do be silent." This time, it was an order, not a request. In the moment of quiet this brought him, Mr Clack made up his mind. He walked back into the room, his expression one of a soldier of Christ going into battle with the Devil. We stood to our feet, but were ignored.

"As God's representative in this parish, Mr Lowe, I cannot shirk my duty. Present fashion dictates – even the Bishop shares the opinion – that a little reading, with the content strictly supervised, does no harm to the lower orders, but there I take my stand. A little reading is all I will allow in my parish." As though in the pulpit, the vicar was now in full flow. "I am, sir, the appointed vicar of this parish and, as such, I have the God-given duty of protecting my flock from the attack of wolves, albeit," he stressed, looking directly at Mr Lowe, "they come in sheep's clothing." He turned and walked out.

At this point, Bumble was quite certain that the last command to, "Be silent, Bumble," had expired. We could hear him, his voice becoming fainter and fainter, declaring, "Learning has its place, sir, as I'm sure you'll agree. But learning is for them with a head for it. Paupers ain't got the head for it, sir, as no one knows better than me." He was out of our sight, but we knew that he would be nodding his head in agreement with his own views.

"Their heads," the beadle went on, "is as thick as their hides and who knows better than me how thick that is? You can't beat proper habits into their hides and you can't beat learning into their heads."

We surmised that Mr Clack's determination was deserting him, now some action was needed, for he said, in a low, hesitant voice, which we could hardly hear, "The problem is, Mr Bumble, that Mr Lowe is paid by Miss Aldbury. The cost comes from private charity, not from taxes. I am not sure of my position in this matter."

Bumble did not quite appreciate the point being made, but he did have an opinion on taxes.

"Charity is a fine thing," the beadle stated with feeling. "Charity is when the rich puts their hands into their own pockets. Taxes is quite another matter. Taxes is when the collector puts his hand into my pocket. Charity is a good and Christian thing."

While Mr Clack canvassed the opinion of his more influential members of his flock, we continued our lessons.

CHAPTER SIXTEEN

William John Bull White sat in the library, a solitary candle lighting the sheets of paper covered with columns of figures and estimates, which lay on his desk.

William John Bull White sat alone, or, to his mind, as good as alone. His servant, sitting upright on a hard wooden chair in the shadow, he considered little better than a dog in terms of understanding or ability to communicate. Indeed, he thought a beloved dog he had owned in childhood, which had understood his every word, would rank above his servant in the animal world. One advantage the servant did have, in his master's eyes, was that, being deaf and dumb not only in speech but also in intelligence, he could be a constant companion without overhearing conversations and spreading gossip like other servants. Another advantage was, that, as a strongly-built young man and a skilled pugilist, he gave his master protection from any attack.

Looking at his servant, the master saw that, as usual, he was alert and gazing directly at him as though waiting, like a dumb dog, to follow his every move. William did not smile at his servant, he felt no warmth for him. Nor did he dismiss him. Servants did not sleep while their masters were awake.

There was no noise from the rest of the house and William began to pace the room impatiently. For his poor relief plans, he needed money and this had forced him to consult his father, the only source of finance. His father had asked for a copy of his plans and costings and had been looking at them for two days. Surely, he had made up his mind by now! At last, as she passed the door on her way upstairs, William heard his mother's footsteps. His father would arrive soon. True to the son's expectations, the father walked in, throwing back the door and marching in to assert that this was part of the family house and not his son's private domain, as he appeared to consider it. At other times, the son would have remained seated at the desk, but wanting to keep in favour, he rose on this occasion, gave up his seat and signalled to his servant to bring another.

"Send the lad to bed," Mr White ordered his son.

"He's deaf. There's no fear of his hearing us."

"That's not what concerns me. When will you learn servants deserve consideration if they are to give you loyalty and unstinting service! He's treated like a dog – a dog with a bad master."

Once again, although considering his father too familiar with the servants and too ready to tolerate those who were old or inefficient, the son yielded to his father. Or rather, he did not argue, but just did not do as he had suggested. What he did, was to indicate to the servant that books should be cleared from the desk to give his father room to spread out the papers he had been studying.

"What do you think of my plans, sir?" William asked, leaning forward as though genuinely interested in his opinion and not just his money.

"You should have had that servant of yours clear away all the books before you wrote it and used your common sense instead of the theories of men who have never come face-to-face with a poor man in their lives."

"A knowledge of political economy is essential to any man interested in the country's affairs," the son asserted, defensively.

"Fashions come and go, son. Believe me, I have seen them all. Some I have seen repeated two or three times as they come round in a circle again and again," his father retorted. "This feller Jeremy What's-'is-name won't last more than a decade."

About to supply the name 'Bentham', William stopped himself. His father knew the name perfectly well and was just baiting him. Taking a deep breath, he lied, "I would value your opinion, sir."

"Let's hope that you do know the value of advice. It's clear that you don't know the value of money," the father snorted. But then, as he had promised his wife, he tried to be calm and patient. It took a few minutes for him to reach that state, and, before he had, he could not resist adding, "It seems I was the last to hear of your plans. You consulted your Aunt Mann first, I hear. Did you think that she wouldn't tell me?"

"I merely mentioned it in passing, father. You are the only one to have seen my detailed plans."

His complaint off his chest, Mr White told his son, "That's as maybe. I'll be honest, I am only helping you for your mother's sake. You well know that I want you to concentrate on the business and the great changes ahead."

"My being in Parliament, father, can only do the business good."

"That may be the case. I cannot see it myself. As I was saying, I'm doing this for your mother. Over the years, I have come to value her opinion. If she thinks this scheme will make your name and make you happy, I'll go along with it for her. Now, let's get down to details."

Mr White referred to his notes. "There's one point on which I'm not clear, William. You plan to take over both the workhouse and also outdoor relief for those who ask for just a loaf and a few shillings to tide them over."

"Yes, Father. If I take over just the workhouse, the overseer will send everyone requesting a crust of bread into the workhouse to sleep and eat at my expense. More than one man trying that plan has been bankrupted."

The frown on the old man's face deepened. "Forgive my stupidity, William, but is not that the same as you taking over both, refusing any outdoor relief and forcing everyone into the workhouse?"

Impatiently, the son answered. "There will be no overseer for the idle to appeal to. No overseer to give them a ticket demanding that I accept them. No one to interfere in the way I run my system. In my plan the workhouse will be what it was meant to be, a place where the idle are made to work for their bread. Word will soon spread that life is no bed of roses and that it is best not to seek outdoor relief in the first place."

For the first time, Mr White realised that his son would find pleasure in making it a bed of thorns. "I have to agree that it may do some lay-abouts some good, but you are forgetting the distinction between the undeserving and the deserving poor. Some folk live so close to poverty that an illness, an accident, a death in the family or any little extra expense will tip them over the edge to where they are in danger of dying from cold or hunger."

"I agree with half of that, father. There are the undeserving poor, the idle and feckless, who waste their wages on drink and gambling. But where are the deserving poor? They all bring poverty upon themselves. They marry too early, have more children than they can afford, and waste money they do not have on family Christenings and funerals. They pamper themselves when they are ill with useless medicines from any charlatan passing through the town. The list is endless. If they have a penny in their pockets, it burns a hole until they have spent it. None put it aside for a rainy day."

Looking at his son, Mr White saw a stranger, who only now and again reminded him of the young boy who, once upon a time, had so eagerly come to the Yard with him. At heart – what was he at heart?

Dismissing such thoughts, Mr White returned to the plans. "Let me tell you my suggestions, William. There are practical advantages in distinguishing between the deserving and the undeserving poor. Such a distinction may mean the difference between success and failure of your experiment."

William appeared far from convinced, "How, father?"

"If you force all the poor into the workhouse, it will burst at the seams and the cost to you will be considerable. For centuries, the deserving poor have been helped by private charity and, to cut your bill, you must let that continue – even encourage it to continue."

Now, the son was really listening to his father's words, as Mr White explained, "I have suggested to your mother that she sets up a charity for those who fall on hard times. I shall give the initial donation to set the fund rolling and then she and the other ladies of the town will raise more and supervise its distribution. That will spare them, especially women and children, the hardship and shame of the workhouse.

The son, hearing this, wondered how the poor could feel shame when their whole lives were so shameful, but the obvious usefulness of his father's plan forced him to keep his opinion to himself. "That will certainly lower the burden on the taxes," he agreed.

"Next point," Mr White said. "We must encourage masters to pay fair wages and not force their labourers to seek help from poor relief. I have always paid a fair wage for a fair day's work, but there are many, especially small farmers, who will pay as little as they can get away with. I see that refusing to hand out cash and making everyone go into the workhouse will stop some of that, but perhaps a good sermon from Mr Clack would shame the farmers into giving more."

The son rightly looked doubtful as to the usefulness of this. Sometimes, he wondered why his father was thought to be such a good businessman.

"I have my own ideas on this point, father. The quickest way to raise wages is to make labour scarce." Carried away with his plan, William did not give his father the chance to interrupt. "I hear that there is ample work in the North and Midlands for anyone, man, woman or child, willing to make the journey. I had thought that we would offer reduced fares on our boats and waggons to encourage whole families to move, but now I see that we could make them apply to mother's new charity for the full fares to be paid to us. Surely, father, you would welcome that idea as being good for business."

"There's more to business than making money, William. Our name would be mud if your mother raised money for charity which ended up in our pockets. I'm not losing the good name it has taken me years to build. I

92

hope that you will remember that when I am dead and gone. What's more, if this clever scheme of yours leads to a shortage of labour in the town, it will be us paying higher wages along with everyone else."

"It was just an idea, father." William thought that, if he seemed to give way now, he would be more likely to win financial support from his father. He could, in any case, later go ahead with the plan, whatever his father said now.

"I have a few other points to make. First, you will never make money from goods made in a workhouse...."

Unable to contain his impatience, the son butted in, "It may have failed in the past, father, but that means it was not carried out by those who knew what they were doing."

"There are some things which never change, William. Unskilled men cannot do skilled men's work. The finished goods will be unsellable and the money paid out for materials wasted. And, if by chance you do produce something worth selling, the local tradesmen will object that you are taking away their trade and sending them into the workhouse."

Stubbornly, the son stuck to his plans. "I have heard you say father, that apprenticeships are too long and that most trades could be learned in two years rather than five or seven." Still annoyed by his father's implied criticism that he had not thought things through thoroughly, he continued, "My plan is to go to the large towns and contract for any unskilled work which is needed. There is often a part of any manufacturing process which requires no skill. The manufacturers will see the advantage of contracting out the work. I shall have a large labour force to complete work quickly and it will save their having to provide factory space for hands to work in. If they already put out unskilled work to individuals, then I shall offer the advantage of their dealing with one man rather than a hundred or so."

Knowing he, himself, knew little of manufacturing and realising the lateness of the hour, Mr White let that point drop and went on to others.

"You can't let any Tom, Dick or Harry, who has a vote in the parish vestry, tell you what to do. If this is your scheme, you need to keep the reins tightly in your own hands."

"That point is covered, father. Some parishes have a small, select vestry running things. I can introduce that and pack it with yes-men."

"Well," his father commented, "you have given the matter some thought. I only wish that you would put the same energy into our family business. But I admire your determination. I might not approve..."

"And the final point, father?" the son interrupted once again. There had to be another point. They had not yet mentioned money.

"It's this, William. You have worked out that you can contract with the parish to manage the workhouse and outdoor relief for twenty five percent less than it cost last year. I cannot see that is possible. In your eagerness to obtain the contract, you are selling yourself short. What if there's a bad harvest? What if it's a bad winter so labourers can't work? What if prices rise? Cut it by ten percent, son, and leave it at that."

"I am sure that I can work within such a budget," the son replied. Then he added, trying to sound as though it were of little significance, "I thought that, if I overrun a little, I could put in my own money to cover the difference."

"And still," his father asked in amazement, "claim to have done it for twenty five percent less?"

"Who's to know, father?" Laughing, he went on, "My aim is to receive the credit for making such a saving, not to actually make it."

"Cheating, in other words," his father stated in disgust.

"Come, come, father, everyone cheats at some time, when the stakes are high enough."

"Is that what they taught you at that school you went to?"

"Yes, father. That is what I learned at the school to which you sent me." Still anxious to have his father's financial support, even if not his approval, William continued, "No one will ever know. It will all be lost in the books in clever accounting."

"But commissioners would go through the books with a fine tooth comb."

"Even a fine tooth comb will not discover anything, I can assure you. They will be here for a day or two, father, taking the opportunity to visit friends in the district. Then they will be off back to London singing my praises. Success is all that matters these days."

"And your mother and me? Don't you think that we care? Our name has always been above reproach."

"And where is your name known, father? In Myddlington and a few dozen miles around. I plan to make my name more widely known."

"Known for what, my boy?" the father demanded. "Cheating and dishonest dealing?" Feeling suddenly old and weary, Mr White brought the discussion to an end. "I assume this money you talk of putting in will come from me. Then my decision is the final one. I will back you only if you cut the cost to ten percent, compared with last year's, and if you admit – should you overrun the costs you have calculated and put in my money – what you have done. Sleep on my advice and conditions, William, and let me have your answer in the morning." Turning, he smiled at the servant, still awake and watchful in the shadows.

As the door shut behind his father, William White swore, "Damn you, father. Damn you."

CHAPTER SEVENTEEN

There were rumours of changes to come in the workhouse, but they float-ed over my head. After all, from Jack's lectures, I had become aware that laws had been made in London concerning workhouses, but I had no evi-dence that these affected my life. In my experience, we were ruled, not by laws, but by the day-to-day mood swings of those, like Mrs Corney and Bumble, who had daily charge of us.

For my part, too, all my thoughts and energies were concentrated on Mr Lowe and the school. Suddenly, I saw opening before me, not just a world of knowledge, but a world of opportunity. I had come to imagine that, if I were a dedicated scholar, I could follow my studies wherever they led. While sufficiently in touch with reality to realise this would cost money, I dreamed of the appearance of a charitable lady or gentleman to sponsor me. Felicity had recently gone into service at Miss Aldbury's and I was sure she would put in a good word for me. The world of learning would be my oyster.

Now, whenever I walked along the High Street, I stopped and read the brass plates proclaiming the presence of lawyers and doctors and of tutors taking pupils as boarders. I noticed every minister of whatever sect whom I passed in the street and even paid attention to the duties Mr Clack per-formed during services. Always, I was weighing up in my mind which of these vocations I would prefer to follow. You might say that I had rapidly passed from the stage of longing for a single book of my own, to imagining myself in possession of a whole library.

Such fancies did not strike me as exaggerated. I was, after all, about to enjoy the prize I had won of tea at Mr Lowe's house. Of all the boys, includ-ing those older than me, I had won top marks. For some weeks I had worn the sash which proclaimed my superiority and had not the slightest doubt that I deserved it. I had won it without having to wait, like Paul, for some-one to whisper the answer to me or help me when the teacher's back was turned. In my own eyes I was the cleverest boy in the class, perhaps in the whole of the country or the world.

From the moment that I had known the treat was to take place on the following Sunday, the days had become longer and longer. Even the nights, which I passed in endlessly practising, "Please, ma'am," and "Thank-you,

Mrs Lowe," dragged so slowly that I was convinced every hour that the chimes of the church clock had broken.

As the moment approached for us to be collected from the gate, my fear of wetting my trousers increased beyond all sane reasoning. If I suddenly needed to go, how, I asked myself, did I make this known in polite company? As a precaution, I had to leave the others, Geogina, Tom and an orphan called Kezzie, watching along the street while I disappeared every five minutes. Jack pointed out that I was not only excited, but over-excited and tried to make me stand still and take deep breaths. It did no good. The very sight of Mr Lowe and his son in the distance forced me to run in yet again.

When I returned, the girls were already seated on one of the horses and Tom was on the other. I was introduced to the son, whose name was Henry and he, taller than Mr Lowe, swung me up behind Tom. None of us children said a word. With the desire to be on our best behaviour had come the realization that we did not know what best behaviour was. It seemed safer to risk no behaviour at all.

"Quite a little family," Henry commented, to break the silence.

"We ain't related, mister, sir." I croaked, my voice having suddenly almost disappeared.

"You must call my son 'Henry', Nathaniel. 'Mister', by itself, is not acceptable."

So this was a lesson as well as a treat. I breathed again, feeling I knew how to behave in a lesson. My confidence returned and, taking my lead, the others relaxed a little, too. We even began to call and wave to the people we passed.

Mr Lowe and his son laughed at our pleasure, until I had to go and call out, "Leathers," to Noah Claypole.

"Do you like to be called 'Workhouse', Nathaniel?"

"No, sir."

"Then please respect the feelings of others."

"I'm sorry, sir."

At the sight of Mr Carson, the local bookseller and his wife, out for a Sunday stroll, our spirits returned.

Mr Lowe and his son raised their hats to Mrs Carson, while Mr Carson raised his to the blushing Gina and Kezzie.

"And where are you young ladies and gentlemen going?" Mrs Carson asked.

The girls giggled and hung their heads, but Tom said, "I improved more than anyone else."

"And I had the highest mark of any boy, even those as old as Paul," I claimed in a loud voice so the whole street could hear me.

"Four scholars, we have here, my dear," Mr Carson announced to his wife.

"I didn't think we had that many in the whole town," she answered. I suppose book sales were not doing too well.

We were all grinning from ear to ear.

"The more people who can read, the better our trade will be," Mr Carson declared, thinking of business on a Sunday, if not actually selling books. "I think we must consider donating a prize ourselves. We must have a suitable book we could award."

We travelled on. Then, I realised, we were turning off along the lane with my house at the end. It was a modest one by general standards, but, as we came up close to it, it towered over us and silence engulfed us again. At the sight of Mrs Lowe and the children waiting to greet us on the steps, I tried not to cross my legs and just hoped I would not disgrace myself just when I might be about to be revealed as their child and taken to live in the house of my dreams. I would keep my identity secret for the moment.

"I shall let Georgina, as the eldest, introduce her friends," Mr Lowe said, whispering to her what to say. I might have guessed that Mr Lowe would know just how to help us in this new situation. We had, after all, never been in a house before.

"Are any of you related?" Mrs Lowe asked.

"No, Mrs Lowe," we replied in chorus. We knew in our hearts that we did not know. I thought I noticed Mr Lowe indicate to his wife to keep off the subject of relationships.

Our skilled hostess had questions ready to ask us to help the conversation along, but, unfortunately, we did not have our answers ready. We either all spoke at once or kept silent. Once silence descended, we were all too shy to draw attention to ourselves by breaking it.

As we ploughed through questions on our ages, Myddlington and our lives in the workhouse, I found the courage to look around. When we first entered, everything had blended into a mist around us, but, now, I realised that I was sitting in a large, solid, leather armchair. It was not as uncomfortable as I had imagined such chairs to be. Without looking down, I slid my hand to feel the cushion and wiggling my shoulders, I leaned back to check whether my head came to the top of this high-backed chair. Then there were the metal studs, where pieces of leather overlapped, to be explored. How very different from the hard, wooden workhouse benches, or even old Sal's ancient, rickety armchair!

"Are you comfortable, Nathaniel?" Mr Lowe's eldest daughter, Emma, asked me.

I jerked my thoughts back from the leather chair. "Yes, thankyou, Miss Lowe." I smiled, hoping I had not missed other questions addressed to me. It seemed the general polite questioning had, at last, reached me.

"What do you plan to be when you grow up, Nathaniel?" Mrs Lowe inquired, smiling encouragingly.

Taking a deep breath, this being the first time that I had revealed my dreams to anyone else, I replied, "I ain't made up me mind between a lawyer, a doctor or a minister of the church. Or maybe," I added, not noticing the silence which greeted my announcement, "a tutor 'oo takes boarding pupils."

The younger Lowe children spluttered as they tried to respond to their mother's severe look by smothering their laughter.

"How interesting!" Mrs Lowe commented.

"Do you know Latin and Greek?" one of the children demanded, knowing full well that I did not. Before I could answer, he ignored his father's frown to state, "I am younger than you, and I can already read Latin and am making a start with Greek."

"Don't be boastful," Henry told him.

Gina, sensing I needed some help, asked sweetly, "Can I 'ave a look at your pictures, Mrs Lowe?"

With some relief, Mrs Lowe gave her permission. Gradually, we were caught up in the activity of examining everything in sight. We had never seen large picture so close before, and pointed to this detail or that. Henry and Emma walked with us, answering our questions.

"Is that an orange?" I asked, stopping at the bowl of fruit. I knew full well that it was, but hoped to be told that I could take one back to the work-house. Knowing that Paul would never win a visit for himself, I had rashly promised to bring him something back from mine.

Tom made straight for the piano. Emma was asked to play for him. He was fascinated by all musical intruments and had heard organs, fiddles and drums, but had never heard a piano. Henry sat him on a second stool and suggested to Emma that she might teach Tom a simple tune.

Georgina found a musical box. She was allowed to wind it and then we stood watching and listening as the tiny pins played tunes for us. "Little things please little minds," Paul would have said. Our confidence rising and our curiosity still unsatisfied, Kezzie asked if she could walk round the patterns on the carpet and, without touching, trace the rings on the wallpaper.

We occupied ourselves with these activities, which had not been among those planned for us, until the entrance of the maid diverted our attention. The Lowe's regular maid, trained for drawing room work, was having her afternoon off and it was soon obvious that the new maid was having her rough edges knocked off by practising on us. She happened to be a young girl from the workhouse. She was called Elizabeth by her employers, but we said straight away, "'Ello, Lizzy, 'ow you getting on?" She immediately forgot that she had come in to announce that tea was served in the garden. Having been stopped from replying, she had to be prompted to make the announcement we had been waiting to hear.

As we walked into the garden, we wondered whether our days of practice in holding our mugs in one hand and plates in the other and eating and drinking from them at the same time would come in useful.

Ever the perfect hostess, Mrs Lowe had anticipated our problems. "I thought," she announced to our great relief," that we would eat in the garden. You children may sit at the table."

As we moved into the garden, under the pressure of urgent necessity, I whispered to Tom, "Jog about a bit, Tom. Please, please." Tom wriggled and moved his weight from one foot to the other.

"I know where you need to go, young man," Mrs Lowe observed. "Show the boys the way, Henry." Afterwards, there was sweet smelling soap to wash our hands, even though they were not dirty. When I got back, I held my hand under Georgina's nose, knowing she would enjoy the perfume and gave Kezzie a turn as well.

Although our minds were on food, we took the time to jump from one stepping stone to another across the lawn, swung to and fro on the swing and dangled our hands in the pond in the vain attempt to catch a fish. We had all relaxed and felt perfectly at ease.

"Sit at the table, children," Mr Lowe told us. We rushed and shoved for places considering ourselves free from the necessity of lining up as we did for meals in the workhouse. Our attention now all on the food, we gazed at it.

"What do you have for meals in the workhouse?" Emma asked.

"Depends," Geogina began, wondering whether to make something up or admit that we had never seen tea like this before.

"Depends?" Emma queried.

Thinking I was being clever, I put in, "Bread and pull-it." I was eating a sandwich as I spoke. The Lowe children, who had turned to me on my reply, turned away again.

"We try to eat with our mouths shut." Mrs Lowe still smiled, but there was little warmth in it.

We all tried, too, but it was all too obvious that they had had a life time of practice. We had difficulty judging the size of the bite which would enable us both to shut our mouths and to chew.

Georgina, trying to curl her little finger while drinking from a cup, spilt most of the tea down her frock. "Bother!" she said, "Mrs Corney'll 'alf kill me."

By this time, Lizzie had forgotten all her training and was joining in our conversation, as though still in the workhouse with us. "Is she still the same bad-tempered old 'ag?" she asked.

We all agreed and added a few more terms of our own.

Having been used to only one item at a meal, or two if it were bread and cheese, we were anxious to try everything, even if it meant dropping the remains of those things we did not like on the lawn. It was not like dropping it on the carpet. Lizzie, having dipped into everything in the kitchen, advised us on the tastiest delicacies.

When we had finished or had realised that we had not been expected to finish everything at one sitting, it was suggested that we might play in the garden, while Lizzie cleared the table. We stood up and began to play, but, as soon as all the Lowes had disappeared into the house, we gathered round the table again.

"D'yer think we could take some away with us?" Georgina asked. There was an orphan boy whose attention she wanted to attract and a gift of food would do the trick. We all wanted to know the same thing.

"Go and ask, Gina," I begged.

"Why me?"

"You're the eldest."

"And you're the eldest boy."

I saw the sense of this and ran into the house. Lizzie directed me to the room where I would find the family. Entering one room, I could hear their voices in the next. As they became clearer, I stopped to listen.

"I hope you have not been encouraging Nathaniel to think that he has the same choice of a career as our sons would have, my dear," Mrs Lowe was saying.

"You know," her husband replied, "that I believe our country has an open society, in which a man may rise on his own merit, but large advances in one generation will always be rare, especially from the lowest classes of society."

"Then where did the child obtain such an idea, Father?" Henry asked.

"He may have misunderstood me. My aim is not so much to raise some children above the others, as to raise the lowest level of society as a whole. Every society must have its labouring classes, but there is no reason why they should live in ignorance and poverty. With a little education they can achieve a modest comfort and pride in themselves."

"But," Emma pointed out, "Nathaniel seems to believe nothing is beyond him."

"He is young," Mr Lowe told her. "He will come to realise that, with hard work and dedication, he can be a teacher in a school for the poor. He will be an example to the children there."

"He will never be a teacher of elocution," one of the younger children laughed.

"Nor of table manners," Mrs Lowe observed. They all, including Mr Lowe laughed at these remarks.

"You must admit," Henry said, "that if he has not yet learned to eat with his mouth shut, becoming a lawyer, doctor or man-of-the-cloth is likely to prove beyond his talents."

"I am not sure that this experiment of yours is a good one, my dear. It is such a bad example to our children."

"Yes," one of the younger children protested. "We would be sent to bed if we behaved so badly."

All my dreams fell away, shrivelled to nothing in the light of reality. Gone, too, was the dream I had never even admitted to myself – the dream that I belonged to a family like Mr Lowe's and that he would come to treat me as a son of his own.

Running back into the garden, I called out, "Mr Lowe says we can 'elp ourselves. We can eat as much as we want now and take the rest back to the work'ouse for Paul and the others."

They did not need telling twice. With no one watching, we stuffed handfuls into our mouths and handfuls into our pockets.

"What you doing?" Lizzie inquired in disbelief when she came with a tray to clear the table.

"Mr Lowe told Nat we can have it all," Georgina mumbled through a mouthful of cake.

"Are you sure?" Lizzie asked, rightly doubting what she was being told.

"Gawd's truth," I mumbled, half choking as I spoke.

Tom was the first to be sick, but I was not far behind. As we recovered from this initial bout, looking as green as the others, I ordered them, "Just stuff your pockets."

"Children!" a stern voice called.

I was sick again. So were the others. Within a minute, the sight of us and our soiled clothes was considered only fit for Lizzie's eyes. She was ordered to take us away and clean us as best she could.

We half expected a caning but, when Mr Lowe said, "Let's take these children home without more ado," I assumed 'ado' was another word for a beating and was greatly relieved.

The next day at school, we were made to confess our sins before the whole class and it was made clear that we were to blame for the withdrawal of any future invitations to Mr Lowe's home.

"I am especially disappointed in you, Nathaniel," Mr Lowe told me. "I was deeply saddened to see such behaviour in a boy whom I had thought to be my best pupil. Superficial cleverness will never make up for seriousness of mind and consideration for others."

How I longed to shout, "And I was deeply disappointed in you, Mr Lowe," but I was too unhappy to say anything.

CHAPTER EIGHTEEN

Not so very long after the meeting between Mr White and his son, Mrs White sat at her husband's bedside. He had collapsed a few days earlier and both doctors, who had been consulted, agreed that he had not long to live. The day had passed in alternating bouts of lucidity and confusion, but now her husband looked at her with clear, intelligent eyes.

"Martha," he began. Not used to hearing her name said with such tenderness, Mrs White thought that her husband's mind had wandered back to the days, long ago, when they had courted on the river bank. The river had, some years ago, been cut through by the canal and had become, just like their affection for each other, formal, lacking its natural spontaneity.

"Martha, are you listening?"

"Of course, William. I have been sitting here day and night listening to your every breath. Your breathing has become more even. Are you feeling more comfortable now?"

"Martha, I must tell you my plans."

Mrs White smiled. Who, but her husband, would be making plans when he was about to die?

"You may have thought," he went on, "that I have always gone my own way, without concern for you, but it has all been for you and William."

"I am sure that William is deeply sorry for causing you distress, my love."

William White's breath became more laboured. "Let me say what I have to say in my own words, Martha. I may not have much time in which to say it."

Martha White was silent.

"Every thought I have had, every plan I have made, I have rehearsed with you. You may not have been aware, my dear, but a word, a look, a nod from you has caused me to go ahead or to think again."

Listening in silence, Martha regretted that her husband had never said these things before.

"There have been three times when I have not heeded your advice or not sought it." Pausing for breath, William White forced himself to continue. "Once when I sent our son away to school, once when I refused to take him away from it and now, when I have rewritten my will."

Amazed at this news, Martha still remained silent. She had, of course, been aware that the lawyer had called several times, but she had imagined they were simply sorting out a few details.

So near death, William White had not considered blaming his wife for making him support their son's plans, but he had realised that he must protect her future and his business from being ruined by his son. By now, the effort he had in speaking made it clear that any breath he took might be his last.

"The details.... you are taken care of, my dearest." Realising he would never finish his explanation, William White stopped and struggled for breath.

"Hush, my love," Martha said gently, wiping her husband's brow. She took his hand and, making the greatest effort of her life, smiled at him.

For a brief second he squeezed her hand. "I have loved you more each day...."

William White died, as the carving on his grand tomb proclaimed, at the age of sixty seven on the third of April, 1832. All those who lined the streets to see the great black carriage with its jet black horses pass by or squeezed into the churchyard to stand at a respectful distance from the burial, commented on the deep distress of the widow and the coldness of the son.

In his will, having committed his body to the ground and his soul to God, William White had decreed that two thousand pounds should be set aside for his wife's sole use, the only restriction placed upon it being that it was not to be used to support their son's plans in regard to the workhouse. Another thousand pounds was left to establish a charity for the deserving poor. On condition that he worked in the business, his son was to be given an ample salary. His remaining wealth and his business were tied up in a trust with clauses and sub-clauses covering every eventuality to ensure that his son could not use any assets or borrow against his future inheritance to put money into running poor relief in the town.

The business was to be run by "my dear son, William John Bull White, my old and honest friend, Robert Campion, and my beloved wife, Martha, on whose advice, support and affection my business was built." When the reading of the will was completed, William White stood and faced his mother.

"You never did stand up for me, Mother. You saw me go to that prison of a school, to that torture chamber and said nothing." He marched from the room, to continue with his own plans, whether he had financial support to fall back on or not.

However busy Mrs White was establishing the charity for which her husband had made provision, she never missed a day visiting the graveyard to leave fresh flowers on his tomb. But she was not the only visitor to that sad and silent place.

CHAPTER NINETEEN

At a loose end, I wandered down to see Jack Star.

"Ain't you a pal of Oliver Twist's?" he asked, as soon as I appeared. At that age, being a friend or not being a friend was a serious business. I played for time.

"I only met 'im twice, at bird scaring and on the first day of school. 'E don't come no more."

"Well, 'e ain't your worst enemy, is 'e?" Jack demanded impatiently.

"No. Suppose not. Why d'yer want to know?"

'E just come by the gate, all solemn like, and said, 'Please, sir, can you tell me where my dear mother is buried? She died in the workhouse around eight years ago.' I 'ad to tell 'im, didn't I?"

Puzzled as to why Jack should hesitate to tell Oliver where his mother was buried, I waited for an explanation.

"I'd 'ave liked to say there were a neat, tidy place with a 'eadstone above it with 'is ma's name on, but there ain't."

"What's there, then?" Graveyards were eerie places to be avoided unless with someone to look after me.

"Well, they put all the paupers right back in the far corner, where no one 'ardly ever goes. And there ain't separate graves. They're all dropped in together, cheek by jowl, to keep down the cost."

"I ain't going to die in the work'ouse, then, Mr Star." They had told me I had come close to death with measles and even closer with diphtheria. That I had not died, along with all the other missing letters of Bumble's alphabet, I put down to Sal's nursing and my own determination to survive.

"'E's a strange little feller, that Oliver Twist. 'E looked so disappointed when I told 'im about them all being in a grave together, that I told 'im to pick some wild flowers to lay nearby. I told 'im that 'is Ma would 'ave liked that. Then 'e asked me if I 'ad met 'is mother. I were glad to be able to say that I 'ad seen 'er and given 'er me seat when she fainted in the street. Told 'im she thanked me kindly and that she were a real lady and very pretty."

I tried not to feel jealous that Jack had seen Oliver's mother and not mine.

"Why don't you go after 'im. 'E'll be upset."

"Don't take much to upset 'im. You can scare 'im by just saying 'Boo!'" I replied, jealous again that Jack was taking such an interest in Oliver.

"You'd scare easy, if you was brought up by Mrs Mann," Jack replied, adding, "You're not as kind and considerate as you used to be, Nat. I'm sad to see that."

"What d'yer want me to do?" I asked, grudgingly.

"Go and sit with 'im for a bit. 'E'll be by 'is ma's grave."

"Wouldn't 'e rather be by 'imself, to remember 'er?"

"Ain't you got no feelings? Is that what school does for you?"

I turned to go, muttering, "'E's lucky to know where 'is ma is, even if she is in the graveyard." I had spoken without realising that the gate was shut and that I would have to wait for Jack to open it for me.

As he swung the wicket open, the porter said, "'Eard about your trouble at the Lowe's. Per'aps you'll tell me one day why you did it."

"One day," I said.

"And," Jack added, ruffling my hair, "There ain't no ghosties waiting for you in the churchyard. Would 'is mother 'urt 'im?"

"She might 'urt me," I replied, remembering how I had dragged her son all around the Yard when he had just wanted to go back to Mrs Mann's. I hoped, if his mother was looking down on us, that she would realise that I was no worse than any other boy.

It was not my lucky day. When I reached the churchyard, Oliver was not in sight. Once, I had walked all around the churchyard, even round the dark, shadowy side for a dare, but doing it all on my own was a very different matter. Yet Oliver had done it on his own. I had to admit that, for all his being green and crying so readily, he was made of sterner stuff than I was.

You had to be made of stern stuff to take the walk to the very back of the churchyard. The far side of the church always seemed to be in shadow whatever the time of day. The silent church, with its heavy, square tower threw a deep darkness over the scene. Two great, brooding yews, which appeared for ever twisted in agony, added to the grimness of it all.

I looked along the path which ran with the church on its left and the graveyard on its right bucking up courage, then, putting my head down, tucking in my elbows and making myself as small as possible, I ran hell-for-leather. At any moment, the effigy on a tomb might lean over, its face moss-green and crumbling, to grab me and pull me down to the dank ground beside it. Or the heavy, oak crypt door might open and a hand reach out to pull me inside to the unspeakable horrors which lay in the blackness. Would they keep me, imploring me to free them from the eternal darkness, or would they push and turn me from one to the other, mocking me with their hollow, ghostly laughter?

My wild imaginings almost making my legs turn to jelly beneath me, I reached the end of the path and struck out, treading carefully, between the graves. As I went, tombs were replaced by headstones of less and less impressive size and decoration, until only humps of grass and weeds marked where bodies lay.

"What are you doing here, Nathaniel?" a welcome voice called. "Is your mother buried here?"

I spotted Oliver in the corner of the graveyard. He seemed almost hidden by nettles and brambles, but, as I drew closer, I saw that the space around him was clear. The regularity of funerals for paupers, especially babies from the baby farm, did not allow the weeds to grow on this patch of sacred ground. Oliver looked as happy as I had ever seen him look.

"Is your mother buried here, too, Nathaniel?"

For a moment I realised how friendless poor Oliver was and how I would miss my friends if I were separated from them. He could not imagine that I was there just to be with him and for no other reason.

"No, she ain't buried 'ere," I told him, suggesting that she was buried somewhere else. None of us admitted that we were foundlings. It was like admitting no one wanted you. To divert attention from my parentage, I asked, "Your ma is buried 'ere, ain't she?"

"Yes, I haven't been here before, but I came to town on an errand. I must hurry back soon, but it is so peaceful here. I am sure my mother is in Heaven, looking down at me."

"Like a guardian angel, d'yer mean?"

"Every one says she was just like an angel."

"Where's your pa, Oliver?"

Oliver tried to fight back the tears which welled up in his eyes. "Nobody knows. He'll come for me one day, I am sure."

Eager to prove that I was not afraid of graveyards, I lay back, careful to avoid the pauper grave.

Suddenly, Oliver asked, "Do they beat you in the workhouse?"

Proudly I showed him a bruise on my back. "Only when you're naughty, but it don't take much to make 'em decide you've done something wrong.

'Ow about you?"

As was usual with Oliver, he had come straight out with a question as it occured to him, without thinking that he might not want to say more. He was silent, unwilling to tell a lie or admit to the truth.

Exploiting his unwillingness to lie, I demanded, "'Oo beats you, Ollie?"

"Mr White. He only beats me when I am lazy."

"'E don't live with you, does 'e?"

"No, but he's Mrs Mann's nephew. Mrs Mann says that he is a gentle-man." Always eager to tell the precise truth, he explained, "Well, she calls him 'a gent', but she means that he is a gentleman."

"If gents or gentlemen beat you, I'm glad I don't know none at close quarters," I announced. Realising Oliver was avoiding the main subject, I asked, "Why does 'e beat you?"

"Mr White went to a very expensive school, where he was taught to behave like a gentleman. He is very well educated. He is teaching me to speak like a gentleman."

Having, myself, abandoned all hope of growing up to be like Mr Lowe, I told him, "I'd rather speak rough than get a wapping. Tell 'im you don't want no more lessons."

"But that's not true, Nathaniel. I do want to speak like my mother did and, when my father comes for me, I want him to be proud of me. I came here to tell my mother how hard I am trying to be the son she would have wanted me to be."

"Where do 'e whack you, Oliver?"

Rolling back his sleeve, Oliver showed arms covered from wrist to shoulder with bruises.

"Gawd, did 'e do that to you? No one beats us like that in the work 'ouse."

Unable to restrain his tears, Oliver sobbed and sobbed. "My back is so sore. I expect it is bruised, too."

"Let's 'ave a look."

As gently as I could, I raised his shirt to his shoulders and examined his back. It was covered with bruises. Even I knew that it had taken more than an occasional caning to inflict that much damage. There were fresh black and blue ones and older green and yellow ones with hardly a space between them.

"Gawd!" was the only comment I could think of. As carefully as I could,

I put my arm around his shoulders. "'Ave a good cry," I urged, as Old Sally told me, when I had fallen over. "You ain't slow, Ollie. You speak like a gent – gentleman and you're only as old as me. 'E must like 'urting you. There was a bully stayed in the work'ouse once and 'e liked 'urting people just for the sake of it. Let's tell Mr Star. 'E's the porter 'oo you spoke to at the gate. 'E'll know what to do."

"No, Nathaniel, swear that you won't. I must learn and no one else can teach me." Between his sobs, he added, "It's getting worse. He always seems in a bad mood these days, but I must be strong."

"You should tell Jack, honest you should. Mr White'll injure you one day. 'E could break your arm."

"Swear, Nathaniel, swear not to tell Mr Star."

"I needn't mention your name. I could just ask the best thing to do."

"No. Please swear you won't tell the porter."

Reluctantly, but solemnly, I swore not to tell Jack Star.

It was only later, as I lay in bed thinking about poor Oliver, that I realised that I had only sworn not to tell Jack Star. I had not sworn to keep the secret from anyone else. I could tell Mr Lowe. He was probably the best person to tell in any case. He was a gentleman and people would listen to him, when they might not listen to Jack. I turned the matter over in my mind for several days and nights.

When I told Mr Lowe, he listened in silence. Then he questioned me closely.

"This is a very serious accusation, Nathaniel. Are you telling the truth? Are you exaggerating just a little?"

"Cross me 'eart and 'ope to die, Mr Lowe."

Mr Lowe was so deep in thought, that he did not reprehend me for my oath.

"Leave it to me, Nathaniel. Tell no one else."

CHAPTER TWENTY

It was soon common knowledge that William White, although visiting the Yard every day and insisting on taking over his father's office, contributed little to the running of the business. His mind was firmly set on his poor relief venture. To embark on this, he was staking all he had, or even more than he had, on his own ability and intelligence. William White saw no risk in doing this.

Canvassing support in the town took up all of William White's time. It was clear that while he had, as his father had pointed out, little understanding of how to get the best out of men, he showed a seemingly instinctive talent for appealing to the worst in them by addressing their pockets and prejudices.

Surprisingly, for those who knew that he had read every book and pamphlet and attended every lecture on the faults of the present system of poor relief, he had no use for long and intellectual arguments. Short and simple statements, repeated often enough to bring people to think that they were true, were his first line of attack. Taxes were too high. Paupers were too numerous. People brought poverty on to themselves by being idle and feckless. Feather bedding in poor relief was encouraging these vices.

After slogans, came sticks and carrots. Sticks were used on anyone employed by White and on anyone having a contract with the firm. It was made clear, beyond any doubt, that opposition to him would lead to dismissal or loss of contracts.

Carrots came in a variety of guises. A small farmer, who doted on his strapping young son, was promised that the son could test his brawn and bravery against Seize-'im. A gentleman, given to spending beyond his means and looking to remedy this with a good marriage for his daughter, was told how beautiful she was, how any bachelor fortunate enough to gain her affection would be a very lucky man and how eagerly William White, himself, was looking forward to his next meeting with the young lady in question. There was more than one father ready to nibble these particular carrots.

Tradesmen, whose daughters William could not contemplate marrying even in theory, were afforded the honour of dining at the White's home or promised contracts for saddlery, building and repairing wheels, carts, waggons, coaches and canal boats. Others were half promised agencies for corn or coal or the dozens of items in which the Whites dealt. Lesser beings were bought pints of ale and given the pleasure of chatting with a member of the wealthiest family in the town, a man who condescended to speak to them and allow them to claim him as a personal acquaintance.

The vicar, Mr Clack was not forgotten. The promise of a generous donation to the church was dangled beneath his nose. It was mentioned that the money could be put to any use Mr Clack wished. It did not have to be set aside for church repairs or charities or even to pay the curate. It was further mentioned that Mr Clack was free to consult Mrs Clack on its use, the vicar's wife being renowned for her taste and her desire, long frustrated by lack of money, to refurbish and refurnish the vicarage. Mr Clack, by his smiles, extravagant thanks and subservience, showed himself ready to follow this dangling carrot even to the Mouth of Hell.

With these examples, I think that I can leave you to imagine the forms other bribes and incentives took and how quickly they provided a large pool of voters ready and eager to support William White. From this, he felt certain that he would be able to build a select vestry, or board, to act as yes-men to his plans.

As any opposition to his plans evaporated, it was clear that three potential centres of resistance, as William White had predicted, remained. One was a tenant of William White's, a small farmer called Ebenezer Long. He worked his farm with his son, but, at haymaking and harvesting and other busy times, Long, and those in a similar position, employed labourers. He found it hard to find their wages and still make the farm pay and looked to outdoor relief for his men to supplement the low wages he paid them.

A second, and greater, threat was Robert Campion. A life-long radical and fighter for the rights of the common man, Campion was popular in the town, even amongst those who had no time for his fancy theories. Amongst the rights of man, which Campion supported, was the right of the poor to help from the community. White had long despised him, as having no understanding of the real world and of men's base natures. Now, as a fellow partner in the business, who could block his plans to extract money from it by fair means or foul, White despised him even more.

After long consideration, White came up with a plan to kill both of these birds, Long and Campion, with one stone. That left the third possible source of opposition, Mr Lowe. White found that no one knew much about him, but the very fact that he was prepared to lower himself to teach in the workhouse suggested he held some strange beliefs. He was a possible threat, White decided, but no more than that.

It was a few days later that William White found that Richard Lowe was, in fact, a serious threat, if not for the reason he had anticipated. Wanting to know what his views and beliefs were, William White rode over to Lowe's house to invite him to dine.

To William White's great surprise, Richard Lowe replied, "I think, when you have heard me out, you will not wish me to enter your house, let alone dine there." Richard Lowe did not return William White's smile and saw that smile disappear as he continued, "It seems honourable to inform you that I have recently received a complaint that you have regularly and brutally beaten a young boy, Oliver Twist. I intend to investigate this complaint and, should it be proved, I shall ensure that you never have control of the workhouse."

For a moment, White was lost for words. He was desperately wondering who had lodged this complaint and how he could discredit them. While his aunt occasionally made a feeble protest, he was sure she would not have spoken to anyone else. As for Oliver himself, he had ensured that the boy never came in contact with others.

"Have you nothing to say?" Lowe demanded,

"As you see, I am taken completely by surprise. That particular child is lazy and disobedient and, after all the care and affection my aunt has bestowed upon him, repays her by ignoring her orders and her reprimands. She has asked me to punish him on several occasions in the past, and I have done so in moderation, allowing the punishment to fit the crime, no more and no less."

"From the description of the injuries reported to me, it would appear that these punishments have been anything but moderate."

"So you do not claim to have seen these imagined injuries yourself, Mr Lowe?" The relief in White's voice was obvious. Gaining in confidence, he claimed, "The child is a great spinner of tales. Fact and fantasy are all one to him. From what you say, it would seem to me that I have been too lenient with him. I did not punish him sufficiently to stop his lying and deceitfulness. How often my aunt has commented to me that the boy will hang one day! Now, I must say that I agree with her. I cannot imagine that you will find one man in the whole town who would not agree that sparing the rod was certainly spoiling the child in Oliver Twist's case."

"We shall see," Richard Lowe said, adding, "After great thought, I have decided to ask the workhouse doctor to examine the boy."

This remark only added to White's confidence. If the doctor wanted to keep his contract with the workhouse, he would not dare to suggest that the bruises were inflicted during a beating. Aunt Mann would soon think up an excuse about the coal-hole steps. "I trust I may be present," he said, calmly.

"I shall, of course, inform you of the place and time."

The two men separated.

As he rode home, William White considered how fortunate it was that he had not seen the boy for a few weeks. All he had to do was persuade the doctor to delay the examination just a little longer and the bruises, if they remained at all, could easily be explained away.

CHAPTER TWENTY ONE

All his planning, of course, went on in William White's head and I can only write about it by working back from the conversations reported in my hearing and from his actions as they unfolded over the following weeks. Little by little, I became caught up in these plans and so came to learn the means by which he sought to eliminate any opposition.

My first intrusion into White's schemes was my reporting of his treatment of Oliver to Mr Lowe. Unfortunately, by the time action was taken, the bruises had faded and the workhouse doctor assured Mr Lowe that the few remaining discolourations could well have been caused, as Mrs Mann swore, by an accident on the cellar steps. Oliver, when questioned in the presence of William White, merely trembled. Mr White was able to claim that he was frightened by all the questioning and the doctor's examination. While Mr Lowe accepted that I had told him the truth, he could do no more than warn William White that he would at once report to the authorities any bruises he found upon the children he taught. By his complaint and this threat, Mr Lowe became someone whom Mr White felt he must destroy.

My second involvement, in this destruction as it happened, arose from my talking to Mrs Bumble. It is clear, from his biography of Oliver Twist, that the only Mrs Bumble known to Charles Dickens was the woman the beadle eventually married. For most of my story, the Mrs Bumble we knew was the beadle's mother.

Mrs Bumble seldom, if ever, left her cottage, yet she knew not only everything which actually occurred in the town, but also every rumour and every hint of an occurrence. Stored in her mind were the branches and roots of every family tree, including all born on the wrong side of the blanket, and the value of every inhabitant of Myddlington down to the last silver spoon or threadbare shirt.

Although Mrs Bumble never ventured out, she would sit, spider-like, by the open window until someone passed by. Then, with a greeting and promises of secrets to be shared, she would draw them into her web. People had been known to attempt to creep past, but she was not to be avoided. There was little doubt, as everyone said, that she had chosen a cottage in a location to see the greatest number of people passing by on their daily business. And she made discovering their daily business her daily business.

"How's your husband, now?" she would inquire of any woman whose husband had not been to work. "Is your daughter keeping well?" was the question addressed to any mother whose daughter was courting or had just married and might be expecting a baby. "How are the children?" was asked of almost everyone in the expectation that all were either proud to talk about their children or at their wits' end and ready to tell more than they intended.

Direct questioning, however, was only one of Mrs Bumble's methods of exacting information. While those who were questioned might pass on along the street feeling they had faced the Inquisition, been tortured with thumbscrews or stretched on the rack, they revealed far less than those who were gently nudged into telling Mrs Bumble all she wished to hear.

By this, I mean Mrs Bumble was skilled in nudging and edging her victims into a position where they either believed they were giving nothing away or were only too pleased to give the information required. Nudging information out of people did not involve the use of elbows, but required, first of all, knowing the direction in which to nudge. Some hint, rumour or lead was required as a starting point. This often came from her son, the beadle, whom she interrogated daily on who was in financial difficulty, who had requested aid, who had been granted it and who refused. Another source was the parish doctor, who made frequent house calls to tend to her hypochondria and his own canvassing for the parish contract. From him, she knew almost every sickness and injury suffered by the people of the town.

Armed with this basic knowledge and her carefully honed skill at nudging, even grownups were putty in Mrs Bumble's hands, so what chance had I to resist? We children had passed the cottage many times, but had never been called over to the window. I suppose Mrs Bumble knew that Felicity and Georgina would give as good as they got and foil her attempts to extract information just for the fun of it. Paul, although a chatterbox, might have stolen any small object not nailed down and the younger ones would have been into everything. But, on this particular day, I was on my own and the grapevine would have let her know that I enjoyed showing off my knowledge on any subject under the sun and, once started on a conversation, could be led by the nose into revealing anything anyone wanted to know.

A voice called, "Nathaniel Swubble." I stared at the window, but the sun was striking it and I could see no one.

The disembodied voice called again, "Over here, Nathaniel Swubble."

Moving to where I could see from a different angle, I made out Mrs Bumble, smiling at me. A finger on the hand she put through the barely open window, beckoned me. I went closer. Mrs Bumble was all smiles. "Come on in, my dear."

Just as I put my hand on the door and realised that it was locked, a key fell beside me.

"Let yourself in, there's a good boy. Hurry, or I'll catch me death of cold by this open window."

As ordered, I let myself in and found myself in a large kitchen, which seemed to serve as her information gathering office. Somehow, she had managed to hurry ahead of me and was sitting, a small, alert old lady, at the kitchen table on which was a cup of milk and a small cake. She was all smiles.

Already, had I realised it, I was at a disadvantage. She appeared to have known that I would be passing, knew my name and was aware that a little old lady with her smiles and gifts was a comforting figure.

"You've been weeding, I know," she commented, increasing the impression that she knew everything there was to know and I need have no fear of letting any secrets excape my lips. "I felt sure that you would welcome a little refreshment on your way back."

I thanked her and drank some of the milk. It had no doubt been watered down, but I had seldom tasted milk, watered down or not. Already, I was in her debt.

"They don't give you little treats at the workhouse, I know. The Parochial Beadle does what he can."

At the end of a long and tiring day it took me some time to work out that she was referring to her own son. The milk had been very welcome and I decided everyone else was wrong about this dear little old lady.

Her next question came out of the blue. "What d'yer think of that Mrs Corney, my dear?"

"She's our matron," I replied, not yet having dropped all my defences.

"And does she take good care of you?"

"We don't see much of 'er, ma'am."

This reply was given some consideration, before Mrs Bumble answered.

"That's as it should be," she replied at last, with approval. "She's in charge. She ain't there to do the hard work. And her rooms, what are they like? I asked the Parochial Beadle, but he says he never goes there." Her eyes boring into mine, she demanded, "Does he?"

"Not that I know, ma'am. It's out of bounds to us."

"Come Nat," she began, then changed tack. "Now that's a good name, Nathaniel Swubble. The Parish Beadle is so good at names. He finds pretty ones for the girls and strong ones for the boys."

"But what does Swubble mean, Mrs Bumble?"

"Mean, my dear? Names don't have to mean nothing."

"Not 'mean', exactly," I tried to explain. "But where did it come from?"

"Perhaps it was one I thought up," she said, pausing to think and giving the impression that she would do her very best to answer any question I posed and I should answer hers in the same spirit of generosity. "I recall. We were going through words which began with S, Sa, Sc and so on and came to St. Do you know your alphabet, Nat?" Her question allowed me the joy of showing off.

"Yes, ma'am."

"Right through?" Mrs Bumble allowed me to claim even more credit.

"A right through to Z, ma'am," I declared.

"The Paroachial Beadle is very alphabetical. Uses it all the time, especially when fulfilling his duty of naming brats…children what people leave for him to take to his generous heart."

Here, in order to obtain my information, I tried to smile sweetly at the thought of the beadle caring for us in even the smallest way, but managed only to suppress my true feelings.

"Yes, I recall it now. The Parochial Beadle was sitting there, just where you're sitting now. He was rubbing his chin and thinking, when he suddenly announces, 'Stubble, how about Stubble? It is a boy, after all.' 'No, my love,' I replied. I was quite definite. 'That name is far too prickly. It don't have the usual ring to it.'"

I began to wonder when she would get to the point, but she finally arrived there. "We went on and reached Su, Sw and it came to him. I suppose Stubble was in the back of his mind and he says, 'Swubble! That's what we'll call the little bast….baby. And that was your name. A good, manly name, if ever I heard one."

I did not point out that, if I married and had children, the females in the family would not appreciate such a name. Perhaps, when I was found, no one anticipated my living that long. My opportunity seemed to have come. Mrs Bumble was said to know all that had happened in the town since her arrival ten years earlier and even, some claimed, for many years before that. "Do you know 'oo my parents are, Mrs Bumble?" My heart was racing.

"Let me look at you," she said, putting a hand under my chin and holding my face to the light. "No, dear boy. If I did know, believe me, I would be the first to tell you." She was making me feel grateful to her. "You can take my word for it, your parents didn't come from Myddlington." To make her appear even more helpful, she added. "I'd say you had a London face. That's where I'd look if I was you."

Having never had any suggestion offered before as to where I should look, I did feel grateful at that moment.

Seeing this, and having let me ask questions for a while, she returned to hers. "Now, Nat, about Mrs Corney's rooms. She has two, I hear."

As she already knew, there could be no harm in agreeing. I agreed.

"And how are they furnished?"

The only information I had on this had come from Felicity, who had done Mrs Corney's sweeping and dusting, and I was not certain that I should pass on the details she had given me.

Making a good guess, Mrs Bumble told me, "Felicity described them to me once. She's quite a friend of mine. I know she's a friend of yours and will have told you all she told me."

How was I to know that sweet old ladies could be deceitful? I told her all she wanted to know, with promptings such as, "And how many silver spoons is it she has? Was it three of four Felicity said?"

When I had described Mrs Corney's room and the contents of every drawer and cupboard, she muttered, "She'll be a good catch for him, but not in my life time. Oh, no! Not in my life time!"

I was about to ask Mrs Bumble what she meant, when she stood up, saying, "I mustn't keep you, young man. Don't want you to miss your supper."

I rose, too, but Mrs Bumble had not yet quite reached the question towards which she had been nudging her way.

"I heard you had been invited to tea with the Lowes. You must tell me about it."

I clammed up at once. Observing my embarrassment, she immediately took me further along the same route, in order to increase my relief and loosen my tongue when she suddenly returned to a more congenial one.

"You were in trouble, I hear."

I avoided answering. It was not a question, after all.

"Now," Mrs Bumble said, opening the door and then pausing to think. "Where did they come from, them Lowes? I was told, but it must have slipped my old mind."

Relieved to leave the embarrassing subject of my behaviour, I was all too anxious to reply. "Warwick, ma'am," I told her. "There was a print of Warwick Castle. Mr Lowe told us 'ow to pronounce it and one of the younger children said that were where they 'ad lived at one time."

As if by magic, I was transferred from the inside to the outside of the cottage and Mrs Bumble was sitting at the window again.

It pleased me to think that, when I related all this to Felicity on our next meeting, I could tell her that Mrs Bumble had got nothing out of me, except things about Mrs Corney, which she had already known, and she had answered more of my questions than I had answered of hers.

As I closed the cottage gate behind me, Mrs Bumble shouted after me, "Nat, call in the Yard on your way back and tell Mr White that I'd like to see him. I'd offer you a halfpenny for going, but I know the Parochial Beadle has seen that you're too well brought up to take it orf an old lady."

CHAPTER TWENTY TWO

My next encounter with William White's plans came when Paul and I were walking along the track by Ebenezer Long's farm.

"'Ere, boy," Mr Long called to Paul, "You're enjoying an expensive education, I 'ear. Let's see you put it to some use. What's this 'ere paper say?" As he spoke, the farmer tore down a notice nailed to a tree.

Paul slowed his pace and fell in behind me. He did not want the paper to be put in his hand so that he was forced to confess that he could read only the easy and less important words. Once the notice was safely in my hands, Paul leaned over my shoulder and, as I read, joined me in reading the easy words while simply mouthing those in between. I had no hesitation in reading out all the words, even those I was not certain about and had never seen before.

"To the Farmers of Myddlington," I read. "The Blackguard Persecutors of the Poeple. Them farmers as dont pay ther men a fare wage will pay with ther ricks. My army shell bern every rick and farmouse down to ashes. Signed Captain Swing."

"Blackguard!" Ebenezer repeated. "Far mouse! What do them words mean?"

We all thought. "Blaggard," I guessed. "And farm 'ouse. Captain Swing ain't a very good speller."

Paul and I had never heard of Captain Swing. That was not too surprising. He did not exist, but was just a made-up character, like Ned Ludd, used to represent thousands of working men and their frustrations in a changing world over which they had no control. Captain Swing stood for all those agricultural labourers trying to work and feed and clothe their families in desperate times. Landowners and farmers had heard that gangs acting under the name of Captain Swing had been active in other parts of the country, but it had seemed that a few heavy sentences by unsympathetic judges had put an end to them. Now letters and notices had appeared around Myddlington.

"Captain Swing," Mr Long protested. "What's 'e got to do with us? We ain't got none of them new threshing machines. We ain't putting men out of work. We try to give them work whenever we can."

As Paul and I could not answer his questions, Mr Long set off towards the field where his son was working. "Come along with me," he told us, "'E can't read, neither."

Paul whispered to me, "Shall we charge 'im a penny?"

I felt outraged, as though some God-given gift were being exploited and contaminated. "It's our duty," I announced primly, putting Paul in his place, "To 'elp them as is less fortunate than us and can't 'elp theirselves."

"'Oo's that then?" Paul muttered, but did not object.

Mr Long's son saw us approaching and walked towards us. "Is it one of them Swing letters in your 'and? Someone's been busy this morning around all the farms."

"Didn't no one see 'oo it were?" Ebenezer demanded.

"Mrs Bumble might know. She don't miss much, but no one else 'as seen anyone." Removing the grass stalk he had been chewing, he stated more clearly, "I thought per'aps we 'ad better talk to Mr White. They've bin our landlords for the past few years."

"Old Mr White might 'ave given us some good advice, but I don't know this young one will be any 'elp at all."

"Let's go back 'ome first. These boys can take us through the words a few times. No reason we should let that stuck-up feller know we're ignorant."

In the farmhouse, Paul and I helped the two men learn the words by heart and were given some refreshment as our reward.

"I tell you what," Mr Long said, "'Ow would you like to tutor me grandson? I don't want 'im growing up 'aving to show 'is ignorance to men like William White."

"I ain't got no patience with little 'uns," Paul said, "but me friend 'ere will be more than willing to 'elp you for a little something in return."

Ebenezer knew Paul, who had worked on his farm, but had never spoken to me before. "What's your friend's name, Paul?"

"Nafaniel."

How I hated being called 'Nafaniel.' "Call me Nat," I suggested quickly.

"I'll pay what I can, but it won't be much, Nat. We pay in kind for most of what we 'ave. We'll see you get something to eat and drink. 'Ave you ever 'ad a fresh egg?"

I said that we had not. It was not quite the truth. I had tried an egg, which Paul had acquired while working on this very farm. We had eaten it raw and, although we had pretended to enjoy it, I had found it very slippery. I hoped cooked ones would taste better, but it would not have mattered. Eagerly, I told the farmer, "I'll tutor 'im for nothing, sir."

Patting my head, the farmer told me, "Your 'eart's in the right place, young man, but you'll never get on in this world."

"I mean it, Mr Long. When d'yer want me to start?"

"Mrs Long'll sort it out. If 'e ain't a good pupil, just tell me and I'll sort 'im out."

Paul and I returned to the workhouse. I was on top of the world. I was not yet nine and I was a tutor already. That would show the Lowe children!

Ebenezer and his son went on to see Mr White in the Yard.

"What's it got to do with us?" Ebenezer demanded, having given Mr White a few minutes to think about the contents of the letter. "I thought Captain Swing were after them as was giving work to machines instead of to men. I give work to men."

"But do you give them a fair wage for their work?" Mr White asked, in a tone which suggested he knew the answer was that the man did not.

"I give 'em what I can afford. I make it up with milk and eggs and a bit of cheese when I can."

"And other farmers," William White asked, "do they give as much as they should?"

"Can't speak for anyone else," Ebenezer replied, defensively. He knew full well that many farmers could afford to pay more, but would not dream of doing so as long as their men could get hand-outs from the overseer.

"I suggest you farmers hold a meeting and decide on a fair wage to pay your men. That is, if you want Captain Swing to keep away from your stacks and your farmhouses."

"I can't see how we can all pay more," Ebenezer commented. "I work thirty acres. Some 'ave got several 'undreds. But if they pay more than me, I'll be left with only the old and lame wanting to work for me."

"If you cannot make a profit," Mr White told him, "perhaps you might consider giving up your lease. If I leased it to one of the bigger farmers, I could charge a higher rent."

"But you don't make your money in rents," the son protested. "You've only got a couple of farms your father acquired when 'e were enlarging the canal basin."

"I look to make a profit from all my assets," William White assured them.

"We'll manage," Ebenezer put in quickly. "Per'aps nothing will come of these 'ere threats. Sorry to 'ave troubled you, sir. We'll bide our time and see what 'appens."

"Time will tell," William White agreed, beckoning to his servant to show the two men out.

CHAPTER TWENTY THREE

Once again, William White had reluctantly taken his place in the office at the Yard, but he had no intention of working on business affairs. He had not arrived until mid-afternoon and, immediately, he had been joined by one of the boatmen. This man, Gideon Raven, was greatly disliked by Jack Star and many others in the town. He was rumoured to be involved in every criminal activity in the triangle between London, Birmingham and Myddlington, on land or canal. Sometime before, he had worked for the former Mr White and people had said that he was kept on only on the principle that poachers make good gamekeepers. He informed on all those stealing from or defrauding the business. Eventually, his own crimes had cost the firm more than his information saved them and he had been dismissed. The general belief was that he was now trading in any goods, animal, vegetable, mineral or human, which gave him a profit.

As soon as the older Mr White died and the younger took over, he had returned, like a bad penny, and had immediately been employed on personal business for William White.

As Raven came through the door, he demanded, "Ain't this a bit public?"

"You work for the firm again, don't you?" White sneered. "I could be confronting you with the goods you stole yesterday."

"What goods?" Raven demanded, ready to deny any knowledge of a theft. Spotting the servant standing silently in the background, he asked, "What's 'e doing 'ere?"

"Standing. He seldom does anything else."

"Is 'e in on our business?"

"What could he do?" William laughed. "He's deaf and dumb." Looking straight at Seize-'im, he said loudly, "All brawn and no brain."

The servant did not flicker an eyelid. As a further demonstration, White approached his servant even more closely and said clearly, "We're planning to ensure that Robert Campion keeps as silent as you do."

"You mean 'e don't 'ear a word?"

"Not a single word and, if he could, he is dumb and could not understand as well as a child could."

Joining in the fun, Gideon stood with his face close to the servant and shouted, "We're going to 'ave ourselves a bonfire and then we'll never 'ear a squeak out of Long or Campion again."

"Leave the fool," William White ordered, fearing the clerks might hear, "He has his uses, but making plans is not one of them. Nor is it yours, Raven. You are to do exactly as I say. I do not want you to change my plan by one iota."

"'Ow can I," Raven smirked, "when I don't know what one of them iotee things is?"

William White set out his plan in detail and Raven was ready to leave. "Remember," White warned him, "I do not want any little details or trimmings added by you just for the fun of it. I know you find it hard to resist going further than you are told for the sheer devilment of it."

When Raven had left, White decided to pass the time by provoking Robert Campion. He hated the man and could not get the thought out of his mind that his father had placed him as a partner in the business simply to frustrate the poor relief scheme. Campion even had power to, and did, cut his salary when he did not work in the family business. Pointing at Campion working in the Yard, White indicated to his servant that he should fetch him up to the office. White watched them return. He would show Campion who was master.

When they arrived in the office, Campion asked curtly why he had been brought from his work.

Without replying, White signalled to the servant to remove Campion's hat.

As though he had simply been asked to take a guest's hat, the servant stepped forward, gave a bow and held out his hand. Although he had his back to William White, the master knew, from Robert Campion's warm smile, that the servant was also smiling. How could he ever make this deaf and dumb young man know that he was to obey his orders, take on his moods and never cross him?

"Knock it off his head, you fool, if needs be." Frustrated by the servant's lack of understanding, he shouted, "You are no bull dog. You could not seize a mouse, whatever they call you. You are no more than a toothless mongrel."

Unexpectedly, Campion removed his own hat and handed it to the young man. "I'll not get you into trouble for something so petty. Now," he demanded, turning to White, "was that all you wanted me for?"

Already feeling the man was getting under his skin and irritating him, William White leaned back in his chair, trying to remain as calm as possible. "I hear that you are spreading your pitiful ideas among the workmen. It seems......"

"It seems to me," Campion interrupted, "that I recall your father made me a partner in this business. I shall deal with the men in any way I please. You are only too willing to let me deal with them when, as so often happens, you are not here."

"Liberty!" White mocked. "What do workmen know of liberty, but liberty to avoid work and still demand a wage? Fraternity! To them that is no more than gathering in the ale house to drink each other's health until they stagger home. Equality! They think that means sharing the money in their masters' pockets. As for democracy!"

Campion interrupted again. "I want no lectures from you. You put yourself before everything and everyone...."

It was White's turn to interrupt. "I hear the Campion cub is preaching the same nonsense."

"My son is no concern of yours," Robert snapped.

William White smiled. He was in charge again. Campion's annoyance confirmed his belief that the way to attack him was through his precious son. Some ten years earlier, when a fever had spread through the town, Campion had buried three young children, along with their mother, within a week. The one remaining child, Francis, was the apple of his father's eye.

"I called you here," White announced," to inform you that my lawyer has advised me to challenge the will."

"Lawyers will advise any course which brings them a fat fee."

"Your son is to be a lawyer, I hear."

"I say again," Campion said,"that my son is no concern of yours." Taking his hat from the servant, he walked out and resumed his work.

"Your son is very much my concern," White stated, once his partner was out of earshot.

Left alone with his servant, William White sat at his desk, making brief notes of his earlier conversation with Gideon Raven, while it was fresh in his mind. From time to time, as though expecting something to happen, he looked at the clock. But it was not until it was turning dark that William rose and walked to the window. From there, he saw that, as usual, Robert Campion's son had arrived to walk the rest of the way home with his father.

As usual, too, while he helped his father with the final load of the day, Francis had placed his hat and scarf on some empty crates. Tearing out the page of notes he had made, White pushed them into a drawer and, finding the key missing, signalled to his servant to see that no one opened it while he was away. Then he went down into the Yard.

For a brief moment, the servant struggled with his conscience. The short struggle over, he opened the drawer, read the notes and another paper beneath them.

Moving to the window, he looked for his master. Careful not to be seen, he watched William White approach Campion and his son and talk to them. Then the servant's eye was caught by a movement a few feet from the crate on which Francis had placed his belongings. It was Raven and he was clearly anxious not to be seen. He had placed himself where he was hidden from most of the men in the Yard and, from there, was checking that none of the men in the other gangs was looking directly at him. Finally, satisfied that he was not being observed, Raven moved quickly from his hiding place, snatched up the scarf and, dropping it into a sack, placed it out of sight.

By the time William White returned to the office, the servant was waiting, respectfully, for his orders. William White indicated that they were going home. As they mounted their horses, Francis called out to ask whether anyone had seen his scarf. Ignoring him, William White rode out of the Yard with his servant riding a short distance behind.

CHAPTER TWENTY FOUR

Felicity Fidget sat very still in the wood. Had Bumble known how she would grow up, even he might have chosen a more suitable name for her. She seemed to have been born sensible and calm, and not long after, it would seem, she had set out to plan her life. This plan was to obtain a good job in service, learn how to manage a house, find a kind, hardworking young man, marry him at a sensible age, around twenty two, have a family and live happily ever after.

The first of these aims, Felicity had achieved. She now worked as the most junior maid in Miss Aldbury's house. Miss Aldbury, a charitable and kindly lady with an independent turn of mind, had, for some time, taken into her employment any poor or workhouse girl who showed signs of wanting to better herself. She took them into her care, as well as into her house, took an interest in their training and, when they married, gave them a few pounds to set up house. When babies arrived, as they inevitably did, each was given a half sovereign.

Although the scrubbing and cleaning was almost as hard as her work-house chores had been, Felicity loved her new position, but she was struggling not to feel lonely. While the people around her were kind, if strict, she missed her friends at the workhouse She worried whether Paul and I were behaving ourselves and how Georgina, with no one to talk sense into her, would ever manage to keep her feet on the ground and fancy ideas out of her head. The other young maids had gone off to regale their families with tales of life in a big house, but she had no home to visit. She wished that she could come to see us in the workhouse, but there was a ritual, which everyone leaving the workhouse went through, of swearing, in front of all the others, that they would never set foot in the place again.

Felicity's only hope that day was that we would be able to get away and meet her in the wood. She had been listening for sounds of our laughter. as we approached but, having given up hope of our arrival, was trying to per-suade herself that listening to bird song and watching squirrels was the best way in the whole world to spend a half day off. All of a sudden, she became conscious of strange noises. It sounded like someone shouting, but the voice had a strange quality to it, which she had never heard before. The words, if they were words, came out in short, harsh bursts, instead of a rhythmic stream.

The thoughts of anyone else alone in the woods might have turned to fears of ghosts and spirits, but Felicity decided that it was us coming at last and trying to frighten her. When the sounds came no closer, she clambered from her log and decided to creep up on us and pay us back for trying to frighten her. As she made for the noises, Felicity did become anxious, but not out of fear. She began to wonder whether someone was in pain or trying to call for help. The strange utterances were not ones she had heard us ever make before.

Who, or whatever, it was, was in a little clearing, hidden from her view by a circle of trees. Creeping forward, still hoping to take us by surprise, Felicity saw a movement and stopped, hidden by one of the trees. William White's servant stood all alone, uttering sounds which, at one moment, seemed to be words, but then became a string of disjointed sounds.

Feeling guilty at spying on him, Felicity moved forward to make her presence known. The second he saw her, his face became a mask, but, as she stepped forward and smiled, he gave a nervous smile in return.

Now she had approached him, Felicity had no idea what to do next. There seemed little point in speaking and yet she felt sure he was in distress and needed her help. For want of anything better to do, she said, loudly and clearly, "Good afternoon, Mr Seize-'im." Then she realised that she did not know his real name.

Reaching out, the young man turned her face towards him and then touched his lips. Felicity was outraged. She would resist, by any means, being kissed by a total stranger. She was ready to put into practice any of the tricks she had learned in the workhouse. Her face showed her anger.

Shaking his head, the young man thought for a moment. Then he pointed to his eyes and back to her lips, gazing intently at them.

"He thinks I have pretty lips," Felicity thought, blushing.

Quick to read her thoughts, the young man nodded in agreement, but then he shook his head and stood thinking. At last, as though with little hope of success, he took some paper from his pocket, wrote on it and handed it to Felicity.

Indignantly, Felicity wrote, "Yes." The written message had been, "Can you read?" Had she not wanted to save paper, she would have expressed her indignation at such a question at greater length.

The young man's smile lit up his whole face. Felicity could not help laughing too. Sensible as ever, she tried to push back the ideas rushing into her mind of romantic messages passing between them. If he wrote any such message, she would have to leave immediately.

How disappointed Felicity was when the young man wrote, "I work for Mr White." Felicity nodded to indicate that she already knew that.

"My name is Martin Horsley."

Felicity, writing "Good-morning, Mr Horsley," could not help thinking what a lovely name Martin was. She wrote her name and Martin seemed equally thrilled by that. Remembering the noises she had heard, Felicity asked,"Can you talk?"

Hesitating, Martin wrote,"Once upon a time. I went deaf seven years."

Felicity was not sure whether that meant that he went deaf when he was seven or seven years ago.

As an after thought, Martin wrote,"My mother understands."

At once, Felicity wrote,"I will understand. Please talk to me."

Shaking his head, sadly, the young man wrote, "Time. Takes time."

"Please," Felicity wrote.

Pointing to a fallen tree trunk, Martin uttered a word which she could recognize as 'log', but other words he said, she could not even guess. Martin looked so disappointed that she was spurred into having a bright idea. She wrote words, one at a time, and he spoke them as best he could. After a while, Felicity began to make out what he was saying, but she realised that he was right and it would take a little while for her ear to become accustomed to his voice.

Seeing that his new friend was disappointed, Martin, as kind as Felicity, tried to cheer her up by showing her that certain movements with the finger could represent letters which could be built into words and he showed her that certain gestures could also replace the spoken word and be understood.

Felicity was trying to ignore the fact, all too obvious, that the sun was already setting, but Martin told her she must go home and he would walk back with her. He helped her over stiles and through the kissing gate, where Felicity modestly hung her head and was grateful Martin was the kind of young man to respect her modesty.

Felicity insisted that Martin walk her right to the servant's door. She knew that Miss Aldbury, with an eye to their welfare, liked her servants to be open and honest about their friends and the people they were walking out with.

At the door, Martin took his paper and began to write. Felicity was certain that he was arranging their next meeting, making quite certain, by writing, that it was clear to her. When she read, "Mr White will hurt Mr Campion's son," she was very surprised. All she could think of to write was, "Tell Mr Campion."

Martin was about to write more, when the door opened and another girl pulled her in and told her that the housekeeper did not like long farewells on the doorstep. Martin left, neither of them knowing when they would meet again.

Felicity lived in a glow for several days and, more than once, she had to speak to herself severely and tell herself not to let her imagination run away with her. She and Martin had met only once and who knew what the future would hold? As time passed and reality replaced the glow, Felicity began to think she had imagined all that had happened. Feelings are elusive things, which can so easily be lost in the mists of memory, even after a few hours or days.

For his part, Martin walked back to the White's house as though walking on air. There had been some girls ready to walk out with a strong, handsome fellow, but they had been warned away by parents and brothers, who thought him big and stupid and, therefore, dangerous. None had been able to read or been ready to bother to learn how to communicate with him, content to share the general opinion that he was not capable of thought or understanding. Now, he was certain that he would court Felicity, marry her and live happily ever after. It had taken only an hour or two to discover that she could take away the loneliness he had felt since the dreadful illness, which had deprived him of hearing, and greatly hindered the development of his speech. Then he recalled that he had to help Francis Campion. It would cost him his job and he could not think of courting until he could support a wife. Suddenly, it was a difficult decision to make, whether to warn Mr Campion or keep his job.

CHAPTER TWENTY FIVE

As William White, like most other people, saw only what he expected to see he did not notice a change in his servant. He did not see a smile in the young man's eyes and a lightness in his every movement which had not been there before. Continuing to see his servant simply as part of the furniture, the master, about to go off on a journey which would take him a day or two, called in his foreman, Jeremiah Clarke.

"Set this fellow to work and make sure it is hard work. He is becoming soft and flabby."

"I'll see 'e pulls 'is weight, sir. Leave it to me." As inquisitive as everyone else about White's destination, he added, "So you're not going anywhere where you'll be needing "im, then?"

He received no reply.

Martin spent the day happily enough. He was glad of the opportunity to have some exercise, instead of standing all day waiting for instructions. As he did more than his share of the lifting and carrying, the other men in the gang smiled and patted him on the back, encouraging him to lift even heavier crates and carry them even further.

Many times, Martin looked over to where Robert Campion was working and thought that he must tell him that William White and Raven were planning some harm for Francis. He was held back, not so much by the thought that he would surely lose his job, but by his fear of not making himself understood. He had become used to being excluded from everything which went on around him, and it took a great effort to draw attention to himself and probably make a fool of himself, too. It was not until he saw that Robert Campion was becoming anxious that his son was late in coming for him, that Martin could put the matter off no longer.

Unable to ask for permission to leave the gang in the middle of loading a waggon, Martin just walked off, took Campion's arm and led him up to the office. Curious as to what was happening, Jeremiah followed them. In the office, the two men seemed willing to humour Martin until, finding the drawer locked and unable to find a key, he began to try to force the drawer open. Then, as they tried to restrain him and seemed about to call up men to help them, Martin snatched up a pen and wrote the words he had read in his master's notes. "Long, Captain Swing, Raven, burn ricks." It was

Campion who finally forced the drawer and found the notes and a copy of the Swing letter.

Jeremiah had stood by, watching Martin write with as much amazement as if he had seen the same feat accomplished by a dancing bear. It was a minute before he remembered, "White and Raven had their heads together in 'ere this morning."

"So White's behind these Swing letters." Campion had already began to think that William White, free from the restraint his father exercised over him, was capable of anything, but he could not, at first, see the point of such action.

"Why?" Jeremiah asked him.

"To frighten Long and the other farmers into paying higher wages, when White takes control of poor relief?" Campion suggested. Jeremiah did not look convinced.

Martin had not followed what they had been saying, but what he feared seemed to be happening. They did not understand that there might be a link with Francis. Taking Campion by the arm again, he led him out into the Yard and to where he had seen Raven throw the sack. Having expected to find the sack still there and triumphantly reveal the scarf, Martin almost wept with frustration when it was not there. However, committed totally by now to the task of making the others understand, he acted out a mime of Francis arriving, taking off his hat and scarf, helping his father and then returning to find the scarf missing. Finishing, he looked, hopefully at the two men.

"What's 'e trying to tell us, Bob?" Jeremiah asked his friend.

"I'm not sure whose been doing what," Campion replied. "White was talking to me at the time." Speaking slowly and clearly, he asked Martin, "Raven?"

Although he could not hear, Martin lip-read the name and nodded in agreement.

"What's Gideon Raven setting fire to ricks got to do with your Francis?" Jeremiah asked. As Campion strode off along the tow path, Jeremiah found himself talking to his friend's back. He followed and signalled to Martin to do the same.

A little before Martin had made up his mind to let Campion know what he suspected, on the canal bank Gideon Raven had began schooling his son in the art and science of assault. George was making a poor pupil. While he had no moral scruples about the task ahead, approaching it with enthusiasm, he always had difficulty in learning a sequence of actions and recalling them in the correct order and without omissions. Gideon, with his habit of proving his own superiority by making others feel inferior, was not proving a good teacher. Having told his son that he was a useless idiot, Gideon then threw doubt on the fact that he was his son.

"Now let's go through this for the last time," Gideon said. He paused and there was a deep silence. "Go on, then, you great slab of lard. Tell me."

"I cut a cudgel, wait be'ind the 'edge and ...."

"Jump out on 'im," Gideon hissed. It took all his self-control not to scream the order for all the county to hear.

"That's right," George recalled, smiling. "Then I 'its 'im on the 'ead. And," he added, with some satisfaction, "I makes sure I've knocked 'im out."

"Then," Gideon concluded, "We drag 'im to Long's farm, find ourselves a 'andy rick and set it and sonny 'ere alight. Let's see you get started then."

Cutting a cudgel from the hedge, George chose the one the thinnest to cut and the simplest to prepare. Gideon made his opinion known in no uncertain terms.

"If you want anything doing right, do it yourself," he muttered, cutting a good, stout stick with a heavy knob at the end, which would have brought down an ox. He took to giving his son orders and, eventually, they were both hiding behind the hedge, waiting for Francis Campion to come along the path. At last, they spotted the young man in the distance.

"Wait till I give the word," Gideon whispered, hearing footsteps close by.

That was more than the eager George could do. He sprang out a second too soon, giving Francis time to dodge the killing blow, but striking him with a heavy blow, none the less. With a great splash, the young man fell into the water and appeared to be drowning.

"Pull 'im out. Pull 'im out," Gideon cried. "We don't want to get caught in the middle of this."

Father and son pulled the victim out of the water and began slowly to drag him through the gap in the hedge and off towards Long's farm, just on the other side of the field.

At Long's farm, Paul was growing impatient. He had finished his work and, as the Longs had not invited him in while I was teaching their grandson, he was anxious to get off and not miss supper. I had told him before that he fidgeted and distracted us from the lesson and so he was not really surprised to be left to his own devices in the farmyard. He had put his head over the half door of the pig sty and grunted at the inhabitants, snuffling in their trough, patted the horse's head and breathed up its nostrils to see whether it would immediately obey any order he gave it. He had even banged on the door of the shed where the bull was settled for the night, hoping to hear it snort and charge.

Failing to rouse the bull, Paul wandered off across the home field, rounded up a few stray hens, shoo-ed them into the coup and dropped the little door down behind them. In the nearby orchard, he searched for eggs and put the one he found into his pocket. Fearing, on second thoughts, that it would crack, he retrieved it, cracked it against a tree trunk and swallowed it down.

Returning to the farmhouse, Paul pursed his lips as though whistling. I had told him about whistling by the window of the room in which I was teaching, but Paul could never completely comply with any request to behave himself. Not quite daring to annoy me, he moved off for another try at the bull's door. When leaning on it and kicking his heels against it brought no response, Paul gave up trying to get attention from man or beast and made for the barn. There, the ladder to the loft always held out an invitation which he could never refuse, and he climbed up. For a few minutes, he chased the rats back into their holes and then, out of habit, placed his eye to a knot hole in the wooden wall and looked out, not expecting to see much in the darkness.

"What's going on 'ere?" he muttered to himself. By the hay rick he had spotted a flickering light. Never one to miss anything, Paul hurried down the ladder and, in a couple of minutes, was creeping towards the stack for a closer look. He could just make out two figures and heard one, who seemed the older, say, "You're more bother than you're worth. You're all thumbs. Give it 'ere."

A spark spluttered near the ground, bursting into flame as it landed on a trail of straw leading to the rick. The two men ran off as fast as their legs would carry them.

"Gawd!" Paul exclaimed. In the flames he could see the body of a man, flames already licking his clothes.

Without thought or hesitation, Paul rushed forward and pulled the body clear. It was Francis Campion. Afraid the two men might return and

137

add him to the funeral pyre, Paul screamed. As Mr Long and his son, with me behind, came from one direction, Mr Campion, Mr Clarke and Martin Horsley came from the other. What exactly happened in the next ten minutes, I cannot recall in detail. With Robert Campion, Jeremiah and Martin trying to ascertain whether Francis was dead or alive, Paul and I rushed for buckets of water from the pond, while Mr Long and his son raked the burning hay to the ground to stop the flames spreading and save as much of the hay as possible.

By the time we had finished, Martin was picking up Francis, who seemed barely alive, and Mr Campion asked Paul and me to run ahead, find Jack Star and ask him to send a cart or carriage to take Francis to his home and to send the doctor there too.

Our instructions carried out and our supper devoured in the kitchen, where Sal had put some by for us, I longed to tell everyone how Paul had saved Francis Campion's life, but Jack had told us to keep our mouths shut.

"Wasn't just me, anyway," Paul said, modestly. "If 'is clothes 'adn't been soaking wet, 'e'd 'ave been on fire 'fore I got to 'im."

CHAPTER TWENTY SIX

Today, reading such a story as I have related, you would have expected Ebenezer Long and Robert Campion to have gone to the police and demand that they bring William White to justice, but, even today, bringing a wealthy man to justice is no easy matter. As Jack Star observed at the time, you would think, by looking at the inmates of our prisons, that wealthy men never commit crimes. In fact, it is just that they persuade poor men to do their dirty work or pay lawyers to paint them as saints rather than sinners. You must remember, too, that all this took place before Peel's bobbies were enforcing the law throughout the nation. In Myddlington, we still had an old constable and watchmen, who spent more time chasing their own tails than pursuing criminals.

As it was, with all those involved having decided White had paid Raven to burn the rick and implicate Francis Campion, Ebenezer was the first to make up his mind about what action he would take.

"This farm 'as been my life's work and I want it to be my son's after me. If White wants to use my rick to teach other farmers a lesson, so be it. I shall not go against 'im. I'll tell everyone it was Swing's men as done it. 'E's me landlord and I'm 'is tenant and that's the way I want to leave it."

Robert Campion went as far as to confront William White and, in his anger, demand to know whether White had paid Raven to do his dirty work.

"Are you mad?" White demanded in return. "I realise you wish to take over the business completely and this would fit in with your plan, but you shall not involve me in this way. I was away on business if you recall."

"The notes and the Swing letter, they set out your ideas clearly enough."

Leaning back in his chair, White laughed derisively." So it was you! I found the desk forced and suspected my servant. I dismissed him immediately. He disobeyed me."

"Martin had no part in this," Campion claimed. "Take him back into your employment."

"'Martin' is it? Did he tell you his name? I had his belongings searched and found that he can write and, no doubt, read. He is no further use to me. But don't worry your head about him. That mad old spinster Miss Aldbury has taken him into her service."

Suddenly, White stopped smiling. "Evidence, Campion. Where is your evidence? You have none. You say my notes and the letter prove that I was giving Raven instructions. I say that Ebenezer Long passed on the letter to me and I suspected Raven might be behind it. I demanded an explanation from him."

"Why?" Campion asked, interrupting White's speech. "Why would Raven do such a thing on his own?"

"Why? Since when has Raven needed a reason to indulge in mischief? Perhaps he wished to punish farmers who have not paid him sufficient wages in the past."

Seeing that Campion was unconvinced, White continued, "But I ask you, where is your evidence against me? There were three of us in the room. Raven has disappeared. Horsley is stone deaf. That leaves me and I tell you that I was trying to prevent a crime, not pay for one to be committed." Smiling again, he enquired, "How is Francis? I trust that he is quite recovered from his ordeal."

Not bothering to answer this, Campion looked directly at White. "You swear you had nothing to do with the attack on Francis?"

Facing him and looking straight back at him, White replied, "I swear it."

"Perhaps," Jack Star said, when Campion related all that had been said, "White had his fingers crossed be'ind 'is back. For my part, I'd swear it were all 'is idea."

"What more could I do?" Robert asked his friend? "Martin cannot tell us what was said. We have no evidence. We cannot take the matter further. Besides, what Martin told us about the scarf suggests that all White intended was to place the scarf by the rick and implicate Francis. There would have been a fuss for a few days and then people would have realised Francis was not involved. As far as White was concerned, it was just a warning not to oppose his plans for the workhouse."

Jack Star was not surprised by the conclusion his friend had reached. From the remarks Campion had made, he had suspected from the beginning that this was how things would be left. There had been remarks such as, "Thank God no real harm was done," and, "I must consider Mrs White and the good of the business my old friend entrusted to me in his will." Then there had been, "Give William White enough rope and he will hang himself," and, "It's true, we have no evidence against White, or even Raven, come to that matter. Francis cannot identify his attackers and that young lad Paul cannot swear to its being Raven he saw in the dark."

But Jack Star realised that, behind Robert's decision to let the matter rest, was his concern for his only child, Francis. When they had been talking, Robert had said, "When I was young, Jack, we wanted to save the world. Now Francis is my world. Once he is out of harm's way, then we can deal with William White." Immediately, Campion had begun to make plans to send Francis to live with his uncle in America.

That was how William White silenced two of his three sources of opposition, without any reflection on himself. That left him free to silence the one remaining source – our teacher, Mr Lowe. Meanwhile, Gideon Raven, disappeared from view, taking George with him. It was said he had joined his two other sons in their criminal activities in London or Birmingham.

CHAPTER TWENTY SEVEN

Rumours about the fire and the attack on Francis Campion circulated for a few days, but, with the perpetrators and the victims maintaining complete silence, they died away. Conversation turned, instead, to the coming charity dinner to be held in the town. Such dinners were common in those days, as they are now, with unexceptional food, long speeches and over-priced tickets, purchased by both those who genuinely supported the charity and those wishing to rub shoulders for a few hours with the gentry and aristocracy of the area. This particular dinner was in support of the Society for the Reclamation of Fallen Women. The strong demand for tickets suggested that this charity, or social climbing, was a cause dear to the hearts of the middling classes of Myddlington.

When the day of the dinner arrived, everything was progressing excellently. Those who attended were gratified to see that, amongst the crowd of onlookers packing the pavement outside, were some servants, sent by their mistresses and masters, to see who had managed to aquire tickets when they had not. Inside, couples paraded up and down and, in case this had not been sufficient to draw attention to themselves, waved and called noisily to their friends. The search for place cards then began. Mr and Mrs Lowe were surprised to find that they were seated quite close to the noble patron of the event. They had not even paid for their own tickets. These had been an anonymous gift, but, to have obtained such seats, someone must have paid a good deal for them. Next to them were two empty chairs and they were surprised to hear an official, fearful that offence might be given by their remaining vacant, tell the patron that the seats had been bought by Mr William White, but it was probable that it was too close to their bereavement for Mr White and his mother to attend.

The dinner over, the speeches began and continued until even the most minor notable in the town had expressed his opinion on the importance of the work relentlessly pursued by the Society. The patron was heard to comment, as each speaker arose, "Seen that feller there," referring to the town's house of ill-repute.

Many were nodding off, when William White entered and, as though about to take his seat, walked to the top table. But, reaching his chair, he did not sit down. Instead, he asked for the patron's indulgence in allowing him to bring an important matter to the attention of the assembled company. This spark of excitement made most sit forward eagerly. White waited until the rustling of gowns and the scraping of chairs had finished, before continuing.

"It was only my belief in the urgent need for the charity you are all supporting by your presence here, which persuaded me to buy tickets to attend, instead of simply giving a donation. But, imagine the outrage I felt, then, to learn that one of the women, I cannot bring myself to call her a lady, whom I was expected to sit beside, might better be considered as a recepient of our charity than a supporter of it."

The tension in the hall was so great that you might have heard a pin head drop, let alone a whole pin.

"Perhaps I should have made this announcement before the dinner began, but this would have ruined the event for all those who have contributed so generously," White went on, knowing that he had rejected this idea in order not to alienate those who had looked forward to the event with such enthusiasm. "Indeed, I was reluctant to raise this matter at all, but I am a man who knows his duty and does not shirk from it."

Get on with it, man," the noble patron muttered, glancing at his watch.

William White bowed, and went on, "I have little to say, your lordship, except to draw to everyone's attention that the woman seated on my right has brought shame on her sex. I fear that Mrs Lowe cannot, in honesty, claim that title. She is, in fact, Mrs Barton, a woman who left her husband and child to run away with this man. Mr Lowe reckons himself to be a gentleman, but no one of rank, knowing his history, would bestow that title upon him."

"That makes two of you," the patron mumbled.

From the expression on the couple's faces, there was no doubt in anyone's mind that what William White said was true. Breathlessly, they waited for Lowe's reply. Would it come to blows?

Furious, Mr Lowe stood up. "My wife, for that is what she has been to me for six years, was, indeed married, but her husband beat her cruelly. In my eyes and, I think in God's, that dissolved the marriage vows."

"Come, come," the patron commented, clearly this time, "if every woman who was struck by her husband up and left him, where would the country be today?"

"Marriage vows are made before God and before man," Mr Clack, being the Lord's representative, announced. "They are not to be broken without fear of punishment from God and from man."

By this time, Mrs Lowe had risen to her feet. Taking Mr Lowe's arm, she stated with dignity, "I have no wish to cause offence. We shall leave immediately."

"Fine woman!" the patron muttered, taking the opportunity to leave with his party.

There was uproar. Everyone had suspected that there was something not quite right about the couple.

"To think I invited them into my house!"

"What an affront to those of us who keep our vows!"

"What duplicity to pose as man and wife for all that time. He has even ridden out with the hunt!"

"Did he not teach those poor, dear children in the workhouse? Mr Clack, you must see that he has not corrupted their innocent minds."

Many clustered around William White to hear more details, which he supplied gladly. "Mrs Barton lived in Warwick. I have met her unfortunate husband, whose heart she broke. The couple have lived abroad for a while, in America, I believe." His listeners looked at each other knowingly. What else was to be expected from people who had rejected British rule, but deceit and infidelity!

One man, lowering his voice asked, "Then the youngest children are bastards?"

William White nodded. "No doubt about it. The older ones are Lowe's. He is a widower."

Later that night, stones were thrown at the Lowe's house and several windows broken. The hostile crowd dispersed only when the people were told that Mr Lowe and Mrs Barton had left an hour before, leaving no forwarding address. The house at the end of the lane was empty once again, ready to be filled with my dreams.

CHAPTER TWENTY EIGHT

It was no surprise to anyone that the vestry meeting, at which William White unveiled his plans, was poorly attended. There were present only the yes-men from whom White wanted to form his Board and those he had brought in to vote for them. Mr Limbkins was elected chairman of the Board, but no one doubted who was really in control. To cut a long story short, after the vestry meeting and the signing of contracts, William White took control of poor relief in the town in return for a sum twenty five percent less than the cost of poor relief in the preceding year. William had not heeded his father's advice.

At the first meeting of the Board, only one member raised a question to the embarrassment, if also the secret relief, of the others.

"I hope there'll be no comeback on us, if you go bankrupt, White. Is my money safe in me own pocket?" Having been assured that it was, this member, along with the others, agreed that there would no longer be outdoor relief, that all in want must enter the workhouse and that they would do a day's work each day they were there. They also agreed that children, adults and the elderly should be separated from each other and that, within each of these groups, males should be separated from females. The Board members then removed to the inn for an ample meal provided by Mr White.

The character of the workhouse building presented no hindrance to the execution of these plans. It had been built with these very policies in mind. After all, the policy on poor relief, as in other cases, does not advance to a solution so much as go round in circles from humane to lax to strict to cruel, as fashion and forgotten memories of past failures dictate. In Myddlington, the fashion had come full circle. William White had nothing new to add. Like many other so called reformers, he had merely taken old, worn out ideas and expressed them with renewed enthusiasm and conviction to a new generation.

It was about this time, that reports, which could often be traced back to those working for William White, were received of the success being enjoyed by those who had left the town to seek work elsewhere. In the North and Midlands, it was claimed, there was so much work for the taking that a man, his wife and his children could all find employment the very day they arrived. It was further claimed that, on the excellent wages paid, they could afford good lodgings, meat every day and a set of Sunday clothes in which to stroll around the town. Such a picture would have appealed to some at any time, but when the alternative was entry to the workhouse, many of those who were unemployed were drawn from the town by the magnetic pull of Birmingham, Nottingham and Manchester. All were transported for a reduced fee in White's carts, waggons and boats. No return tickets were issued.

True to her nature and her promise to her husband, Mrs White, with the help of other influential townspeople, set up a fund for the Relief of Poverty amongst the Deserving Poor. Everybody who was anybody and anybody who wished to be somebody supported the venture.

The rules of the Charity stated that help should be given in kind rather than cash. Applicants, it was decreed, had to have a letter signed by their priest or minister and by one other respected citizen vouching for their need and their respectability. Having appeared, with their letters, before the committee, applicants were approved and given help or rejected and told to apply to the workhouse. The ladies of the committee visited those who received help to make sure that they were who they claimed to be and practised strict household economy. By the supporters of the charity, this was considered an enlightened and excellent scheme. Some even spoke of the success of the scheme at meetings in neighbouring towns and saw it established in many of them. For those who received help, it was a lifeline which saved them from starvation, but which demonstrated that charity was indeed cold.

CHAPTER TWENTY NINE

Almost over-night, our lives changed for the worst. At one and the same time, many more children were admitted and, no longer having the run of the whole building, we children were confined to one wing. In the over-crowding, bullies flourished. The oldest picked on the youngest and the strongest preyed on the weakest. Gangs formed and, just for self-protection, you had to choose one side or another.

In an attempt to impose order, Mr White gave an old army sergeant, who had himself been admitted to the workhouse, absolute power over our little kingdom. At first, Sergeant Stamp did bring a measure of order, but we despised him. Before he entered the workhouse, we had passed his cottage many times and knew him to be very different from the picture of a love-able old soldier, who gathered children around his knee to tell them tales of battles. We knew him as a grumpy old man, whose natural bad temper had been made worse by his wounds and poverty. With Sergeant Stamp in charge, in the long run, bullying increased. He not only indulged in it him-self, as a matter of course, but appointed corporals from among the older boys to put his methods into action when he was not there.

Our day, now, began with a bugle call and a whack of the sergeant's stick on the buttocks for anyone who did not jump out of bed on his com-mand. Then it was quick march to the yard, with the heads of the slowest half dozen being held under the pump until they felt they were drowning. In the same way, the last children to march into the dining hail were given only half measure, when full measure was barely enough, and the slowest to finish had the remaining mouthful eaten by a corporal. Sergeant Stamp was a great one for making an example of those who did not reach his standards.

Our chores began immediately after breakfast and continued through-out the day. I need not say that we were no longer allowed to leave the workhouse, unless we had a job outside to bring wages in to pay for our keep. There were, however, plenty of chores to do. Extra pairs of hands did not seem to make up for extra pairs of feet marching over the stone floors. There was cleaning and sweeping, scrubbing and scraping, fetching and carrying, gardening and cleaning shoes. Everything had to be done in dou-ble time and every order, however pointless, obeyed immediately. If the task was not performed to the sergeant's standard, or to that of his corporals, they would throw dust on a newly swept floor or dirty water on one freshly scrubbed. Were the sergeant or his minions in a bad mood, this could be repeated two, three or four times.

We also found ourselves repeating tasks over and over again, simply because the sergeant could find nothing else for us to do. The theory was that the Devil found work for idle hands, but, even at that age, I felt certain that he was more likely to find work for idle minds. My thoughts screamed out against the mind numbing tasks on which we spent our days.

Confined within our wing, we spoke to no one except the sergeant, Old Sal, Martha and Jack Star. Jack we saw as he rushed about sorting out the problems caused by having too many men confined in the workhouse. Frustrations boiled over, and he was forever racing to stop a fight or protect the workhouse master. The former master, from the navy, had been replaced by one who, although large, was flabby and cowardly. He could not face up to men who were in the habit of using their fists on the least provocation outside, let alone when cooped up together in one wing of the workhouse. It was fortunate that the porter had not only learned to fight while in the navy, but had also learned how to win, no holds barred.

We were glad to have Old Sal and Martha appointed to look after us at night and in illness, but not as glad as we would have been had Sal been her former self. But Sal's sole purpose in life had been to raise a family and see her children, and theirs in turn, do the same. With the death of her last child, and having no grandchildren, Sal's whole world had collapsed. She seemed, too, to have something on her mind, lost for minutes on end in her own thoughts.

As I have said, while our hands were busy, our minds were numbed by repetitive tasks, which required no thought and provided no interest. I need hardly say that Mr Lowe was not replaced. The nearest thing approaching food for the mind was a Sunday school. This, set up by Mr White to show any Commissioners, who might visit, that attention was being paid to our moral and religious training, consisted of the teacher's reading moral and religious stories to us and our answering questions. Mr Clack, seeing no use in even this mite of education, gave the task of supervising this to his curate. That was, until the arrival of a new archdeacon. This gentleman, a keen supporter of Sunday schools, announced that he would preach a sermon at any church taking a collection in support of a Sunday school. Not to be left out, Mr Clack arranged such a service and arranged for us all to attend.

When the Sunday in question arrived, Mrs Corney paid special attention to sprucing us up, not with her own hands, of course, but with Sal's and Martha's. I listened to every word of the service and the sermon, devouring words and ideas like a starving child.

Paul spent his time, next to me, mastering the art of slowly slipping down the back of his pew, disappearing onto the ground and slowly reappearing again. When he became bored with this, he spent his time catching flies, which, unaware of his spider-like skills, were foolish enough to walk over him. It was clear, from this and Paul's behavoiur when we were lined up as a kind of guard of honour for the archdeacon, that he was feeling bored and frustrated by his life and sought a little excitement.

"I wonder," Paul announced, in a voice which all could hear, "why they pray for King William and Queen Adi-what's-er-name and not for us. They got money and servants and clothes and 'orses. We ain't got nothing."

"There," the archdeacon commented, showing his Christian-like patience with children by not clipping Paul around the ear, "is an opportunity for a lesson. Which of you gentlemen will answer this child?" As he spoke, he glanced along the line of Sunday school teachers, lined up beside us. They all, even the women, seemed very flattered to be addressed as 'gentlemen' and very embarrassed to be called upon to give a lesson in public. Some looked as though, despite all they taught their pupils, they did not know whether to speak out or raise their hands and wait to be asked.

While the others looked from one to the other, a teacher did step forward. As he was a man who sought attention and approval, I had noticed him before, pushing to the front and keeping close to the archdeacon.

"I shall be happy to answer, sir." He turned to Paul. "Look at me, young man, when I speak to you." He raised Paul's chin so suddenly, that Paul bit his tongue. Ignoring Paul's squeals, he continued, "Two reasons. Note and remember them. One, as head of the nation, the King has great responsibilities. You, as a pauper, have none. Two, where there is wealth and power, there must be temptation to abuse them. Not," he added as an aside, "that His Majesty would give in to temptation." Looking back at Paul, he concluded, "You, on the other hand, being poor and leading a simple life, may more readily follow the honest, simple life of the Carpenter, who is Our Saviour."

"There, young man," the archdeacon told Paul. "There is your answer. He stopped to have a few words with the teacher, asking him which town or village he came from and where he ran his Sunday school, but the teacher had not finished.

"Might I point out, to all those teachers who have not had my experience—I am a teacher in a day school as well as a Sunday school – that children should be taught not to seek attention as this boy does. Were he in my class, he would be punished for calling out and seeking to have everyone notice him."

The archdeacon smiled his thanks and was about to move on, but the teacher had not finished.

"Where I find attention-seeking boys, I look for girls, who encourage such behaviour with their giggles and smirks. See," he declared, in the tone of a prophet foreseeing the downfall of the world, "these girls are immodestly gazing around them to see whom they may entice from their duties. Their eyes should be cast down in the modest manner, which becomes a woman."

The archdeacon, who, after many years of experience, knew that a man once riding a hobby-horse would not quickly dismount, walked on, making a mental note that he would try to avoid visiting the Sunday school in the town, twenty miles away, where Mr Edward Kilsby ran the Sunday school.

We had to stand and listen to the rest of his tirade against women and hope that he would not then embark on another against children and yet another against everyone who was not Mr Edward Kilsby.

"Their hair hangs down immodestly around their shoulders. Some might say that their locks might be hidden under their caps. I say that they should be shorn. We must always remember that, without the temptations of Eve, we should yet be in the Garden of Eden." Holding firmly to Mr Clack's arm, so that he could not escape, he went on, "Why do you allow the girls to walk in front of the boys? Do you allow your wife to precede you? It is our duty, as God-fearing men, to teach women their place as set out by God. Look to the Old Testament! And look to the New! All is laid out for those who have eyes to see and ears to hear. Get thee behind me Satan!" He seemed to be looking directly at Georgina. She immodestly stared straight back.

"Thank-you, sir, for bringing these matters to my attention," Mr Clack said, wrenching his arm free. He walked on and we were about to follow.

"And your name, boy?" the man demanded of Paul.

"Paul Quince, sir."

"And yours," he demanded, looking at me.

"Nathaniel Swubble, Mr Kilsby."

"Foundlings, I can surmise from your names." To our relief, he walked off to tell Mrs Corney that he would make sure Mr Clack understood that the girls' hair was to be cut short. She told him to mind his own business. We knew why. At regular intervals, she cut and sold the girls' hair to a wig-maker, and their hair was not, at the moment, worth harvesting.

On the way back to the workhouse, we managed to dodge out of the line and took the chance to talk to Georgina and Virtue. They had been shut up in the girls' wing, just as we had been isolated in the boys'. We were soon discussing the story, which had been told at the service. As usual, it was the type of tale aimed at turning us into God-fearing, hard working adults.

In the story, a girl, brought up in the workhouse, had been employed as a maid. In the kitchen, washing up after the family had taken tea, she had been tempted to steal sugar from the bowl. Had she not attended Sunday school, she would have given in and eaten it, only to die a violent death, the sugar having been mistakenly replaced with arsenic. We had all waited eagerly for the next part of the tale, where there were horrible screams from the drawing room, where the master and mistress, having eaten the powder, were dying. Much to our disappointment, the fate of the family was not revealed.

"What," the vicar asked us, demonstrating the question and answer method used to impress the story upon out minds, "is the moral of this story?"

Paul hissed, "No one answer."

I could not resist showing how quickly I grasped the point of stories. Old habits die hard. "Our loving Father," I began, avoiding the title which always came out as 'Gawd', was watching over 'er and saved 'er from sin."

Mr Clack winced at hearing such low speech uttered in church. "No, Nathaniel Swubble," he declared, with the certainty of one to whom all has been revealed, "God was watching to punish the girl if she sinned. This story teaches that God is ever watchful. Have no fear, your sins will find you out! Even when there is no earthly being to see you or hear you, God, all-seeing and all-hearing, knows all and will surely punish you for your sins. When you are a child and sin out of sight of your parents, God knows. When you become servants and labourers and sin out of sight of your masters and mistresses, God knows." Pausing for emphasis, he finished, "And God will surely punish you.

As we walked along, we discussed what we had heard. It was, after all, the only story we had heard for some time.

"I bet 'e can't," Paul announced.

"'Oo can't what?" I demanded, liking to get facts clear.

"God can't see and 'ear everybody in the world all at once."

We took the feeling of the group and found we were four to two in favour of God's being able to see everyone in the world in one glance. Georgina and Paul were on one side and Virtue, Tom, Peter Pace and I on the other.

Mindful of Jack Star's reference to William White's using carrots and sticks, I remarked, "God don't seem to use carrots in the stories they tell us. She would 'ave got punished if she 'ad eaten the sugar, but she didn't get nothing when she didn't."

"Yea," Paul agreed, "when she didn't eat it, it should 'ave turned into diamonds."

"That would 'ave been a punishment," Georgina pointed out. "She might 'ave choked on 'em."

"And," Peter, the moral one amongst us pointed out, "they would 'ave belonged to the master and mistress. It were their sugar."

"The reward was," Georgina explained, after some thought, "that she didn't drop down dead."

We all agreed that was not a real reward, but, then, there were not any carrots in the moral stories we were taught, only sticks or the absence of sticks.

We walked back, chatting about other things, unaware that an event was about to take place which would prove that God, perhaps looking in the other direction at the time, did not always punish the sinner and spare the righteous.

152

CHAPTER THIRTY

A few weeks later, in October, an Irishman was brought into the workhouse, having fallen down in the road and suffered a bruised head. Naturally, having had experience of gangs of Irishmen descending on the area at harvest time and still having memories of the navigators who dug the canal, it was assumed that he had drunk too much. He sat for a short while in the porter's tiny lodge, while it was agreed that he should be admitted into the infirmary.

We, Paul, Peter and I, were sent to help the man into the workhouse and up the stairs. As he staggered across the yard, he moaned that he was too hot and demanded that we took off his top coat and put it around his shoulders. Going through a door, it fell off, but he did not seem to notice. Paul picked it up and followed us, as though carrying it upstairs for him. But, at the bottom of the stairs, Paul dived off and disappeared. Seeing what had happened, I left Peter to struggle upstairs with the man and followed Paul.

"What you doing?" I demanded, already knowing what the answer would be.

"'E's drunk and injured, ain't 'e? 'E won't remember where 'e lost it."

"That's thieving."

"Fancy knowing that. Clever, ain't yer?" Turning the tables on me, Paul added, "Are you pretending you never stole nothing yourself?"

Rather than add lying to my sins, I gave up my feeble protests, turning my attention to checking that we had not been seen. Having helped the Irishman to his bed, Peter came and found us in an old outbuilding. Realising what had happened, he at once told Paul to give the coat to the workhouse master or matron. "They won't give it back," Paul claimed truthfully. "I might as well 'ave it as give it to them."

"They'll catch you when you wear it," Peter said, realising Paul was unmoved by being told it was wrong to take the coat, but might be restrained by the fear of punishment.

"Shan't wear it, shall I? Ain't that stupid. I'll 'ide it till I leave this place or sell it."

"Will you give us sixpence when you sell it?" I asked.

"A farthing, more like."

Having found a place to hide the coat, we could not resist trying it on first. Filling the pockets with small stones, Paul swaggered towards me, took stones from the pocket and, placing them in my hand, ordered a gin, a brandy and a pint of ale. Having poured the imaginary contents of imaginary glasses down his throat, he rolled about as though drunk.

Peter tried to take the coat, but he was not as old or strong as Paul was. Knowing right from wrong, but having fallen in the habit of following Paul in everything, I stood by and said nothing. The coat having been hidden, we went back into the workhouse, Peter still trying to persuade Paul that, if he did not want to give the coat to the master or to Mrs Corney, he should hand it to Jack Star.

We expected Peter to continue his protests next day, but he seemed to have realised the impossibility of making Paul do the right thing. He seemed to be keeping to himself, and Paul, with me in tow, made no effort to seek him out. Then Sal told us he was ill and had been put in the little room off the boys' ward. She told us that he was sleeping and that we must not disturb him. These days, we had begun to feel we were too grown up to take orders from an old lady and we obeyed her only when it suited us, but, having fallen out with Peter, on this occasion we followed her advice.

In the night, we woke to hear someone scurrying to and fro and the hideous sound of someone retching his insides out. I realised it was Peter.

The woman, who was sitting by his bed to give Sal a few hours' rest, had expected to be free to nod off herself.

"You naughty boy," she shouted at him. "I'm run off me feet 'ere." Very soon, she told him, "I warned you. Now you'll stay in your filth."

I kept my eyes shut. Opening eyes or showing that you were awake meant becoming involved, being sent on messages or even being asked to clear up the mess. Eventually, the noise subsided and I fell to sleep.

It could not have been long before we were jolted awake.

"Good Gawd,' 'e's dead!" Martha exclaimed. "Go and fetch Sal."

The woman rushed past us and, soon, she returned with Sal. Sal sent the woman away and she and Martha had a hurried conversation.

"We'll leave 'im 'ere till the morning," Sal decided. Once upon a time, she would have prepared the body immediately, but she was old and tired these days.

By the light of their lanterns, Sal and Martha made their way past the rows of beds. As their lanterns fluttered in their trembling hands and their old feet shuffled across the uneven floor, the shadows of these bent little old ladies were further distorted by being thrown against the angle of the wall meeting the ceiling. They loomed over us and, as their trembling hands and shuffling feet made the lanterns swing erratically, the huge shadows jerked and pointed to first one bed and then another. It was as though the shadow of the Angel of Death was passing through the ward, selecting those who would be the next to die.

My heart was beating rapidly, but I still obeyed Paul's call to come and look at the body. We were used to seeing dead bodies, but they still both attracted and repelled me. I could feel more than relieved that it was not me, lying there, but I realised life was a lottery and it might well be me next time. And dead bodies, themselves, had an unearthly quality, of this world and yet not of the next. Curiosity and bravado always made me look at them and even, if dared, touch them, but I always knew that, under cover of darkness, they would return. I would have to lie awake, holding my breath to listen for their breathing, peeping beneath my eylashes to see their dull, lifeless eyes looking back at me and holding the blanket tightly around me to block out the touch of their thin, icy fingers.

Some of the boys were still asleep and most of those who were awake chose to wait and see if we discovered anything worth leaving their warm beds to see. I tried to shove Paul forward, while he grabbed my arm and dragged me with him. This suggested that, for all his bravado, his thoughts on dead bodies were similar to mine. As it happened, Paul reached the door of the little room a second before me.

"'Oly Mother of God!" he exclaimed, having caught the saying off some of the workhouse's new inhabitants. As he had seen them do, he crossed himself, but only having seen this procedure executed when he was facing them, it came out back to front, as it were.

Taking a step to draw up alongside him, I uttered, "Gawd Almighty!"

Only a few boys came running to see what had startled us. The others sat up, pulling up their blankets and peeping over, or remained lying down and pulled their blankets over their heads. There was pushing and shoving in the small group inside the door. When it settled down, the smallest found they had been pushed to the front and the tallest were looking over their heads. Through it all, not one had taken his eyes off Peter's body.

The body was lying on top of the bed. In the candle-light, his skin seemed pinker and less bloodless than our idea of the average dead body we were used to. But it was not this which had arrested our attention. Twitching muscles, on every part of his body it seemed, caught our eyes and drew them here, there and everywhere, up and down the body. Then, before our eyes, the left leg was slowly raised off the bed of its own voli- tion. Then, by its own weight, it dropped back. We half knew what might happen next. As the second leg raised itself, "Gawd," escaped from all our lips in unison.

"'E's still alive," one of the corporals whispered, in the quietest voice we had ever heard him use.

"'E ain't dead, that's for sure," another boy agreed.

We were all breathing again, but gently and quietly, so as not to draw attention to ourselves. After all, a body lingering between life and death was worse than a completely dead one. I realized that someone was clutching my hand. It was Tom.

"They're going to bury 'im alive," the same corporal announced.

"They won't stop at 'im," Paul hissed through his teeth. "It'll be our turn next. It's William White wanting to get rid of us all."

We were all shivering.

"It ain't 'alf cold tonight," the corporal declared, to cover his fear.

"We got to save 'im," Paul said, stepping forward and touching the body. "'E's warm," he announced and then drew back his hand quickly. "Ugh! 'E looks a bit black to me."

Forcing himself to stay by the body, Paul began to lift off the pennies placed on Peter's eyelids to keep the eyes closed.

"You little devil," Sal shouted as loudly as her old voice would allow. She pushed through to stand by Paul. "Stealing from the dead now, are you, Paul Quince?"

"'E ain't dead, Sal," Paul stated firmly. "We all see 'im move. We ain't going to let 'em bury 'im."

"Over your dead body, eh?" Sally cackled. "Give us them pennies. Placing them back on Peter's eyes, she told Paul, "'E's as dead as a door nail, take my word for it. I seen more dead bodies than anyone in the country, I shouldn't wonder."

"'Ow d'yer know 'e's really dead, Sal?" I asked. "'E keeps twitching and jerking."

"You'll twitch and jerk in a minute, if you don't get back to bed."

Looking at the shrivelled body, Paul asked, "What did 'e die of, Sal?

Don't look natural to me. Were 'e poisoned so they don't 'ave to feed us no more?"

Old Sal seemed to sink into her own thoughts, muttering to herself. I thought I caught the word cholera. I did not need to hear it twice.

"Is it cholera, Sal?" I demanded. "'As it reached Myddlington? Are we all going to drop down dead?"

Most of us had heard of cholera. It was talked of as the modern plague. It had swept across large parts of the world, leaving death in its trail and, in 1831, it had crossed the sea to England. For a year, it had spread here and there, touching this one and that one without rhyme or reason, but those it touched died in agony, quickly, if God was merciful, slowly if He were not.

"Cholera!" Sal said, gazing accusingly at us. "'Oo said anything about cholera?" Then she seemed to recover her wits and laughed. "Cholera, we seen that many a time, ain't we? Good old English cholera. Upsets you for a bit, but you don't die."

"But there's another kind now," I said. "I read about it in a newspaper what I caught sight of."

"You and your reading," Sally laughed. "You and your fantasies, I should say."

"Why were 'e jerking about" Paul demanded. "I ain't never seen that before."

"When you're as old as me, you'll 'ave seen everything."

"'Ave you really seen it before, Sal," I asked, seeking reassurance.

"Ain't that what I'm telling you?"

"Yes or no, Sal?" Paul demanded, trying to pin her down. No one knew better than him how to avoid confessing the truth.

"Cross your 'eart, Sal," I said.

"Yes," Sally stated. "I'm telling you I 'ave seen it before. Cross me 'eart and 'ope to die." It was the truth. She had seen the Irishman die a few hours earlier in the same way. Seeing we were still not completely convinced, she added. "That Irishman were weak from a life of drinking and loose living. The Paces, they always was poor stock. 'Adn't the whole family passed away? Now Peter's in 'Eaven with 'em."

"Why were 'e kicking?" Paul persisted.

"Getting ready to come back and 'aunt you, I shouldn't wonder. Just trying his legs out, 'e were."

Sally left us and we had hardly got back in bed before Jack came and carried out the body, thickly wrapped in blankets. Before daylight, Peter and the Irishman were buried in a deep grave in the corner of the work-house garden.

Peter, the boy who knew right from wrong, and practised only right, was dead. Paul, who seldom resisted temptation, and I, who followed him against my conscience, were fast asleep in our beds.

CHAPTER THIRTY ONE

News of the deaths, with added twists and trimmings, spread from wing to wing. The very air within the workhouse seemed to vibrate with tension, threats and demands. What, the women wanted to know, had happened to their children? Were they lying, untended, on their sick beds waiting to die? And their husbands, were they dead like the Irishman? Unless they were allowed to see their families with their own eyes, some threatened, they would throw themselves from the top windows.

The men, confined to their wing, demanded to know what illness had taken the lives of the Irishman and the boy. Fearing it was cholera, or, as some said, the plague, many declared that they would rather starve outside the workhouse than stay and die that terrible death inside.

We children, when we had time to think about it, found we had sore throats, headaches and pains all over, signs of the onset of serious illness. Many, who had parents, cried to be with them and those who had none, wished, not for the first time, that there was someone to place an arm around them and kiss away their tears.

William White had not gone home that night. The parish doctor had told him of his fears and saw himself, as the hero of the hour, taking precautionary measure to prevent the illness spreading into the town. He had read all the theories regarding cause and cure and had his own favourite one. With two dead, William White had asked him to consider the matter very carefully and then give his opinion.

"It would appear to be cholera. The Asiatic variety, that is," the doctor stated, feeling important to have been the only medical man in Myddlington to have attended the Irishman and examined the boy's body. "The symptoms are identical with those described for this dreadful disease."

"Appear to be! Described!" William White mocked in a sneering tone. "Have you no first hand knowledge? Have you never seen such cases before?"

Feeling less heroic, the doctor agreed that he had not.

"And you are, of course, simply an apothecary, not a physician or surgeon."

In other circumstances, the parish doctor would have protested that he knew just as much as they did, but he felt on less sure ground where cholera was concerned.

"You realise, Mr Thomson, what will happen if you claim that there is cholera in the town? If this news spreads," White warned the medical man, "no one will enter the town and many will leave it. Trade will slump. Tradesmen will be bankrupted and you will be blamed. And," he added, looking directly at the doctor, "if you are wrong in your opinion, you will not only be the butt of all this anger, but the butt of every joke made by physicians and surgeons for miles around." Pausing to let the doctor consider the terrible possibilities, William White demanded, "Are you ready to take this burden upon yourself, based only on your unsupported opinion of what you have read?"

The doctor, dejected as his dreams of recognition had come up against cold reality, hesitated. If he had known, for certain, what was the best policy to follow to prevent the spread of the disease, he was certain enough of his diagnosis to make it public. But he did not know and he was not alone in that. In this particular case, if he advised that no one should be let out of the workhouse, many might die inside it and there would be a riot put down by troops. On the other hand, if people were allowed out of the workhouse, cholera might spread through the town. Either way, he would be blamed.

The apothecary's hesitation was so obvious, that William White decided to push him further towards a decision to say nothing.

"You know as well as I do, that once it was known that you had, or claimed to have, been within a mile of a case of cholera, no one else would consult you on any other matter. Tradesmen provide your bread and butter. They will not only turn against you for ruining their businesses, but will avoid you as a possible source of the disease.

Seeing the apothecary, who had a conscience, still tottering between telling and not telling, White said, kindly, "No one shall ever know that was your private opinion. We shall both say, and I shall ensure that everyone else says, that the man and boy died of English cholera. That old woman, although she is in her dotage, still has a great deal of influence. She shall tell everyone it was English cholera."

"Old Sal? Yes, they take more notice of her than they do of any medical man. She brought many of them into the world in her younger days."

"That is settled, then," William White announced briskly. "No more need be said."

To salve his conscience, Mr Thomson insisted that the bodies were buried in lime and that all bedding and clothing were burned. Then he returned home and sent his family to stay with relations in the country.

When told that they were free to leave and starve in the town, if they wished, some changed their minds, but some did leave. Amongst them was the woman who had sat with Peter Pace and had treated him so unfeelingly. She died, but not before she had taken cholera into the filthiest part of the town, the part Felicity had taken us to a few years before. From there, it spread from the dark courts and miserable hovels to the more respectable streets in which we had met the Browns and nearly lost Gina.

Perhaps William White had thought that, by releasing people into the town, there would not only be a temporary drop in the number of mouths to feed, but also, as people in the poor parts of town dropped like the flies amongst which they lived, a long term one. How wrong he was! While a number certainly died, some were not taken ill and some survived. It was not always the smallest and weakest who were taken, but the oldest and strongest, who were the bread winners. As cholera passed, it left in its wake widows and orphans from families who had never sought help before. By White's own rules, they had to be admitted into the workhouse. Whether or not he recalled his father's warning that no one could predict what disasters might occur, we shall never know. White's response was to try to rid the workhouse of the children, who placed such a burden upon his resources. As usual, he called a meeting of the Board to agree to all his proposals.

For this meeting, as for others, a boy was chosen to stand ready to run messages and bring people before the Board. I was chosen, not because I was particularly fleet of foot, but because I was one of the few considered to have enough sense to remember the message, deliver it and, where necessary, bring back the answer. Perhaps more importantly, I was one of the few boys who could make out what William White said and make myself, generally, intelligible to him. When he spoke, on account of the plum in his mouth, most boys stared blankly, mouths half open, wanting to ask, but not daring, why he did not speak English, like them.

When boys spoke to William White, he usually said, "Take a deep breath, boy, and fill your lungs. Stand up straight and speak out. Don't hang your head and mumble." Here he would mimic the way they stood and the noise he imagined they made. "Can you not speak your own mother tongue? Are you some heathen savage?"

At the meeting, William White would have been happy to let me stand close by the assembled Board. To him, I was a servant and, by definition, invisible. It was the members who, afraid that I would repeat things they said or agreed to, insisted that I stood by the door out of earshot. But they were all elderly and earshot for them was yards less than it was for me. Even when they dropped their voices, I could hear every word. Always, I pretended to be looking down at a spot on the floor or studying my hands, giving the impression that I was not listening.

The minutes of the last meeting having been agreed, Mr Limbkin, the chairman, asked William White to put forward his proposals.

"We have attempted," White said, "by separating parents and children in the workhouse, to take the children from the evil example and evil influences these parents present. But, I am afraid, older children can influence younger ones to evil. For the good of both older and younger children, I propose that they be separated, the older being sent to learn, as soon as possible, that they must work for their living."

"I have noticed," Mr Clack intoned, "that children as young as five and six are already servants of the Devil."

"If we stand by and do nothing," one of White's most loyal supporters asserted, "it will mean prison, transportation or hanging for all of them."

Just in time, I stopped my hands from going to my throat at the thought of the noose tightening around it. I was not supposed to be listening.

How many times had I heard Mr Clack's next remark? "What we are seeking to produce are hardworking, obedient and God-fearing labourers. The sooner the children start work, the more readily may they avoid temptations."

"'Ear! 'ear!" the Board members agreed as one.

William White moved on to his solution. "I have been approached," he stated in firm tones, intended to brook no disagreement, "by an agent who apprentices boys and girls in factories in the North and Midlands. He will take as many children as we can supply."

"What will be the cost to us?" Limbkins usually asked that question.

"No cost will fall upon us. In fact," White added, beaming around the table, "he will pay us two shillings for each boy and one shilling for each girl. It would have been more, but there is the cost of transport to take into account."

"They'll say we're selling our children," a member muttered.

"Did you speak?" White demanded.

The member decided that he had merely coughed.

"And that's the end of the cost to us?" Limbkins asked, as predictably as ever.

"Certainly. They will be boarded in a hostel, fed and clothed by the factory owners."

Mr Clack and another member spoke at one and the same time.

"And the girls," the vicar asked. "Are they to be closely supervised by a matron? One hears such stories of the fate of young girls in the mill towns."

The member's question was more down to earth. "Are we talking about orphans or all the children? Parents'll want to see a shilling or two in their palms if they send their children off."

As he had been prepared for the member's question, William White answered that first. "Where there are parents, the money paid by the agent will go to them. The parents can then leave the workhouse and survive for a while on the money they have been given."

Having had time to think, William White went on to answer Mr Clack. "They will be supervised no better and no worse than they would be at home."

"Oh dear!" Mr Clark replied, "Will it be as bad as that? Open to all the sins of the flesh."

"They'll be better off," White's supporter claimed. "They'll be so tired when they get to the 'ostel, they'll not 'ave time to get into trouble."

The vicar was not happy. "I would like to know that they are supervised."

"I shall make that plain to the agent," White told him, knowing he had committed himself to very little. Looking round the table, he asked, "If there are no more comments, may I take it that we all agree to children of' nine and over being apprenticed in the factories."

There were a few hesitant coughs and muttered words.

"Well?" White demanded.

"I'm afraid," Limbkins said, taking his role as chairman seriously for the first time, "that the local employers will say that we have taken away their labour. Don't forget that the deaths from cholera have reduced the number seeking work. If we get rid of the children, labour costs will shoot up and remain up for a generation."

"We've fed some of 'em from birth," another member dared to point out.

"Just as they can pay the town back, don't make sense to send 'em away."

"You see, they're Myddlington children," another member explained, coming down on the same side as the others.

William White did not see. "The town seldom raises a hand to help them."

"That's another matter," Limbkins tried to explain to White, "but you send 'em away and there'll be an outcry."

"But the cost of feeding and clothing so many children is excessive," William White protested.

No one replied. They were not bearing the cost.

"Some people," Limbkins explained further, "almost make pets of 'em. That Paul Quince is quite a favourite, with his cheeky smile."

William White looked around at the members, whom he had never seen before as anything but puppets. They had no arguments worth listening to, but he could see stubborness on the faces of these yokels. They could not reason. They could not win an argument, but they were as immovable as the donkeys they were.

"Then," he said in his most reasonable tone, "you will agree to our apprenticing the older boys to local masters, if they can be found?"

With obvious relief that their opposition had brought no retaliation, they all agreed.

Having dared question William White's decision once, the Board passed the next two items on the agenda, without discussion. Inmates were to be put to work picking oakum and gruel was to be provided for a second meal in the day. The reason for the first proposal was not set out in detail by William White, but the Board members were well aware that no local tradesman could be found to teach the paupers, that goods produced by the workhouse lowered prices and that much expense had already been incurred on materials, which had been spoiled by untrained paupers. The reason for the second proposal flowed from the first. William White was finding his enterprise far more costly than he had imagined.

CHAPTER THIRTY TWO

Not for the first time, recently, Paul was thoroughly angry and dissatisfied with his lot in life. On an inadequate diet, he was sent out to work in the fields and, to add insult to injury, he was expected to bring back the few pence he earned and hand them over. And this was only a stop-gap until, if rumours were to be believed, the older boys were handed over to any masters in any low trades to be apprenticed for seven years whether they liked it or not. As he saw it, and it was no doubt true, there were seven years of slavery stretching ahead before he was a free man. The food would be as bad as we had in the workhouse and his lodgings, probably in an outhouse, worse than we had known.

Neither had Paul's temper been helped by his having to watch the top coat he had stolen going up in flames. Jack had realised the Irishman's coat was missing and had guessed where he could find it. He had tried to explain to Paul why it had to be destroyed, but Paul had demanded to know how a coat could pass on any disease, when coats cannot catch diseases in the first place.

On Saturday, Paul said, as he was leaving for work, "Today's me last day with Mr Long. 'E promised to give me a few coppers for meself. I'll be finished early. Meet us about four o'clock, Nat, outside Mr Limbkins' shop."

With no doubt in my mind as to what Paul planned to do, I thought about it all day. There was no doubt that I could time a delivery of a message for around four o'clock, but I knew that Paul did not intend to spend his coppers in Mr Limbkins', but in the gin-palace next door. The truth was, Paul had a fondness for gin. Even Jack admitted that her tiny charges acquired nothing at Mrs Mann's baby farm except a disease, which killed them off there and then, or a taste for gin, which took a little longer to finish them off. He said they were given a drop of daffy to stop them crying and, for the rest of their lives, they turned to gin for comfort.

For as long as I had known him, Paul had sought out Sal's bottle of supposedly medicinal gin. We all stole things in a small way. We took fruit from orchards and from stalls and potatoes and turnips from fields. We were hungry and these things were there for us to take. It seemed the natural thing to do and, in general, such activities were not planned, but were the impulsive actions of bored and unsupervised children. Only Paul put his mind to planning raids on the gin and the daffy. When one of his tricks was discovered, he thought up a new one. I was quite young when he took to topping up Sal's bottle with water, so as not to be found out.

Do I need to say that, although I had decided to meet Paul to take him straight home, we ended up in the gin-palace? The effect gin had on Paul and on me on this occasion will illustrate the differences in our characters. I tried to refuse it as something to be viewed with suspicion. What would it do to me? Would it make me ill? Would it turn me into a raving lunatic? Urged to accept it and not be a spoilsport, I snatched the glass from Paul when there were only a few drops left in the bottom, declaring that was plenty, even too much. Then I did nothing but gaze at it for as long as possible, as though it were poison and, at the first drop, I would fall down dead.

Paul mocked me until, holding my nose and closing my eyes, I unwillingly forced it down my throat. Then I stood very still, fearing that, if I moved, I would fall over or disgrace myself in some way. All my strength and thoughts were concentrated on keeping control of myself, my actions and my words.

What a contrast this was with Paul. He held his glass, urging the pourer to give him more. "Go on," he said, "let's see 'ow much I can drink 'fore I falls over." This was a very crafty trick, which Paul must have thought out before hand. Onlookers were certain to provide the pennies and take bets on how much he could take before falling flat on his face.

"Give us another, you old miser," Paul demanded, after the first drink, playing to his audience. "You're keeping 'alf of it for yourself. There ain't enough in there to wet me whistle." After singing Rule Britannia, he offered to sing anything the crowd demanded. All this time, I was tugging at his sleeve, trying to make him come with me. Usually, someone said he had had enough, but, this time, a stranger kept the gin coming. It seemed an age before Paul staggered out, with his arm around my shoulder.

"'Ow long," he demanded, "'as old Gamfield 'ad two donkeys on 'is cart?" Stopping dead in his tracks and nearly toppling into the road as he peered across, he exclaimed, "Gawd! Mr Gamfield's got a twin brother." His arm slipped from my shoulder and he dropped to the ground. I had barely pulled him to his feet, when he darted across the street. I prayed that we would not end up under the wheels of a carriage. It seemed highly likely that we would. On the other side, he embraced the sweep's donkey like a long lost friend. Feeling the soot which had transferred from the donkey to his face, Paul fell about laughing. "Better get a wash, or they'll sell me off as a slave in....where is it I'll be sold off, Nat? You knows everything."

"The West Indies." There had been much talk of freeing slaves at this time.

In a second, his mood changed from laughter to tears. "Won't make no difference. You and me is slaves already, ain't we, Nat?" Here, I was embraced and the soot on my clothes spurred him to laughter again.

"Shut up, Paul," I urged, trying, quite in vain, not to attract attention. I felt the whole town was staring at us. "Come on. Let's go 'ome."

"'Ome!" Paul roared, "We ain't got no 'ome, Nat." He seemed on the point of tears once more, but suddenly brightened. "You and me ain't got no 'ome, Nat. We ain't got no parents what nags us. You and me, Nat, can do whatever we likes."

"Is that so?" an angry voice demanded. "You'll do what you're told and like it, my boy." Jack Star stood blocking our way. "You, Nathaniel Swubble, get back to that work'ouse 'fore they know you're missing. Keep your mouth shut, or there'll be no more errands to run."

I did not need telling twice. Much as I wanted to help Paul, I wanted to keep my job as errand boy as well.

Taking Paul by the collar, Jack dragged him back along the street to the gin-palace, pushing him in front of him through the doors. Shoving his way through the crowd, Jack propped Paul up against the counter and leaned over to grab the barman.

"Listen and listen good," he spat out. "You ever give any of these children intoxicating liquor again and I'll see you suffer for it."

"Now, now, Jack," the barman smiled. "Weren't me. That gent over there. 'Ee's from London. 'E paid for the gin. I told 'im Paul 'ad 'ad enough."

Turning to the stranger, Jack told him, "Everyone 'ere knows to keep an eye on these boys so no 'arm comes to 'em. We all acts as Ma and Pa to 'em. May be different in London, but, while you're 'ere, you better do it our way."

People hastily stepped aside, backing into each other and treading on each other's toes, rather than stand between the two men. Even the most drunk seemed to sober up for a moment and fell silent. Only the Londoner made no effort to move.

"Let them be," the man urged. "They ain't yours are they?" He winked and smiled around the room.

Not wanting trouble, the barman called, "Come and 'ave a drink yourself, Jack. No real 'arm done. The boy'll sober up soon enough."

"See," the Londoner smirked, "You're making a fool of yourself, cluck-ing like an old mother 'en."

Lifting Paul from the floor, where he had settled quite happily, Jack said, "I'll finish this some other time." He knew full well that brawling in a gin-palace would not be viewed lightly by the Board.

"Any time, me 'eartie," the Londoner called after Jack and then began to sing Hearts of Oak.

At supper time, I tried to rouse Paul, who was sleeping, snoring noisily.

"'Ere," I called to some of the boys going in to our evening meal. "'Elp me get 'im in, but don't let no one see."

While several closed in around us, another boy helped me drag Paul into the hall. He hovered between groaning and resuming his singing. Every now and again, he sighed, "Gawd, me 'ead!"

It took all the strength of two of us to prop Paul up on the bench, pulling his elbows onto the table to support his head. Elbows on the table was a deadly sin. Punishment was swift and sudden.

"Get them elbows orf the table," the sergeant yelled. "Did you think I couldn't see what you was up to?" Swinging his cane, Sergeant Stamp swept Paul's arms from beneath his head, so that his face smashed onto the table.

With blood running from his nose, Paul shouted belligerently, "'Oo done that?" Swearing and cursing, he put up his fists as though ready for a fight. No one had ever been less ready.

"What did he say? What did he say?" Bumble demanded. He knew full well what Paul had said, but, if he had forgotten, we were not going to remind him. "Fetch the master somebody."

It was Paul's bad luck that the master was just outside the door talking to William White. They both hurried in. While William White walked along the row to stand facing Paul, the master took up his position behind him.

"Stand up, you young idiot," White ordered. As Paul was barely capa-ble of doing that slowly, let alone at speed, the master helped by grabbing his collar and lifting him to his feet.

"What? 'Oo? Get orf!" Paul mumbled, trying to turn and face the mas-ter. When he succeeded, he was suddenly sick all over him.

For Paul's sake and our own, we tried to continue eating and pretend we had not noticed. We leaned away from him as far as possible.

"You think you are grownup, do you?" William White demanded. Paul. being in no state to reply, White went on, "Those who behave like babies shall be treated like babies." Turning to Bumble, he ordered, "Take him to my aunt's. Tell her to put him on the floor with the babies. The three mile walk will do him good."

Bumble hesitantly put forward the opinion, which his expression told more clearly, that the task of dragging a drunken child through the town was beyond his ability and beneath his dignity.

"Take the porter with you," White ordered.

At the baby farm, Mrs Mann cursed her nephew under her breath. How could she manage this lout on her own? She could manage Oliver, who was small and submissive enough to carry out her orders and reel under her blows, but this one was shaped like a square piece of granite and was all too likely to hit her back. She was happy to let Paul lie down on the floor among screaming, wet and smelly babies and fall into a deep sleep. Susan and Oliver could clean him up in the morning.

That was, indeed, Susan and Oliver's first task in the morning. Paul did not thank them for it and appeared to have trouble working out where he was. The only thing that he was certain about was that he could not face the spoonful of congealed gruel they offered him. Later, with Mrs Mann's saying that the sooner he returned to the workhouse, the better she would like it, he grudgingly did the few tasks she gave him to occupy his time.

It was not until evening that William White arrived and everyone melted away. He held a stick in his hand and, when Paul put up his fists to defend himself, he laughed. Stunning Paul with blows on his outstretched fists, he spun him round and pushed him forward over the table. Then he beat him, with ever increasing ferocity, until Paul fell to the ground, senseless. White left the room, replaced the stick in the hall and went out of the front door and back to Myddlington.

"Is he dead?" Mrs Mann asked, peeping round the door. She seemed to think that, by keeping her distance now, she would avoid any blame. Susan and Oliver undressed Paul, revealing deep weals across his back and buttocks. They rubbed him gently with ointment and revived him with sips of cold water.

"Ma! Ma!" Paul sobbed, as returning consciousness brought returning pain. "Ma! Ma!"

"You ain't never had no Ma," Mrs Mann pointed out.

"Sh! Sh!" Susan whispered, "You can cry for anyone you want."

"He'll have to stay here now," Mrs Mann grumbled. "Can't let no one see you with them marks all over you. You'll have to do as you're told, while you're here, or I'll tell me nephew."

Paul barely had the strength to mutter what he would do to her nephew, but he made a supreme effort. "I'll kill 'im," he swore. "When I'm older, I'll kill 'im."

CHAPTER THIRTY THREE

Late one night, a family of a man, woman and four children presented themselves at the workhouse gate. They said that they had been on their way to the North, but that one of the children was ill and they had taken longer on their journey than expected. As a result, they had no money or food left and needed assistance. The father said that he had been at Waterloo and had not been employed for more than three months at a time since his discharge.

"We was 'eros on the battle field, but, once we'd sent Napoleon packing, no one wants to know our troubles."

The master was quite impressed by this and even more impressed by the fact that the man waved a piece of paper under his nose. This stated that the parish of St George in the East in Middlesex would refund any financial burden imposed by the family on other parishes on their journey. Claiming reimbursement could take a long time, but it was always possible to claim a little extra for the master's own pocket.

Jack Star would not have been impressed by the man's claims or the piece of paper. Had all the claims he had heard been true, there would not have been sufficient room on the battle field of Waterloo for a soldier to raise his musket or draw his sword. As for the paper, these were all too easy to forge. What is more, Jack Star would have recognised the man as the Londoner he had met in the gin-palace. But the porter was away, helping Bumble to return some paupers to their parish of settlement and he had no say in the matter.

With the father in the men's ward and the mother in the women's, the daughter was sent to the girls' ward and the three boys joined us.

Sal did question the biggest boy's age, but no one in authority listened to her on such matters. We were not welcoming. We knew it as Gospel truth that Londoners were dirty and had fleas and hair lice. We kept our distance.

The next morning, the youngest boy had such severe blisters, that the master agreed to keep the family for a day or two until he had recovered.

Old Sal looked at his blisters. "'Ow far 'ave you bin walking?" she inquired. "Ain't your feet 'ardened by now?"

"It ain't with walking," the boy told her. "It's 'cos me boots is too tight."

Sally understood such problems, as we all did. Boots could be too tight or too loose. They were rarely just right. Sal let him stay in bed for most of the day.

When I returned downstairs, the oldest boy had joined Paul and Tom at their chores. He had not needed any invitation, but had set out to make himself pleasant to them. His name, he told us, was Jacob. Whenever the sergeant or corporals were not about, he told us stories of London. If Jacob was to be believed, and I did not think for one minute that he was, he was the most accomplished thief in the world and had never been caught. To hear him, you would have believed that the streets of London could easily have been paved with gold from his pockets had he wished to do it. I took a strong dislike to him. I disliked the way he put his arm around my shoulder, as though he were my best friend, and I disliked even more his being so friendly with Paul and Tom. They seemed so impressed by him

"Listen," Jacob said all confidentially, "I've made ten shillings a day many times. If I ain't made a pound, it's been 'cos I had something better to do."

I was glad to hear that Paul was not completely taken in. "'Ow is it you're in rags, then?" he asked, quite reasonably.

"Well," Jacob replied knowingly, "You didn't expect us to turn up in the workhouse in our Sunday best, did you?"

"No," Paul jeered, "We don't expect you to wear 'em, 'cos you ain't got none."

"When we finished this job," Jacob said, "if there ain't nobody about, just foller me."

Once the task was finished, we did just that. Somehow, Jacob had found our hiding place in the derelict outhouse. With a flourish he produced a silk waistcoat, beautifully embroidered. Paul and Tom were even more impressed. I tried not to show that I was. They felt it and Paul held it up in front of him to see how it looked.

"Try it on, friend," Jacob urged. "But swear you won't breathe a word about it to anyone."

We all swore not to tell a soul.

"Go on, sir," he told Paul and then admired it, like a tailor eager to sell his wares. But that was not what he was selling.

Sensing my hostility, Jacob concentrated his efforts on the other two.

"Hey, presto," he called, pulling a golden sovereign from one of the pockets. Paul and Tom were allowed to admire and touch it, but I was not invited to join in.

"Now, young Tom," Jacob said, patting Tom's head, "wouldn't you like to earn a few of them nice glittering little things?"

Tom, his eyes shining as brightly as the gold in Jacob's hand, smiled back at him and nodded his head. "Wouldn't arf buy a lot of things," he murmured. I could see that he half hoped Jacob would give him one

"You ain't wrong there," Jacob grinned, holding the coin out to Tom and then pulling it away again.

I had seen enough. Neither Paul nor Tom noticed when I walked away.

A few minutes later, I passed Jack Star. "You look as though you've lost a shilling and found a farthing," Jack commented. "Where's Paul and Tom?"

"Went off with a new boy."

Jack looked puzzled. "New boy? I didn't know we had any new inmates."

I walked on, pretending that I wanted to be on my own.

Later, I watched as the three approached me, talking happily together, with Paul and Tom looking admiringly at their new hero. When Paul and Tom tried to talk me round, I ignored them.

I did not speak to them on the way up to the ward that night, nor when we prepared for bed. As we were locked in for the night, I lay silently wondering if the others would call out to me. I had not made up my mind whether or not to reply.

"Cat got your tongue?" Paul called out.

I would have answered, but Jacob's laughter made me realise that Paul was playing up to him as much as wanting to make friends with me again. I remained doggedly silent.

After a few minutes spent trying to make me talk, with other boys telling him they wanted to get to sleep, Paul pulled his blanket around him, ready to settle down.

"Don't speak, then," he muttered. "You'll be sorry you didn't speak to me when I've gawn."

"Sh!" Jacob hissed and added in a more openly aggressive tone than I had heard from him before, "I told you not to blab." Jacob's annoyance with his new friends, who were my old ones, cheered me up. I decided to make an issue of it.

"Where you going?" I demanded, sitting up and addressing Paul.

173

Before Paul could reply, Jacob snarled, "Mind your own business'

"It is my business," I told him. "Paul was my friend before 'e were yours."

In the pale moonlight glowing through the windows, I saw Jacob get out of bed and come towards me.

Paul jumped out of his bed, and stood between Jacob and me.

"Leave 'im alone, Jacob. 'E don't mean no 'arm, honest 'e don't."

"Let's 'ear 'im say it, then," Jacob demanded, the threat in his voice undisguised. In the moonlight, Jacob's long shadow seemed to hang over the whole ward.

In a voice full of pleading, Paul urged me, "Go on, Nat, tell 'im you didn't mean nothink."

Here, it seemed to me, was the chance to turn Paul against the intruder, Jacob.

"Ain't going to talk to the likes of 'im," I replied, trying to keep my voice firm and challenging.

Jacob tried to move closer to me, but Paul gently placed his hand on Jacob's chest to stop him in his tracks.

"Come on," he told Jacob, "'e ain't worth bothering about." Then he turned to me. "Look, Nat, why are you trying to get 'im worked up?" In a lower voice, he added, "I'm just thinking of going back to London with 'em. It'd be a better life for me. Don't you want me to get away from this place and better meself? There ain't nothing for me 'ere, is there?"

Too jealous of Jacob to show much sense, I sneered, "So it's London they're off to is it. Thought they was telling everyone it were Manchester. I'll 'ave a word with Jack tomorrow about their lies and their...."

Afraid that I was about to tell about the waistcoat and the money, Jacob pushed Paul aside and made straight for me. Paul dragged him back.

"You don't understand, Jacob," he said, "we been in 'ere together for years. 'E wouldn't grass us up, you got my word for it."

In my eagerness to stop Paul leaving, I ignored all the signals that Jacob was becoming increasingly angry and was not one to let anyone stand in his way.

"What do you 'ave to do for a waistcoat, Paul? Be a thief like 'im and 'is family."

Jacob did not move, but looking at his expression, Paul fell silent, concentrating on the boy's next move. He realised that Sal had been right to question his age. This was no boy, but a young man. I had not finished.

"And young Tom," I demanded, "what does 'e 'ave to do to earn a sovereign?" My voice trailed away as Jacob passed me and approached Tom's bed. Tom was sitting up, his frightened eyes all that was visible over the blanket. As he reached Tom, Jacob looked back at me. His eyes seemed ablaze, but I shall never find words to describe his expression. It was a smile, but not one which made you smile in return. His lips were parted and his teeth showing, certainly, but so are a mad dog's before it attacks.

As he leaned over Tom and his brothers held off Paul, he smiled more sweetly. "I'll just whisper to 'im what you 'ave to do for a sovereign."

Tom tried to run away, but Jacob held his head and whispered in his ear. Tom fell back on the pillow sobbing loudly.

"'E don't really understand," Jacob, said, shaking his head sadly. "But that's all the better."

Paul tried to lunge at Jacob and, being bigger and stronger than the two boys holding him, managed to grab at Jacob.

"Oh," Jacob said, "did you want me to whisper it in your ear?"

As Jacob whispered what Tom would be expected to do for a sovereign, Paul exploded in fury. I leapt out of bed and, terrified but realising that I had started all this, I joined in the fight.

I did not know what had been said, but, suddenly, from the fear and guilt which welled up inside me, I sensed that we were in that world of mixed half truths, lies, mystery, ignorance and guilt which surround children, but into which they are forbidden to enter by grown-ups.

I had first been made aware of the existence of this world as a young child, when, gazing at a woman holding a baby to her breast, she had stared back at me accusingly. "Ain't no one taught you not to stare?" she had demanded. "You'll grow up to be a peeping Tom, if you ain't one already." I had hung my head and felt ashamed like Adam and Eve in the Garden of Eden.

Growing up amongst men and women, boys and girls, I had learned something of these mysteries, of the difference between boys and girls and what went on between grown-ups, but many uncertainties remained. The old people, who willingly told us so many other things, and Jack, who thought it his duty to educate us, never brought the subject up in our long discussions and avoided answering our questions. Men and women joked and teased each other in our presence, but soon berated us if we tried to join in. Women grew large and screamed and swore in the infirmary until we heard a baby cry, but they told us babies were found under mulberry bushes or in the cabbage patch. Felicity had looked for one many a time, yet she had never found one.

We did know that there were fancy women and wanton women and men who spent their time with them, for what purpose we were not sure. Sometimes children giggled and sniggered in little groups and told unbelievable stories. To avoid looking silly, you had to pretend that you knew what they were talking about and you had to be careful not to make a remark and reveal your ignorance. If you raised the matter with adults later on, they told you, "You keep away from children like that," or, "You'll find out when the time comes."

Had the time come now? Or was I mistaken? What could Tom have to do with these things?

"Tom's coming with us, ain't you, Tom? If you don't, you'll be sorry. We're off tomorrow and we'll take anyone what wants to make a good living away from this stinking place."

Tom jumped out of the other side of the bed and ran round to me for protection. I was wetting myself and in danger of soiling myself, too. I put myself between Tom and Jacob.

"Joining in the fun at last, are you?" Jacob laughed.

"I ain't coming with you," Paul declared, trying to draw Jacob's attention from us. The three brothers laid into us with heavy punches. No one came to help us. Most boys in the ward were new to the workhouse and quite indifferent as to who won, as long as they were not involved.

Tom ran to the door and battered on it, only to be grabbed by Jacob. It was clear that he thought, as Tom was coming to work for him in London, he would take this opportunity to show him who was boss. He ordered us to stop fighting his brothers, or he would make Tom pay for it.

"Right," Paul agreed breathlessly, "We'll stay 'ere, but don't touch 'im."

"I'll do what I like," Jacob laughed and we knew that he could.

Then the key was gently turned in the lock.

Had we not been standing almost frozen to the spot, we would not have heard the sound of the door handle rattling very quietly and turning very slowly. As it was, we all turned to see who was entering so stealthily. As the door opened inch by inch, I prayed for it to be Jack, or even Sergeant Stamp. As the door was opened, the light of a lantern was thrown in a wider and wider shadow on the floor. Any second, it would reveal the face of our saviour.

Old Sally stood blinking at the scene. This was no six foot giant, or even a bent old soldier with his cane. This was a bent and shrunken old lady, with a lantern in one hand and her gin bottle in the other. Her eyes, half blind and half dimmed by drink, stared blankly, reflecting, it seemed, a mind incapacitated by age and suffering.

Jacob and his brothers laughed in relief and in expectation of the fun's being increased by baiting Sal. They watched her wobbling from side to side as she bent to place the lantern on the floor.

"Everything alright boys?" she grinned happily and toothlessly, peering at each of us in turn. There seemed no point in answering.

Only Jacob replied. Going over to her he reached for her gin bottle. "Give it 'ere you old 'ag."

Smiling, Sal obediently held out the bottle.

"Makes you forget all your troubles, son. 'Ere, take some."

Jacob reached out for the bottle. Tense as we all were, we jumped like released springs at the sound of the dull thud as the bottle hit the side of Jacob's head. He dropped to the ground and lay there without a moan or twitch.

"Still got the touch," the old woman chuckled. "Told you it would make you forget your troubles, young man." Then she addressed Martha, who had entered close behind her, "'Ow many times did I 'ave to do that to me 'usband?" she asked.

"More times than we've 'ad 'ot dinners," Martha laughed.

"You're right there," Sal agreed. "I could 'it the right spot even when I were a bit under the weather meself."

Highly pleased with herself, Sal sat down on the nearest bed. She took a swig from the bottle. "I earned that. Now, shove 'im and is brothers into that little side room and lock the door." There was no lack of volunteers now the trouble was over.

"The trouble with youngsters is," she muttered, half to herself, "they think we was always old. We was young once. We've lived life day in day out." Beginning to lose the thread of her speech, she finished, "That's why we're old, 'cos we've lived long enough to see everything."

I ran and found Jack.

By morning, the family had been run out of town. The beating the father and Jacob received at the hands of Jack Star and his friends ensured

177

they did not return. As he slunk off, the man swore that he had been told to come by Gideon Raven, who had told him that William White would be all too grateful if he could persuade some children to go to London. Jack was inclined to believe him, but believing was not evidence.

It was only hours later that it was discovered that Georgina had disappeared. From what we could make out from Virtue, the girl in the family had befriended Gina and given her pretty ribbons and described a life in London, where a beautiful girl could take the fancy of a rich man and live happily and wealthily ever after. Gina was not the only one to disappear. With a life of a skivvy in service stretching before them, two others went with her.

CHAPTER THIRTY FOUR

Through all these events, I was, as all children do, storing each one away, piece by piece. Each was being fitted into the image I was building up in my head of what life and the world around me was really like and how I fitted into the picture.

The piece I slotted into the picture after the tea party at the Lowe's represented my growing awareness that society was made up of many, many layers. There were quite deep layers from outcasts and paupers, through labourers and artisans, through clerks and shopmen on to master craftsmen and manufacturers, doctors and lawyers and merchants, up to the gentry and aristocracy and right up to royalty. Within each of these, were dozen upon dozen of thin layers, scarcely recognisable to the outsider, where people were divided and labelled on the basis of skill, occupation, wealth, birth and connections. And matters were arranged so that men, by birth, by education and by all the advantages or disadvantages they received as children, were ordained to stay within their own level or struggle to live a respectable life and take pride in rising just the tiniest degree.

The piece fitted in after Peter's death and the spread of cholera, showed that, in this life, death was never far away. It might tap you on the shoulder at any time and no man, be he doctor, clergyman, local dignitary, lawmaker or king, had the power to stand against it.

The third piece, stored away after our encounter with Jacob and his family, reflected the fact that there was evil in the world. The young and the weak were at the mercy of those who were older and stronger. It reflected, too, the dawning realisation that children could be twisted and distorted, like Jacob, to resemble those who abused them.

I am not claiming that, as I lay in bed on the eve of my ninth birthday thinking back over my short life, I had arrived at a clear, complete and final image of the world in which I lived. At such an age, many of the pieces were still missing. Moreover, like the colours in a kaleidoscope, the pieces could be shaken and rearranged in many different ways. I rearranged them day by day, according to the last view on the subject I had heard expressed, be it by a clergyman, a radical, Jack, Old Sal or anyone else. Often, without realising what I was doing, I would rearrange it according to my mood. When I was cheerful, the world was an exciting place. When I was sad and lonely, it was a frightening one.

On this eve of my birthday, I had arranged the pieces with God at the centre. He could make miracles happen, so that I could find I was the son of a wealthy family at the top, rather than at the bottom, of society. He could save me from death or, alternatively, grant me Eternal Life. He might not keep me from meeting another Jacob, but He could give me strength and comfort in times of trouble. Most of all, I suppose, the appeal of a Heavenly Father was overwhelming to a child with no Earthly one.

If God would be my Father, I decided, I would be His kind, perfect and obedient son. I would not only obey all His commands myself, but, by my example, single-handedly convert Paul to the same way of life.

The next morning, there was no Jack Star waiting for me before breakfast. Recently, I had been disappointed that he was always too busy to worry about me. Today, I was disappointed that, when I did see him on my way out to deliver a message, he said he could spare only one shining, new penny as a present. I did not know that he was lending the little he had to Old Sal.

The sparkle had already gone out of the day and I was walking sluggishly along the High Street, when I spotted Paul running like the wind in the direction of the workhouse. Nearing it, he dived into the churchyard and disappeared from view. He must have found one of our old ways out of the workhouse that was still open. What surprised me, in my low mood, was the speed at which he had been running. Our poor diet left us all lacking in energy and slow in all our movements. But, in the cold, wind-driven rain of January, I supposed it did make sense to hurry. I pulled my threadbare jacket tight around me and pulled my cap forward to keep the rain out of my eyes. At least, with so many women in the workhouse, our clothes were well mended. Indeed, there were more darns and patches than original material.

At midday, as we waited for dinner, Paul managed to work his way along the line until he stood next to me. He looked very pleased with himself. Our bowls in our hands, we reached the huge copper from which food was dished out. In the old days, wheneveryone knew everyone else in the workhouse, I would have expected an extra piece of vegetable, or even meat, floating in my bowl. Now there was not only little solid material in the stew, but no one slopping the liquid into our bowls who knew it was my birthday. To be honest, I doubt whether the woman by the copper even knew her own birthday. Many people had no call to remember such dates

and had lost count of their years on earth long ago. That suited the authorities, who could add on a year or two when children approached the age to
go out to work. Paul tried telling the woman that it was my birthday. She
stared at me as though I were some strange and unusual creature.

"What d'yer want me to do about it?" she demanded, sulkily. "If I give
'im an extra spoonful today, tomorrow will be everybody's birthday.
Anyway," she added, truthfully enough, "there ain't no good bits in 'ere to
pick out, even if I were Little Jack 'Orner."

As we ate our stew, Paul whispered, "Don't look down, but I'm slipping
you a present what I got you."

"I spotted you running through the churchyard." I was playing for time.
It would be something Paul had stolen, an apple perhaps, and I would have
to refuse it. Then I would have to point out to Paul the error of his ways.

"'Ere, take it from me." From his coat, Paul produced not an apple, but
a book.

"Did yer buy it?" I asked, hoping against hope that he had at least been
given money for going an errand or found it in the street with no hope of
identifying the owner.

"Buy it! 'Oo d'yer think I am, the King of England?"

My heart sank further. I wanted that book like a man in a desert needs
water, but Mr Carson, the bookseller, was one of my friends. He let me
stand at his stall and, as long as I did not get into any customer's way, read
anything I liked. I could not steal from him.

Paul saw the expression on my face. "Oh dear! Goody-goody's pouting."
He illustrated this statement with a girlish pout.

"But Mr Carson is our friend."

"'E never were mine," Paul hissed in a fierce whisper. "Calls me a gutter-
snipe. Anyway," Paul added, "you 'aven't stolen it, 'ave you? It were me what
stole it. That makes it mine and I'm giving it to you of me own free will."

My hand on the book Paul passed to me under the table, I found this
argument totally convincing. The small voice of conscience was completely stilled. My only worry now was not to spill greasy stew on it. I pushed it
under my jacket. There was plenty of room for it and the fact that I was
being half-starved seemed to help justify my acceptance of Paul's gift.

"Are you pleased with it?" Paul asked.

"Course I am. Ain't never 'ad a book of me own before, 'ave I?"

"'Ide it," Paul advised. "There ain't many as'll want to read it, but there's plenty as'll want to steal it."

Later, as I examined the book in our secret hiding place, Paul sat beside me. He said nothing, but he seemed to be going over what he wanted to say. The speech had clearly been planned beforehand.

"If I were your brother and I were rich," he began, "I could give you a 'undred books, but it wouldn't 'ave cost me nothing." He stopped to collect his thoughts. "Well, I mean, I would 'ave 'ad to pay for 'em, but I wouldn't 'ave missed the money. I could just ask me rich Pa for some more. Now," he continued with greater confidence, seeing the end in sight, "that book did-n't cost me no money, 'cos I ain't got none, but I risked me liberty to get it." Feeling he had not made himself clear, Paul added, "That's more to me than a few shilllings to a rich man."

Gazing from the book to my friend, I hesitated to kiss his cheek in thanks. We were too old for that. I put my hand on his arm for a second.

"It's worth a lot more than money to me, Paul." I found that I had tears in my eyes.

As I examined every inch of the cover, Paul asked, "What's it called?"

That presented some difficulty. I knew some of the words, but had to sound out others with great care. Finally, I read, 'Chronology, or the Historian's Companion, being an authentic Register of Events, from the Earliest Period of Time, comprehending An Epitome of Universal History with A Copious List of' the Most Eminent Men in all ages of the World.'"

Paul let out a whistle. "Let's 'ave a look at the picture."

We looked at the one picture in the book, opposite the title page. It showed two figures, one clearly a woman sitting writing and the other, like an angel without wings, who was not clearly male or female. The second figure was kneeling on a large, open volume and held a burning torch in his hand.

"'Oo's that, then?" Paul asked.

Not for the first time, his faith in my learning was misplaced. "Chronology," I read the one word printed beneath the picture.

"Didn't know it were about nobody," Paul commented.

I suspected he had just grabbed the first book he could without being seen and had no idea what it was about.

As I looked inside, I told him, "It ain't about nobody, it's all dates and things I can learn. It's lovely, Paul. It'll take me years to learn 'em all."

Looking pleased with himself, Paul took the book from me. "What's that say?" he demanded, pointing to a line.

"Straw used for the king's bed, twelve hundred and thirty four."

"Didn't know that, did yer?" Paul demanded, with pride.

CHAPTER THIRTY FIVE

Soon after my birthday, Jack Star sent for me.

"Nat," he said, "that young friend of yours, Oliver Twist, is coming in today. Will you 'elp 'im out? Settle 'im in and show 'im the ropes? Be a friend to 'im?"

I agreed readily enough. Oliver was a bit green, but he was easy to talk to.

The next piece of news pushed Oliver's imminent arrival and my promise right out of my head.

"You know," Jack began. His voice was gentle, but he spoke briskly to suggest it was something I should take on the chin. "Paul's gone orf to work. 'E won't be 'ere no more."

Paul and I had talked about this. If anything, as he was strong and useful to the workhouse, he was late going out to work. He had told me that we would always be friends and that he would visit me whenever he could.

"You mean 'e won't be in the work'ouse no more?"

"'E might not be in the town no more."

"But William White said that 'e'd apprentice all the boys in Myddlington, itself."

That was news to Jack Star. "Well, I suppose you could say he's been apprenticed in Myddlington, but 'is job is going to take 'im further away."

"'Oo's 'e been apprenticed to? Will 'e be 'appy working with em?"

"I think 'e'll like the work well enough. 'E's 'elping out on a boat."

"In the Yard with White's?"

"No, Nat."

"'Oo then?"

"Simon Smith."

"'Oo's 'e?"

"To tell you the truth, Nat, I don't know. No one told me about it. I saw it in the register. It just said, 'Paul Quince apprenticed to Simon Smith, boatman'."

"What's the name of the boat?"

"I've told you all I know, Nat."

I felt panic rising inside me. "When did 'e go, Mr Star?" I could not keep my voice from trembling.

"Mr Bumble took 'im first thing this morning. Mr Bumble's gone straight to pick up Oliver, so I ain't seen 'im since."

Never before had I abused Jack's trust in me, but the gate was open and I dashed past him and straight through it. Blindly, I headed across the street, ignoring the traffic, and took the short cut across the Yard to the canal. I nearly crashed into Mr Campion overseeing the loading of a boat.

"Where are you off to in such a hurry, young man?" he asked.

"'Oo's Simon Smith?"

"Never heard of him, Nat. Why do you ask?" Then he recalled, "Bumble was here asking for him a while ago. He was with that friend of yours, young Quince."

"Where did they go?" I demanded.

Mr Campion stopped what he was doing and placed a hand on my shoulder. "What's wrong, Nat? Should you be out?"

"Where did they go?" I repeated angrily.

"Ask that fellow over there. He spoke to them. Shouldn't you be getting back to the workhouse before they miss you?"

Running as fast as my legs would take me, I sprinted over to the man, whom Mr Campion had pointed out.

"Where did Mr Bumble go?"

The man looked up from his work. "What are you in such a state about?"

Tears of frustration and anger flooded my eyes. "Where did Bumble go?" I demanded again.

"I told 'im to try along the towpath. I don't know no Simon Smith. The beadle come past me again, later, without the lad."

I was off down the tow-path in a second. As the frost melted, the mud was becoming slippery and I fell several times. Each time, I picked myself up and ran on.

"'Ave you seen Mr Bumble?" I asked everyone I saw. Panting for breath as I was, they often had to ask me to repeat what I had said. Everyone and everything seemed to be against my finding Paul.

Slipping over, I crashed into a boatman. "Did you see Mr Bumble go this way?" I sobbed.

"Steady yourself and remember your manners, lad. You don't come rushing along 'ere where we're all working and busy."

"I've lost my best friend," I cried, feeling no one in the whole world cared that Paul had disappeared.

"Now, lad, stand still for a minute, take a deep breath and let's start again."

I did as I was told. "Mr Bumble's taken my best friend to be apprenticed and I shall never see 'im again."

"Never see Mr Bumble again. You're lucky there, lad." Pushing into my hand the grubbiest rag I had ever seen, he told me to dry my eyes. "They come along 'ere asking for Simon Smith. I didn't know no Simon Smith, but I knew this feller what gives 'imself a different name every day." Watching my reaction, the boatman told me to dry my eyes again. "Bumble went up to the man I pointed out and a couple of minutes later, 'e come back on 'is own."

"What man?" My hopes rose that I had found Paul. Again, they were dashed.

"The feller went orf a couple of hours or more ago."

Suddenly realising how exhausted I was, I was past crying. Still I clung to some hope.

"What was the man s real name? Does 'e come and go round 'ere."

"'E comes and goes, alright, but not on a regular basis. Works anywhere on the big canal what joins up with our little un. 'E might be back next week or 'e might be back next year or….." He had been about to add, "never," but was too kind to do so.

"What's 'is name, mister?"

"Your guess is as good as mine. I've known 'im by 'alf a dozen names. If what people say is true, it's likely to be Simon Raven."

"What people say?" I echoed in disbelief.

"They say 'e's Gideon Raven's brother and everyone knows what a villain 'e is."

All I could think of to say was, "William White promised the boys would be apprenticed in Myddlington."

"'Fraid 'is promises ain't worth a farthing, lad." Looking round, he commented, "'Ere's someone looking for you, I shouldn't be surprised."

There was Jack, coming along the towpath. Without a word to me and with just a brief nod to the boatman, he put his hand on my arm and began to walk me home. He had obviously decided to leave the lecture on my bad behaviour in running out of the gate until later. I hung my head and said nothing to him.

We had almost reached the spot where we turned off the towpath into White's Yard before he spoke. I hunched my shoulders and prepared to let the words run off me like water off a duck's back.

"It's time you grew up. You're not a baby any more."

"I'm only nine."

"Only nine! I were at sea when I were nine. I saw a lad beaten to death and chucked overboard when I were nine. When are you going to grow up? Ten? Twenty? Thirty? Never? As for Paul, he was certainly old enough to go out to work."

"But not to work for Gideon Raven's brother."

For a moment, Jack appeared at a loss as to what to say. It was clear that he was surprised by what I had told him. Then, for my sake, he tried to brush his doubts aside.

"Paul can look after 'isself. If the worst comes to the worst, e'll run away. 'E'll find some way of letting you know where 'e is."

With his arm on my shoulder, the porter continued, "I've always ad 'igh 'opes of you, Nat. I thought you'd make something of yourself. Don't disappoint me, will you?"

"What shall I do, Mr Star?"

"You're one of the oldest, now, Nat. It's your turn to look after the youngsters, just like Paul looked after you. You 'ave to step into Paul's shoes."

"I ain't a fighter."

"That's 'cos you let Paul fight your battles for you."

We walked a few steps in silence, before Jack took up his theme again. "This is a cruel world, Nat. It's cruel what happened to Paul. It's cruel what beatings Oliver suffered. It's cruel Matt and Mark were apprenticed to old Gamfield a day or two ago and 'ave to climb chimneys. But people like you and me can help to make it a little bit better by what we do hour by hour, day by day through our lives. The church don't seem to make a lot of difference. A great revolution in France just seemed to make things worse, by all accounts. But small people, like me and you, can make things better in small ways. We can make it bearable for those we meet."

As we stood outside the workhouse, with Jack's arm on my shoulder, a stern voice ordered, "Leave that child alone, Star." William White was standing next to us. "We want no friendships with the boys, Star. Get back to your post." Turning to me, he asked, "Are you the boy who takes messages?"

"Yes, sir."

"Look at me, when I speak to you."

Standing quite still and staring him in the face, I hated him. He had sent Paul away. He had let Jacob into the workhouse and now he was insulting Jack. Why, I wondered, should I look at him, when he never did anything but address me over his shoulder or while looking down at his desk. Then, I decided, I would play Jack's game of keeping out of trouble, so that I was at hand to help the younger children.

"Did you want me for an errand, Mr White?"

As I hurried about my task in the town, I saw Matt and Mark. They were carrying heavy bags of soot out of the houses for the sweep, Mr Gamfield. They were already as black as the ace of spades, except for their blue eyes and the streaks of white down their faces, where they had been crying, and down their legs, where they had wet themselves in fear. Once, I saw them tied to the cart outside the inn. In the January cold, they shivered in their rags. The clean, carefully mended clothes in which they had left the workhouse had probably been sold already. The clothes they wore now represented not only Gamfield's meanness, but his claim that he was thinking of the boys. With little clothing, they were less likely, he claimed, to become stuck in chimneys. I spoke to them, but they seemed in a world of their own. When the sweep emerged from the inn, they flinched in case, like the donkey, they felt his whip.

Sometimes, a man or woman shouted at him. A woman told him he would end up in Hell. People knew any clothes they gave to the boys would be sold straight away and no one gave them any more. A man threatened what he would do to the sweep one dark night, but Gamfield only laughed and replied, "I'll see you first, 'fore you sees me in the dark."

But no one did anything. The boys were his property to all intents and purposes. They were no better off than the donkey. If I were grown-up, I thought, I would pull him off the cart and beat him to within an inch of his life.

Meanwhile, Oliver had returned to the workhouse with Bumble. As Dickens describes this day, Oliver's ninth birthday, in some detail, there is little point in my adding to it, especially as I was out most of the day. I must, however, refer to two matters, which Dickens touches upon. At the interview with the Board on his admission, Dickens refers to Oliver's being confused on being told that he was an orphan. Of course he was. As far as Oliver, or anyone else knew, his father was still alive.

Commenting on the Board meeting, Dickens also suggests that Oliver had been given little religious training. This claim goes against Dicken's own description of Oliver's friend, Dick, who spent much of his time longing to go to Heaven. Dick had also been brought up at Mrs Mann's and received the same training as Oliver. While their training was far from perfect, it was not completely neglected and what there was appealed strongly to children in such unhappy circumstances. While Mrs Mann had not an ounce of Christian charity in her bones, she, like most at that time, had a good grasp of the theory, especially as it could be applied to keep children good and busy. She made it clear to all her charges that there was a Heaven and a Hell and that, unless they behaved themselves, they would all burn for ever in the latter. Oliver also attended church now and again and learned of the gentler side of the Church's teaching from the young maid, Susan, who found great comfort in it herself.

Apart from this, I need simply describe my meeting with Oliver that evening. Going into our evening meal, he spotted me and ran forward along the line to greet me.

"Nathaniel!" he cried out in pleasure, "We can be friends now." Oliver could not have chosen a worse introduction. All my determination to be kind and considerate to others faded away.

"I ain't nobody's friend. I ain't never going to be nobody's friend ever again."

The boys around us pushed and shoved Oliver to the back of the line, some jeering at his speech and others complaining that he was pushing in, I ignored him and fought back my tears. Paul was the only friend I wanted.

That night, in the ward, Oliver was not the only one to cry himself to sleep, but I had my dream house in which to escape. There, I told my father, a wise and powerful man, of my troubles. In my imagination, Paul was brought back and I let him ride my horse in the fields behind the house at the end of the lane.

CHAPTER THIRTY SIX

When not running messages, I sat crosslegged on the floor with the other boys picking oakum, or, in other words, unwinding and unpicking old ropes. It was a task which made out brains numb and our fingers red and sore. Stray hairs of rope choked our mouths and noses and irritated our skin. We all hated the work, but had no choice in the matter. We welcomed almost any diversion, but not the one which occurred when a boy ran in calling for Sergeant Stamp.

"Sergeant Stamp. Sergeant Stamp," he shouted, forgetting all the little niceties, which had to be followed in talking with the sergeant. "The porter sez will you come and mind the gate? 'E 'as to leave it for a while. Please come quick, 'e sez."

"You'll never be a soldier," the sergeant roared. "Screaming and shouting gives your position away to the enemy." Taking his time, he went on, "'Aste is all very well in its place, but I can't see no call for it now. Where's 'e going?"

"There's some commotion down the street, sir."

That was more appealing to the sergeant. From the gate, he would be able to look along the street and see what was happening. Having put a corporal in charge of us, he left. We took the chance to suck our fingers to try and relieve the pain and shake the strands from our clothes.

Some time passed before the sergeant returned. The corporal dared to ask him what was happening.

"A good sergeant lets 'is men know what's going on, so I'll tell you," was the surprising answer from the old man. He was obviously dying to tell the story. "One of the boys what was apprenticed to the sweep got stuck up a chimney."

"'Ave they got 'im out yet?"

"In a manner of speaking. They got 'is dead body out."

"'E's dead, sir?" I asked.

"Ain't that what I said?"

We were silent, wondering who would be chosen to take his place. I prayed that I had grown too big.

"Get on, then," the sergeant urged. "Life ain't no different from war. There's sure to be casualties. Can't be 'elped."

Later, Jack Star told me something of what had happened. On hearing the news, he had sent for the sergeant to take over his duty until, knowing the urgency of the case, he had just left his post and run down the street. At first, the servants had refused to let him in, but he had argued that he knew the boy and could calm his panic. And, he had said, being tall and thin, he could reach up into the chimney further than any of them.

Inside, the housekeeper was near to hysterics. "Mr and Mrs Dell are away," she cried. They aways go away while the chimneys are swept. The soot is bad for Mrs Dell's delicate throat and Mr Dell doesn't like the smell and the nuisance."

"The fire is still alight," Jack protested, in disbelief. It had made it impossible for any one to shout up and reassure the child. The smoke and heat were enough to choke him.

"It's damped down," the housekeeper replied. "The maid lights it the same time every morning and then has other things to get on with."

"Shove the hot coals into that coal bucket," Jack ordered the footman.

"They'll burn the bottom out of it," he protested.

Jack did not tell me the exact words he used next, but the footman removed the coals and threw water from the vases onto the remains.

"We've already tried to smoke him down," the footman commented, thinking, from the steam which arose, that Jack was trying that method again.

Mr Gamfield assured everyone, "Burning damp straw usually brings 'em down. 'E's only panicking. It's the lad's fault, not mine."

Jack stood in the grate and could hear the boy whimpering.

"We can't stand around discussing what to do next," Jack decided. "Get a builder round 'ere quick and let's 'ave that wall down."

The smallest and newest servant in the room, who had not yet learned that a servant's first and only duty was to his master and mistress, ran to fetch the builder. The housekeeper collapsed in a chair. "The carpets," she moaned. "They cost a fortune. It's more than our jobs are worth to let you smash the bricks all over them."

"Are you offering to pay the builder?" the butler demanded of Jack. "It will cost money to knock it down and money to put it back."

"And it's not coming out of our wages," the butler declared.

"If there's a spot of dirt, I'll be dismissed," the housekeeper wept.

"Ain't come to that yet," Mr Gamfield told everyone. He was holding a rope in his hand and held it out to Jack. "'Ere, tie that round 'is ankle so as we can all tug 'im down."

Jack edged his head and shoulders into the chimney, talking gently to the boy and ignoring Gamfield's order. He discovered from the sobbing and terrified child that the lad was stuck with his arms tight by his sides and his legs twisted under him. Then he heard the child returning to whimpering like a trapped animal.

"'E's too far up to tie any rope and it wouldn't be no use if we could," Jack concluded. "I'm going for the builder meself. Don't waste any time while I'm away. Find out exactly where 'e's trapped and where we need to break in."

"'E's just there," Gamfield declared, not wanting to break into the wall and lose a customer in a town where sweeps were two a penny. "If I were as tall as that feller, I'd 'ave 'ad 'im out by now."

Jack found the builder with the young lad from the house still pleading with him to come. His reluctance to come did not lessen with Jack's arrival.

"I've been in this situation before," he told Jack. "You can't just attack someone's property with a pickaxe, you know. When the servants are too frightened of their masters to give you permission, there ain't nothing you can do, 'cept wait and think of the poor mite dying up there." Seeing the contempt on Jack's face, he went on, "I ain't got the money to pay for new bricks and for the cost of all the damage. It's alright for you, but I got a business and a family to think of."

Jack grabbed up a pickaxe and turned to hurry back to the house. The builder followed, protesting at what would happen to him if it was thought he had lent the tool willingly. At the door of the house, the footman refused to allow Jack in again. Jack pleaded and then threatened, while the builder tried to pull him away and persuade him there was nothing to be done.

The situation was saved by the arrival of Miss Aldbury, who had been shopping when she heard of the commotion.

"Let the builder in at once," she ordered in the tone which only ladies born and bred can use. "Unless you obey me at once, I shall see that your precious Mr and Mrs Dell are never invited to a social event in this town again. I shall take full responsibility for this and, if your employers are too mean or too poor to pay themselves, I will pay for everything."

"We'll have to roll up the carpets," the butler said, trying to maintain his authority.

"Rubbish!" Miss Aldbury replied, having reached, by now, the room nearest to the trapped child. "It's a bedroom, isn't it? Throw down a sheet or two, if you must, but I'll brook no further delay. You, builder, set about your task."

In the circumstances, the builder was only too happy to comply with the order. The butler fussed around, telling him to hurry and rescue the poor, dear child. Miss Aldbury's arrival had changed the whole situation. Miss Aldbury represented old money, and ranked well above Mr and Mrs Dell, who were definitely new money.

Working very carefully and painfully slowly to avoid hurting the boy, the builder broke a hole through into the chimney.

For a moment, he stopped working. "Can't 'ear nothing." They all listened. Miss Aldbury had been praying.

"Be quick," she urged. "Porter, and you, footman, help him pull out the loose bricks."

"At least 'e's got some air now," Jack observed, as he worked.

When the hole was large enough, Jack reached in and lifted the child out. Matt's broken legs dangled unnaturally and his head was lolling to one side. It was too late. His eyes were wide open in terror, as though, even in death, he could still feel the agony of that suffocating prison. Miss Aldbury resumed her prayers, but it was to ask for mercy on his soul, not for his life to be saved. Life had left his limp body some minutes before and could not be recalled.

I had never seen Jack cry before, but, as he finished his story, he sat down with his head in his hands and wept, not only in sorrow, but also in frustration and anger. I crept away, not wanting to embarrass him.

While the builder set about rebuilding the chimney, creating a tomb for another child, Sowerberry came to take the body. Immediately, at the sight of the undertaker, Gamfield left, muttering, "Ain't up to me to pay for the funeral."

The muttering continued until master, donkey and remaining boy arrived at the inn. The first went in, leaving the other two outside. Mark, tied to the back of the cart, cried silent tears. No one tried to comfort him or even explain what had happened to his twin brother, Matt. At night, in the shed, he would hug the donkey for comfort, but here, in the street, he could not even do that. He stood all alone in the cold, crying for his brother and for himself.

Only when Gamfield was settled and had been given a drink by those cronies eager to hear the whole story, did the sweep stop his muttering. Even then, his voice, emerging through a throat, which seemed lined, like some old chimney, with years of soot, croaked and creaked.

"Lost count of the numbers I've seen go like that in me lifetime," he wheezed. "Nearly went meself when I started at six or seven." He took a slow and deep swig of ale. "You might say it's an 'azard of the work. All jobs 'as their 'azards."

His cronies all nodded in agreement.

"What 'appened, exactly, then?" one asked, wanting value for the money he had spent on Gamfield's drink.

"What 'appened? Nothing 'appened. The boy got stuck, didn't e? Ain't what you might call an 'appening, no more than a boatman falling in the water now and again ain't an 'appening. If 'e'd 'ave listened to me, I'd 'ave 'ad 'im out of there in a trice. Panicked, 'e did. Weren't my fault 'e just got stuck tighter and tighter, were it?"

"Was it 'is first time up?"

Gamfield took another deep gulp of his ale. "Got to be a first time, ain't there? 'E wouldn't do what I told 'im. Once they're up the chimney, you ain't got no control. You can't reach 'em to give 'em a whack."

Dreaming of the old days, Gamfield continued, "I were born and bred to it. Us Gamfields 'ave been sweeps for generations. But me sons is sweeps and they keep their own boys to use theirselves. I used to buy other children orf their parents, you know. If you buy 'em, you can choose just the right size and ones with a bit of discipline to do what you tell 'em."

After a pause, Gamfield continued expounding the theory of chimney sweeping. "You see, you don't just need 'em small. Any boy is the right size at some time or another. You needs ones what is small for their age, if you get me meaning. Ones what is still small, but 'as more understanding of the skill of the trade. And ones what ain't going to grow too quick, so they're too big for the work just when you got 'em trained up right."

The man who had bought Gamfield's drink decided he was not getting his money's worth and dared to raise a delicate matter.

"'Ear they might not let you use boys much longer."

"'Oo says? Chimneys ain't straight up and down, you know. They got twists and turns, narrer bits and wide bits to be taken into account. And it ain't me what wants boys to do the job. It's them ladies and gents what say,

'Do yer use a boy, Gamfield? I must 'ave a boy to do a thorough job. Me 'usband 'ates smoke in the rooms and it don't do the furniture no good neither.'" Gamfield had tried, but failed, to pitch his voice to the level of a demanding female customer.

The others nodded. Customers could be unreasonable.

"So you don't think nothing will come of the clamour them societies is making about climbing boys?" a fellow drinker asked.

"Never," Gamfield declared with confidence. "Private property, them boys is and Parliament don't like meddling with private property. They'll never stop it in my lifetime."

"That might not be too long," another drinker laughed. "You're no spring chicken."

"I'll live to be a 'undred," Gamfield claimed. "Ain't me what goes up chimneys."

They all shared the joke.

CHAPTER THIRTY SEVEN

For the rest of that day and as I lay in bed, I felt anger against the world. Nobody cared about Mark. Nobody cared about Matt. There was only one thing to do and I had no hesitation in making up my mind to do it. After all, in my own imagination over the years, I had been Robin Hood and a Knight of the Round Table and now I saw myself as a follower of Christ. In all those roles, I saw the world through the clear and simple eyes of a child. Right was right and wrong was wrong and I would do what was right without fear of the consequences. I must free Matt.

There was no doubt that, although I did not realise it, the task presented me with the challenge for which my brain had been yearning. I planned carefully. I would have only one chance and must not simply free Matt, but see that he was not recaptured.

My first step was to learn more about knots. I needed to be able to untie the one securing Matt to the cart without attracting attention. Old rope to practise on, we had in plenty.

One day, as we picked oakum, I said to the sergeant, "Do soldiers know how to tie knots, or is it just sailors like Mr Star?"

Here was a challenge Sergeant Stamp could not resist. Picking up a piece of rope, he demonstrated one knot after another.

"You ought to teach us, sir. I might become a soldier like you was, sir, and then it would come in 'andy."

All the boys decided they longed to join the army and, within a few days, I had learned how to untie the knot the sweep used and several others I have never found a use for then or now.

Meanwhile, I had prepared Matt for what was in store. No one bothered to look at me as I patted Gamfield's donkey outside the inn.

"Matt," I whispered, "pretend you ain't interested in me." The command seemed unnecessary. If I had ever seen an expression devoid of hope and interest, that was Matt's. "Just listen. I'm going to set you free."

"Please no, Nat. 'E'll catch me and beat the 'ide orf me." he pleaded.

"No, Matt. I've got it all planned from start to finish. You ain't got nothing to do, 'cept run like 'Ell when I untie you."

"Don't think I can run, Nat." In support of this, the sweep's boy pulled up the ragged legs of his trousers to reveal his legs raw and bleeding. Blood trickled down from his sore knees and mingled with the soot.

"Gawd, they look sore."

"Me elbows is the same. Mr Gamfield rubs 'em with salt to toughen 'em up, but it don't seem to work."

"You'll 'ave to run, Matt, when I come for you. Think of Mark. You'll end up like 'im if you stay."

"'E's in 'Eaven," Matt said, almost with envy.

"That's what Mr Clack would say. Don't see 'im rushing to get there."

"I've 'ad enough, Nat. Life ain't worth living."

"It will be, Matt, I promise. Just wait for me to pick the right time and then run like the wind."

I wanted to stay and cheer him up, but I did not want to attract attention. I had to leave him and hope all my planning would not be in vain.

For the next part of my plan, I had to enlist Virtue's help. Girls had easier access to the kitchen and the laundry than boys and were viewed with less suspicion. At first, she refused to help me, but, when I explained what I had in mind, she agreed readily and swore to keep my secret. One by one, Virtue stole the garments and scraps of food I had asked for.

To give myself the free time outside the workhouse, I played upon the habit into which the Board members had fallen of making me do their private errands while I was out on Mr White's business. Instead of waiting for them to ask me to go here or there, I poked my head round their shop doors and asked," Any errands for me today?" There were always several eager for a free service and I ran so many errands no one knew where I was supposed to be from one minute to another. When Virtue told me she had collected everything, I took the little bundle from its hiding place, threw it out of a window and over the wall and made for the gate.

"Where d'yer think you're orf to?" Jack asked.

"Mr Limbkins told me to call in and run an errand for 'im." It worked. Once out, I dashed round and picked up the bundle. Checking no one was following, I ran across the fields to a derelict house near the wood. There I left the bundle, praying rats would not eat the scraps. In the rubbish and debris, I found an old bucket. It had no handle, but it was just right for Matt to take to the stream and wash himself. A black and sooty sweep's boy would be all too easy to recognise and return to Mr Gamfield. Then I collected straw blown against the building in the wind, made a rough and ready bed and returned to the workhouse.

Impatiently, I waited for the next day to complete my final task. When it arrived, I took my book, which Paul had given me, felt it in my hand and turned the pages for the last time. As I stuffed it into my jacket, I told myself that I had learned every word and did not need it anymore. Whether I needed it or not, I knew that I still wanted it, but sacrifices had to be made. Hiding the book under my coat, I ran down to a small shop by the canal. I could hardly sell the book back to Mr Craven, but this shop was well known for buying things, no questions asked. The shop-keeper bought and sold just about everything, mainly trading with boatmen going up and down the canal. Boatmen felt safer selling away from the scene of the crime. They also found it useful to claim, if they were questioned about anything in their possession, to say that they had bought it at the canal shop in Myddlington, safe in the knowledge that the shop-keeper would say he could not be expected to remember everything he sold. If a man said he had bought something there, he would not argue with him.

Until the moment I walked through the door of the shop, it had all been something of an adventure. Suddenly, I was a nine year old pauper standing all alone with a stolen book and was going to try to sell it to a man who had been a fence for years before I was even born. I prepared to take my turn, but it never seemed to come. Men and woman bustled in and pushed me aside. It seemed a very long time before I found myself at the counter, the only customer in the shop.

"Well, lad?" the fence asked.

For a moment, I fought back my longing to turn and run. Would he hand me over to the law? Would he make me steal more in return for his silence? I tried to think of Matt.

"Please, sir, would you like to buy this book?"

"Let's 'ave a look at it. There ain't much call for books in these parts." Turning it over, he held it away from him and stared at it disdainfully.

In the hope of increasing its value, I assured him, "It's very interesting." I was horrified to hear my voice trembling as I spoke.

"I'll give it to me grandson. 'E's a scholar like you and just as much of a rogue."

It was clear he knew it was stolen. I tried, but failed miserably, to protest my innocence.

"Can't pull the wool over my eyes, lad. I'd say it's your first time trying to sell something, but you'll get 'ardened and braver if you keep going."

He took a few coins from a purse under the counter. "Well, I'll give you your first lesson out of the kindness of me 'eart. You never get what a thing's worth from a fence. We 'ave to make a profit, you know. 'Ere, take this four pence. It's all you're getting orf me and you'll do no better anywhere else."

I took the coins and ran. I knew I had been fleeced, but I had never had four pennies in my hand at one and the same time before.

I am afraid to say that those pennies burnt a hole in my pocket. As I hurried back to the workhouse, I worked out how many sweets or cakes I could buy with them. But Matt would need money to travel out of Myddlington.

Deliberately, I had avoided Jack Star, but he approached me as I returned.

"What is it, Nat?"

"What?" I queried, looking as innocent as I could.

"What are you up to, Nat?"

"Me? I ain't up to nothing." Had he heard the pennies jingling in my pocket?

"I can read you like a book, Nat."

I knew that to be true, but I asked, "What's me title, then?"

"Being cheeky won't 'elp you. At a guess, I'd say it's got something to do with Matt."

Stopping myself from asking, "'Ow did yer know?" I said nothing.

"Don't do nothing on your own, Nat, I'm begging you. If you elp 'im get away, 'e'll soon be in trouble. 'E'll 'ave to steal to get by. Don't want to see 'im 'ang, do you? And what about the boy 'oo 'as to take 'is place? Might be Tom."

I did not answer. I was not going to give up my plan.

"Be careful, Nat. You could get yourself into serious trouble."

Walking away, I still saw myself as a hero. What a pity I did not have an impressive name or something short and simple. When people told my story, Nat Swubble would not have the ring of Robin Hood.

When the appointed day came, I walked over to the sweep's cart and began to untie the rope securing Matt. It was not as easy as it had been in practice and my fingers were sore from picking oakum. At last, the rope came away and I lay it carefully on the cart, so it did not fall to the ground and give the game away. When I had imagined this moment, I had seen my.self standing in the street shouting to Matt to run and run. Now it was happening in reality, I heard myself saying, "Count to fifty while I go and hide. Then run like 'Ell to the old 'ouse by the wood. That one where Paul and me wouldn't let you orphans play."

Matt seemed anchored to the spot.

"I can't count to fifty."

"Count to ten five times, then", I told him impatiently.

I ran, hid behind a stall and watched. For what seemed like minutes, Matt stood without moving a muscle. Then he ran. Dodging horses and wheels, he ran along the opposite pavement, weaving through passersby, until he dived right into an alley and disappeared. Suddenly realising what was happening, people had cheered him on and stepped aside to leave him a clear path.

I breathed a deep sigh of relief. For the first time, I noticed where I was hiding. I realised that I was kneeling down by Carson's bookstall. Mr Carson was looking down at me. Reaching out for my collar, he dragged me to my feet.

"You've come into some money, I understand. Sixpence, to be precise." The fence had not only split on me, but had made a small profit as well.

Mr Carson let go of me, as all hell broke loose. The sweep rushed out as fast as an old, bent man, who has drunk too much ale, can rush and stood screaming in his croaking voice that he had been robbed.

"'Oo done it?" he demanded. "I done up them knots meself 'fore I left 'im. 'E couldn't 'ave undone 'em 'isself."

No one answered, until a man said, "An angel took 'im up to 'Eaven, like 'e took the other one."

"Spirited away by the fairies 'e were," another called. Gamfield stamped up and down the road, swearing and cursing. "Where is 'e? Where's 'e 'iding?" Spotting me, the sweep demanded, "Is this your doing? Someone 'ad to 'ave untied 'im."

"This lad has been here all the time," Mr Carson told him. "I've a score to settle with him, as it happens."

"'Oo done it then?" The sweep looked oddly pathetic, more a victim than a cruel master. He wandered up and down being abused by some and ignored by others. Defiant, none the less, the sweep promised, "I'll 'ave the 'ide orf 'is back, when I catch 'im. And I'll catch 'im, mark my word."

No one would help the sweep look for the missing boy and a few, guessing my part in the adventure, congratulated me on what I had done. It was not the popular acclaim I had hoped for and I still had to face Mr Carson. Although he had let go of my collar and lied for me, he had remained by my side.

"You owe me sixpence. That is what I had to pay to recover my book."

"'E only give me fourpence," I protested. "And it weren't me as stole it, sir." As I spoke, I felt disloyal to Paul, but he was out of harm's way.

"You sold it, Nat, knowing it had been stolen. I had planned to hand you over for the law to take its course, but you have done what we grown-ups should have done ourselves and helped the sweep's boy. Just hand back the fourpence and we shall forget the matter."

"I give it to Matt, sir."

"Where is the lad? He cannot be left to fend for himself. He has other friends beside you and we shall see that he is safe."

"And you won't give 'im back to old Gamfield or to Mr White?" I told him where to find Matt and found myself relieved to have the responsibility taken from my shoulders.

"Just remember," Mr Carson told me, "that you owe me sixpence. And you will not be welcome at my stall for a very long time."

"I didn't mean to steal it for ever, sir. I were just going to learn it off by 'eart and then give it back."

"The road to Hell is paved with good intentions, Nat."

Later, I heard that Mr Carson had taken Matt to Miss Aldbury's and, from there, the boy had been sent around the country to make public appearances at meetings of all kinds of societies for the rescue of sweeps' boys. Miss Aldbury and her friends planned to apprentice him, when he was older, to a reputable master in the trade of his choice. He was better off than I was.

CHAPTER THIRTY EIGHT

It turned out that it was Oliver who was selected to take Matt's place as Gamfield's boy and that it was I who, unwittingly, put him in this position. Events were set in motion when we made Oliver the victim of one of our jokes.

Some children, who came into the workhouse, had been in the habit, while at home, of waiting hopefully for second helpings. Such children had been given small helpings to start with and had to watch their fathers and working siblings eat the lion's share of any meal. Then, if there was a little left over, the young children were asked if they wanted to finish it up. Eagerly, they passed their plates up for second helpings.

We old hands had long learned to laugh at newcomers who sat with their empty bowls in their hands and their eyes fixed on the master, waiting for him to ask, "Who wants to finish this up?" When he never did, their looks of disbelief and utter disappointment seemed so comical to us, who had long ago learned that what was put in our bowls the first time round was all that we were getting.

"Why don't no one ask for more?" a new boy wanted to know. He was bigger and fatter than the rest of us and had clearly been accustomed, in his father's cookshop, not only to a second helping, but to a third and fourth as well.

Holding our hands over our ears and our bottoms to indicate the whacks and cuffs such a request would lead to, we rolled about laughing until the sergeant approached with his stick. Later, at bedtime, we gathered around this boy, commonly called Pudding, who swore that his stomach felt as though his throat had been cut and he feared he would fade away. He was not so far gone, however, that he was unable to go around poking his fat finger into the arms of other boys, feeling, in vain, for any spare flesh which would make the owner worth devouring. Then he had a brain wave.

"Let's get someone to ask the master for a second 'elping. Just for a laugh," he added, seeing the horror on our faces.

"The master ain't got a sense of 'umour," I told him, to the agreement of all the other long-time inhabitants. "You do it, if you think it's such a good idea."

I suppose we all thought about it later, wondering if anyone could be persuaded to do it. It would be a laugh both to trick someone into asking and to watch the master's face as it happened. We all came to the conclusion that there was only one boy to do it. That was Oliver Twist, with his unique mixture of naivety and obstinate courage.

"Oliver," Pudding began, throwing his arm around Oliver's shoulders. This was an action which would have scared any of the regulars, except Oliver, into denying any request the boy was about to make. But Oliver smiled with delight and attempted, without success, to throw his thin little arm around Pudding. Even Pudding hesitated for a moment, but he could not resist treating Oliver like the sitting duck that he was, just waiting for the loaded catapult to be released.

"We ain't arf 'ungry," Pudding began again, "Ain't you Oliver?" Winking at the rest of us over Oliver's head, he continued, "We've all been talking, Ollie, and we've come up with the idea of asking the master for more. We could all do with a second 'elping."

Even Oliver had the prudence to ask, "Won't he be angry with us, Philip?"

It was probably the gentlemanly tone in which this question was uttered and his refusal to call Pudding by the name the rest of us used, which made us suspend any doubts we had entertained on urging Oliver to this task.

"To make it fair," someone declared, "we'll draw lots."

"That's right," Pudding agreed. "All collect any bits of straw you find and we'll draw for the winner tonight."

"How does that work, Philip?" Oliver inquired politely. His speech sounded strange to our ears.

"Hi 'old the straws, Holiver," Pudding explained, trying to imitate Oliver's accent. "Hand everyone takes one. The one what gets the shortest is the one what does the deed." Pudding waited for a brief moment. "Are you game for it, Nollie?"

"I'll take a straw," Oliver agreed eagerly, "but, if I win, I'd like to exchange my extra gruel for someone's piece of bread."

"Anything you say, Oliver," Pudding agreed, slapping him on the back.

I knew, and tried not to think about it, that Oliver planned to give the piece of bread to Dick, his old friend at Mrs Mann's.

Before we drew straws that day, Pudding told us to take the one he pushed towards us. It was no surprise when Oliver drew the shortest. Apart from turning a little pale, he took it like a man. I determined that, if I managed to steal anything from the garden or kitchen in the week, I would give it to Oliver for his friend. My conscience was easily satisfied.

That evening, the master must have sensed, from the absolute silence in the room, that something was planned. Perhaps he feared a riot, for he had Bumble standing by and Bumble panicked and sent for Mr White.

You know from Mr Dickens' account something of what happened when Oliver asked, albeit very politely, for more. Oliver was punished, confined on his own and offered as an apprentice. He did not tell of Mr White's pleasure in seeing Oliver brought before the Board for punishment. That gentleman's expression was that of a cat who, having seen the mouse escape out of reach, puts out his paw again to recapture its prey. Nor did Dickens tell that, when Mr Gamfield spoke to the man in the white waistcoat outside the workhouse, this was by appointment and no accident. The final humiliation for Oliver, the would-be gentleman, William White had concluded, would be for him to walk the streets tied to the sweep's cart and live in fear of the dark, airless chimneys he was forced to climb.

Dickens did not know, moreover, that Jack overheard a conversation telling how Oliver was to be taken from his punishment cell to be apprenticed before the magistrates to Mr Gamfield. I knew of this when Jack came to find me and tell me that, just as I had helped Matt, I must now help Oliver. Ignoring the solid door of the room in which Oliver was confined, Jack took me round to the yard, where a chute led down into the very same cellar.

"No one must see us," he told me. "You can slip in quite easily, but you'll need Oliver's help to get out. If you're caught, for any reason, I'll take all the blame."

Having called quietly to Oliver to put down any sacks he could find to break my fall, I took the short, but exciting, slide down the chute and landed at his feet. He stood shivering, gazing at me. Perhaps it was all the beatings he had had in his life, which had convinced him that he was, indeed, guilty of offending everyone. Just as I was thinking this, Oliver shamed me by putting my safety before his.

"Please don't get yourself into trouble on my account, Nathaniel. My mother is always by me and gives me courage to bear my suffering."

"Look. Ollie, I ain't got much time. Mr White is planning to apprentice you to the sweep. You know what 'e's like. 'E killed Mark and 'e'll beat you and maybe kill you, in the end."

Oliver looked petrified.

"It ain't come to that, yet. Mr Star sez as 'ow you'll 'ave to go before the magistrates to 'ave some papers signed. 'E sez you must tell 'em straight out you don't want to be a chimney sweep. Say you 'ate the thought of chimney sweeping and want to be a tinker, tailor, anything you can think of 'cepting a sweep."

"What if the magistrate doesn't ask me, Nathaniel? I must not interrupt my elders."

If this was what being a gentleman's son meant, I knew I would never be one.

"Look, Ollie, this is serious. You'll just 'ave to speak up for once. They might be your elders, but they ain't necessarily your betters."

Oliver still looked doubtful as to his ability to make himself heard.

"Would your Ma like you to be a sweep's boy?" I demanded, playing what I saw as my trump card.

For a moment, I thought he had accepted what I said, but, after careful consideration, Oliver answered, "I think that my mother would want me to be honest and hardworking in any calling I might undertake."

"Gawd 'elp us!" I cried in desperation. "Calling! Chimney sweeping ain't a calling. God don't call you to it. The Devil pushes you into it. 'Ow many real ladies do you know 'oos sons are chimney boys?"

Oliver appeared overwhelmed and tears sprang into his eyes. This gave me an idea.

"That's it, Ollie. If the worst comes to the worst and you can't make yourself 'eard, cry like you've never cried before." Taking his hand, I tried to joke. "All 'ands to the pumps, Ollie, all 'ands to the pumps."

Oliver did try to smile through his tears. "Thank you, Nathaniel. I know you are trying to do your best for me."

"Mr Star sez as 'ow you must make 'em realise you don't want to be a sweep." It was always reassuring to have an adult to back you up.

"I'll try my best, Nathaniel, I promise." He admitted, "I don't want to be a sweeps's apprentice." Then he made me despair by adding, "But if I have to be, I shall do my best to be hardworking and obedient."

"Give us a leg up," I told him. I had done my best. Now it was up to him.

To his credit, Oliver, small as he was, put all his strength to the task of hoisting me back onto the chute. I scrambled up and then turned back to look at Oliver. He thanked me politely for coming, as though I had just called in for tea.

You will know from Dickens' account that Oliver did not speak up at the court, but he did let the tears flow and saved himself from Mr Gamfield's clutches. Soon after, as you will have read, Bumble apprenticed Oliver to Mr Sowerberry, the undertaker. If Noah Claypole had not intervened, Oliver might have become an undertaker in his turn and a very kind and sympathetic one he would have made.

But, in my need to relate the feelings and concerns of the young child I once was, I have run ahead of the whole story. Now I must turn back to an event which took place in the town just before my ninth birthday and Oliver's return to the workhouse.

CHAPTER THIRTY NINE

Behind all these events I have related was the shadow of William White pulling the strings. In bad times, and the poor of Myddlington had certainly experienced these, people look for someone to blame. The poor had long since identified this person as William White. To the poor, this man was the very Devil. Looking back through the mistiness of memory, they claimed there had been a time when the workhouse had been a refuge for those who survived to old age and for the orphaned children of those who did not. They recalled how a few shillings, a little food and medicine given as outdoor relief had seen them through bad times, while allowing them to retain their independence and dignity.

But the anger and disgust of the powerless poor was not even a minor irritation to William White or to anyone else who had power to influence events. Some sympathized with the poor, but most, privately or publicly, were more than willing to give White his head while they counted the money they had saved in taxes. It was an event which took place as the Old Year of 1832 gave way to the New Year of 1833, which swung the views of those who mattered against the man in the white waistcoat.

By midday on the last day of the year, one set of weather prophets, going by the menacing sky with its low, grey clouds reflecting a strange and unearthly light, swore it would snow within the hour. Opposing prophets, basing their prophecies on their twinges and the icy chill in their bones, declared with equal certainty and shaking of their heads, that it was much too cold for snow.

As he looked at the heavy, grey sky, John Baxter's anxiety for his family increased. At daybreak, he had left them in the deserted, derelict cottage where they had taken refuge on their arrival in the town the evening before. He had told them that, if he had found no work by midday, he would go to the overseer and seek outdoor relief in the form of a little fuel and a loaf and cheese to see them through another night. Since leaving their home fifty miles away to seek work in London, they had used up the little money they had put by for the journey and had been forced into this hand-to-mouth existence. As winter deepened, a carpenter's work had been harder and harder to come by and there was more than enough local labour competing for odd jobs. Today had been a repetition of the last ten days. There was no work. He would have to seek relief. And, by the look of the weather, he would have to plead for a few pence for the family to find a room in a lodging house.

By the time the first covering of snow had proved the first group of prophets to be correct, John Baxter had visited the overseer. As usual, he had been directed here and there in pursuit of that official as he moved around on his own business. He had been forced to tell his story over and over again and absorb the contempt or indifference of those he spoke to. When he had, after trudging half way round the town, caught up with the overseer, he had received the unexpected news that there was no outdoor relief to be had in Myddlington.

To receive food and shelter, he was told, he and his family would have to enter the workhouse. Having received this news, John Baxter should, by now, have been on his way to fetch his family, but his feet just would not turn in that direction. His hatred of the workhouse made him cling to the vain hope that help could still be found outside. When the overseer had said that he did not make the rules and it was William White and the Board who did that, Baxter had demanded their names and set off to visit each one and explain, simply, that he could not find work once he was confined to the workhouse. If they would give him nothing for himself, he would go without yet again, but they would surely not begrudge relief for his wife and his three children.

As the snow fell faster and faster and thicker and thicker, he set out for William White's house, but, when he asked directions, he was told it was well out of town and, unless he was familiar with the area, he would miss the turning and landmarks, now being rapidly disguised by a blanket of white. He decided to concentrate on the Board members living within the town, only to find the first two he visited shrugged their shoulders and said they could do nothing. They directed him to Mr Limbkins' shop.

By now, the town was engulfed by a blizzard. The streets were emptying rapidly. Even had people been able to keep their eyes open against the blustering wind, they would not have been able to see their way through the thick, whirling flakes, which appeared to be uniting into a solid mass even before falling upon the roofs and ground. With the snow's falling upon the previous night's ice, the roads were treacherous and it was against all reason to remain in the open. But John Baxter's hatred of the workhouse over-rode reason.

Outside Limbkins' shop, he paused to brush snow from his coat and kick snow from his boots. It gave him time to realise that the snow had penetrated through both coat and boots to his flesh.

He welcomed the warmth of the shop, which hit him as he opened the door and stepped inside, but the smell of hams and cheese assailed his empty stomach, making him feel faint and confused.

"May I be of service, sir?" the shopman asked, eyeing his new customer up and down and deciding he was good for no more than a halfpenny worth of broken odds and ends of something or other.

John struggled to collect his wits about him. "I've been directed to Mr Limbkins' to ask for a small amount of outdoor relief for my family."

The shopman made a noise which might have been a low whistle or a sucking in of air between his teeth. The shaking of his head, which accompanied this sound, made it clear what the answer would be. "'E won't welcome you coming in and asking in the shop," the man said, but, seeing the weariness which showed, not only in Baxter's face but in his whole body, he added, "I'll call 'im and you can ask."

Limbkins came from the back of the shop, where he had been counting the day's takings. "This weather'll cut into my profits," he muttered, as he emerged. He must have heard what was going on for, without waiting for Baxter to speak, he announced, "If you want help from the parish, this ain't the place to find it. My business and the parish business is two separate and different things."

Bending forward to replace a ham, the shopman smiled to himself. Mr Limbkins would not have concerned himself with parish affairs, but for the orders he received for substandard goods for the workhouse and best quality ones for the Whites.

"You ain't from this parish, are you?" Limbkins demanded, making it clear from his tone that outsiders had no right to help.

"No, sir," John replied. Even he could see that the situation was hopeless. The little strength he had left seemed to ebb from his body, but he struggled to continue. "I'm passing through looking for work. It's my wife and children what need 'elp, sir." He began to explain his position, but Limbkins intervened.

"No outdoor relief. No exceptions." As Baxter tried to speak, Limbkins raised his hand and continued. "I've heard all the stories what have ever been spun by your kind. Half of 'em ain't true. I've discovered that."

Baxter was too tired to argue or to make a decision about what to do next. He just stood, looking as wretched as any man had ever looked. Eager to get rid of him and put up the shutters against the storm, Limbkins added, as though he were being considerate and generous, "Tell you what. Try Mr Clack at the vicarage. He's on the workhouse Board and on the Charity Board what gives help to the deserving poor. He'll be able to sort something out for you."

Past making up his own mind what to do, John Baxter felt grateful for being given advice on what to do next. A great anxiety for his family filled his mind, but he was too confused by hunger and tiredness to realise that he should give up his search for that day and return to them.

Leaving the shop, he made for the church, its tower now just a faint outline in the blustering snow. As he approached the vicarage, it did not even occur to him to knock at the front door, but he trudged wearily to the back and rang the bell. The door was opened by a young maid, who heard John out and then shouted the request, as she understood it, to the cook in the kitchen.

"It's a scruffy man 'oo sez 'is wife and children need food and shelter. 'Is wife's expecting another any day. They're passing through to get work. 'E's a carpenter and ain't worked in no more than odd jobs for a month nor more. No one won't give 'em nothing. Mr Limbkins told 'im to come and ask Mr Clack."

As the warmth of the kitchen flowed over John, he felt suddenly sleepy. The girl seemed to be talking about someone else and he was detached from everything around him.

From the kitchen, the cook's voice sounded out loud and clear. "Well, don't stand there with the door open and all the cold blowing straight in. And don't let 'im come in 'ere with wet boots. The floor's just been done for the 'undreth time. Tell 'im to go to the front door and I'll let Mr Clack know 'e's there. 'E's wasting 'is time, though. Some people think they can get anything at this time of the year when it's the New Year coming up. And a bit of snow! Well, that brings all the beggars out, don't it?"

Obediently and without question, John dragged his feet to the front door and waited. For minutes, no one came. Then a servant came, but did not open the door. He was waiting for Mr Clack to arrive and ask for it to be opened. Suddenly, to John Baxter, the world seemed to spin out of control. As if it were from afar off, he heard a stern voice order, "Stay close by,

Jones. These beggars can become quite violent when they are refused money, especially if they have been drinking in the ale house."

The door was opened the smallest degree, and Mr Clack peered out reluctantly into the blizzard . In his effort to stop himself falling, John leaned against the wall and, in an effort to clear his head, closed his eyes and shook his head from side to side. He was about to relate his story yet again, when Mr Clack exploded in disgust, "The fellow is drunk. He can no longer support himself on his own two feet." With all the dignity of his office in the church, he went on. "The charity is for the deserving poor, my man. Seldom has an applicant appeared less deserving."

With a great effort, John struggled to tell his story again. Mr Clack listened impatiently for a short while and then held up his hand for John to stop.

"I have wasted enough time here. Let me reach the point at once. Have you a letter signed by two local and respectable people to say that you are a case deserving our aid?"

Not wanting to see all his chances of help disappearing by a straight, "No", John Baxter tried to protest that he had only just arrived in the area and knew no one. "Please,sir," John pleaded in desperation, "let me have just a little food for my wife and family."

"The workhouse," the vicar said firmly, "will provide you with a simple meal in return for honest work picking oakum."

"I'm a skilled man and 'ave always paid my own way until now. I 'ave done all that's 'umanly possible to find work," John told him. Then he added, "I've my pride, sir. I was brought up in the work'ouse and I swore when I left that I would never return. That proves I have always tried to be independent and support myself and my family." John was swaying slightly with tiredness and his voice expressed his exasperation with the vicar's response.

"Don't use that tone to me, my man," Mr Clack told him. He expected men to respect his office, which he, himself, held in high regard. "The matter is closed. You have clearly been drinking and now seek to replace the money you have wasted. You should have thought of your family when you passed your money to the inn keeper. If you are really in need, you will take your family into the workhouse."

"But I 'ave my pride, sir." Stubbornly, with all other arguments becoming muddled in his tired brain, John repeated the point again.

"Pride!" Mr Clack declared. He was on his own territory now. "Pride is a deadly sin. It is to be condemned in a rich man, but it is even worse in a poor man, who has no cause for pride." Shivering in spite of the thick coat around his shoulders, Mr Clack ordered, "Shut the door, Jones. God has inspired me yet again. I was sitting in my library considering my sermon. Now I have the subject. Pride and all the evils to which it leads."

With the door shut in his face, John leaned against it for a moment and wept. He felt as weak as a child and as helpless. All he longed to do was fall on the snow and let it envelop him in sleep. With a great effort, he stood upright and trudged off, back to his wife and children.

CHAPTER FORTY

It was dark and long after the only sounds were the whistle of the wind and the clanking of shop signs, when an urgent tugging at the bell of the workhouse gave rise to a muffled sound and scattered a hail of frozen snow. Jack Star rose at once, threw on his greatcoat and stepped gingerly across the ice to peer out of the gate. Under the dangerously swinging lantern, now in shadow and now in light, stood a man with a child in his arms and his wife with two young children huddled around her skirts. It was clear from the woman's size that another birth was not far off.

"Can you let my family in, mister? They're starving 'ungry and starving cold."

In a second, Jack decided that he would let them in without authority and that he would not, as he had been ordered, poke the woman's stomach to make sure she was really expecting a child.

"Come in. I'll open the wicket "

When the gate was opened, John Baxter ushered his family in, but made no effort to enter himself.

"Come on," Jack urged impatiently. "It's bitter tonight."

"'E won't come in," the woman sobbed. She was clinging to her husband's arm.

Irritably, like a man at the very end of his tether, but making a great effort to speak gently and reassure his wife, John said, "It's only for a few hours, Beth. I'll be back outside at daybreak, ready for you to come out."

"You can't leave," Jack began, but no one was listening.

"Come in," the wife pleaded. "We must stay together." Her tone was almost as weary as her husband's and suggested she knew her pleading was in vain.

"It's only for a few hours," the man answered again. He was past all reasoned discussion and could only stubbornly repeat the same thing over again. He kissed her. "I'll be back for you at daylight." Patting the children's heads, he turned and made off into the night.

"Let's get you in, at least," Jack told the wife, "or you'll all be frozen statues by the morning." It was the wrong thing to say. That was what the wife already feared would be her husband's fate. Her sobbing became louder and more desperate.

With a great effort, as Jack pointed out that the children needed food and their beds, the woman struggled to dry her tears and lead them inside.

In the kitchen, Sal sat with her cronies debating which winter had been the worst they had known. Ignoring their own aches and pains, they rose and made way for the family around the fire.

"What'll we give 'em to eat?" Sally asked. "Everything's locked away these days."

"Fetch the keys," Jack ordered. "It'll be my 'ead what rolls and not yours."

Old Sal thought for a moment. "No, Jack. Get orf to bed. We're inmates. They can't sack us. We'll get the food."

"You're a good 'un, Sal, as I've said before, but I've got to find out what's 'appening 'ere."

Sal brought some bread and cheese, but the woman too concerned for her husband to eat.

"You must find 'im, sir," the wife told Jack.

"Where's 'e gone?" Sal asked.

"'As 'e got somewhere to go?" Martha wanted to know.

"I don't know where 'e is," the woman sobbed. "'E won't never set foot in a work'ouse 'owever bad things is. 'E sez 'e's taken an oath on it."

"A parish boy 'isself?" Jack asked, knowing the answer already. He took up his coat.

"'E'll not come with you," the woman told him. "If 'e won't come in for me and the children, 'e won't come in for you."

"Leave it to me," the porter reassured her. "There's many takes that oath as lives to break it."

The children, watching their mother, were weeping, too, by now. Like her, they had been hungry for so long that they had almost passed the stage of wanting, or being able, to eat. Sal cut up their bread and cheese into small pieces, the better to make it slip down.

"There, there, dearies," the old nurse urged. "You eat up and get to your beds. Leave it to Jack Star. 'E's the man what'll find your Pa."

In our ward, we were all awake by now. Sal had sent up a younger woman to warm a bed with Mrs Corney's warming pan full of hot, burning embers. It had long since been used to warm Mrs Corney's bed, but she insisted, for fear of fire or the scorching of her carpets and furniture, that it was removed from her room when she went to bed. She had no idea how frequently it was put to use long after she was asleep.

The rest of us had had our beds warmed by hot flat irons, but even two in a bed and wearing all our clothes, we felt the damp cold reflected off the stone walls. It seemed to eat through to our very bones. In the candlelight, as the children were brought to bed, we could see our breath turning to mist and no one even considered peering out far enough to ask what was going on. We tugged the blankets around us and could feel the damp where we had breathed onto them.

Even with the covers wrapped around our ears, we could hear the children's crying. After seeing their father leave, they had clung to their mother, only to be separated from her when they were sent to the children's ward, while she went to the women's. The workhouse was proving to be the dreadful place their father had always told them it was.

Jack Star had been wise to set off after John Baxter as soon as possible. Only by doing so had he given himself any chance of tracking the man's footsteps. Already, new snow had almost covered the mark of his boots, but, as Jack held the lantern high, it threw into relief the slight indentations, which remained. Following step by step to White's Yard, he paused to look around. It was impossible, in the wind, to hold the flame steady. As it spluttered, light and shadow lurched across the snow in rapid succession, but Jack could see that his quarry had walked to the gate and then retraced his steps to the lowest point in the wall. Here crushed and disturbed snow showed that John had climbed over, but it showed, too, that he had climbed back.

Making his way to the bars of the gate, Jack gazed through. It was too dark to see where the man had walked, once over the wall, but he guessed that he had been searching for the night-watchman and his fire. The watchman would have been forced inside one of the buildings and would not have heard, against the storm, anyone who called out. The man must have given up the search and returned to the town. Jack wondered why he had not chosen to shelter amongst the warehouses, but he knew tired and starving men could make foolish decisions.

Without wasting more time, Jack searched again for the trail leading along the High Street. He found John Baxter had walked along the middle of the road. Again, this had been a foolish decision. The wind howled through the tunnel made by the shops and houses, battering his body. A path along the side of the street would have offered some slight shelter. Jack struggled on, following the tracks down the centre of the road. He was becoming more and more concerned for the man. Anyone, with the least sense, would have knocked at a door and sought shelter on a night like this. His own eyes ached from the reflection of the lantern on the stark white snow and his limbs ached with the effort of moving forward in the thick drifts. He walked wearily on and on, until he suddenly realised that, in this strange world of silence and of featureless white, edged by deep blackness, he was no longer using his reason, but simply repeating the same action, the same step, over and over, long after any trace of footsteps had disappeared. Forcing himself to stop, he tried to think what was the most sensible thing to do. The man could have knocked at any house. He could have slipped into any side lane or court seeking shelter or even broken into a shed to get out of the biting wind. Weary himself, Jack hardly felt able to work out where an even more weary man had gone. Long ago, the church clock had chimed in the New Year and there was no sign of life, no light from any window and no sound, but that of the storm. Frozen and exhausted, Jack returned to the workhouse to sleep for a few hours and thaw his frozen bones.

CHAPTER FORTY ONE

It was Jack, the first person up and about in the morning, who found John Baxter's body. The carpenter had sort some refuge in a shop doorway, but starved of food and warmth, had fallen first into slumber and then, imperceptibly, into unconsciousness. All life had ebbed away in the bitter cold of the night.

Kneeling down beside him, Jack tried gently to brush the snow from his face, but the snow had frozen. Pausing, Jack realised that he had been trying to reveal the man's features, hoping for some clue as to why John Baxter had died in this way. Had he, cold, hungry and confused, struggled to fight off death? Or had he welcomed it as an end to his suffering in this life where people did not take care of their neighbours and good Samaritans were nowhere to be found.

Abandoning such pointless thoughts, the porter tried, in vain, to straighten the man's twisted and frozen limbs. It seemed important that, in death at least, John Baxter should have some dignity. He knocked at the door of the shop, but the milliner refused to let him lift the body inside.

"My ladies," she explained, curling her nose in disgust, "do not expect to see a dead body when they come to buy a hat." She ordered the shopboy to fetch Sowerberry.

"Suppose it'll be a pauper funeral," the undertaker moaned, in a tone which suggested it was hardly worth his coming out on a day like this. "Still," he went on, "it's all business."

"Thank God for small mercies," Jack said, contemptuously.

"What happened to respect for your betters?" Sowerberry asked. Everybody, dead or alive, was strictly ranked in social order in Sowerberry's world. A porter ranked well below an undertaker in his eyes.

"What happened to respect for the dead?" Jack countered.

"He'll have to go back to the workhouse," Sowerberry decided.

"That's where I were taking 'im," Jack said, "but I were trying to spare his wife the sight of' 'im trussed up like an animal."

"The relict," Sowerberry corrected him in a voice of authority. "In the trade, she is known as the relict."

At that moment, Mr Carson pushed through the gathering crowd. "Take him into my shop."

As Jack and the bookseller lifted the body, an unmistakable voice uttered in a solemn and commanding tone, "Leave that body. Paupers is my business." Bumble was taking command.

"He was never a pauper," Jack Star pointed out.

"Thanks to you, sir, his wife and children is. We'll have to give him a pauper funeral and pray we get the money back from his parish."

Sowerberry made a mental note to charge a little more if another parish was paying.

Turning to Sowerberry, Bumble commanded, "Bury him smartish, sir. The sooner He's buried, the sooner we can send his family back to where they come from." He added, in a tone which suggested he found such behaviour in paupers most unreasonable, "'Is wife won't go 'til he's buried."

"It's a good job I had the forethought to leave the pauper hole open after the last interment," Sowerberry congratulated himself. "There'd be no opening it up in this frost."

Jack, still anxious to spare the wife any more distress than necessary, took the body, with Mr Craven's help, into the workhouse. "

Doesn't she know?" Bumble asked. "I'll warn Sally there's a job for her." He rushed off in the direction of the workhouse. "Loves to be the bearer of dramatic news, that one does," Jack commented.

He was right. Ten minutes later Mrs Baxter arrived, distraught with grief, one minute blaming herself for letting her husband wander off into the night and the next minute blaming him for deserting his family.

"It was 'im made the choice 'isself," Jack told her. "You must never blame yourself nor 'im. 'E 'ad 'is pride. Now, go back to your children, while I bring your 'usband back for Sal to lay 'im out."

To Jack's surprise, once they were back at the workhouse and Sal was laying out the body, the old nurse muttered to herself and wept as she worked.

"I've done this 'undreds of times," Sally told the porter. "Strong men, frail old women, babies not a day old and never thought twice about it. Lately, I shivers at the sight of a dead body. They seems to stretch in a long line over the years and I sees meself on the end of the line."

Helping her, Jack let the old woman talk. There was clearly something on her mind.

"That pallor," she went on, "and the cold of the flesh. Death's coming for me soon, Jack. I feel 'is 'and upon me sometimes, as though it was another 'uman touching me."

"We've all got to die," Jack remarked, for want of something better to say.

"But will we all go to 'Eaven, Jack? I used to think I would. I lived as best I could and looked after me family and neighbours best I could."

"You're no worse than the rest of us Sal."

As though the corpse might hear, Sally lowered her voice. "I'm going to 'Ell for me sins, Jack. I wronged an innocent young woman what trusted me. I ain't going to 'Eaven."

If Jack had ever imagined the conversation he would have had with Sal while laying out the body, this was not it. To encourage her to talk and as he could think of nothing to say to comfort her in this mood, he kept silent.

Sal continued to mutter, half under her breath. Jack thought he heard the words 'ring' and 'locket', but could not make out any more.

At last, Jack, seeing her so distressed, asked, "Whatever it is, can't you put things right, Sal?"

"Put things right?" she asked herself and considered the question. "I'm too old to own up, Jack. They'll put me away. No, Jack, there's no owning up without getting me punishment 'ere on Earth. Sooner take me chance that God will 'ave mercy on me than expect it from a magistrate."

"Can't I 'elp you some way, Sal?"

Sally seemed not to have heard, but she was silent and Jack guessed that she was thinking the matter over.

Suddenly, Sally said, "Yes, you can 'elp me, Jack. But not yet. When I know me time 'as come—and please God I get more warning than this poor soul—I'll send for you and tell you the 'ole story. Come straight away and I'll give you something as'll put everything right. You're a man of the world, you'll know what to do with it."

Wondering what she meant, Jack recalled the number of times he had seen the old woman visiting the pawnshop and the pennies she had borrowed.

"What did you do, Sal, take something as weren't yours?"

Sal put her finger to her lips. "Shush! Someone might 'ear. Lowering her voice so that Jack could hardly make out her words, she whispered, "I ain't no thief. It were given to me to keep safe and it's still as safe as 'ouses. I still got it, in a manner of speaking. I ain't sold it. I ain't no thief, but some might think I am." Suddenly, she became her old self, busying herself with her task. "See 'e gets 'em back, that's all that's needed. You sort it out for 'im Jack and I'll get me through them pearly gates after all."

The funeral over with undue haste, Mrs Baxter gave birth, before time, to a baby girl. Both mother and child died in the cold, infection-ridden infirmary. The children were sent back to the parish from which they had come to grow up in the same workhouse their father had hated.

CHAPTER FORTY TWO

As bad luck would have it for William White, it was just at this time that, after repeated requests from that gentleman, visitors from London arrived to observe the working of White's scheme and report back to the Commission inquiring into the working of' poor relief throughout the kingdom. As good luck would have it, this brought my interests and William White's together for the one and only time in our entire lives.

The coroner's jury had just decided, as Dickens reports, that the tradesman, John Baxter, who had died in the shop doorway, had, "Died from exposure to the cold, and want of the common necessaries of life." William White knew all his one-time allies would desert him. They would forget all the advantages they had received, often at his expense, and fall over each other to free themselves of any blame in the case. To save his scheme, he required a spy to tell what these people said when interviewed by the visitors.

While William White was fuming over his problems, I was growing more and more restless. After just five minutes of picking oakum each day, I wanted to throw the stuff in Stamp's face and rush, screaming in anger and frustration, out of the workhouse and into the outside world. There, I was sure, I could find my best friend, Paul, and satisfy the need, which seemed to grow more and more desperate over the years, to find my parents. I needed to be free of the workhouse and, as I saw it, begin my life.

This was the situation when William White sent for me. Looking me up and down, he seemed to see me for the first time. For the first time, he addressed me by name.

"People tell me, Nathaniel Swubble, that you are a clever boy, older than your years. Quick to learn, with a good memory. And you can read."

"Yes, sir." I stood up straight, with my arms at my side, sure that I looked smart and alert.

"Let me tell you something about life, boy. You are nobody without powerful friends. If I had had such friends, I would not have been forced into this plan, into dependence on idiots, to make my name. Now, I can be such a friend to you, if you make yourself useful to me."

Not sure what comment this called for, I remained at attention and tried to look even more alert.

"Once these men have left Myddlington," White explained, "I intend to put all boys over ten years of age out to work in what," he sneered, "are euphemistically called apprenticeships. Such apprenticeships, Swubble, are nothing more than unpaid drudgery in unpleasant trades. They lead to nothing in life except labouring work. Do you understand?"

"Yes, sir," I replied, just to show that I was paying attention. I sensed that a carrot was about to be dangled before me.

"I need a lad like you to act as messenger for these visitors. A boy who can be always at hand. A boy who can listen, remember and repeat to me all that is said. Do I make myself clear? Are you such a boy, Swubble?"

In anticipation of a reward, I was quick to say, "I can do that, sir." I had, after all, been doing much the same as errand boy to the Board. I had listened and remembered, even if I had not repeated everything.

"Do this well, Swubble, and I shall be your friend. I shall give you work in the Yard. Just an errand boy to start with, but it will be up to you what you make of your chance. Work hard and, at fourteen, there will be a real apprenticeship for you with any of the craftsmen who work there." Obviously searching his own past to think of something which might appeal to a ten year old, he went on, "Or you might want to be a boatman or the driver of a coach."

"Could I be a clerk, sir?"

"Why not, Swubble? This task I am giving you will be good training. You must try to read anything the gentlemen write down about what they see and are told."

"I'm your man, sir," I told him. This would put my foot on the first step of the ladder of my career. I saw a future stretching up to manager, or even owner, and I would be able to hear news of Paul from men travelling to and fro on the canal. I would be free to search for my family.

Even before the delegation arrived, the gossip was that no one of importance was being sent to Myddlington. It was said that all the important evidence presented to the Commission elsewhere had, in fact, been mulled over and proposals for the future already decided upon. No one would have been sent, it was said, but for the Commission's wish to keep those who ran the workhouse happy, so that they would willingly apply the new law, when it eventually came into force.

On the appointed day, two clerks arrived. To me, they looked very severe and important, but I gathered that, in London, they were very small fish. I did not accompany Mr White and his guests around the workhouse and was not present when they examined the books. Afterwards, I did hear them expressing their private doubts on the total cost. They guessed that Mr White had put in some of his own money to make it appear that he had successfully cut the cost of poor relief in the town by a considerable amount.

It was the afternoon, after they had asked Mr White to leave, that I was sent to make myself useful to them. This was the time when members of the Board were lining up, eager to rid themselves of any blame for John Baxter's death.

Mr Limbkins came first, bringing with him some choice cheeses as a gift for the clerks. To my surprise, and even more to his, they politely declined the gift, saying they wished to remain above any accusation of bribery. Mr Limbkins, playing his role as the bluff, honest tradesman with no other aim in life but that of serving God and his neighbours, decided that expressing outrage at this suggestion might offend the men and merely sat with an expression of hurt and innocent confusion on his face. But the strain of the situation made him reach for a large handkerchief with which to wipe his brow.

"Well, gentlemen, what would you like to ask me?" he enquired, in the tone of a simple man with nothing to hide.

"We understood, the more junior of the two clerks replied, "that it was you who requested to see us."

"Only to answer any questions you might have, sirs, and clear up any little misunderstandings which may have arisen." Uncertain as to whether to bring up the subject of John Baxter or hope the men had not heard about this death, Limbkins sat awkwardly, and applied the handkerchief to his brow with some vigour.

"You are referring, Mr Limbkins, to the death of the unfortunate tradesman, who died recently in a shop doorway?" the senior clerk asked, in a voice which seemed neither to condemn nor rage at the event. It gave Mr Limbkins the impression that one death in a little town was nothing to these men who, if born with any emotions, had seen them wither long ago.

At once, he decided that no form of apology or explanation was required. An expression of regret would be enough to put him in a good light.

"All the town, sirs, is in deep mourning for the poor man. A tragedy! A tragedy for his whole family. A tragedy for the town. We are well known as good Christian folk."

"You think the jury's verdict was mistaken?" The clerk's tone was as unemotional as ever.

"I think, sirs," Limbkins continued, reciting the speech he had prepared with his friends beforehand, "It did not go far enough. The culprit went unnamed and unpunished."

"The culprit, Mr Limbkins?"

"Certainly, sir. There is one man to blame for the policy which led to the man's death. That man," he added dramatically, "is William White."

"But you, Mr Limbkins, are the chairman."

"In name only, sirs. In name only." This defence, having been rehearsed by Mr Limbkins many time before the mirror and to his wife, was spoken in a firm voice. It was only the quick wipe of his brow which revealed that he realised he was not out of the woods yet.

Continuing his speech, Limbkins turned to condemning White's whole scheme. "No outdoor relief! We, in Myddlinton, have never begrudged an applicant outdoor relief. We ..."

"You sir, the citizens of Myddlington, allowed taxes to rise to the skies with your previous policy."

In his turn, Limbkins was quick to interrupt, delaying his next wipe of his brow until he had finished. "It was our wish to correct this, sirs, which made us reluctantly go along with Mr White's heartless plan."

"I think I might say," the senior clerk announced, "that the Commission sees the withdrawal of outdoor relief as the possible solution to the high and unsustainable cost of relief."

Feeling the need to wipe his palms as well as his forehead, Limbkins played for time.

"It's a case, sirs, of keeping the balance, gentlemen," the grocer began again, as though revealing a deep truth known only to grocers. "That's what I've learnt in my trade. No tipping of the scales, that's my style, sir. My customers get what they are charged for. Ask anyone in the town. Honest Limbkins they all...." Limbkins had not noted that he was rambling. It was second nature to him and it was so much less worrying to talk about groceries than the death of John Baxter. But both clerks were coughing to signal their impatience.

"Tell us simply, in your own words, how this death came about, Mr

Limbkins. The man came to your shop, we understand." The grocer, having relaxed sufficiently to replace his handkerchief in his pocket, took it out again.

"Yes, he came to my shop, gentleman," Mr Limbkins began slowly, wondering how he could return to his carefully prepared defence. "But me hands were tied. Tied tight, you might say, behind me back. Mr White, he's the one who runs things. He made the rules. No outdoor relief. There were no funds, sirs, no funds to cover a case like that. I ain't got no funds to hand out over the counter." A thought occured to Limbkins. "Even if we had had outdoor relief, I weren't the person to hand it out."

"You do not believe in private charity, Mr Limbkins? You could not have handed the man a few pence from your own purse or goods from your shop? Mr White has no say over your own finances."

Mr Limbkins busied himself with his handkerchief, which now served the dual purpose of drying his skin and giving him time to think. His face and voice expressed his relief when an answer came into his mind at last.

"Oh dear no, sir. Reluctantly, most reluctantly, us tradesmen have had to refuse to give private charity to them as asks for it. If I was to give a man sixpence or a bit of ham or cheese just 'cos he asked, you'd find he went straight to the butcher for scraps of meat and to the baker for a pie and round the whole town for anything he could get." Mr Limbkins laughed in contempt of the very idea. "No one'd pay for anything and the town'd be full of beggars. That's real life, sirs, something what I suspect you don't see much of up in your offices in London."

The two clerks smiled grimly to themselves.

"Don't mean, mind," Limbkins went on with growing confidence, knowing these men could not verify his claims,"that we don't give money to charity, but we give it through Mrs White's charity, official like, not haphazard."

The clerks' faces expressed no emotion or thought.

"You sent the tradesman to this charity to ask for help, we understand."

"You are informed correctly, gentleman." Limbkins replied with confidence and with the handkerchief returned to his pocket. "I considered him a upright character with an independent turn of mind. Considered him an ideal candidate for the charity."

"But the charity required a letter of recommendation. Did you provide him with one?"

The handkerchief reappeared and was put to use for some seconds. Smiling and shaking his head to imply that the clerks could have no idea of the situation at the time, Limbkins replied, "Gentlemen, there was a storm. I knew Mrs Limbkins, in her poor state of health, would be worrying about me. And me children would be worried for their Pa. I was trying to put up shutters and secure the shop. I sent him over," he explained and then, with sudden inspiration added, "I told him to say he had my recommendation. I thought that way would be quicker for him and for me than writing a letter." Inspired once again, Limbkins confessed, "To be honest, sirs, writing ain't something I can claim to have mastered to any great degree. Mrs Limbkins does all the accounts."

"But it seems to have appeared to the vicar that you had simply sent Mr Baxter to him without sending him, if you take my point," the younger clerk said. "The important point was to make it clear that he came with your recommendation. Did you do this?"

For a few seconds Limbkins looked puzzled and then realised this was his way out. Sighing, the grocer agreed, "That, sirs, is where the confusion seems to have arisen. I sent him to say as how I were behind the request, but Mr Clack thought as how I had – well, how I had just sent 'im."

"Precisely," the elder clerk stated. The other nodded.

In obvious relief, Limbkins wiped his head and hands and returned the handkerchief to his pocket.

"So, what is your conclusion about this affair, gentlemen?" Limbkins asked, convinced he had cleared himself of all blame.

"We are not here, sir, to place blame on one particular case. We are here to take evidence and that is not complete."

"Of course. Of course," Limbkins muttered, wondering whether he could ask the one question he had come to ask. He decided that he could. "I hope there will be no bar on me giving me services to the town on the Board when the new law comes into force."

"That will be up to the electors as it has always been, Mr Limbkins."

Limbkins went away happy, the late John Baxter dismissed from his mind. Few others wanted the thankless task of running poor relief. It had always been left to those tradesmen with something to gain. That was the way it was to continue, new law or no new law.

Other townspeople, one after the other, tried to tell the same story. Mr White deserved all the blame. Eventually, with the last one gone, the senior clerk told the junior, "Let us return to London with all speed and shake the dust of this place from our feet."

"We must dine with William White, first," he was reminded.

I remembered that I had to report immediately to Mr White. Tidying away chairs, I made enough noise to remind them that I had not been dismissed. Once they indicated that I was, I turned to go.

"One moment, lad," the junior called after me. "How would you describe life in the workhouse?"

Where was I to begin? As I shrugged my shoulders in confusion, I turned up the palms of my hands, red and raw from picking oakum.

"The child has hands like a prisoner," one observed in a low voice.

"It ain't just me 'ands, sir, what's suffered. If I could show you me mind, you'd see it were empty."

"Have you never been to school?"

I told them all that had happened. They listened patiently and sympathetically and then each gave me a penny for my trouble.

After I reported every word I could remember to Mr White, he looked far from pleased. As I finished, he muttered angrily, "Rats all of them, deserting the ship they caused to sink."

"You ain't sinking, are you, sir?" I asked, like everyone else looking out for my own interest. "They say you own 'alf the town and could own the other 'arf if you put your mind to it."

To my surprise, Mr White laughed. "Worried that I cannot keep my promise? Report to Mr Campion in the Yard first thing in the morning."

Of course, I can not give a personal account of all that happened at the White's house that evening. In general, servants only reported what was unusual and let everything else float over their heads. They did not report, for example, that Mr White had repeatedly hinted that it would be to the clerks' interest to promote his name to their masters in London. They did tell people the surprising news that the senior clerk had spoken up and said, with great dignity, that they did not accept gifts of any kind from anyone. In the same way, they were not surprised that the clerks agreed with White's refusal to give outdoor relief, but were amazed that they pointed to the lack of schooling for children.

Jack learned something of their overall impression from the butler, an intelligent man and one who could understand the speech of educated men. According to him, Mr White repeatedly asked their opinion of his experiment, as he called it.

Eventually, after raising several particular points, the senior clerk replied, "We have learned one important lesson from our visit. It is that there is a vast difference between the letter and the spirit of the law. We have little quarrel with the letter of the law you have put into practice here. The death of the tradesman, however, is a stark symbol of everyone's failure to bear in mind the spirit of the law. The spirit of the law is to help, with reasonable expense to the taxpayer, those in dire distress and to train children and adults to be independent of help and contented in their work."

Mrs White, the butler reported, then defended her son, saying the death was not his fault and Mr Baxter would have been helped by her charity, had Mr Clack not misinterpreted the rules.

"Exactly, madam," the younger clerk had exclaimed. "Again, we see the letter of the law winning over its spirit."

"I can see," the senior man continued, "this is our greatest problem. However well we frame the new law in London, there are people who will keep to the letter of that law, forgetting its spirit."

"Inspectors will go some way to correct this," the other clerk put in.

"Not as long," William White had complained, "as there are fools like Limbkins and Clack enforcing it."

Of the conversation which took place between William White and his mother when the guests had left, little was known. It was reported, that, in the morning, White had commanded the servants to burn a pile of books he had thrown around the library. They were all concerned with the poor laws and suggested remedies for the evils of poverty.

It was clear Mr White had given up his plan to make his name by that route.

CHAPTER FORTY THREE

Early next morning, I dressed in my new clothes. They were new to me, that is, but second or third hand in anyone else's eyes. Each workhouse child was given such clothes on going out into the world. My smile, as I approached the gate must have stretched from ear to ear.

"'Appy to be leaving us, then?" Jack asked, knowing full well what the answer would be. "Let's inspect you to see everything's shipshape."

I slowly turned around, keen that I should look the part on my first day at work.

"Tuck your shirt in, Nat, and see you do it every day when I'm not there to remind you."

This reminded me that, happy as I was to be leaving the workhouse, I would miss seeing Jack whenever I needed his advice or support. Awkwardly, I held my hand out to him. The short speech he had so carefully prepared slipped out of his mind. As we shook hands like men of the world, he blurted out the few parts of his speech he could recall.

"Be a man, Nat. Stand up for yourself and for others when they need your 'elp. Try not to do anything in the 'eat of the moment what you'll regret later." Selfconsciously, he added, "Try and make England a better place."

"Yes, sir," I replied, realising this was what he tried to do himself. I was keen to be off, but suddenly remembered Old Sally. Telling Jack that I would not be a moment, I ran up to the infirmary. The old woman was dozing in a chair. More and more, since the death of her son, she had seemed to escape into her own world, created from her memories of happier times long ago.

"'Oo is it?" she demanded, apparently irritated at being recalled from the past.

"It's me Sal, Nat Swubble."

Smiling weakly, she asked, "'Oo could forget someone with a name like that?"

"I'm orf, Sal," I told her and heard myself add melodramatically, "to make me way in the world."

"Rather you than me," she mumbled. "Me, I've seen and 'eard enough of the world to last me a life-time." But, for a moment, her old curiosity

229

returned. "Where you orf to, then?"

"To White's Yard."

"One of me sons went there. Can't recall which one it were. 'Ope you stay longer than 'im. A week and they give 'im 'is marching orders."

I did not comment. I had heard he was sacked for stealing. Once again, the old woman seemed lost in her own world. Awkwardly, I kissed her cheek.

"Bye, Sal, be good."

This brought a toothless grin on Sal's face.

"Weren't I always? Not," she smirked, "like that porter down there." In a hurry not to be late on my first day, I ignored this little private joke of hers and turned to go. Her next remark brought me quickly back to her side.

"Ain't Jack told you 'oo your parents were yet?"

"Does 'e know?" Suddenly, I found it hard to breathe.

"E knows something, that's for sure. Watched 'im meself come down the street that morning with you in 'is arms. Watched 'im put you down on the ground by the gate. Then 'e come into the work'ouse. Suppose 'e just waited for someone to find you and bring you in."

Perhaps I had misunderstood her. Demanding reassurance that I was not imagining what I was hearing, I tried to make her repeat everything. "Jack? Jack Star put me down outside?"

"Ain't that just what I said?"

"But your memory," I suggested as tactfully as I could, "ain't it a bit.... well, don't it give you a bit of trouble now and again?"

"'Bout what 'appened yesterday, maybe," she claimed impatiently, "but ten years ago? I remember that like it were yesterday."

Sal's mind wandered off again. Perhaps it had been wandering all along. Like a sleepwalker, I went downstairs and out of the gate. Fortunately, Jack was not there at that moment and Mr Campion was just passing.

"Move yourself, Nat," he told me. "I've been telling Mr White for weeks that you're the kind of bright boy we need in the Yard. Here you are looking as though you haven't woken up fully yet."

This remark brought me back from the confusion into which Sally's remarks had thrown me. I hurried along by his side.

"Now," Mr Campion told me, "Make a good impression on Mr White. Couldn't get him to agree to your working in the Yard until yesterday. Didn't want any boys from the workhouse. Don't know what made him change his mind."

I did and I hoped he would stick to his word to be my friend. Not my real friend, that was, but the man to further my career. The man himself, I hated as everyone else did.

CHAPTER FORTY FOUR

Perhaps I had imagined everyone in the Yard would know of my arrival and be ready to welcome me. Instead, I was assigned general duties by a foreman, who then handed me over to one of his men, who passed me down the line without even asking my name. Eventually, I reached the end of the chain, a boy called Edward Reddy, whose father worked in the Yard. Edward made it clear, by his every action, that he had been forced, against his will, to follow in the paternal footsteps. For a few days we edged around each other like young stags establishing our positions, but I had little real choice. I was the younger and the newcomer and tradition stated that I had to do as ordered by this young tyrant. As soon as he realised that I would do anything rather than be dismissed, he soon had me doing his work as well as my own.

As to accommodation, to start with I boarded with a widow recommended by Jack. She had impressed him as kind and friendly and eager to help a young parish boy. It did not take me long to realise that these virtues were extended only to Jack and that I was tolerated as a route by which she might become better acquainted with him. Mrs Hodges had a son, Charles, a charity school boy, who was the apple of her eye. To me he was friendly and accepting, but, as the lion's share of any meal and all the tit-bits were put on his plate, I could see no reason for him to be anything else. Somehow, Mrs Hodges had it firmly fixed in her mind that, as her son was so easygoing, he would, without a father's influence, be led astray. In other words, she was looking for a husband. More particularly, as she did not want other children in the house, she was seeking a single man or a widower without children.

In the evenings, she quizzed me about Mr Bumble and about Jack, both candidates on her list. She tended to favour Bumble as a better class of person, but I encouraged her to find out as much as she could about Jack. Ever since my last meeting with Sal, her words had crept back into my mind a hundred times a day. Not wishing to give the impression of being a daydreamer in my new work, I had forced such thoughts to the back of my mind. Did I want Jack to be my father? I was not sure about that. When I thought about it, I felt, to be honest, that there was nothing to be gained from this. I respected Jack, but he was already my friend and mentor, whether he was my father or not. Now I realised that, secretly, I wanted my father to be a scholar and a gentleman and, even, to find myself advanced in the world by finding him. Still, if Sally was to be believed, it was Jack who would lead me to my real father. I did all I could to encourage Mrs Hodges to inquire into his personal affairs.

"Does Mr Star have a lady friend, Nat?" she asked one day, in her most innocent voice.

"Never seen one," I laughed. It was a kind of joke, that I did not fully understand, that Jack was not interested in ladies. He had to put up with a lot of jokes about sailors and would often get very angry with people who teased him in that way. My latest theory, since my talk with Sal, was that his wife, my mother, had died in childbirth and that was why he had brought me to be near him in the workhouse. With my warm endorsement of Jack's good qualities and Bumble's bad ones, I persuaded Mrs Hodges to make it her business to discover all she could about him. I hinted that his heart might have been broken and that was why he had not married.

It was a few days later when the subject was raised again.

"Well, well," Mrs Hodges announced one evening, as I washed the dishes. "Your Jack Star knows how to keep a secret."

"What about?" I asked, trying to keep my voice as casual as possible, even though my heart was racing.

"Your precious Jack has a lady friend. I see you didn't know that, did you? Had one these twelve years. Almost as long as he's lived in these parts."

"Where?" I demanded eagerly. "'Oo? When's 'e see 'er ?"

"I wish," Mrs Hodges sighed, "that you would take a little more trouble with your speech. I'm coming to think that you are a bad influence on my dear boy."

Charles pulled a face and winked at me, but I was concentrating on his mother's words.

"I promise I'll try to speak proper," I said. "Just tell me about Jack's friend."

"I don't know that children should talk about such things. If Jack Star chooses to lead innocent women on, that is no concern of yours."

With an instinct above my years, I fell quiet. Only a minute later, Mrs Hodges took up her story again.

"She's the housekeeper to Miss Aldbury. Though what a respectable woman in such a position can see in a workhouse porter, I'll never know."

"Why ain't... 'aven't they got married then, Mrs Hodges?" I asked in my most polite way.

"That's it, isn't it? That's why he's so taken with her and she, foolish woman is taken in by him."

Once again, I waited silently for her to continue.

"It seems that some years ago, now, Miss Aldbury was very ill and Miss Frampton, that's the hussy's name, looked after her. Miss Aldbury made her promise to stay and look after her as long as she lived. In return, if the housekeeper gave up all thoughts of marriage, Miss Aldbury promised her a cottage and a good pension in her will. She'll want for nothing. What man could offer more than that? And, meanwhile, she has good food and accommodation and, I'm told, an excellent salary. Miss Aldbury calls the woman a treasure."

"So she won't marry Jack?"

"Not until the old lady dies. A nice little set-up he'll walk into. Well worth waiting for, but," she added, with some satisfaction, "I don't expect they knew Miss Aldbury would last so long."

I sat thinking all of this over. I knew women could have children only up to a certain age. Perhaps Miss Frampton and Jack had decided to have me while there was still time and keep me a secret. Jack had always said that I could live with him when he had a place of his own. He must have known that meant the three of us would live together one day. I was mulling all this over, when Mrs Hodges spoke again.

"You had better go and pack the few belongings you have into a bundle. I've decided you're a bad influence on my boy. I don't want him to end up speaking like a parish boy."

Charles pulled a face at me, to show me he did not care how I spoke. And he laughed when I poked out my tongue behind his mother's back. Perhaps she was right that he would go his own way, one day when he summed up the energy.

CHAPTER FORTY FIVE

Once again, Mr Campion promised to find lodgings for me, and I was about to look for him at the end of the day when Edward Reddy called to me.

"'Ere you," he yelled, aiming to attract everyone's attention as well as mine, "You're coming 'ome with me."

"Why?" I demanded in astonishment. If anyone had consulted me on where I wanted to stay, Edward Reddy's house would have been the last place I would have named.

"Why? Why?" he mimicked. "You sound like a baby. 'Cos you're lodging with us, that's why."

"With you?" I queried, reluctant to accept this as the truth.

"And look smart about it," Eddy advised, no doubt repeating the words he had heard from his father many times. "Or your'll go without and learn manners that way."

As I walked slowly towards him, he added in his gravelly, loud voice, "Ain't me what wants a work'ouse brat in the 'ouse. It's me Ma. She's soft 'earted, ain't she?"

The way his friends, from whom he had sought confirmation of this fact, laughed, I guessed her tender-heartedness did not even extend to her own son let alone to me. Casually, like a slave master, Edward ordered me to carry his box and to walk behind him.

"If I want to talk to you, I'll yell at you over me shoulder. You don't speak unless you're spoken to." Without looking back, he added by way of explanation, "It's me duty to learn you 'ow to be'ave, seeing no one else 'as done it. It's up to us to teach you your place, me Pa says." As though I had not spent ten years learning that my place was at the bottom of the pile!

"And it's 'is Ma's place to spend the money what you give 'im," a friend laughed.

"Yea," Eddy recalled. "Me Ma sez I ain't to bring you 'ome unless you've got your money."

I felt in my pocket. There were all the coins I had in the world. In the usual course of things, Eddy would have tried to relieve me of a copper or two, but he knew his mother aimed to take them all for herself.

On our arrival, Mrs Reddy looked me up and down. Nothing she saw removed the look of distaste and disapproval from her grimy features.

"Empty your pockets onto the table and be quick about it. No one eats in this 'ouse without paying their way."

I could see even Eddy was wandering why his father was given anything, let alone the lion's share, if this rule were strictly applied.

Several sharp nudges in the back propelled me to the table. Trying to establish that this was a contractual agreement to which I was a party, I inquired, "'Ow much do I 'ave to pay?"

"Don't give me none of your cheek. You give me all you've got. That won't cover it, but," she added with a sign to indicate what a charitable woman she was, "it will just 'ave to do."

In vain, I tried to leave a few coppers in my pocket.

"All of 'em, I said," my keen eyed landlady ordered. "Or I'll turn you upside down, big as you are, and shake 'em all out of you."

"Me Ma knows everything," Eddy whispered in the conspiratorial tone of one who has tried, but also failed, to outwit a mutual opponent.

"Wash yourself, Eddy. And you," she added, without even looking at me. "It's our 'abit to wash our 'ands before meals in this 'ouse. That'll be a new experience for you, I'm sure."

It was not as novel to me as it was to Eddy. Grumbling, he made me hold the bucket of water high enough for him to wash, or dabble, his hands without bending down. Telling me not to dawdle, he marched inside.

By the time I arrived, they were seated, on a variety of ill-matching stools and chairs, around a rickety table. A glance told me that an old, broken-spouted teapot had been taken down and replaced a little out of its old position. That would be where my money, as I still thought of it, had been hidden.

When I looked back at the table, I noticed a new face and a look of resentment on Eddy's. A great discussion was taking place. It seemed that they had taken a young apprentice as a lodger on that very day. Eddy, who was really enjoying having me to bully, was very put out, but Mrs Reddy was making a great fuss of the lad.

"'Is Pa's a 'ighly skilled man in the Yard. Got 'is papers to prove it."

Mr Reddy, from his expression, shared Eddy's opinion of the youth. Mr Reddy had no papers, unless they give them to men who have served time for petty theft.

"Where's 'e going to sleep, then?" Eddy mumbled, his resentment of the intruder obvious in his tone and expression. He clearly had a fair idea what the answer would be.

"In with you? Where else?" The look his mother gave Eddy must have been backed up many times with a clip round the ear, for he smothered any protest he was about to make. There seemed no place for me at the table and they were all devouring a meal from piled up plates.

"Come 'ere and 'old your plate out," Mrs Reddy ordered.

I held out what she chose to call a plate, but which I would have described as an old, stained and dented metal dish. The family supply of plates, as with chairs, had not stretched to encompass the demands made upon them by two lodgers.

As Mrs Reddy dropped a few scraps onto my plate, she announced, "Best meal you've ever 'ad, I'll be bound."

"It ain't as good as the work'ouse," I mumbled. "And I weren't paying for that."

For a heavy, lazy man, Mr Reddy moved with astonishing speed. As the blow landed, it was all I could do to keep the food on my plate. I strove to do so, knowing that if I dropped it, they would either make me pick it up and eat it or let the dog have it. Not that he seemed too keen on stealing these pieces of gristle.

"Where shall I sit?" I asked.

"Where do I sit?" Eddy mocked in a childish voice.

"In your room," Mr Reddy told me. "And don't let's 'ave another sound out of you until the morning."

"Up the stairs as far as you can go and then some more," Eddy giggled.

Holding my plate as best I could, I climbed two flights of stairs and then clambered up the ladder into the roof space. I will not flatter it by referring to it as an attic. There were no windows, but streaks of light came through holes and splits in the thatch.

After a hard day's work, even that food slipped down without too much effort. What did stick in my gullet was the thought that I was paying good money for this, only to be treated as a charity case.

Putting the plate down, I looked around and listened. By the look and sound of it, the thatch was home to every kind of insect and small mammal to be found in Myddlington. The floor was rough boarding, sufficiently thin and rotted to make me fear falling through

What should I do? Tell Jack Star and ask him to sort it out? Was not that what fathers were for? Go down and demand my rights and be bowled over by a clout from the master of the house? He had the heaviest hand of the many I had experienced in my life. Still trying to settle on a plan, I fell asleep.

Early next morning I awoke, knowing exactly what I was going to do. As quietly as the rickety ladder and creaking stairs would allow, I made my way downstairs. I helped myself to a couple of slices of bread. I could find no milk and smiled at the thought of Eddy's having to go and fetch some for the apprentice before he could have anything himself. Having settled for a mug of water, I drank that and then looked for the teapot with the broken spout. It was on top of the dresser, not a hard place to reach when you are an agile boy of ten. Tipping all the money out, I took back all that Mrs Eddy had taken from me, less a penny for the food I had eaten. Then, recalling how scrappy and foul the meat had been, I took another happenny back. Wiping my feet on the mat, silently, but with great energy, I walked out.

At work, I went straight to Mr Campion. He was no doubt busy with his problems, but mine loomed larger in my mind.

"Please, sir," I asked,"don't they say 'im as pays the piper calls the tune?"

"They do, Nat."

"Then, please sir, I'd like to change me lodgings."

As I explained how I had been treated, my words and tone expressing the disgust I felt, he listened intently, as though he had no other concerns of other workers or of the business to worry about.

"Quite right, too. Sounds as though another young man was given what I had arranged for you. You can't afford much, but you deserve better treatment than that. Leave it with me, Nat. I'll have something else fixed up for you by the end of the day. See me then."

When Eddy arrived at work, he was intent, like his father, on teaching me manners.

"Wait till you get in tonight. Me Pa ain't 'alf going to wallop you."

"Ain't coming back." Smug delight oozed from every syllable.

Eddy's mouth fell open, as it so often did. "You've got to."

Raising my voice so all the other boys heard, I asked, "What! Back to that pig sty and to that pig swill you call food? I was used to better in the work'ouse."

Edward rallied all his mental resources to think of an answer. At last, as usual, he fell back on what he had heard his father say.

"We don't want your sort in the Yard," he announced. "Me Pa sez as 'ow these jobs should go to the sons of honest working men, not to parish orphan 'oo ain't got no parents what wants 'em."

The jibe about my parents not wanting me hurt as much as usual, but I resisted the urge to fly at him and make him take it back. I kept my feet firmly on the moral high ground.

"That ain't what Mr Campion thinks, nor Mr White. They both been particular to get me work 'ere. I know Mr White quite well. I worked for 'im before. 'E's keeping an eye on me, so it's you and your Pa 'oo'd better watch out. When 'e asks me 'ow I'm getting on, you don't want me to mention what I think of you and your family, do you?"

By the time Eddy thought of a reply, I had started on my work for the day.

CHAPTER FORTY SIX

That evening, full of self-importance, I waited outside the office for Mr Campion to come. When Eddy passed on his way home, I waved cheerfully to him and called to him to make sure he held the bucket steady while the apprentice washed.

Time passed and one by one the men departed, each for his own familiar home. I did not worry too much. I convinced myself with every passing minute that Mr Campion had decided to give me lodgings in his own home. My hopes were dashed when one of the foremen hurried up to me.

"Don't know why you're getting all this attention, Nat Swubble," he managed to blurt out between breathlessly gulping air. "I was twenty one 'fore the master even knew me name and 'ere you are, 'aving the master worrying about your lodgings."

"Where am I to go?" I demanded, still clutching at the hope that it would be to Mr Campion's house.

The foreman had not had his say yet. "You'll 'ave to learn to stand on your own two feet, young man, like we 'ad to when I were young. You'll ave to sort something long-term out for yourself."

"Did Mr Campion say that?" I asked, all too ready, as usual, to feel rejected.

"No, 'e's too kind 'earted by 'alf, but you mustn't take advantage."

"Where am I to sleep tonight, sir?" I tried to sound business-like, but longed for him to reply that he was taking me to Mr Campion's.

"Well, that's a good question, son." The man's tone softened as he had to tell me, "Mr Campion left it to me to find you somewhere, but I've been rushed off me feet more than usual. Just for tonight, it will 'ave to be in the old stables. That'll do for now. I've brought you a couple of blankets."

It was still midwinter and seeing my face fall and tears coming into my eyes, he put tuppence in my hand.

"'Ere, get yourself something warm inside you. Then 'op straight in between them blankets. See you in the morning." Still feeling pangs of guilt, he added in his most cheerful voice, "There's Bob by 'is fire. 'E'll keep an eye on you."

At that moment, two opposing reactions fought to control me. One, rising from the deep well of past experience, saw this as yet another abandonment. Here I was, like the Baby Jesus, rejected and despised and forced to sleep in a stable. But it was Bob, the night watchman, who urged me in the other direction of seeing it as a place of my very own.

"Ain't nothing to look at now," Bob pointed out, only too truthfully, "but a few days and a bit of work and you can turn that into the comfiest little spot in the whole kingdom."

"Or the world," I joined in, entering into the spirit of it all.

"Or the 'ole world," Bob echoed, as though endorsing the truest and most reasonable statement ever uttered.

Inside the stables, Bob, never one to hurry, gave the problem a few minutes thought, while I surveyed the huge building, divided into separate boxes. The floor was covered with puddles and ingrained with horse droppings. The stink of horses and horse manure still hung heavy in the air and great cobwebs, weighted in dust and dead insects, trailed from every ceiling and high window.

"Just for now," was the advice I received after all this thought, "find yourself the warmest spot, where the wind ain't blowing the snow in. Them old blankets'll keep you warm. Wouldn't mind one of 'em meself."

"You're a good boy," the night watchman nodded, taking the blanket I offered. "Tomorrow, you can sweep it out. Then you can 'ammer a few bits of wood over the big 'oles and fill the cracks with a bit of mud and 'orse 'air. There's still plenty of that blown into the corners. Add a lime wash on the walls and you'd never recognise the old place. Yea, there's plenty you can do to turn this old stable into a little palace. Best of all, there'll be no woman bothering you and telling you you've got to eat when she says so and 'ave what she chooses to give you."

I was about to tell Bob that this was to be temporary accommodation for one night, when I saw the place, as Bob seemed to see it, transformed beyond belief. By now, I had found the best spot to leave my blankets while I went to eat. We walked as far as Bob's fire together.

"And look at it this way, young feller, it ain't everyone what 'as 'is own night watchman within call."

When I returned, Bob had retired into his own little hut, but I found some hot coals placed in a little make-shift grate of bricks by my blankets. I fell asleep a contented child.

Only those who have never possessed anything of worldly value will understand how I felt about my new home. It was, in fact, no more than a shelter from the worst of the elements. It kept off the direct rain and snow, but leaked as the snow melted or rain collected on the roof. It kept off the direct rays of the sun, but allowed the air within to become stuffy and oppressive. None of these faults mattered. To me, they were like faults in a friend, to be ignored where possible and forgiven when noticed. To me, the old stable was, indeed, a palace.

First, I selected a stall in which to create my central room. I already had plans for expanding into others. Next, I swept out the whole place as thoroughly as any servant has ever swept a mansion. Wherever I worked or walked, I collected pieces of wood and metal in case they might prove useful. I had learned from our clothes in the workhouse that everything in the universe, once it has served its original purpose, can be reincarnated to play another role, not on a higher plane, but lower and lower down the social scale. All the pieces I found, even if rotten in places and white with mildew, could be cut and trimmed and shaped to new uses. A little limewash made all the difference to the cleanliness and brightness of the place. After a while, friends and well-wishers heard of my searches and would leave items for me which might prove useful. That was how I came by a two-legged table and broken chairs, with a few ill-matching legs with which to mend them.

Living like this, with no rent to pay, I could spend or save all my wages as I wished. Having my own money in my hand for the first time in my life, for a while I felt loathe to spend it. I gave up eating out and bought myself food reduced at the end of the day and cooked it in old pans collected for me by a friendly tinker. I was king of my own castle.

Although a major aim was still to find Paul, a wonderful part of working in the Yard was the use of the library, which old Mr White had set up for his workmen. I could borrow a book, take it to the stable like a precious trophy and settle down to read, often delaying feeding my body until I had fed my mind.

It is only looking back, that I realise how lonely I was. Although I told myself that I had to take a walk each evening for the good of my health, I noticed every passerby, helped old women across the street and, even, admired babies, just to have someone with whom to exchange a few words. If anyone spoke more than a bare sentence to me, I would make sure I bumped into them again at the same time the next day, hoping the conversation could be extended each time.

I always had some excuse which would allow me to go to the work-house gate and talk to Jack without admitting to myself that I was desper-ately in need of company. I would linger by places where I knew fellow workhouse children worked. Often, I would look into Mr Sowerberry's to see if I could have a word with Oliver, but to preserve the appearance of solemnity he presented to the outside world, he was not allowed to come out with me or even to speak to me. Mr Sowerberry, with very little capi-tal, had never been able to invest in horses and cater to the gentry, but, with such an accomplished mute in Oliver, he was able to appeal to parents will-ing to give the few shillings they had to show the town how dear their child had been to them.

It was such a funeral which came along one day as I stood by the Yard gates. What attracted my attention to it was not the gleaming black coach and fine black horses with great, waving plumes, which Mr Sowerberry must have hired from a wealthier undertaker, but three or four children run-ning alongside it and resisting all of Mr Sowerberry's efforts to shoo them away. Ignoring the adults, who told them to show respect for the dead, they were intent on teasing Oliver.

Dressed all in black, which emphasised his pallor, with a long black rib-bon hanging from his top hat almost to the ground and with the face of an angel, Oliver walked slowly and solemnly at the head of the procession. Beside him, the urchins ran, yelling in chorus, "Left, right, left, right, left." Then some continued with that rhythm, while others changed to, "Right, left, right, left, right." Having failed to make him trip with these tactics, the children called, "Watch that ribbon, goody-goody. You'll trip over it in a minute."

Anyone else would have fallen over his own feet, but not Oliver Twist. Looking straight ahead and keeping perfect time, he walked serenely for-ward. I knew that he would be thinking with sympathy of the dead child, whose small coffin followed behind, and trying to do his duty to bring com-fort to the parents. Green and soft as he might appear, Oliver had a quiet bravery, and, as he was soon to show to Noah Claypole, a fighting spirit.

CHAPTER FORTY SEVEN

When I did talk to Jack, I could never resist dropping at least one hint or reference to Miss Frampton and his marriage plans. Once, I dared to ask if he would have lots of children, and, man to man, if he had ever had any in the past. Much to my disappointment, all these leads were brushed aside or met with the reply that it was not for a child, even one old enough to go to work, to ask such questions of grown-ups.

Drawing a blank on my paternal side, as I thought, I decided to investigate what I had come to believe was my maternal side. If Jack would tell me nothing, perhaps Miss Frampton would.

One Sunday, when Felicity and her beau had come to visit me, we walked in the woods and then returned to my home, as I called the stables, to eat the treats they had brought for me. Convinced Miss Frampton had made sure that Felicity had such things to bring me, I broached the subject of my visiting them on the following Sunday.

Felicity was none too sure. "It ain't like I've me own room, Nat. It's not like your sta…your 'ome. I 'ave to share with two other girls and it's only a small room to start with."

A great deal of signing took place between my two visitors before Felicity finally said, almost defiantly, "Come to think of it, Nat, Betsy had her mother come over last week and she sat down to tea with us all in the servant's kitchen. I'll ask Miss Frampton and see what she has to say about it."

I had no doubt she would agree. What mother would not be longing to see how her son was growing up?

"It will do you good to meet a few civilised people. You know I always wanted you to come and work alongside of us."

I started to pull a face to indicate that serving was not a real man's job, but stopped hastily in case of hurting their feelings.

Having guessed what I felt, Felicity was annoyed enough to make this an excuse for a lecture on my manners, or lack of them. People who lived on their own let standards drop, she was always telling me. Today, she added that mine had little further to fall to start with.

During the week, I took some of the money I had been hoarding like a miser, and bought myself some clothes, not absolutely new, but not as old as the ones I usually wore. When Sunday arrived, I put them on and made myself as presentable as possible. It was even a day for a little spit on my hair to keep it in place.

The quickest route to Miss Aldbury's, and so to her housekeeper, was through the wood. For once, I did not even notice the woodpeckers and squirrels, let alone stand and stare at them for minutes on end, as I usually did. I was quite certain, in my own mind that this was to be my first face-to-face meeting with my mother. It did not occur to me to wonder whether she would be harsh or kind. All I wanted was that she should love me.

Straightening my jacket and scarf, I knocked at the back door. A young kitchen maid opened it and looked me up and down with approval, before blushing and looking down at her feet.

"'Ello, Nat," Betsy greeted me. She was an orphan from the workhouse.

"'Ello, Bets," I answered, suddenly as shy as she was. I was of an age to be aware of girls, but not to know how to behave with them.

"Come on in, Nat. Felicity's busy for a mo'."

The kitchen was full of people and they all seemed to be looking at me. Perhaps they had heard rumours of who I really was. Those who missed their little brothers smiled and even patted my head. Those who had been pleased to leave home and little brothers just stared. My head and eyes seemed suddenly to be beyond my control and I found myself looking at my feet, while others were commenting, "Isn't 'e shy for 'is age," and, "I suppose no one has ever taught him how to behave in company." All of which increased my embarrassment and made me almost wish that I had never come.

Felicity stayed close by me, eager to protect me.

"'E'll soon learn, won't you, Nat? Sit 'ere by me." Turning to the other servants, she boasted, to make up for my awkwardness, "'E's ever so clever with 'is books. Reads and writes as well as any grown-up."

I was not so overcome with embarrassment, though, as to completely forget the secret purpose of my visit. There was much giving way to and putting chairs for this person and that, but I could not be sure who was at the top of this pecking order. Whispering, I asked Felicity if the large lady with a shiny red face was Miss Frampton. Even Felicity laughed at me and whispered that she was the cook.

A very self-confident boy, not much older than me, turned to Felicity and spoke as though I were not there.

"'E's a shy one, your brother, ain't 'e? Are you going to get 'im work 'ere?"

Before Felicity could reply, I answered without hesitation and to prove that I was not shy, "No, I work in the Yard."

"And where's that going to lead to?" the young lad asked, defensively, having noted the pride in my answer. "Me, I'm going to work my way up the ladder to be a butler."

Guessing I might express my well-known opinion that this was not man's work, Felicity rested a firm hand on my shoulder.

"'Oo is the butler?" I whispered.

The others laughed. One said, "'E don't 'ob-nob with the likes of us, although per'aps 'e might show 'imself to us slaves seeing as 'ow it's Sunday."

"At least Miss Frampton always comes and sits with us after Sunday tea," the cook commented.

I was very pleased to hear that and tucked into the food with a will in order, just in case my table manners were not up to scratch, to finish before she arrived.

"Suppose you've 'eard about Miss Frampton from Jack at the work-house," the cook said, addressing me. "Everyone seems to know about them all of a sudden, although they kept it secret for long enough."

"Knew about what," I thought. "What did they keep secret?"

"Could do a lot better for 'erself, I say," the young man put in. "She's more of a lady than 'e'll ever be a gent."

Before I could think of a reply, Felicity thrust a plate of cakes at me. Then she went on to stick up for Jack. "Mr Star is as much of a gentleman as any man I've ever met," she stated very firmly and, staring at the young man, dared him to dispute it again.

"'Ave you taken Miss Frampton 'er tray?" the cook asked.

Felicity told her it had been taken some time ago and they had better hurry and clear away before she arrived for her Sunday visit. The conversation became more general, and I played the role of a child being seen and not heard. I was waiting for the click of the latch and the entrance of Miss Frampton, my mother, as I thought of her.

When a lady eventually entered, Felicity poked me in the back to indicate that I should rise to my feet. The lady smiled around graciously, but naturally and with ease, and thanked them for the tray they had sent up to her. I thought that she had the sweetest and kindest face that I had ever seen. I loved her at once. Whatever she said or did was going to seem wonderful and extraordinary in my eyes.

Having addressed a kind word to each of the staff, enquiring about their relations by name, she turned to me. My eyes did not look down. They were fixed on her face with such intensity that Felicity gave me a surreptitious poke to bring me to my senses.

"This is Nathaniel Swubble, ma'am," Felicity answered, no doubt wishing that she had never agreed to my coming.

"Well, well," Miss Frampton said to me, holding out her hand and smiling at me. "So this is the Nathaniel Swubble I have heard so much about."

Taking her hand, I held it in mine. It was soft and her grip on my hand gentle, but firm and reassuring. It was as though I were being welcomed home after a long journey. All too soon, I realised that Felicity was shaking my arm to and fro, like someone trying to persuade a stubborn dog to drop what it was holding. Reluctantly, so reluctantly, I released my grasp, but continued to stare up into the housekeeper's face. To me, her expression was one of sweetness and affection. Felicity saw it for what it was, one of puzzlement and surprise, mixed with not a little amusement.

Embarrassed for herself and for me, she explained, "'E's a good boy, usually, Miss Frampton," adding, as she was always strictly honest, "On the whole, that is. And 'e's clever with 'is reading and writing."

"Indeed. When you have both finished your meal, Felicity shall bring you to my room for you to display your skills, Nathaniel."

"Yes, Miss Frampton," Felicity replied. Unable to remove the sentimental smile from my face by poking or shaking, she gave a barely suppressed groan. All this time, I continued to stand gazing at Miss Frampton with a fixed, glowing smile all over my face.

Seeming to think my strange behaviour arose from shyness, Miss Frampton laughed and assured me, "I won't eat you, you know."

At this point I recalled where I was and went back to blushing and hanging my head on my chest. Felicity moaned audibly this time. As the door closed behind the housekeeper, Felicity muttered the usual threat about waiting until she got me outside. Telling the others that she had to spruce me up before taking me to read to Miss Frampton, she resorted once again to poking me in the back in order to encourage me out of the room.

"Whatever come over you, Nathaniel Swubble? Are you going soft in the 'ead? You've embarrassed me in front of everyone."

I had no other defence but to blurt out the truth. "She's me Ma, Felicity."

Seeing the look of utter disbelief on her face, I added, "Honest to God, Felicity."

Having learned to take whatever life threw at her, including young lads with wild ideas, Felicity dragged me into the nearest room and demanded that I explain myself. As I related all Sal had told me, she listened patiently. I could see she knew nothing of this.

"And did you ask Jack about all this? No, I can see you didn't. That would be too sensible and simple a thing to do for someone with your cleverness and imagination."

Handling me more roughly than she ever had before, she treated me to the threatening look I had sometimes seen on the face of mothers when they would like to slap some sense into their children, but are not in a place or the company to do so.

"Look, I've got to take you up to Miss Frampton. There ain't no getting out of that, but you say just one word out of turn or mention this daft and wicked idea to her and I'll never, never speak to you again. Is that clear, Nat Swubble?" She sought for words to knock my fancies on the head once and for all. "Miss Frampton is a real lady and real ladies don't go around 'aving babies without being married and married to the father and all. And Jack, do you think as 'ow 'e would leave you in the workhouse to be brought up if you was 'is son?"

Revealed to the light of day and to Felicity's common sense, the whole idea did seem impossible. Tears came into my eyes.

"Now stop that!" Felicity's tone was only a little more gentle. "You go in there, read to Miss Frampton and come out again. Next time I see Jack, I'll ask 'im for an explanation. And," she added with feeling, "it won't be the one you come up with."

In her room, it being a Sunday and not a day on which anything else could be read, Miss Frampton had the Bible ready for me to read. As I mechanically read the familiar words, I had to admit to myself that, when I thought about it, I just could not see her indulging in the activities which Paul had told me were necessary for making babies. But Oliver's mother had been a lady and she was not married.

Once busy reading and showing off, I began to take an interest in the room and realised the walls were lined with books.

"'Oo reads them, then, ma'am?" I asked.

Miss Frampton laughed, "I do Nathaniel."

I laughed with her. "No, honest, Miss, 'oo reads all them books?"

Without laughing this time, she replied, "I do."

"But they're men's books!"

"I did not see that written on them," she answered, smiling again.

"You can tell by the titles," I pointed out. "They're all about science and religion and things. I shall read them all when I'm older."

"Well, Nathaniel, women are allowed to read them when they are as old as I am."

This was news to me, and I was about to say so, when Felicity announced that it was time for me to go home.

"You wouldn't allow women to have minds of their own, Nathaniel?" the housekeeper asked.

"Oh yes," I said magnanimously. "Old Sal 'as a mind of 'er own and Felicity. But," I added, "Sal always did what 'er 'usband told 'er and so will Felicity, won't you?"

Blushing, Felicity mumbled, "Just you wait and see," and ushered me out. "It ain't 'alf seemed a long afternoon," she commented, relieved it was almost over.

CHAPTER FORTY EIGHT

After the intense interest I had shown in Miss Frampton, you may find it hard to believe that my desire to find my parents subsided, but that was the way it was. You might compare my desire to discover who they were with the lava in a volcano, always there beneath the surface, but remaining hidden for long periods before rushing forth and sweeping all before it. In the cold light of day and of Felicity's common sense, the idea that Miss Frampton was my mother gave way to other, more mundane, concerns. Felicity's telling me that she had told Jack what Sally had said and that he had dismissed it as the wanderings of an old lady, helped to lay the matter to rest for the time being.

To be honest, I was more or less content with my life. Independence and the freedom to do what you like when you like has a great appeal for a boy growing into manhood. All too quickly time passed without a great deal worthy of note happening in my personal life.

Despite my oath never to set foot in the workhouse again, I called in just about every day. Visiting Jack and Tom and Virtue was not, after all, like being an inmate. Taking the two children sweets, and more substantial food when they were hungry, I tried to act the big brother to them, just as Felicity acted as my big sister and Paul had protected me as my big brother. On Sundays, I took them for a walk, solemnly instructing them to turn to me for any information they might require on flora and fauna or life in general, but we usually ended our outings as three children, hiding and chasing and generally playing about on our way home.

Once, I took them to the house at the end of the lane. Wishing to appear grown-up, I did not mention my belief that I was born there. Instead, I said, "One day I'm going to live in that house. I've made a good start in the Yard and I'll work my way up, you'll see. You two can come and live with me. Would you like that?"

Virtue and Tom, peering through the railings, nodded their heads in agreement.

"Will it be yours, Nat?"

"Maybe. Maybe I'll just rent it, like Mr Lowe did. I'll be travelling round the world, you know."

"Who'll look after us when you're away, Nat?"

"There'll be servants," I answered airily.

Looking back, I can see that I did all this as much for my own sake as for theirs. Together we were a little family, each with two siblings to fall out with and care for. Both Tom and Virtue were bright as buttons and I tried to help them with their lessons, especially later when a school was established in the workhouse. It was a monitorial school, with the master drilling the quickest and brightest children in fact upon fact for them, in their turn, to drill the younger and slower ones. Not that Virtue or Tom objected to this hammering in of the bare bones of facts with no covering of reasoning or discussion. It was all that was offered and their starving minds lapped it up to the last drop. Both spoke eagerly of being monitors and then pupil teachers and, eventually, fully certificated workhouse teachers. Although I would not admit it, with so little formal education myself, I learned something from them. Having discovered the bare bones of a subject with the children, I could go to the library in the Yard and put the flesh of detail on them.

More had happened in Oliver's world than in mine. A couple of months after I had started work, Oliver ran away from the undertaker. Knowing the slyness and meanness of Noah Claypole, I did not blame him, but, having so often been warned of the perils in store for children loose in the world on their own, I feared for him in the Great Wen.

What I did not know at the time was that his disappearance and fears for his well-being played on poor Sal's aging mind to the extent that she confessed to Jack how, on her death bed, Oliver's mother had entrusted a ring and locket, proof of his real identity, to her for safe keeping. She confided how she had kept them safe for the boy, but had then pawned them to pay the guinea for the doctor to save her own son's life. Although neither had the money to redeem the ring, Jack tried to reassure her by saying that knowing the name engraved within the ring was as good as having the ring itself. This would enable him to make enquiries about the boy's parents. Once he had found them, Jack told Sal, they, with the influence and wealth of the gentry that they were, would soon find Oliver.

It was common knowledge that Oliver's mother had arrived in the High Street, fainted and been carried to the workhouse where Oliver had been born. Jack reasoned that she must have been given a lift into the town by some kind-hearted carrier, who had passed her as she trudged along the road. He duly began his enquiries in White's Yard. Knowing the drivers, he began with those who, having had daughters who found themselves in the same unfortunate position as Oliver's mother, had supported and cared for them instead of following the common practice of throwing them out of the house.

Sure enough, the second man Jack questioned admitted, in confidence, that, fearing the lady would die by the roadside, he had broken the rules and let her ride beside him into town. He added that she had seemed not to know where she had come from or to where she was going. It had been on his mind these ten or eleven years and, if it would help the ill-treated little lad, Oliver Twist, he would give Jack a free ride and take him to the very spot where he had seen the unfortunate woman in distress and offered her a ride.

"If you ask me, Jack," the driver declared, "I'd always thought there was a married man somewhere in the case. When she found out what wrong he had done her, the poor lady almost lost her reason. But, desperate as she was, she would not accept charity. She said that she would sell her most precious belongings and lodge with a nurse until the baby was born, then she would find work. Now I ask you, what work can a lady do that anyone would pay good money for? Suppose she could have become companion to an old lady with means, but what old lady wants a yelling baby about competing for attention?"

As it happened, Jack did not need the free ride, having been told to go to the very same town and collect a pauper, who was being returned to her parish of birth. But he made sure that he rode with the driver who could show him the spot where he had met Oliver's mother. In the short break the driver had in the little town, he introduced Jack to the people at the inn and asked them to give all the help they could. They were all ready to help, but most had been too young to work in the same jobs ten or eleven years ago and those who had been there could not recall seeing the woman to whom the driver offered a ride. The driver continued on his way, telling Jack that he would pick him up the next day and hoping he would yet meet someone who knew of the woman.

Left to himself, Jack visited every shop and stall, seeking out the meanest and cheapest, where a woman with little money might seek to buy food. At long last, returning to the inn, he feared the trail had gone cold. A friendly waiter brought him a plate of food and, as he commiserated with Jack on his failure to find out anything at all about the woman, he bent over and whispered that a stranger had followed him in and sat close enough to him to overhear what was said. Jack silently ate his food, but, seemed to feel the man's eyes piercing his back. In a last bid for information, Jack went and sat by the listener.

Trying not to provoke or annoy the man by suggesting he was eavesdropping, Jack asked, "Would you be searching for the same woman, sir?"

The man, whom nature had not endowed with beauty and life had not brought a pleasant expression, kept his head bent forward, but eyed Jack keenly with a sideways glance. He seemed about to speak, but could not find the words.

"Forgive me for approaching you, sir," Jack apologised, picking up his plate to resume his original seat.

Irritably, the man signalled him to stay where he was. "Why do you ask? What do you know?" His tone, expression and gestures suggested that he resented Jack's intrusion into a private matter and yet still wished to obtain any information he had. "Where is this woman now?" he demanded, still not raising his head.

"You have as many questions as I have, sir," Jack told him. "Perhaps we could begin by exchanging names and telling of our interest in this matter."

"There is no need for you to know anything of me," the man replied shortly. "Just accept that I have a justifiable interest and tell me what you know."

Straight away Jack jumped to the conclusion that Oliver's mother had been related to a well-to-do and well-regarded family, who did not want to reveal their names in connection with a scandal.

"Who are you?" the stranger demanded. "A sailor once, I see," he commented, looking Jack up and down. His words seemed always accompanied by a sneer.

"I'm the porter at Myddlington Work'ouse," John said, looking intently at the man to gauge his reaction.

The man appeared impressed and even more interested in what he had to say. It was clear that he wished to receive information without giving anything away. That seemed understandable to Jack. The man probably thought the woman had disgraced the family name and did not want it mentioned.

"Come," the man coaxed, with a leer, which this time he seemed to intend as a smile. "Let's have a drink together. I'm seeking such a woman on behalf of her family. A delicate matter, you understand and I cannot reveal their name."

Pleased with himself for guessing correctly, as he thought, Jack prepared to answer the man's questions. After all, he concluded, there was no need for him, or for Sal, to know the family name. All that was required was for him to give the family the information he had, so that they could trace Oliver and restore him to his rightful place in the family and in society.

"Where is the woman now?"

"She died, sir. In my work'ouse."

Jack noted that the man's face seemed twisted and deformed. It almost seemed as though he had smiled at the news.

"Describe her to me."

The porter did so and asked, "Is that the lady you're seeking, sir?"

"Maybe, maybe." The man appeared to smile again. Then, as though holding his breath for the reply, he half whispered, "And what of the child she was bearing?"

"'E survived, sir, to be brought up a pauper in the work'ouse itself."

The stranger cursed, but eagerly sought more information. "So he's a useless, lazy little thief?"

"No, sir," Jack said, annoyed with this remark and becoming suspicious that a detective, seeking unadorned facts, should pass such a comment. "There's saints and sinners among paupers, just as among other men."

"And which is this one? No better than he should be, I'll be bound, with a mother not married and his father already wed to another."

"He was a strange little lad, but badly treated by life." Pushed into a wish to annoy the man, Jack added, "A real little gentleman. Everyone who had seen the mother said the child took after her to an amazing degree."

The man had not listened to all Jack had been saying, having eagerly picked up on the first few words.

"Was, you said? Is he dead?" The leer, which served as a smile, fought with a frown to spread across the man's features.

"No, not dead, sir," Jack answered firmly, gratified to feel this was not what this stranger wished to hear.

"Then why do you speak of him as though he were dead?"

"'E ran away, sir. I've been seeking news of him, too, sir."

Again, the man seemed to curse under his breath. Not trusting him, but still convinced he was the only lead to Oliver's family, Jack said, "Please tell the family to search in London, sir. They will not regret it."

"He'll fall into the wrong hands," the man muttered. Half to himself, he added. "He'll end up in court."

Reluctantly, Jack had to agree. "'E 'ad very little money for food. 'E'll 'ave been tempted."

"Indeed he will," the man commented with apparent satisfaction. "And whoever heard of a workhouse child resisting temptation?" Rising, the man went on, "I must just speak to a companion and then you must tell me more of the boy." He summoned the waiter and ordered and paid for two more drinks. Then, he paused to ask casually, "What name does the boy go by?"

"Oliver Twist."

"Is that the name his mother gave him?" the man demanded in evident amazement.

"No, sir, she died giving birth. 'E were named by the beadle, Mr Bumble."

"Will he and others have more to tell me, if I go to Myddlington?"

"I very much doubt it, sir," Jack replied, lying. He felt this man should not get his hands on the jewelry at the pawnbrokers.

The man stared at him. He seemed well aware that Jack was hiding something.

"Who was at the woman's death?"

"The usual old women," Jack replied, keeping Sal's name to himself. "What will you do now, sir?" he asked.

"I must talk to my friend," the man said impatiently and walked into the yard, leaving his full glass on the table.

Lost in thought going over the conversation and thinking of questions he must ask before telling the stranger any more, it was some minutes before Jack jumped up and ran into the yard, cursing his own stupidity.

The man had disappeared. No one could say who he was or where he had come from. That was how Monks came to know of Oliver's existence and to know of his name and the name of the beadle. In London, he hung about magistrates' courts, where he was convinced the child would turn up and, although Oliver was charged under a different name, recognised him from his likeness to his mother. Monk's connection with the underworld brought him to Fagin and the rest you know.

It was almost a year later that Bumble returned from a short visit to London with the news that Oliver had been befriended by a kindly gentleman, Mr Brownlow, whom the child had rewarded by stealing his books and money.

CHAPTER FORTY NINE

In telling of Bumble's visit to London, I have, once again, run ahead of myself. On the day Jack met Monks, his real reason for the trip had been to pick up an inmate from the local workhouse to return her to Myddlington. On the morning after his meeting with Monks and in preparation for collecting the pauper, he went to the Black Bull, where White's office was situated, to check on the exact time the waggon would leave. As he approached the inn, he saw a beggar outside. Her appeal to the public was made, she was saying, with the greatest reluctance, on account of her blindness.

Those who had good use for their own money, who thought all blind beggars to be fraudsters or who were simply tight-fisted pushed her aside. Ready to join the few who placed a coin in her hand, Jack took one from his pocket and then stood watching to see if she were, in fact, blind. Observing her, Jack saw how she moved the coin around in her hand clumsily, gazing at it as she did so. Also observing this, the person who had given her a penny snatched it back, berating the beggar for being a parasite, who lived off hardworking, Christian people and exploited their kind hearts. For a moment, the beggar looked about to protest, but, instead, felt her way to a low wall where she sat, weeping silently.

Experiencing the same annoyance that all felt with beggars who traded on others' emotions, be it of pity or fear, Jack was about to return the coin to his pocket and walk on, when something made him hesitate. Perhaps, he admitted to himself, it was because she was a young woman who, in better days, had been and still could be, very pretty. He stood where he was, silently observing her. She certainly seemed unaware of his presence.

Looking at her, Jack noticed that, as her hand relaxed on her shawl, it fell a little open to reveal gaps in the opening of her dress, where buttons had been wrongly matched to button holes. From her mop cap, which had been pulled on at an awkward angle, tresses escaped. Some had been carefully combed, but others had been left unbrushed and tangled to hang down in disorderly array.

Clearly, the woman had attempted to wash her face, but grubby spots, here and there, remained untouched. If this was a fraudster, she had been well trained. Jack continued to observe her, noting freshly healed scars around her eyes of the kind he had seen on foolhardy young men who had challenged a pugilist at a fair. Suddenly, the woman turned her head to gaze unseeingly in his direction. In a brief second, he realised why he had been loath to pass on by. Stepping forward, he gasped in astonishment.

"Mary? Mary, ain't it?"

"Who is it? I can't see you and I ain't learnt to use my ears instead of my eyes?" Then fear overcame her frustration. "Did Fred send you? I ain't never going back. I'd sooner be dead."

"There, there," Jack murmured soothingly, placing his hand gently on her shoulder to calm her. "It's me. Jack Star from the work'ouse at Myddlington. You remember me. I won't 'urt you."

For a moment, the young woman relaxed, but life had taught her to be suspicious of others' intentions.

"How do I know?" Her helplessness becoming all too obvious to her, she began to cry again, her tears a mixture of anger, frustration and hopelessness.

"'Ow can you be sure? 'cos I reckon you was once Mary Abbott and that you cared for that little scrap Nat Spratt, as you called 'im."

For the first time, the young woman smiled and Jack knew for sure that she was Mary Abbott.

"How is the little scamp?" she asked.

"He's growing into a bigger scamp," Jack laughed and then admitted, "You'd be proud of 'im, Mary. It was you as set 'im on the right road." Putting his hand under Mary's elbow, Jack continued, "'Ere, give us that bag and let me 'elp you to the inn. It's my guess you're the woman as I've been sent to collect and take back to Myddlington."

At this, Mary shook her arm free of Jack's hand. "I ain't going back to the workhouse. I hate it and what's more, he'll find me there."

"Let's go to the inn and you tell me all that 'as 'appened to you. Then we can decide what's best to do."

Once they were seated and Jack had obtained refreshments for them, Mary told her story. "You know when I last saw you, Mr Star? I was about to marry and I come for young Nat. Fred wouldn't take him and being young and foolish, I went ahead and married him, thinking I could get him to change his mind. That was all I was marrying him for. Thought I could change him once I was his wife." Mary laughed at her own foolishness. "He wanted his own children and said it was my fault when we had none."

Taking a deep breath to stop herself crying, Mary continued, "Then someone who had known me in the workhouse told him as how Nat was my baby. I denied it, but he wouldn't believe me." She paused, seemingly unable to go on.

Jack patted her hand. "There's no need to tell me, if it causes you pain."

"I've had no friend to speak to since I left the workhouse, Mr Star. Let me tell you, now I've started. I've longed to have someone to tell."

"As you please, child. If I can take any of the weight off your mind, I'm only too willing to do so."

"Well," Mary began again. "I knew it was the truth to deny that Nat was mine, but I still felt I was telling a lie not mentioning the child I had had. He went on and on about Nat being mine and I blurted out the truth."

Once again, Mary stopped in her story to try to compose herself, but this time it had no effect. Crying, she came to the reason for her blindness. "When I told him I'd had a baby, he just stared at me then he smiled, like in triumph."

"I knew it," he yelled. "Me ma was right. No woman never pulled the wool over 'er eyes. She said you trapped me into marriage. She said you wasn't good enough for me."

Crying uncontrollably and scarcely making herself heard, Mary came to the final act of her story. "Then he beat me, Mr Star." Pulling herself together with an effort, she looked round out of habit and whispered, "Ain't everyone staring at us, Mr Star?"

"No, Mary, they're all busy with their own stories," Jack assured her, never having been one to hesitate in telling a white lie to save someone's feelings. "Calm yourself. You don't 'ave to tell me the details. I see your 'usband when 'e come to see Nat. Now I can tell you, I didn't like the look of 'im. A big bull of a man as 'ad never been crossed and 'ad been spoiled to death by 'is mother."

"He knocked me to the ground," Mary wept. "Then he kicked me until all my senses were knocked out of me. When I come to, hours later...." Mary's words trailed away. She could not bring herself to say that, when she awake after this dreadful beating, she was blind.

She began again. "It was not all his fault, Mr Star. I never loved him and he knew it. He knew I only married him to get a home for Nat." Perhaps she could not admit the awful harm he had done her and so live with the hatred which must have followed.

To himself, Jack thought what a lucky escape I had had, but aloud he said, "There, Mary, it's all over now. All we got to decide now is what we're going to do with you."

"I ain't going to the workhouse." Mary stated without hesitation and Jack was left in no doubt that she meant it.

"That was why," Mary explained, "I was trying my hand at begging to support myself." There was bitterness in her laughter. "But I ain't got the hang of it yet, even I can see that."

Jack knew why Mary would not go back with him to the workhouse. There would be no outdoor relief and she would be kept in the workhouse, or even, as there was a modern way of separating and labelling everyone, she might be sent to an asylum for the blind miles away from anyone she knew.

A waiter, concerned that Mary's tears were making the other customers eager to eat and be off as quickly as possible with money still in their pockets, indicated to Jack that they must be on their way.

Taking Mary's things and helping her into the street, Jack suggested, "We'll go back to Myddlington together, Mary. I'll fix you up with lodgings for a day or two with the driver of our waggon, a kind man with a wife 'oo's just as good and kind as 'e is. Then we'll think what's to be done with you." As Mary still hesitated, Jack added truthfully, "It can't be no worse there than 'ere, can it?"

As they prepared to leave, Mary asked where they were going.

"To White's office," Jack told her. She appeared to flinch and, for a moment, Jack thought she had changed her mind and would not come with him. To urge her along, Jack laughed, "Nat Spratt'll be 'appy to see you. 'E's always going on about 'ow Mary looked after 'im and when will 'e see Mary again."

To Jack's surprise, his comments had the opposite effect from the one he intended. Mary stood stock still on the pavement. "I ain't coming if you tell him, Jack. He'll want to help me and I'll hold him back in life."

To try and persuade her, Jack pleaded, "But to be quite honest, Mary, the boy's a bit selfcentred and it would do 'im good to 'ave someone to care for. You'd be doing 'im a favour."

Mary stayed firmly fixed to the spot. "I ain't coming back if you tell the boy and that's final."

"If that's what you want, Mary, that's 'ow it'll be. Now let's get you back to Myddlington with someone to look after you. Shouldn't think anyone's done that for quite some time. You look pale and worn out."

Mary commented bitterly, "Do I, Mr Star? I ain't never going to see how I look again."

As they journeyed back to Myddlington, Jack told Mary all about me, hoping this would persuade her to change her mind about seeing me. Although she listened eagerly, once again the words did not have the desired effect. She continued to insist that I was to be told none of this and I was to remain in ignorance of her presence in the area.

Late that night, as Jack lay in bed going over the events of the day in his mind, he came back again and again to the way Mary had flinched at the sound of the name of William White. Was it simply, he asked himself, that hearing the name of the carrier made her trip back to Myddlington seem close and unwelcome, or was it the name of William White, himself, which had brought back terrible memories to her? Thinking back, Jack recalled that White had been a friend of the son of the house where Mary had worked. Was it that he, and not the young son himself, had fathered her child?

CHAPTER FIFTY

Looking back, I can see that, all my life, I have felt both the attraction of the busy, bustling world and the need for solitude and privacy. My life at this time provided both, with the Yard bursting with people from dawn to dusk, followed by the privacy of my own little home in the stable. All I missed was the closeness of a special friend. While I had many workmates and acquaintances, no one had taken Paul's place as my best friend.

Jack, afraid that I would one day go off to London or Birmingham to find him and fall in with bad company, had made me promise not to take off without telling him first. He also warned me about going on any boats without his express permission, but, while I kept my promise about going off, what boy would not be happy to go on boats if offered the chance?

Most evenings, I took to walking along the canal bank and offering to lead a horse on my way back to the basin, when horse and boatman were tired and longing for their moorings. I would take the harness off the horse, give it its nosebag and tether it for the night. It was something I enjoyed doing, and the farthings, or apples and oranges from the cargo, I was given were more than enough payment.

There was one independent boat, which came by from time to time, with a boatman of about twenty five or six. Eager to get off to the inn and the girls in town, he was always ready to accept my offer of help. He said his name was Fingers Arthur, which I thought was a strange name, but boatmen, like gypsies, have their own favourite names and ways of doing things. There was a woman on the boat with him. Fingers called her "Ma", but it puzzled me that she seemed too old to be his wife and too young to be his mother. It was clear to me that Mrs Arthur, as I called her, was over fond of the bottle. She managed to do her work of cooking and cleaning and helping with the boat, but her moods veered from tears to giggling, each emotion as embarrassing as the other.

"Is she your real Ma?" I asked Fingers one day.

"No, she died years ago."

"She married your Pa, then?"

"No, 'e don't 'old with marriage. Common-law wife 'e sez she is." Being in an unusually communicative mood, he added, "Don't know 'ow she can be any sort of wife except to the 'usband she left to go off with me Pa."

"Where's 'er real 'usband, then?" I asked, being a gatherer of information on any subject.

"That miserable old toad! 'E didn't 'ave a chance, once Ma 'ad seen me Pa. All the women go for Pa." Shaking back his curls, Fingers added proudly, "They say I take after 'im and they ain't wrong."

I thought I was going to be told all about his conquests, but Fingers looked me up and down and decided I was too young to fully appreciate his stories. Eager to receive instruction in the subject, I tried prompting him.

"Do you know many girls in Myddlington, Fingers?"

Fingers smirked, but said nothing.

Thinking of my own origins, I asked, "Do many men.....well, do many 'ave babies and leave the woman to get on with it."

"What," Fingers asked, being quick to spot one reason for my interest, "do you mean is that 'ow babies come to be left by the roadside?"

"I suppose so," I conceded, not certain that I knew Fingers well enough to discuss so personal a subject.

"Now, when you was born," Fingers murmured thoughtfully, using his fingers to illustrate the point, "there were a few young fellers in the 'abit of leaving girls in the lurch as I've 'eard about. There was William White...." Although Fingers found sufficient names to employ all ten of his digits, I heard only that one name and forced it out of my mind. I changed the subject.

"Are you married Fingers?"

"Me? Do I look like a fool to you? Mind you, I'll marry when I get me own boat. A man needs a woman to work alongside of 'im. Won't stop me seeing other ladies, though, if you gets me meaning?"

I laughed, as I knew that was what was expected of me.

"Come and 'ave a bite to eat with us, Nat. Ma 'as 'er faults, but she can cook as good as any other woman." He nudged me in the ribs and asked, "Why else would me Pa let 'er stay with us"

I hesitated for only a minute and dismissed Jack's warnings from my mind. I knew these people. They were up and down the canal all the time. I let Fingers hand me up onto the boat. It was as snug and cosy as all the boats were, with the smell of cooking that would have proved irresistible to any boy.

Fingers watched my face.

"I can see you fancy the life. You can work for us. Can't pay you a wage,

263

but any lad with 'is 'ead screwed on the right way can make a living for 'isself."

Knowing Fingers was offering me a life of crime, I rather primly replied, "No, thankyou, Fingers."

"Please yourself," Fingers commented, laughing at my innocence. "Suppose I'd 'ave that Jack Star after me, if I tried to persuade you."

"I think you would," I assured, him, happy to know he was aware that I was not alone in the world.

"Come on, then, Nat. Sit yourself at the table."

Singing happily, Mrs Arthur had already dished up three large plates of stew. Glancing from one to the other, I realised there was to be no washing of hands or saying of grace and I tucked in with a will. It said something about my meagre diet at the time, that I could devour the whole plateful even though I had eaten all my usual meals for the day.

"And what's your name, my dear?" Mrs Arthur inquired, in between mouthfuls.

Believing that when in Rome I should do as the natives did, I replied with a full mouth, "Nathaniel Swubble, ma'am."

"Nathaniel Swubble," she repeated. "Never 'eard of a Swubble before, 'ave you Fingers?"

"Bumble give it to 'im, that's why," Fingers told her.

"'Ow d'yer know that?" I asked immediately.

Fingers shrugged. "Knew someone as 'ad a similar 'andle."

"Do you know Paul Quince?" I demanded eagerly.

"'Oo?" Fingers asked.

"Paul Quince? D'yer know 'im?" I demanded even more urgently.

"Maybe I do and maybe I don't," Fingers answered, with a serious expression on his face. He had the air of a lawyer, explaining the law to an ignorant client. "On the canal, Nat, you keep yourself to yourself. You never say 'oo you've met or 'oo you know."

"But 'e were me best friend."

As Mrs Arthur appeared to be collecting her thoughts to speak, Fingers put one of the digits which had given him his name to his lips. "You shut up, Ma," he ordered.

"Shut up! Shut up! Shut up!" his mother repeated. "Shut up! That's all I 'ear from you and your Pa these days." But she kept silent after that.

"Take no notice of 'er," Fingers advised. "She'll be crying in a minute."

Sure enough, Mrs Arthur began to weep. My chance of asking about Paul had passed.

"You're watering that stew, Ma," Fingers grumbled. "What you got to complain about?"

"What 'ave I got to cry about? Oh, nothing. Not me. Me life's all sunshine and flowers, ain't it? I'll tell you what I 'ave to cry about," she snorted through her tears. "A man what beats me when 'e feels like it. And a son what ain't much better."

"'Ere we go again," Fingers declared wearily, having heard it all before.

"Me own sweet babies died," the woman spluttered, weeping as though her heart would break.

Fingers' face and bearing reflected not an ounce of understanding or sympathy.

When he failed to give any guidance on the approach to take, I murmured lamely, "I'm sorry to 'ear that, ma'am. Truly sorry."

The woman stopped crying as suddenly as she had begun.

"Ma'am, did you 'ear that?" she demanded of her stepson. "Some people know 'ow to treat a lady with respect."

For a while, I was kept busy with the extra stew doled out onto my plate as a reward and had no chance of returning to the subject of Paul. When at last I did, Fingers promised to keep an eye open for him.

On a later occasion, as I walked along the canal bank hoping for company, Fingers jumped down onto the towpath beside me and gave me a hearty pat on the back.

"You're a good friend, ain't you, Nat? Do us a favour. Walk the 'orse along, feed 'er and tie 'er up for the night. There'll be someone there as'll help you tie up the boat." He tossed me a penny, never imagining for one second that I would refuse. He had guessed right. Of course. I was only too eager to help.

"I've got to run along into town." Winking man to man, he leered, "You know what I means. If you don't now, you will before you're much older."

I grinned and winked back, as that was expected of me. "Sure, Fingers. Anything to 'elp a friend when 'e's got important business waiting for 'im."

As I took the horse's head, Fingers ran ahead of me back to town. Now and again he waved and did a little jump into the air to show what fun was in store for him.

I smiled at his antics. We rubbed along famously together even though we had little enough in common. He was close to becoming my second best friend, after Paul.

All jobs completed, I swung myself up onto the boat like an old hand, hoping another tasty meal would be thrown in as payment. To my delight it was, but, to earn it, I had the additional job of listening to Mrs Arthur's chatter.

She questioned me about myself and, made emotional by the gin she had consumed, shed a tear when I told her I had no parents, letting her assume that they were dead. I never confessed that I was abandoned, who with any pride would? Even though people told me my parents had abandoned a baby before I could have done anything wrong to make them, I still took it very personally.

"You poor little lamb," Mrs Arthur sighed, dropping a tear onto her potatoes. "'Ow they must be looking down from 'eaven now and thinking what a credit you are to 'em."

As I filled my mouth with food to give me an excuse for not explaining more, I hoped that they were not in heaven or they would be listening to me telling lies.

"I know what it means to lose loved ones," she assured me, with feeling. Smiling sadly through her tears at the memory of their little faces, she told me, "My two little ones died minutes after they was born. So lovely they was. So perfect from tip to toe. After I'd carried each of 'em for nine long months!"

Here I took yet another mouthful too large to manage. Talk of carrying babies and the details of birth were embarrassing to a boy of my age. As she continued to weep, I tried to distract her with a question commonly asked about babies.

"Were they boys or girls, Mrs Arthur?"

She looked at me as though something in my question was confusing, then shook her head and answered. "Boys. They was both boys. If they had only lived! The joy they would have given me."

"God moves in a mysterious way," I heard myself say. It was what I had heard the vicar say on many such occasions.

As though I had stopped working a pump, the tears suddenly ceased flowing. Her tone changed to one of scorn.

"I don't 'old with God and all 'Is works. Narrow-minded bigots them as talk of The Almighty." Obviously, I had touched upon a favourite topic of hers, for she continued, "Make 'Im an excuse for their meanness and petti-ness, they do. Can't bear people 'aving fun, so they sez God forbids this and that and just about everything. Well, if God forbids all them things as makes life worth living, the less I 'ave to do with 'Im the better."

Feeling like Peter betraying his Master, I was too cowardly to admit that I was a believer. It was comforting to have one Father in my life, even if He sometimes seemed too busy to look after me. I was not to get off so light-ly.

"Do you believe, Nat? 'Ave they got to you and twisted your little mind?"

Chewing noisily to show I had my mouth too full to talk even in this easy-going household, I played for time. Would God strike me dead if I said, "No"? Equally unpleasant, would he reward me with an early place in Heaven if I said, "Yes"? Neither event was to be anticipated with enthusi-asm.

Under the influence as she was, Mrs Arthur recognised my dilemma.

"You're no martyr, are you?" she laughed, reaching to ruffle my hair in a way I hated. "Good lad! They ain't got you yet. If you wants to believe when it suits you, that's no crime. We often tells a good story to the clergymen where we stays. I got the language off perfect, you see. I can 'ardly stop from laughing sometimes, as I tells me sad stories. I always adds, "But if that's 'Is will, Reverand, then I'll carry me burdens willingly like a good Christian should."

At this point, Mrs Arthur picked up a bottle of gin and, tipping it up and seeing that it was empty, pulled a face. She seemed about to resume her weeping, but she rose and fetched another from a cupboard. Pouring a gen-erous helping into a glass, she commented loudly, "God 'elps them as 'elps theirselves."

The woman chatted on and I had little chance to comment or even reply to questions, but she warmed to me through the haze of drink. "I can see you'll be as clever as our Fingers, one day." Lowering her voice, even though there was no one within hearing distance, she confided, "'E'll be out thieving, I'll be bound. A little thieving, a lot of drinking and a bit of what 'e fancies, that's what our Fingers enjoys and 'oo can blame 'im." All this was accompanied by energetic winking.

Having finished my meal and thinking that I would not know what to do when, as seemed inevitable, she fell drunk to the floor, I suggested it might be time for me to leave.

"Why?" she demanded aggressively, "You ain't got no one waiting for you, 'ave you?" Her mood swung from hostility to amusement. "You ain't even got no 'orse in them stables." She fell about laughing.

When it seemed that she would never stop, I hurried away, leaving her wiping tears of laughter from her eyes.

Making my way back to the stables, I was half way across the Yard when the watchman came hurrying towards me, bursting with news he could hardly wait to tell me.

"Glad you're back, Nat," he called while still some feet away. "I just 'ad to chase orf a young feller as was trying to break in to your 'ouse."

"Did 'e take anything?" I demanded.

"Didn't I say I stopped 'im 'fore 'e could get in? 'E run like 'Ell when 'e saw me, I can tell you."

"'Oo was it?" I asked, knowing the watchman knew most of the local villains both by sight and by name.

"Never set eyes on 'im before. Usually they go for things what are stored in the Yard. Must 'ave thought you 'ad money 'idden some place in there. You been talking to any strangers lately?"

I was not too young and green to guess that it must have been Fingers. But he had nothing, while I had a penny and a free meal.

CHAPTER FIFTY ONE

It was in the depth of winter that Old Sal died. We were all upset by the death of an old lady who, for all her faults, had tried to be a grandmother to us, but Jack was also angry, not with her dying – that was bound to come, of course, – but that it happened when he was out of town. He had been unable to comfort the old woman in her dying moments by telling her that someone was looking for Oliver on behalf of the family. Moreover, in his absence, Mrs Corney had got her hands on the pawn ticket Sal had said she would give to him to see the locket and ring were returned to their rightful owners.

With this, and the next event to take place that year, Mrs Corney thought life was turning out quite nicely for her. This second event was, of course, the consequence of Bumble's thoughts having turned to love well before Spring arrived. Was it love? The crowd which turned up to watch the marriage of their beadle, soon to be workhouse master, and their matron had various ideas, but few, if any, espoused the theory that this was a love match. Most popular was the idea that Bumble was looking for a house-keeper to replace his mother, who had passed over. People said that Mrs Bumble, having made inquiries while yet alive, had found Mrs Corney to be a good cook and housekeeper and had given her son, from her deathbed, permission to marry the matron. Bumble, having been fussed over and wait-ed on hand and foot all his life, saw an urgent need for a replacement and, having from his own investigations discovered her to be the owner of a small quantity of silver, settled his affections on the matron. Being pompous, self-opinionated and egotistical, it had never occurred to him that his mother had gained complete control of him with her smothering or that another woman would have her own, less congenial, ways of control. Mrs Corney certainly did not want him tied to her apron strings. She want-ed him under her thumb.

Little did Bumble know, as he arrived at the church, resplendent in his beadle's uniform, that his insistence on wearing it at the wedding was the last time he would put his foot down without having it stamped on by his wife. His uniform, as clean and shining as the inmates could make it with Bumble breathing down their necks, the beadle felt pride in himself and pride in his office. As he told anyone who would listen, it was a great shame that he would have no uniform as master of the workhouse, but a man of his character was in no real need of outward signs of office.

Mrs Corney followed her betrothed into the church only a few minutes behind him. After all her scheming and flirting, Bumble was not going to slide through her fingers at the last minute. She had not been foolish enough to invest so much effort into hooking him without having checked all his mother's possessions.

"There goes the lamb to the slaughter," one bystander commented. No one questioned who was the lamb and who the slaughterer, but one added, "'E might be the lamb, but she's the mutton dressed up as lamb."

"Or a wolf in sheep's clothing," another laughed. "'E'll find out her true nature soon enough."

"It'll be a savaging more than a quick slaughtering for 'im," yet another sage observed. "'Eard they found claw marks on 'er last 'usband's body."

The couple, emerging from the church, were flattered to see so many smiling faces.

"They hold me in great respect," Bumble whispered to his new wife.

"More than I do," the new Mrs Bumble replied, beginning as she meant to go on.

It was soon common knowledge that their very first quarrel occurred when they arrived back at the late Mrs Bumble's home to carry off the spoils back to the workhouse. Assembled there were six Bumble sisters, whose existence had been hidden by their all having married against their mother's wishes and never having come near her since. Now all wanted their share of the estate, or more if they could possibly get it. By the end of the day, Bumble realised, too late, that he had sold himself for a few silver spoon. Only he considered himself worth that much.

Perhaps you would expect me to spend more time describing such an important event involving two local dignitaries, but another happening that day was of greater importance to me. Just as the couple walked arm and arm along the church path, I felt a hand jab me in the back. As I turned to protest at being shoved in that way, a voice said, "'Ello, me old son." It was Paul. He had shot up in height and filled out, to look as stocky and strong as a young bull.

As I stared at him, he looked embarrassed. "Ain't you got nothing to say, then?"

"It's Paul," I murmured feebly.

"Always was a great one for seeing the obvious, weren't you?"

"I've been asking for you."

"So I 'eard," he laughed, pleased to have been missed. The slap he gave me on the back sent me reeling, but I laughed too.

"Where you bin? What you bin doing? 'Oo were you with? We thought Raven 'ad got you."

Putting his arm around my shoulder, as in the old days, Paul urged me, "Give us a chance, Nat. Let's sit over there, where we used to sit and talk."

I'd have followed him to the ends of the earth had he suggested it. This was the happiest day of my life.

"'Ow d'yer get 'ere, Paul?"

"Come with Fingers, didn't I?"

About to sit down, I remained standing in surprise. "'E didn't say 'e knew you. I asked 'im time and time again."

"People on the canal don't go around asking questions or answering em." He sounded as though he had worked the canal all his life. I felt a stab of jealousy to realise that he had built a whole new life without me.

"If you ain't done nothing wrong, questions shouldn't worry you, should they?"

"'Ope you're not still a goody-goody, Nat. Still got that book I give you? Anything you want, Nat, just say the word and it's yours." Wisely, he qualified his statement. "It'll cost you a little, but nothing like what you'd 'ave to pay to buy it somewhere else."

"It's so good you're back, Paul." I still gazed at him and again he looked embarrassed. Only later I realised that, while a few years difference in age had once seemed nothing, Paul realised that, while he had become a man, I was still a child. Things could not be the same now as they had been.

"Let's go to the boat. I've got to 'elp Fingers."

He set off at what was now his usual pace, with me almost running by his side. As we reached the boat, Fingers jumped down and stood beside Paul. Why had I not seen it before? The same dark, curly hair. The same brown eyes. And now the same stocky build. As I stood fixed to the spot, Paul looked even more embarrassed.

"'E's me brother," he mumbled in as casual tone as he could muster.

At that moment, Mrs Arthur called, "Ain't your father with you, Paul?"

"No, Ma. 'E stopped at the inn for a drink with 'is friends. Shall I fetch 'im?"

"No, dear." Unable to resist the opportunity for a drink, she added sweetly, "I'll fetch 'im. You boys sit and talk."

Paul and Fingers quietly exchanged words.

"You know 'e don't like 'er showing 'im up. She'll be singing and dancing 'fore you can say Jack Robinson."

"I can't stop 'er, can I? You stop 'er. You're the eldest."

Pausing in her attempt to tidy herself up, Mrs Arthur wanted to know, "'Ow can singing and dancing and being 'appy embarrass anyone? That's why I come with your father. 'E's a great one for a bit of fun."

"That's the trouble," Fingers sneered. "'E's busy 'aving fun without you now."

I was standing puzzled by all this, scarcely able to believe my ears. Paul had a father and knew him well.

As I looked at them, Paul looked at the ground, gazing up now and again to see whether I had put two and two together or whether he would have to go through the explanation he had been practising, but putting off. Fingers was thoroughly enjoying his embarrassment and anticipating, with glee, my disbelief at the news I would finally hear.

"The truth's dawning on your young friend, Paul. 'Oo's going to tell 'im, you or me? 'Oo's going to put 'im out of 'is misery?"

Paul began to speak and then, realising the truth would bring me even greater surprise and misery, his courage failed him. "You tell 'im, Fingers," he urged his brother.

"Our Pa's Gideon Raven," Fingers announced with pride, as though claiming a relationship to the King, himself. "That surprised you, didn't it?" Rubbing his hand through Paul's hair, he laughed, "'Is Pa's the biggest villain on the canal, ain't 'e, brother? And Paul 'ere is a chip off the old block."

Looking past me to avoid my gaze, Paul muttered, "I got to go. I'll see you later, Nat, and explain."

"'Ang on a mo,'" I begged. "'Ow is it none of you is called Raven?"

"Ma calls me Fingers Arthur 'cos she's usually under the influence and can't recall which is me real name. I were baptized Arthur Raven. They calls me Fingers," he explained, grinning proudly, "'Cos I'm so 'andy with me fingers in someone else's pocket." Giving himself time to enjoy the look of horror which I could not keep from my face, he went on, "Fingers and Thumbs. I'm Fingers and that other brother of mine, the stupid one, is Thumbs, 'cos 'e lets everything slip through 'is 'ands."

"But I called your Ma Mrs Arthur."

"Let you do that for a laugh, I did. Didn't you notice she looked a bit puzzled now and again? She's so drunk 'alf the time, she probably thinks that's 'er real name." Fingers was laughing at me and I could see that Paul was having to hold back a smile, so as not to hurt my feelings.

"I'll see you sometime," I announced, staring straight at Paul so he would know he had betrayed me. Turning on my heels, I left. Paul made no attempt to follow me.

It was not long before Jack, having heard of Paul's return, sought me out.

"So 'e's back?"

"Yes," I answered defiantly, daring him to forbid me seeing Paul.

"Look, Nat," Jack began, trying to be patient and reasonable, rather than just laying down the law. "I know Paul was your best friend and 'e looked after you like a brother, but the Paul 'oo's come back ain't the Paul as went away. That family got their 'ands on 'im at just the right time. Just at the age when a lad like Paul was restless and full of energy and wanting to make 'is mark in the world. They showed 'im that the way to use up all that energy and be somebody was to thieve and part folks from their money in any way 'e can. Now, it ain't no good you sulking. Think about it and you'll see there's truth in what I'm saying."

With shoulders hunched, staring down at my feet, I tried not to listen to what was being said. At least Paul knew who his father was. I knew mine could be William White. It just had to be Jack and, if he would not admit it, I was not going to let him tell me what to do ever again. Seeing my stubbornness, Jack shrugged and slowly walked away.

That evening, I was waiting, hidden in the grass, for the Raven family to go out. I was delighted to see that Paul was not one of the group which set out, noisily shouting and singing, for a night in town. As soon as they were out of sight, he emerged and looked around for me. When I waved, he jumped onto the towpath and we set off in the opposite direction to the one the family had taken. We ended up in the wood on the very same log on which we had sat so often in the past. We both wanted things to be just as they used to be between us.

"Is 'e really your Pa, Paul?" I could not bear to say Gieon Raven's name.

"Yea," Paul answered and embarked on the story which had obviously been told him by his father. "They was always looking out for me, recog-

273

nised me and come and took me to live with 'em and take me rightful place in the family business."

"But," I began to protest, "they abandoned you"

Before I could finish, Paul rushed on as though to still his own doubts on the subject. Once again, I felt he was giving the version carefully planned by his father and told to him.

"They didn't really abandon me," he explained, stressing the word "abandon" to suggest it was not a fair description of what really happened. "Made sense. Me Ma died when I were born. Me Pa was grief-striken and 'e 'ad four children already. There were no woman around to look after me." Smiling, as his father must have done in the original telling of this yarn, at the absurdity of the idea of a man looking after a baby, Paul commented, "'E didn't know what to do with a tiny baby. What man would? So Pa left me outside the workhouse to be looked after and reared by them as did know. 'E waited outside 'til 'e saw I were safely taken inside. And 'e never forgot me. 'E come back for me, didn't 'e?"

"Why didn't 'e come for you when 'e got a new wife?" I demanded.

Paul looked at me as though I had no understanding of real life. It must have been the look his father gave him when he asked that very question.

"Couldn't come and say as 'ow 'e'd abandoned 'is own child, could 'e? 'E 'ad to wait until I were old enough to be 'prenticed and then 'e come and said 'e were looking for a lad to learn the trade and made sure I were the lad 'e got."

"'Ow convenient!" I thought and Paul could see that I did not believe a word of it. I still tried hard not to believe that Raven was his father, but I feared, from the resemblance, that it was.

"'Ow d'yer make your money?" I asked, knowing the answer already.

Tucking his legs in closer to the log to hide his new, expensive leather boots, Paul replied, "Me Pa pays me a wage." Defiantly, wondering why he should answer to me, a child who knew nothing of the ways of the world, he told me, "I've money in me pocket for oysters and beef steaks, for beer and for gin. I always 'ave a pretty girl on me arm and I can spend a day at the races or a fair whenever we come across one. What's wrong with that, Goody-goody?"

"If you can't see for yourself," I told him, primly, "ain't no good me trying to explain." Even more sanctimoniously, I added, "I can see you ain't one for saving your money or your soul."

274

As Paul exploded into laughter, I walked home to find it looked just like an old stable, not the fine palace I had pretended. Perhaps Paul and the Ravens had the right ideas after all.

CHAPTER FIFTY TWO

On one of the few occasions that Paul sought me out in the stables, he marched in, his jacket open to reveal his new embroidered and expensive waistcoat and leaned against a stall post to give me a good view of yet another pair of new boots.

"You better tell that Jack Star of yours that me brothers are planning to 'ave fun and games with that fancy woman of 'is."

Puzzled by this announcement, I rose to my feet.

"Miss Frampton, you mean?"

"No. What's she got to do with it? That woman 'e visits in the little cottage on the edge of Miss Aldbury's land."

"Jack?" I queried. "A woman in a cottage...?"

"Don't repeat everything I sez like you was stupid. You're a real baby sometimes, Nat. 'Ow d'yer think a grown man spends 'is spare time?" Brushing a minute speck of dust off his boot, he repeated slowly and emphatically, "Yes, Jack, even at 'is age, and yes, a woman in Miss Aldbury's cottage."

I was about to protest that I did not believe him, when Paul urged, "If you waste time they'll be there before Jack is and 'e won't thank you then."

Snatching up my jacket, although still confused by the whole thing, I walked beside Paul out of the Yard, only to have him stop just outside the workhouse and tell me to go in on my own. He well knew that Jack had not welcomed his return.

"What'll I tell 'im?" I wanted to know.

"Tell 'im me brothers is planning to visit 'er cottage. 'E'll understand. 'E always thinks the worst of us Ravens and this time 'e's right about two of 'em."

A few minutes later, I was back by his side. "'E ain't there and no one ain't seen 'im."

"We'll just 'ave to get over there ourselves, then," Paul said, reluctantly. He knew that, if he tried to stop them from harming the woman, it would mean a beating from his brothers and a falling out with his father. He added hopefully, "Perhaps Jack's there already."

We ran and ran until our sides ached as though they would split. Paul could run faster than me, but too much beer and too many late nights left him panting and scarcely able to keep up with me in the long run. He certainly had no breath for speech and I had to hold back all the questions racing through my mind about who this woman could be.

At the cottage, to Paul's relief, there was no other Raven in sight. He leaned, panting heavily, against the fence. I stood, holding my side and taking deep, steady breaths. It took us a few minutes to recover.

"Let's 'ave a nose around while we're 'ere," Paul decided. Not waiting for me to agree or disagree, he crept up to the house, under cover of hedges and trees. Watching him, I realised this was no new activity for him. Quickly and silently, he fixed on the room from which voices emerged. Gently, he eased himself to the ground and, sitting beneath the window, beckoned me over.

Jack was just finishing speaking and I did not catch what he said, but I caught what the woman replied clearly enough.

"How did you know, Mr Star? Who told you William White was the father of the child I lost?"

"I only 'ad to see your face when I mentioned 'is name. It looked like you 'ated and feared 'im."

I'll hate him 'til the day I die. I try not to hate, not just 'cos it's not Christian, but 'cos it eats you up and destroys any happiness you may still find in this world. He still has power over me through the hatred I feels for him."

"'E should pay for it, Mary. I'll go to Mrs White if you like and tell 'er the 'ole story. She's a fair woman and a generous one."

"You ain't listening, are you? I don't want nothing that ties me to that man. Everything to do with him is tainted, Mr Star." Her voice softened, "Except for young Nat."

Paul dug me in the ribs. He had no need. The conversation already gripped my attention. My stomach tightened and I feared I would be sick.

"What's Nat got to do with it?" Jack inquired.

"If my baby had lived, I'd have loved him with all my heart, with no thought for who his father were. When he died, I took Nat in his place. I often felt he might have been my little one's brother, having the same father, perhaps."

Jabbing me again, Paul mouthed, "Mary Abbott. It's Mary Abbott."

I shook his hand off and silently swore at him to be quiet. Any feelings I had on Mary's return were as nothing to my desire to hear Jack's reply. It came only after a long pause.

"It's time the boy knew 'oo 'is father was. I'm just working out in my mind the best way to tell 'im."

Paul looked at me with concern. He could imagine all the questions which were racing through my mind. Was William White my father? Was it Jack? Or was it someone else?

Again, Paul jabbed me in the ribs, this time to signal that I was to sink closer to the ground. It was clear from Jack's voice that he was standing up, looking out of the window across the garden.

"I can't stay no longer, Mary, but I'll leave Titan with you. Keep 'im close by you and no one will touch you. It was just a rumour about the Raven boys' coming, in any case."

"I'll be quite safe," Mary assured him.

As Jack and Mary went to the front door on the other side of the house, I pulled Paul's sleeve. "Come on," I told him, dashing for the copse at the bottom of the garden. I wanted a chance to sit and talk over all we had heard. Were Paul's conclusions the same as mine?

"Don't you want to see Mary?" Paul asked, as we sat down in the shadow of the trees.

"Why? She ain't asked to see me, 'as she?" I was hardened to being abandoned, I told myself, and was not going to poke my nose in where I was not wanted.

We talked and talked and finally I had to admit that Jack's remarks had not advanced me an inch in the search for the truth about my parentage. Paul was quite keen on my being William White's son.

"One day," he pointed out, "'e'll be dead and you could in'erit all 'is money. You could be lucky there, Nat."

With a total lack of enthusiasm for promoting my claim, I told him, "We don't know 'oo me Ma is and I doubt if 'e knows, so 'oo's to stand up and swear as ow 'e is me Pa? Me Ma is the only person 'oo knows for sure 'oo me Pa is."

Paul looked at me and was clearly debating whether to explain to me that even she might not be certain, but he let it pass. Even so, he was unwilling to let any opportunity for making money slip through his fingers.

"If you went to Mrs White, she'd 'elp you. I bet she'd love a grandson and there ain't a legit....a proper one to be seen. If you went to 'er with that 'butter wouldn't melt in me mouth' look of yours, 'er 'eart would melt and she'd adopt you for sure."

I didn't bother to reply. In the silence, we heard the catch of the back door being lifted and Mary appeared, a bowl of corn under her arm. As she scattered the grain for the hens clucking around her feet, Titan stood in the doorway sniffing the air.

"'E's got a whiff of us," Paul whispered.

"Stay, Titan," Mary ordered, fearing he would send the chickens flying in all directions.

Ignoring her, Titan made straight for us and taking not the least notice of our urgent signalling to go away, the great mastiff lollopped over to us. As we tried to fend him off, he licked our faces with his great, wet tongue until we rolled about on the ground laughing and begging him to go back to the house.

"Titan, Titan, where are you?" Mary called, but the old dog had never played for hours with her, as he had with us in our days in the workhouse. Mary walked back into the house, but soon returned outside. "Where are you, Titan?" Her tone was pleading now. "Where are you, boy?"

Titan ran back half the distance to her, torn between our old friendship and obedience to his master's orders. Mary looked straight at him.

"Are you inside or out?" she asked, almost in tears.

In the same split second, we both realised that Mary Abbott was blind.

"Go back, Titan," I ordered, raising and sharpening my voice to show the dog that I meant it. He ran back to the house and licked Mary's hand. Praising him, she went back into the house, but soon came out again, shutting the door behind her. She had heard us and knew it was someone Titan knew.

"Who's there? Who is it?"

"You've done it now," Paul murmured. "She's 'eard you." Once we knew she was blind, we both felt guilty about hiding from her.

Mary called again, "Who is it? Is it you, Jack?"

"No, it ain't Jack," a rough voice answered. "It's Tom, Dick and 'Arry come to visit you."

Mary turned to look in the general direction of the voice. The raucous laughter revealed that the Raven boys had been drinking before setting out. Arthur lurched along in front of George.

"No, it ain't Jack. 'E's busy, so 'e sent us to 'ave a bit of fun with you tonight. Can't keep you all to 'isself, can 'e now?"

As his two brothers approached Mary, Paul jumped up and joined them.

"Come on, lads, there ain't no fun to be 'ad 'ere. She's blind, can't you see?"

"All the better," Fingers giggled, "She won't be able to tell anyone 'oo it were." Lunging forward, he asked, "'Oo d'yer prefer, Mary, me brother or me? Or," he suggested, pushing Paul forward, "You can 'ave this green young brother of ours."

"Please go away," Mary begged and I could see that she was too confused to know in which direction the house and safety lay. "I've nothing worth stealing."

Arthur broke into wild laughter, which George immediately imitated. "We'll be the judges of that, missus. We'll tell you if it were worth taking when we've took it," Arthur sniggered.

Paul tried to head them off, but was pushed vigorously in the chest and sent sprawling.

"'Ere, me dear," George called. "'Oo d' yer want, Arthur, Paul or me?"

Had it not been such a serious situation, I would have laughed, but Paul tried to use George's stupidity to our advantage.

"There, now she knows our names. We better get out of 'ere and back to town, so we can swear we was there all the time."

"If she do tell our names," Arthur warned, the grin disappearing from his face to be replaced by a mean and vicious expression, "we'll come back again and again and it'll be the worse for 'er." Saying this, Arthur ran forward and danced around Mary, poking and teasing her and twirling her around. Her cries and pleas for him to stop only increased his enjoyment. Paul moved forward, too, to stop her falling and to push his brothers away. They, who had been jealous of his arrival in their lives, put up their fists to give him the beating they had long wished to give him.

Titan could be heard inside the house, barking and scratching at the door. While their attention was taken up with Paul, I left my cover and skirted round to the cottage door. Seeing what I was trying to do, Paul pushed his brothers aside and then ran in the opposite direction to draw them away.

The second I opened the door, Titan rushed past me at the speed of light and with the power of an engine. With unrestrained use of tooth and claw, he attacked Fingers with such frightening force that George turned tail and ran for home. As Paul pulled Titan off his brother, Fingers crawled away, swearing and cursing and threatening to poison the dog for the damage he had inflicted.

"They've gone, ma'am," I said.

"Who is it?" Mary demanded, trembling and crying after her ordeal.

Running to her side, I announced, "My name's Nathaniel Swubble, ma'am."

Before I could introduce Paul, her sobbing stopped. "Nathaniel Swubble," she repeated, her face alight with pleasure. "My darling Nat Sprat."

Then I knew, beyond any doubt, that this was Mary Abbott. No one else had ever called me by that name.

Awkwardly, she moved her fingers over my face to trace the features she remembered. All she could think of to say, laughing and weeping at the same time, was, "You've grown."

I laughed, too. "Oh, Mary," I heard myself say, "I 'ave missed you." Those were the truest words I had ever spoken.

"And I have missed you, Nat. You will never know how much I've missed you." Her ordeal fresh in her mind, Mary asked, "Have they gone, Nat? Will they hurt you?"

"They've gone, Mary," I reassured her. "My friend Paul, 'e saw 'em orf. It was 'im as saved you."

"Paul! Your friend Paul! Is he still here?"

"'E 'ad to go 'ome with 'em, or they'd think 'e 'ad stayed to tell on 'em and 'e'd 'ave bin in trouble. They're older and stronger than 'im."

"What's he doing mixing with them?" Mary asked.

Not able to admit that he was a Raven, I told Mary it would take too long to explain and took her into the cottage and made her a hot drink.

"Shall I stay 'ere, Mary, and look after you like you looked after me when I was little and 'elpless?"

Mary thought carefully how to frame her refusal. "But I don't want to be helpless, Nat. I want to look after myself and make myself useful to other people. When I can look after myself, then you can come and live here and I'll look after you just as if I was your Ma. That's what I've always wanted, Nat."

"But," I protested, "I'm big enough to look after you. I can cook and keep 'ouse. I've me own place in the Yard."

"I know all about your place in the Yard. Jack tells me every day what you've been doing."

"Was we wrong to spy on you?" I asked, feeling guilty.

"You can do no wrong in my eyes, Nat."

We both laughed, but I had to hide the fact that I was also weeping for her. Assuming the role of her protector, whether she wanted it or not, I promised Mary, "I'll get the Ravens for you, just see if I don't. Paul ain't really one of 'em and 'e never will be."

Mary told me I must not do anything silly and that I must leave it to Jack to settle the score with the Ravens. But when I returned to town and excitedly told Jack all that had happened, he seemed preoccupied. About all he asked was, "And 'ow was it you two were at 'and to 'elp Mary?"

Turning from his inquiring gaze, I replied, "Paul and me was just walking in the woods and we 'eard Mary screaming."

"Is that all you 'eard?"

"Yes," I lied. I knew, at last, that he would soon tell about my parents. I went home and spent the few remaining nights when I would have to lie awake and worry about who they were.

CHAPTER FIFTY THREE

Now I can see that I was both desperate to hear what Jack had to tell me and reluctant to learn the truth. Could I face the fact that William White was my father? Did I want, if Jack were my father, to give up all my day dreams of having brilliant, wealthy and influential parents, who would welcome me with open arms and provide me with that education for which I longed? Torn between these opposing desires, I hung about the workhouse whenever I could, but never raised the subject which was on my mind. I talked to Jack, instead, about how he had found Mary and how we could help her. I was all for insisting on living with her and looking after her, but Jack said that I was being selfish. For once in her life, Mary must decide what she wanted to do.

It must have been about a week later when, having been drawn yet again to the workhouse gate, I saw Jack in conversation with the new master of the workhouse, Mr Bumble. The latter had taken to walking up and down outside the gate, taking in the fresh air and escaping his wife's nagging for five minutes.

"'E likes to make believe," Jack told me later, "that 'e can walk out of these gates to freedom any time 'e chooses. But 'e knows in 'is eart that she's a ball and chain round 'is leg for the rest of 'is life. There ain't much justice in this world, but 'e's a living example that it works that way sometimes."

On this particular occasion, Bumble, an expert on matrimony after just a few weeks, was dispensing advice. "Stay a single man," Bumble advising the porter. "Matrimony is a battlefield, sir, a battlefield, and battle rages day and night."

"Mrs Corney – forgive me – Mrs Bumble, she's an able opponent is she, sir?"

"That lady don't fight by the rules," Bumble complained. "She don't know when she's defeated. I utter a cutting remark, which would have mortally wounded a grown man, and I follow it with another and another. Does she sink under my scorn? No, sir, she don't. She hits me with any weapon she finds handy. Come to my house, sir, and look for any object which ought to be straight, long and in one piece and what will you find? You'll find a broken umbrella, a broken cane and dented pots and pans. And where did they suffer such damage? Where else but on my head, sir, on my head?"

"I 'ope you don't retaliate, sir, seeing as 'ow she's a lady, like," Jack commented, at a loss for anything else to say.

"Seeing as 'ow she's a lady, like!" Bumble echoed. "Mrs Bumble is nothing like a lady. My dear Mother," Bumble went on, looking up to the clouds, where he thought his mother to be, "was a lady. She would have given my wife what for, I can tell you." Giving Jack's comment further thought, he explained, "Retaliate! How could I retaliate, when she turns from a demon to a weeping woman in the blink of an eye? A little nudge, a little push and she weeps buckets and cries blue murder."

"You've met your Waterloo then, Mr Bumble?"

Bumble smiled knowingly. "Not Waterloo, my friend. We haven't reached that particular battle yet. That woman is a Napoleon, if ever I saw one, and, like him, so far victorious in every one." Drawing himself up, Bumble added with fresh resolve, "But Waterloo is to come. My dear wife will find that I am another Wellington. I, sir, am another Iron Duke."

"That's the spirit, sir," Jack said approvingly, hardly taking in what the man was saying, but signalling to me that he wanted me to wait.

As Bumble, his head held high, returned to the fray, Jack beckoned me over. Putting his arm on my shoulder, he asked,"Alright if I come over to the stable tonight? There's something I want to talk to you about."

I nodded briefly without looking up at Jack. He often seemed to read my mind and I did not want him to guess I already knew what the topic of conversation was going to be.

That evening, there was food in the bag which Jack brought with him and he spared no time in sharing it out. Now the moment was here, he came straight to the point. "What has Raven told Paul about 'ow 'e abandoned 'im?"

I repeated the tale, as told by Paul.

Jack's smile was grim. "I might 'ave guessed it. 'E's determined to get 'is clutches on Paul, but I ain't going to 'ave 'im drawing you into 'is evil web. It's time you knew the truth, son."

"You found me somewhere else, didn't you?" I blurted out.

"Yes, Nat. What Sal told you were true. But leave that for a minute. Let's deal with Paul first." Taking my silence as agreement, Jack began to relate his version of events. "One day, I were coming up to the work'ouse to try and get the porter's job, which I 'eard was going. The old porter were on duty and standing there with this yelling bundle in 'is arms. 'E laughed at my surprise. 'E said I'd see more abandoned babies if I get the job. 'E were trying to keep 'im quiet by letting 'im suck 'is thumb. 'E said as 'ow some one just found 'im beside the tow path. A matter of luck whether anyone come by before 'e perished."

"'E got out the book where we 'ave to record everything what appens and, seeing as 'ow I 'oped I'd soon be doing the job meself, I looked over 'is shoulder. There 'e were writing, 'Male child left at work'ouse gate.'"

"I asked 'im why ever 'e were doing that when it weren't true. 'E said it were to confuse them what left the little beggar. Told me some of 'em come to claim 'em back when they can work and bring a few shillings inter the 'ouse. 'E said as 'ow they didn't deserve to 'ave 'em back."

"That's where and 'ow Paul were found. His Pa left 'im by the canal path to live or die as fate decreed. There was no laying 'im carefully outside the work'ouse and no waiting to see if 'e were found and taken inside. And, what's more," Jack finished, "I can assure you there were no knowing at that time that 'is Ma would die a few days later. Was probably knowing what Raven 'ad done made 'er lose the will to live. When she died, there were the evil old grandma living with 'em to look after a baby, if she wanted to."

"Then it was a pack of lies what they told Paul?"

"All except the bit about leaving 'im. And, if someone 'adn't appened by, 'e'd 'ave died that very day." Jack paused, glancing at me from time to time to see whether I was ready for what he had to tell me.

My chest and stomach tightened, so I could scarcely breathe. My heart beat like a steam engine against my ribs. Jack was taking such care in telling me, I knew that it could not be good news.

At last, Jack began, "And now we come to Nathaniel Swubble, or the nameless child you was when it all 'appened."

CHAPTER FIFTY FOUR

Jack had his eyes firmly fixed on me now and, seeing my distress asked, "Are you sure you're ready for all this, Nat? If you don't want to know, now or later, I'll keep me knowledge to meself and take it with me to the grave."

"No! No!" I managed to utter. "I must know. I must face up to it."

Jack looked far from convinced, but began to tell my story. "I'd been 'ome, all the way to Portsmouth. Me Ma 'ad been ill and me sister sent for me. Thank God, I got there just before she died."

My mind racing around to grab at the first clue to my identity, I made a wild guess that I was Jack's nephew, born to an unmarried sister, perhaps. But it was not to be.

"As soon as we'd buried 'er, I 'ad to come back or lose me job. I were nearly at the end of me journey, coming across the fields to the towpath to follow it into the Yard. The early morning mist was quite thick and I fixed me eyes on the lights from a boat, thinking it would guide me across the field and show me when I had reached the path and stop me walking straight into the water. But I were feeling my way, too. The path went through a gap in the 'edge and I were feeling for the branches to tell me I were stepping onto the path. "Just as I felt the 'edge on either side of me and was about to turn into the path, I 'eard voices. It were a man and an old woman. The woman said, 'Be quick, Gideon, someone could come any minute.'"

I was gulping the air, but receiving no breath. Jack reached out and asked me again if I wanted to continue. I nodded. Even if I were Gideon's child, I had to know.

"'So what?' was the man's answer. 'You can't see your 'and in front of your face in this mist.'

"'You always was a cool one, son. But 'urry up. You don't want to get into trouble with the law when this one ain't even yours. Why don't we just drop it into the water and make orf?'

"'Cos I don't want nosey people finding a body."

"'Is it dead, yet?' the old woman asked.

"'As good as. I'll put it in that 'ole under the 'edge what I got ready yesterday. The last one were mine and I give it a sporting chance. This one ain't a Raven, so I'll cover 'im over with earth so no one finds 'im.'

"At this," Jack explained, "I were worried. Thought they might suffocate you 'fore I 'ad a chance to get you out."

So Raven was not my father, but if he had had his way, he would have been my murderer. I began to feel a great hatred, which was never to leave me.

"I struggled to think what to do." Jack continued. "If they knew I were there, they would take you back and leave you somewhere else. I 'urried back as fast as I could along the path, then turned and come towards 'em again, whistling as I come."

"'Leave, 'im, son," the old witch whispered.

"'I'm coming, Ma. Ain't as good a job as I wanted to do, but 'e's covered. Let's get our breakfast." They made off back to the boat, not wanting to be seen. I walked on by, whistling, praying I was doing the right thing and you'd still be alive. I doubled back, found you and held you with your face down while I brushed out the dirt. Thank God you 'adn't cried and swallowed it. Thank God you didn't cry as I sat be'ind the 'edge, cleaning you up and wrapping you in me coat. You was a nasty colour, I can tell you, more blue than pink, but you were as determined to live as I were to make you."

Jack looked at me closely and finished off the story. "That's 'ow it were, Nat. When I were sure you'd survive, I wrapped you in a sack and put you outside. I were just about to go out again and find you meself, when Bumble passed by."

The story was ended before I realised I still did not know who my mother was. Jack, perhaps without realising it, was so reluctant to tell me, he had missed out that little detail.

"So 'oo was me Ma?" I asked, gazing at Jack as he tried to look cheerful and make the best of a bad job.

"You know 'er, Nat. That lady you calls Mrs Arthur. The woman what lives with Gideon Raven to this day. She ain't all bad," he added, this faint praise revealing his true thoughts. In Jack's book, a woman could leave her husband if he were cruel, but not leave a child.

"Just the mother anyone would want," I said bitterly, adding sarcastically, "She's a wonderful cook and 'er washing's always clean and bright. And she can tie up a boat and un'arness the 'orse when she ain't too drunk to stand on 'er feet." But even now, I was truly searching for a redeeming feature in this woman who was my mother. "She thinks I died at birth. She thought they buried a dead baby. She ain't to blame for what they done, is she, Jack?"

Jack looked doubtful, torn between leaving me a strand of hope and making me face the truth, as he saw it.

"A woman knows," he said gently, "whether her baby is alive or dead."

"Per'aps," I argued, "they didn't let 'er 'old me."

"Per'aps," Jack said, without conviction.

"'Oo was me Pa?" Already I knew my mother's opinion of him. But if she went off with Gideon, she would not value, or even see, the strengths of a good man.

"'E's a schoolmaster," Jack began.

Wildly, it entered my head that, if Mr Lowe could live with one woman without marrying her, perhaps he had done it before.

Jack read what was in my mind. "No, Nat, it weren't Mr Lowe." Wanting to keep to the script he had so carefully prepared, he went on, "Let me tell you what I did a few weeks after I found you."

"Saved me, you mean," I put in.

"God was watching over you, Nat, I'm sure of that. By rights, you should 'ave been dead." Not a man given to an outward show of belief, he did not labour the point, but he was none the less sincere for all that.

"Thinking things over, it were clear from what Gideon and 'is mother 'ad said, that your mother 'ad left your father. That meant, I reckoned, that you 'ad a father somewhere, 'oo might bring you up. It would 'ave been better than a life in the work'ouse. Asking around on the boats, I found that your mother come from a place some twenty miles up the canal." Suddenly, Jack broke into his story, "Are you alright, Nat? 'Ave you 'ad enough for now?"

Knowing how, if I knew only half the truth, my mind would pick on every little fact Jack had mentioned and cling to any little strand of hope to be found within them, I asked him to tell me everything. I had to hear the story sometime and it might as well be now. "And don't miss any bits out," I told him.

"I think you're right, lad. Let's get it all out in the open and then you can start to build your own life. There's me and Mary to 'elp you all the time. I'd give the world to be your real father, Nat, and all Mary wants is to be a mother to you."

Giving me a minute to agree, Jack continued, "One Sunday, when you

288

was still a tiny mite, I went to this village and kept me ears open for any mention of the name Kilsby. That," Jack explained unnecessarily, "was the name the woman, your Ma, went by."

It seemed familiar, but I could not place it and it was not an uncommon name in the villages around.

"I'd decided not to mention what I was there for. I didn't want to 'and you over to just anybody. Suppose I were already too fond of you to let you go." Somewhat embarrassed by this confession, Jack hurried on with his tale. "At the inn, I asked the landlord if there were anyone with that name 'oo's wife 'ad left 'im within the last few months. 'E said there were, but when I asked the landlord to point the man out, 'e nearly died laughing. 'What's the joke?' I asked."

"'See all these people 'ere enjoying theirselves with an innocent drink and a bit of gossip? No gin palace this. No one drunk or rowdy – not until late at night, anyway. Well, they're all doomed to go to 'Ell. They've given their souls to the Demon Drink. No singing, no dancing in 'is life. Just praying and Bible reading, and Bible reading and praying on and on, morning 'til night. Mind you, I've nothing against that, if people match the Christian words with Christian deeds.' Barely taking breath, the landlord continued, without me 'aving to ask, 'No wonder she left 'im, – 'is wife that is. She were sixteen. 'E were forty-five. Spring and Winter. Spring all full of life and Winter cold and icy. It were 'er parents pushed 'er into it It were like 'e picked a beautiful bud and stopped it from opening and blooming forth in all its joy and glory.'

"To cut a long story short," Jack summed up, "'e said she met this boatman – in the inn it were – and run orf with 'im. The innkeeper said the boatman, Raven, were an even worse choice than 'er 'usband, but she wouldn't take advice. 'E'd 'eard she'd taken to drink. The landlord said as 'ow that were a sad thing in a woman, 'ow ever good it might be for 'is trade.

"As luck would 'ave it," Jack went on, "'Is brother – not the landlord's, but the 'usband's – come in and told me the rest of the tale. 'E said your Ma 'ad told 'is wife just before she left that she were expecting. Said Raven wouldn't want 'er if 'e knew, so she were keeping it quiet and 'oping 'e'd think it were 'is."

Looking at me, Jack wanted to make sure that I was taking in what he was saying. "I interrupted 'is story at that point, to ask if there were any chance the baby – you – might be Raven's. 'E sez 'is wife were quite sure it

289

weren't. Said she were being sick in the morning before ever Raven come along. Reckoned that was why she went off in such a 'urry, before 'e 'ad any idea." Jack was making the best of my story and going out of his way to assure me I did not belong to Raven.

"It seems," Jack explained,"that when she left, your Pa ordered no one were ever to mention 'er name again. In 'is book, she were a daughter of the Devil and bound for 'Ell"

Grabbing at any straw, I asked, "So my Pa never knew about me?"

"'Fraid 'e did, Nat," Jack answered, determined to have the full truth out for once and all. "'Is brother plucked up the courage to tell 'im, thinking Raven was no man to be a father to you. Your Pa just said as 'ow 'e 'ad said no one was ever to mention 'er name again. 'E just opened 'is Bible and shut 'is ears and 'is mind to everything they said. It seems you were the fruit of an evil woman in 'is eyes and no son of 'is."

There was a long silence between us. Jack watched me closely, anxious that, as the bringer of bad news, he should not be rejected. At last, I had to ask the final question left to me.

"'Oo is my Pa, Jack?"

"I give you 'is name, Edward Kilsey. Thought you might recognise it. 'E's a teacher, Nat. 'E's a clever man and well read, they say. 'Ad things been different, I expect you'd 'ave followed in 'is footsteps." Shuffling a little uneasily, he added, "You 'ave seen 'im, Nat. At the services for Sunday Schools."

Suddenly, I recalled where I had heard the name. Of course, the teacher, whom Paul and I had hated on sight. That was my father!

Seeing the disgust which I could not hide, Jack asked, "D'you want to come back for the night? I can make you up a bed in the lodge. You don't 'ave to go right in to the work'ouse."

I gave no answer.

"I got to go, Nat," Jack told me, reluctant to leave me on my own. "I'm on duty."

I remained silent. What is there to say when you discover your mother is an empty-headed, drunken woman, who ran off with Raven, giving no thought to the baby she was expecting, and your father is the greatest bigot and misery for miles around?

"You know, Nat," Jack said awkwardly, not having taken a step in the direction of the workhouse, "I look on you as me own son. 'Ave done ever since I lifted you into me arms on the misty, cold morning. 'Ow many times

I've wished you was me son! 'Ow many times I've wished I never 'anded you in as though you was a lost parcel! But, if I 'adn't got 'elp for you as soon as I did, you'd 'ave died."

"Then everyone would 'ave been 'appy." For the first time, tears rolled down my face. I could not stop them, even had I wanted to.

Kneeling down beside me, Jack took my hand. He was crying for me. "You'll 'ave me for the rest of me life, Nat, and that's a promise. I'll never abandon you." Rubbing his sleeve across his eyes, he reminded me, "And there's Mary. She loves you like a son. I know now, Nat, you can only think of what you ain't got. But, as time passes, try to think of what you 'ave got. People 'oo love you as much as any mother or father could. People 'oo 'ave chosen you from all the rest of the world. And you've Felicity and Paul, Tom and Verily, brothers and sister what love you as you love them."

It was not Jack, I thought bitterly, who had been as good as murdered. Hate was the strongest of all the emotions, which overwhelmed me now.

"Why didn't you kill 'im, Jack?" I demanded.

"What? And 'ave 'em 'ang me and leave you alone in the world? Don't think it didn't cross me mind."

"Why didn't you beat Raven within an inch of 'is life, then?"

"And 'ave 'em know I'd saved you? I thought of one scheme after another, but staying 'ere to watch over you took first place in me plans."

"I'll kill 'im, if ever I 'ave the chance."

Jack looked worried. "I 'ope I ain't done wrong, telling you all this," he said. Seeing the hatred in my eyes, he added, "I told you all this to keep you out of trouble, not to 'ave to watch you swinging from the gallows." Perhaps to divert my anger, perhaps to make me realise others were even worse off, or because it played on his mind, Jack suddenly asked, "Did you hear young Dick up at the baby farm was dead? They say William White beat 'im to death."

"What if 'e did?" I demanded. "No one ain't going to bother to do nothing, are they?"

CHAPTER FIFTY FIVE

You may have wondered why I have not mentioned the name of William John Bull White recently and you may even have imagined that, after the failure of his plan to make his name reforming our workhouse, he had left to seek fame and fortune elsewhere. That is far from the truth. When the New Poor Law came into being, White remained, now openly chairman of the Board. Some said he had to remain to cover up all he had done in the past. There may well have been some truth in that, but others knew the real reason for his presence in Myddlington.

William White decided that, with a wider range of men having been given the right to vote, there would be more willing to vote for a business man rather than a lesser son of a local aristocrat. He turned his energies to his business. Day after day there were rumours of arguments between him and Robert Campion on how things should be managed. Campion stood for old-fashion values of morality, while White followed the modern theory that any method or scheme which was successful in bringing a large profit was acceptable. Many a smaller man was put out of business, while the Yard prospered as never before.

Although I was still a child, I feel it is to my eternal shame that I fell into the habit, on the frequent occasions that I met him in the Yard, of doing what most people did. I shut my eyes to his faults and, bowing and scraping, hoped that he would use his influence to further my career.

That was how matters stood when news of Dick's death and rumours of its cause spread like wild fire through the town. Susan, the maid at Mrs Mann's, had claimed that she had seen Mr White beating Dick and then carrying his near lifeless body into the cellar to leave it there. She had tried to comfort Dick and dress his wounds, but he had died in her arms.

There was much mumbling about the way the rich were above the law and many comments on what people would like to see happen to White on a dark night, but few seemed prepared to take any action. Meeting together, Jack Star, Robert Campion and a few friends, blamed themselves for what had happened. They should have spoken out about their suspicions about White's involvement in the attempt on Francis Campion's life and confronted him then.

"This time," Jack said, "we must do something before more harm is done." Even so, they knew they would not persuade the authorities to act against him without clear evidence. When the parish apothecary called at the workhouse, Jack drew him aside. He asked what had, in truth, happened to the boy.

"The child fell down the cellar steps," the apothecary replied, but he did so while burying his head in his bag. His shoulders were tense and he remained ferreting in the bag while Jack questioned him further.

"There are few as believe that, sir," Jack told him, "and I'm one as don't"

At last, having prepared his story, the apothecary turned to face Jack and ask, "I thought you above gossip. I did not expect you to listen to the words of a dull and foolish girl. I am right, am I not, that these rumours can be traced back to Susan, the half-witted maid at Mrs Mann's?"

"Dull, she may be," Jack agreed,"but that means she ain't got the sense to lie. She ain't got the sense to watch 'er own back and 'ide the truth because it don't suit them 'oo run the town to 'ear it."

"And I," the doctor answered, with growing confidence in his story, "prefer to believe Mrs Mann, an intelligent woman and greatly trusted by the Board."

"And the aunt of the Chairman of the Board," Jack snorted.

Ignoring this remark, the apothecary continued, "I was called to the house and led at once to the bottom of the cellar stairs, where the child lay in agony." In a sneering tone, the man added, "In such circumstances, in all reason, I could not conclude that he had been pushed off the roof or trapped under a cart."

Keeping his patience only with great effort, Jack asked, "And what were your observations on the child's condition? I am asking for your opinion as a man of science, not as a man employed by the Board."

With relief, the apothecary saw the way to escape this questioning. "As the man of science appointed by the Board, I report to them, not to the workhouse porter."

"It ain't just me as is asking, sir. It's the citizens of Myddlington."

The apothecary's immediate reaction was a snort of contempt. "This is not France. We have no citizens here, interfering in things they have neither the sense nor the education to understand."

Seeing no point in arguing along these lines, Jack changed tack. "The newspapers these days are so full of stories of scandals in the workhouses, and we don't want 'em reporting on what is 'appening 'ere, do we, sir? An inquiry might be the result, with you 'aving to answer to it."

The doctor's confidence was clearly shaken. Once again, he searched in his bag, turning his face away from Jack. When he turned to him again, his expression was one of sweet reasonableness.

"Come, come, my man. Let us keep things in proportion. Had I found anything to support the girl's story, I would have been the first to report it to the authorities."

"What did you find, sir?"

The man hesitated for a second, but decided it was best to appear open and have everything above board. "Broken ribs. A broken arm." Wanting to give the impression that none of these things was exceptional, he spoke slowly, as though having to drag such unimportant matters from deep in his memory. "Bruising of course, as he bounced from step to step."

"And that was sufficient to kill 'im, sir?"

"He must," the doctor explained, as though talking to an idiot, "have cracked his skull as he fell. This resulted in unconsciousness and death." Picking up his bag to leave, the man added, "All perfectly consistent with a fall down the cellar steps."

"And equally consistent," Jack claimed, "with a beating."

"The child was at the bottom of the stairs!" the apothecary stated in the voice of a man who is losing patience.

"'E could 'ave been placed there. Or, more likely pushed into the cellar as a final punishment."

The doctor controlled himself with a great effort, but the fear of an inquiry stayed in his mind. In the newspapers the words of an ignorant man like the porter were given equal weight with his. His own secret doubts as to the cause of the boy's death, made him circumspect. He wanted to be on the right side in an inquiry, which ever side that might prove to be.

"Come, Jack," he smiled, "I am a simple country doctor. I am called to an accident and find a child lying at the bottom of steps. I find nothing inconsistent with this story. What else can I do?"

"Did the boy say nothing to you?"

"Mrs Mann urged him not to strain himself by talking," the apothecary said, his voice tailing off as he realised the weakness of this answer.

Jack smiled and the smile stung the doctor into speaking without thinking.

"If William White had beaten the child, he would have had to have lost all control. Mere correction would not have inflicted such injuries. He would even have had to kick the child. Would that be the action of a gentleman?"

"'Oo mentioned William White?" Jack asked quietly.

"He's the only man who visits the baby farm." Thinking attack the best form of attack, he countered with a laugh, "Unless you are accusing Mrs Mann or me of attacking the child." He added, "Of, course, the girl Susan could have pushed him down the stairs and have thought up this tale to cover herself"

"You know the rumours as well as anyone," Jack said impatiently. "Mr White beats the children and Mrs Mann covers up for 'im. 'E's 'er nephew and puts business 'er way."

In his most dignified manner, the apothecary announced, "I make it a practice not to listen to rumours."

"'Ow convenient!" Jack commented and, before the doctor could protest, added, "So you won't support an inquiry?"

As though giving the matter very careful consideration, the doctor frowned and then announced, "I can see no reason for an inquiry and I doubt that the Board will see one, either."

"How surprising!" Jack put in. "And William White's the Chairman."

"Your manner is offensive, Mr Star. That is a fact I might well draw to the Board's attention. But, even so, to show my own honesty in this matter, bring me one piece of solid evidence to back up these rumours and I shall go straight to the appropriate authorities."

"The child Oliver Twist told of beatings by Mr White."

"Oliver Twist! The child who turned on those trying to teach him to earn an honest and independent living. If he is your best witness, you have a lost cause from the start, Mr Star." Smiling and shaking his head to stress the weakness of Jack's case, the apothecary made for the door. Looking back, he assured Jack, "I have no axe to grind in this matter."

"You're employed by the Board," Jack pointed out, but knew that he would get no support from this man.

"Indeed," the doctor agreed, "but I follow my conscience, not my purse."

At the next meeting with his friends, Jack told them they could expect no support in bringing White before an inquiry or a court.

"How far d'you think we'd get, with Susan as our only witness?"

"There's not even the girl now," one replied. "Her father's been bought off and 'as taken 'er 'ome to keep an eye on 'er."

"And we all know what that means. 'E's beaten 'er 'til she were covered with bruises many a time."

"That's why," Jack pointed out, "if she says Dick had a terrible beating, we know it was worse than she's ever 'ad."

"That's not how the law will see it," Robert Campion remarked. "It's a young, foolish girl making up stories to harm her betters. The lawyers would twist her words until they had her saying that White and old Mother Mann were angels straight from Heaven."

Without speaking, the friends sat down to their weekly game of cards, but the game never started. Jack, still stung by my words that no one protected the weak from the strong and the evil, put the cards he had been dealt on the table without looking at them.

"We all know in our hearts what we 'ave to do, don't we?" When some were still silent, he reminded them of William White's crimes. He did not mention Mary's treatment, but he counted it his own mind. "Then there was his attack on young Francis. The Ravens carried it out, but no one can doubt 'oo was be'ind it."

"And 'ow 'e got rid of that teacher, Mr Lowe," another said, but not all agreed that was wrong. The couple were living in sin.

Jack continued the list. "'E let them villains into the work'ouse to frighten the boys and take away Georgina. Can you imagine the life she's leading in London? And the beatings 'e give Oliver. And putting them young boys into slavery with the sweep and other employers like 'im."

"And look what 'e done to the work'ouse!"

"And still does."

"It was a place to keep children safe and give the old somewhere to live and die in peace. 'E's turned it into a prison for everyone."

"And don't forget," Jack reminded them, the sight of the frozen body still clear in his memory, "there was that carpenter 'oo perished in the snow. A few pennies put into 'is 'and would 'ave saved 'im."

All this listing of White's sins was playing for time. Every one knew why he should be punished, it was what the punishment should be and how it was to be administered which no one wanted to be the first to state. Had it not been for my words playing upon Jack's conscience and his determination to put an end to words and decide upon action, the plan they decided upon might never have been proposed.

"'E needs to be made an example of," one man announced. "There are plenty of others getting away with murder."

"Yes," Jack agreed, "but they are rich and influential men. None of us would ever get away with it. It'll 'ave to look like an accident."

With those few words and nods from the others, it was agreed that William White was to be killed. As to how, suggestions came thick and fast, only to be abandoned as impractical, as pointing to one of them as the murderer or, worse still, pointing to an innocent person.

At last, with all of them committed to ridding the world of William White, Jack put forward his plan, which had been developing in his mind over the past few days.

"'Ow about this?" Speaking as though planning a fishing trip or a poaching expedition, he went on, "Every Friday, there's a Guardians' meeting at the work'ouse. White allows no discussion, so off they all go 'ome about eight o'clock. About quarter past the hour, White's riding through the wood and we are waiting. We leap out, the horse is startled and throws 'is rider."

As Jack paused before the final bit of the plan, one man said, "And 'e'll live and finger us.

"Or," another added, "we'll 'ave to finish 'im off and it'll be clear cut murder and we'll 'ang for it." Like the others, he was willing to risk his own life for justice, but not to make his wife and children suffer.

"I'm coming to that," Jack said. He was finding it more difficult than he had expected to put his plan into words. None of them had ever been involved in cold-blooded killing before. He did not know whether they would agree to go along with his plan or recoil in horror. Forcing himself to go on, he said, "We pick 'im up, one each arm and one each leg, all of us working together and...." His voice hoarse and breathless, Jack continued as best he could, "and we ram 'is 'ead against a tree and kill 'im with that one blow."

No one spoke, but, as they acted out the deed in their minds, all shuffled uncomfortably and sought to stop their hands trembling.

"The blood," Jack explained to break the silence, "will be on a tree and not on a weapon." A shudder ran through him as he went on," It will look as though he fell 'ard against the tree. They'll write it off as an accident. They'll not come looking for anyone to blame."

"We'd have to lead the horse round to make it look like he reared in the right place," Campion, a practical man, said.

"And then cover up our own tracks," another man added.

After a pause, in which no one could fault the plan or add anything more to it, Robert Campion expressed the thoughts of them all. "It's so cold-blooded, cowardly you could say."

"And what was the killing of young Dick?" Jack asked. "Keep the image of that young boy in front of you and what we're planning don't seem 'alf as bad."

CHAPTER FIFTY SIX

"Vengeance is mine," saith the Lord. How many times, in Mr Clack's sermons, had we heard that? We, the humble people, were called upon to do nothing else in life but endure. We were not to have the satisfaction of wrecking vengeance on our oppressors. The trouble with this, I now saw all too clearly, was that God might take his time. While, eventually, William White might burn in Hell for Eternity and Gideon Raven be struck by a thunderbolt, countless, powerless children might suffer and die before that happened.

Vengeance was to be mine. A terrible anger burst from the restraints I had imposed over the years and turned my thoughts, night and day, to how I might punish White, Raven and the two Raven boys.

As I could think of no plan in which I could act alone, my first step was to find an ally I could trust, but I did not have to look far. Once I had repeated Jack's story, with a few embellishments and pointed comments, I had one close at hand in Paul.

"We ain't real brothers, then," had been his first reaction, giving himself time to digest all I had told him and yet conveying to me that we were, once again, brothers in spirit. Trying to salvage something from my story, he added, "'E did give me a chance."

"What more could a loving father do?" I sneered.

"More than 'e give you."

"'E didn't give me no chance," I agreed bitterly.

Suddenly, Paul kicked hard against a tree. "They don't want me, really," he confessed. "They talk about before I come and don't include me in much, except working for 'em and doing their dirty work."

I put the knife in and turned it. "They only come for you when you was big and strong and could earn more than you could eat."

"And 'oo got the profit? It weren't me, I can tell you that," Paul stated. "They just pay me off with a few pairs of boots and a few smart clothes. I ain't living with 'em no more. I'll come and live with you in the stable and work side by side with you in the Yard."

Apart from the fact that Paul would never be given a job in the Yard, this did not fit in with my plans. "You got to stay and watch what they're up to," I told him.

Reluctantly, he agreed. I had not had to tell him what was in my mind. Vengeance would now occupy all his thoughts as it did mine. "And I can 'ear all their plans," he said, "so we can think 'ow to make 'em pay."

We planned one absurd scheme after another, each urging the other on and neither restraining the other. Neither Paul nor I questioned the rightness of our proposals or gave a thought to the consequences. Together, we plunged head first deeper and deeper into our obsession – the destruction of our enemies.

It was some days before Paul came with a piece of information which suggested a plan with a reasonable chance of success. The information concerned rumours, circulating all over town, that a crowd was to gather at the workhouse to protest at the workings of the New Poor Law Act.

"Raven," Paul announced, refusing to call the man his father, "says it'll turn into a riot, and 'e should know, 'cos 'e's going to see that it does. Says by the time it's all over, the place'll be burnt to the ground."

Immediately, I saw, as Paul had done, all our enemies burning in a Hell on Earth. I wanted to make plans there and then, but Paul was eager to get back. For the next few days, wherever Gideon and his sons went, Paul followed. The very skills of choosing a victim, winning his confidence and learning all that could be useful in tricking him, which Gideon had taught his son, were now used against him. Paul kept close to his father, was included in all their planning and aroused not the least suspicion.

During this time, I had another obsession to follow. I had to know whether my mother had known of Raven's attempt to kill me. Had she really thought that I was still-born? When I had mentioned this to Paul, he had offered me no comfort.

"'Aving a baby don't make you deaf," he had said. "If Jack could 'ear what was going on, so could she. And when babies is born," he added from years of experience in the workhouse, "babies yell their 'eads orf. She'd 'ave known you was alive. Even if they told 'er you was dead, wouldn't she 'ave begged to 'old you to weep over you? And she'd 'ave wanted to know where you was buried, to put a few wild flowers on your grave, whenever she passed that way again."

I knew from my experience that he was right. That is what other mothers did. But still I clung to the hope that she did not know. I could not accept the truth as readily as he could. Against all Jack's advice, I visited the Raven's boat again.

"Well, well," Gideon Raven mocked as I climbed onto the boat. "To what do we owe this honour? Thought you was too good for the likes of us."

No smart reply occurring to me, I just shrugged.

"'E's been 'ere lots of times, ain't you lad?" my mother said, signalling me to sit down. "It's just you 'e don't like, and 'oo can blame 'im!" I must have been looking at her closely, as she wiped her hand across her face and asked, "What's the matter? 'Ave I got a smudge on me nose?"

"You've always got a smudge on your nose," Raven mumbled. The sons smirked at his comment. Strangely, I felt angry with them for their treatment of this foolish woman. My feelings for her swung erratically from rejection to sympathy. This blowsy, falsely happy woman smelling of gin could not be my mother, I was certain. But then, perhaps the Ravens had made her this way. Her closeness made me shiver, yet I thought that, if she would leave them and come with me, she might be a completely different person from the figure before me now.

"What you frightened of?" Raven demanded. "Think we're going to tie you up, pop you in a sack and carry you orf to London and a life of crime?"

"'E could do worse," Fingers laughed, joining in the fun at my expence.

"'E 'as done worse," Raven sneered. "Working for a few pence in the Yard. Look at our Paul and try to be a bit more like 'im. What 'e sees in you as a friend is beyond me."

Again, I shrugged my shoulders. Paul came to my rescue.

"'E can't 'elp being a goody-goody, Pa. 'E ain't lucky enough to 'ave Raven blood running through 'is veins. Unless..," Paul added as though struck by a sudden thought, "unless you've got a few more sons in the workhouse you 'aven't told no one nothing about."

While Raven hesitated between pride in the thought of the number of children he might have fathered and fear of claiming to know anything about me, I jumped straight in. "You ain't me Pa, are you, Mr Raven? And you ain't me Ma, are you, Mrs Raven?" As I spoke, I watched her face closely.

Paul seemed to be holding his breath, seeing Gideon looking at me with intelligent eyes.

"What gave you that idea, lad?" Raven asked in a strangely gentle tone. "Someone been putting ideas in your 'ead?"

At that moment, his wife decided to speak. She could have kept quiet

301

and left Gideon to deal with the situation, but then she would have received no attention.

"All me babies died, didn't they, Gideon?" Dramatically, she dabbed at her eyes with a filthy rag, "'Ow I'd 'ave loved children of me own!"

Again, I seized my opportunity. "When was they born?" I demanded, not caring that I was going too fast, too soon. Paul tensed.

"You don't remember things like that," she replied, dabbing energetically at her eyes. "You tries to put all them things out of your mind."

Raven muttered something about "out of your mind", which made the boys snigger. My mother ignored them and, with a sudden swing of mood, sang as she prepared the food.

"You don't look a bit like us," Raven stated, adding, as though it were an insult, "And you certainly ain't got our ways." He paused for the boys to laugh. "Any way, like I told Paul, I only left 'im 'cos there were no woman 'ere to care for 'im."

When it came to his own history, Paul was a reckless as I was. "Didn't I 'ave no aunts nor grandmas?"

"'Oo's been putting these ideas in your 'ead, son?" Raven demanded, his suspicions aroused again.

This time it was my turn to come to the rescue. "You don't need no one to put ideas in your 'ead," I told him, "when you don't know 'oo your Ma and Pa are. You wonder about it all the time, don't you, Paul? You even walk down the street looking at everyone and wondering, 'Is that me Pa?' or 'Is that me Ma?'"

"Yea," Paul agreed truthfully, "I done it as long as I can remember."

"Well, you can 'ave no more doubts now, son. You belong to me and to me first wife what died. But you," Raven glowered in my direction. "You're nothing to do with us and never 'ave bin."

CHAPTER FIFTY SEVEN

Four men stood in a small clearing in the wood and then, solemnly shaking hands, they separated to take up their positions behind trees to be hidden by the trunks and the thick undergrowth of saplings and brambles.

All moved self-consciously, as though acting out a part on a stage, a part in which they were not practised and were unwilling to appear. They did not look at each other, fearing to see in another the doubt in their own minds. This was a serious matter they were about, one which should have been carried out unemotionally and dispassionately by the Law. Each had discovered himself to be neither unemotional nor dispassionate. Each wanted to run miles from this place and this task. Each was stopped by that strongest of all restraints – loyalty to his friends.

As the men waited, the rising gale battered the trees, shaking down the dry, rustling leaves and twigs to deepen the carpet, which crunched beneath their feet. There was the harsh rasping sound of great braches being forced by the wind to scrape savagely against each other. Seeing the young saplings bending to the ground in the teeth of the gale, Jack noticed how their roots clung tenaciously to the earth. Would William White cling as tenaciously to life in the sudden onslaught of their attack?

The violent clamour of the storm was merely the background to the thoughts of the other men. They heard only the violent protests of their consciences. Reason and sound arguments had brought them to their decision, but, over the past few days, these had grown weaker and less persuasive. At night, they had acted out this scene over and over again. Each had acted his part, working in unison with his friends, right through to the second when William White took his last breath, the moment when the deed was done and there was no going back. From that moment on, they had seemed to be whirling and turning, falling and spiralling into a bottomless chasm. Terror and guilt consumed them and they knew they no longer had any control over the future of their own lives.

Campion was the one they were watching. It was he who had positioned himself to see along the path and signal when he saw White approaching. He prayed for the strength to do what he had undertaken to do and not to betray his friends. They prayed that the signal would never come and that they could return to their own homes, the same men as they had left them. But none would be the first to break his word and let the others down.

Time and time again, Robert Campion thought he heard, over the storm, the pounding of hooves or the crack of a whip, but William White did not appear. Seconds dragged by and then minutes. An hour passed before Campion stepped into the path and the other men, as bedraggled and cold as he, joined him. In their relief, having thanked God in their hearts, they chatted and even laughed.

"It wasn't to be," Campion concluded. "It's a sign that we must find another way. Some way where we don't feel like cowards."

It was only as they neared the town that someone thought to ask, "What happened to White? He hasn't passed us, even now."

"Perhaps someone else got there first," one joked, half hoping it were true.

"More likely," Jack suggested, "Raven really meant it when he said there would be trouble soon."

They hurried along, fearful for the children and old people, if Raven had started the riot he had threatened for so long. For the moment, Jack put to the back of his mind the decision he had made that, as the only man with no family, he must take upon himself the task of ridding the world of William White.

As for Paul and me, we had started some hours before to put our plan into action. Over the past days, unlike Jack and his friends, we had felt only excitement and anticipation, not dread. Being, as we saw it, on the side of the angels and of justice, the quiet voice of conscience had not yet been heard by us. Being young and having each to spur the other on, we had, as yet, given no thought to the consequences of our action. Perhaps it helped, too, that we had no detailed plan to rehearse and to bring home to us the reality of our actions. Our scheme, as far as it went, had been summed up by Paul as, "We'll give 'em enough rope and then 'elp 'em to 'ang theirselves." In other words, we would just make sure that Gideon and his boys set about burning down the workhouse and were caught in the act. And while this was happening, somehow, in some way, William White would die.

With a plan so fluid, Paul made me swear to do just as he ordered, without question.

"I'm going to 'ave to think on me feet," he explained, savouring the situation. "I'll be giving the orders and you'll be carrying 'em out. That way we'll know where we are. 'Ave you got that, Nat?"

I assured him that I had and when Paul ran into the Yard that afternoon and told me Gideon and his friends were about to act, I awaited my orders, ready to carry them out, whatever they might be. Sheltered from prying eyes by a pile of barrels, Paul outlined his father's plan and where we fitted in to turn it to our advantage.

"Gideon's going to get people all steamed up and start a riot. Then, when all 'Ell breaks loose, me brothers are going to lift a few tiles and drop burning stuff in on the rafters.

Anticipating my question, Paul went on, "I know. I know. It seems a lot of bother, but wood burns and stone don't. The wood's up in the roof, ain't it?"

"They'll be seen."

"That's where I come in, ain't it?" Paul said, with obvious bitterness. "I'm supposed to light the mattresses in the boys' ward to distract them below from seeing what's going on.

"Then they'll see you instead."

"Yea, and don't that just show what they thinks of me!"

"What do I do?" I asked, ready to take as dangerous part as my friend.

"Pa.... Raven's going to signal to me first, then walk round and signal to the boys. I'm betting 'e'll make orf 'ome then and be sleeping on the boat, as innocent as you like, when anyone comes to ask questions. 'E mustn't get away. That's your job, Nat. You 'ave to be outside, making sure people see what 'e's doing. People what matter, that is. And make sure they see me brothers on the roof Can you do that?"

"I'll try Paul, honest I will. But 'e'll get away, I know 'e will." For the first time I realised that the success of our plan did not lie in our own hands. Other people might do something unexpected and ruin it all.

Paul winked at me. "I've got me plans, don't you worry, little brother." Ordering me to wait before I followed, he jumped up and ran out of the Yard.

I had to be satisfied with that, but I was not of a nature to tolerate doubt and uncertainty without fearing the worst. Once certainty of success was taken away, I viewed every event from every conceivable angle, imagining what might go wrong. Only in the case of the sweep's apprentice had I acted with decision. Now, feeling like a mere pawn in a larger game, I knew

I had little or no control over what might happen. Now, in the cold light of reality, all the certainty I had felt about the rightness of our cause, the euphoria of self-righteousness, the readiness to be a martyr in the cause of justice evaporated like a morning mist exposed to the rays of the sun. Raven would escape, I knew he would. As for William White, I had no idea how he fitted into Paul's plan. What was it like to take a man's life? I had seen many a dead body in the workhouse, looking at it without fear in the daylight, but haunted by it at night. How much worse it would be if I had been the one to extinguish life! Throwing my arms around one of the barrels behind which I was hiding, I clung to it, my mind plummeting, twisting and turning into that bottomless chasm of fear and guilt which the men had faced in the wood. Like them, I knew there was no way out. I could not let Paul down. He was my best friend.

It took every bit of resolve in my bones to make me stay in the Yard. My attention not on what I was doing, Robert Campion, himself as tense and distraught as I was, clipped me on the ear. And he did another thing he rarely did, which was to leave in the middle of the afternoon. Had I known it, he, like his friends, wished to spend time with their families—time they might not have again.

So far, Raven's plans had been known only to his family and a few friends. It was not until late that afternoon and early evening that rumours began to circulate that there was to be an assault on the workhouse that very night. But the workmen around me in the Yard were those of whom some of the middling classes, who believed everyone in the lower classes to be feckless and idle, had never heard. They gave a thought to the morrow, kept their heads down and hurried home. There had been an orderly and well-conducted meeting of respectable artisans a few days earlier at which a decision had been made to petition the local Member of Parliament to have the New Poor Law repealed. That was heady enough action for men in the Yard.

As Campion and his friends sought comfort at home and then made for the woods and as I tried to imagine what Paul was planning, Raven and his cronies were going around the inns and ale houses in the town gathering in men who had no work or labourers returning from theirs. They plied them with drinks to put them in the mood for a night of fun and taught them short, quickly learned and easily repeated slogans to release the frustrations of the oppressed and the ignorance of the uneducated.

Full of ale, the men were armed with sticks and bottles and led, many staggering, into the streets in the direction of the workhouse. As the various groups gathered into a mob, they found the houses and shops in the High Street shuttered and bolted. The fear which seeped through these defences from the terrified citizens within gave the marchers a feeling of power and invincibility. For now, at least while the effects of the ale lasted, they had the town at their mercy.

Tucked in against the wall of the workhouse, I watched the approach of this unruly crowd. To my surprise, Raven was not at its head. None of his friends were. Having worked up the men into a state of drunken fury and drummed into their heads the simple slogan, "Burn! Burn! Burn!" they had evaporated into the night. How was I to ensure that Raven was blamed for all this? How was I to carry out Paul's orders?

I was thrown into an even greater state of confusion when, out of nowhere, Raven appeared and addressed the crowd.

Raising his arms, he called, "Steady, lads! Steady! You're 'alf drunk and don't know what you're doing. Go 'ome and sleep it orf, that's my advice." Then he raised his cap and waved it. "Go 'ome!"

At this point, he was hustled out of the way by one of his own cronies. It had been made to look as though Raven had done everything he could to stop the advancing mob. In fact, by waving his cap, he had signalled to his sons on the roof and to Paul that they were to light their fires. Tears gathered in my eyes. He was too clever for us. Whatever should I do?

Deciding that I could at least make sure that the Raven boys were caught in the act, I ran into the workhouse and, fighting my way against the stream of inmates trying to escape, I sought out Mr White. Unable to believe the crowd would, indeed, attack the workhouse, he had delayed giving instructions to a small group of employees, inmates and tougher towns-people, who had gathered to resist such an attack. He was just on the point of ordering them to close and bolt all the doors when I arrived.

"Mr White," I yelled, pushing through the little crowd, "I've just seen some men on the roof. I spotted them in the flames of their torch. I think they're going to set the rafters alight."

William White looked at me. It was against his nature to trust anyone, but he recognised me and decided to believe me.

Rushing outside, all the helpers stared upward.

"There they are!" I yelled, pointing to Thumbs Raven, who, unlike

Fingers, had not had the sense to hide himself

"A reward for the men who capture them," White announced.

"'Ow much?" came the reply.

"Ten pounds to the first man to lay hands on each of the villains," was the promise.

In seconds, the helpers had disappeared, leaving me standing by White's side. "I saw Gideon Raven signalling to them, sir," I said. "If you ask me, sir, 'e's be'ind the 'ole thing."

Before White could reply that he had not asked me for my opinion, I was amazed to see Paul dashing along the corridor. He was putting on a great show of panting and holding on to his side to give the impression that he was rushing in with a most important message. The exhibition put White in the frame of mind to accept what he said without question.

"Sir! Sir! I've just seen someone going into the boy's ward with a burning torch. 'E were screaming 'e were going to set the 'ole place alight."

For a moment, White looked around him for men to send with Paul, but they were all out seeking the reward for the capture of the Raven boys. Cursing, he set off for the ward, telling Paul to follow him.

"You," White called to me, "find where Bumble has hidden himself. We need every man, even the cowards, if we are to save the building."

Waiting for Paul to indicate that I was to carry out this order, I ran to the master's apartments. Men were carrying their belongings, including the furniture, into the street.

"Mr White wants you, Mr Bumble," I called, standing on tiptoe to see him behind the piled up goods.

"Don't you dare leave me," Mrs Bumble screamed in a voice which would have made even the bravest man hesitate and which caused her husband to sink into a chair, as though hoping to be carried out far away from all his troubles. "You're a useless lump of lard," she screamed, "but you're all I've got."

"I'll never leave you, my dear," Bumble promised, jumping up. "I'm just packing my mother's silver."

"What's left of it after those locusts you call your sisters snatched most of it from under your very nose.

I left without the master, my mind worrying about what Paul was up to. A dreadful gnawing in my stomach told me he was trying to kill White. I should be with him, but my feet would not take me in that direction. I told myself that Paul had not wanted me there and I might upset his plans.

CHAPTER FIFTY EIGHT

How right I had been! Paul, his mind full of hatred and resentment for world in general, had spotted a chance to murder William White and get his own back on at least one member of the human race. Acting out the role of the subservient, dull yokel, he had led William White to the door of the boys' ward.

"I saw 'im coming out of 'ere, sir, I swear I did. And I can smell smoke, sir." He pushed back the door. There, sir, over there. Look over there! I can see smoke coming up, sir. Whatever shall we do, sir? They'll burn the whole place down, sir, and us with it. 'Oo shall I fetch, sir? I'm not staying 'ere."

Up to this point, William White had made no reply, thinking Paul's whining and fear beneath contempt. At last he had had enough.

"Stop snivelling, boy. I see nothing. Have you brought me here for nothing?" Pushing Paul aside, he marched deeper into the room.

Suddenly, Paul abandoned his role of frightened idiot and tossed his lamp on to the pile of flammable waste he had set ready beforehand.

"Burn in 'Ell!" he shouted, as he turned and ran for the door, pausing only to laugh at the uncomprehending expression on William White's face.

Locking the first door, Paul ran along the corridor to the second door, turned the key and heard a satisfying clunk of the lock. That deed done, he leaned against the wall to catch his breath and enjoy the moment. He began to laugh at the look of total puzzlement which had been on William White's face as he had glanced back at him, but the laughter died in his throat. As the realisation of what he had done dawned upon him, Paul found he could not laugh and his limbs were trembling and refused to be still. To his own amazement Paul began to realise the horror of what he had done.

Within the ward, White tried each door in turn. When neither yielded, he kicked them in frustration and cursed himself for being taken in so easily. Sensing Paul had remained outside the door, he attempted to control his anger and speak as though he were the first to see the joke, but now it was over.

"Come, now. You've had your joke, young man. Come, let me out." After a short pause, he added with growing anger, "The prank's over. Let me out at once and I'll say no more about it."

Trembling all over, his words barely escaping his lips, Paul sneered, "Ain't no prank. It's to learn you a lesson for beating me and Oliver and for killing young Dick." Hazy memories of Sunday school returning, Paul controlled himself sufficiently to add, "A eye for a eye, Mr White. Ain't that what the Bible sez? It were you what killed Dick and I'm killing you to make it all fair and square."

As he heard his own words, Paul trembled even more violently. The small voice of conscience, to which he had seldom listened, became louder than it had ever been before, telling him that he should release the man. It was murder that he was committing as surely as if he had put his hands around White's throat and strangled him. But, instead of releasing his prisoner, Paul forced his legs to move him along the corridor, ensuring at one and the same time that he would resist the urge to let White go and would be separated from the terrible thing he had done.

At the top of the stairs, Paul heard men coming towards him. They had seen the flames and come to make sure that no one was trapped. Hardening his heart, he rushed towards them, announcing as he ran, "There ain't no one up there. I've searched everywhere. Let's get out of 'ere while we still can."

The first man turned and passed the message back to those following and, one by one, they turned and were relieved to go back the way they had come without having to put themselves in danger. If everyone were safe, what did it matter if the building were burnt to ashes?

They returned to join those gazing up at the workhouse, pointing and cheering as, in the high winds, new fires burst forth here and there in the roof and a blaze could be seen spreading the length of the boys' ward. The flames lit up faces on which the sullen resentment of some, the melancholic dullness of others and the deep hatred of the rest were turning to expressions of satisfaction and delight.

Then a cry went up. "There 'e is! There! See 'im! The Devil 'isself!"

"And what better place for the Devil than in a burning 'Ell?" someone demanded.

If anyone in that crowd felt like going to the aid of William White, who was looking down from the window, he kept it to himself and forgot all about it when other men moved to the doors to prevent any attempt to go to the rescue.

Without opening the window to issue angry orders or make desperate pleas, White turned back into the room. He could hear the crackling of burning rafters and the crash of debris falling to the floor all around him, but swirling smoke blotted out most of the ward from his view, leaving him in a small, dark world of his own. Standing there, he reflected that it was not the fire alone which isolated him from the rest of the world, but the hatred and spite of the peasants outside. It was their ignorance, their failure to share his vision of a more efficient and prosperous country which would lead to his death. But he would not lower himself to their level to ask for their help.

It was then that White found that he was not alone A small hand was placed in his hand and a small face looked up into his face, while a small voice begged his forgiveness.

"Please, sir," Tom wept, "I never meant to be naughty. I come back for me tin, sir. I won't never do it again." Then the child reached up his arms to White, in quiet confidence that the man would pick him up and carry him to safety.

For a moment, White gazed at the boy in silent amazement, before impatiently pushing him away. Then, suddenly, as Tom's eyes filled with tears, White's angry frown turned to a wide smile. How strange that it should be this particular child who would be his salvation!

Now White opened the window as far as he dare without allowing the draught to fan the flames and held up the child.

"Cry, boy, cry," he snarled in his ear. "Plead! Melt their stony hearts or we'll never get out of here alive."

Tom, his fingers firmly holding on to White's jacket, hung out of the gap and pleaded, but not for himself alone.

"Save us! Please save us! Me and Mr White are stuck up 'ere and we don't want to die." He repeated his calls and then, easing his arm around White's shoulder, he whispered in glee, "They're coming. I knew they'd 'elp us."

"Some of you men," White called, "Come up at top speed and save the boy."

"Ain't you coming, mister?" Tom asked, clinging to him even more tightly.

"Oh, yes," White answered, "we'll both get out, just wait and see."

As White made his way to the door, Tom coughed and hid his face in the man's shoulder. White held him tightly and put a hand over his head to protect it. Then he stood by the door, ready to push past the men and charge down the stairs before anyone could grab the boy and leave him inside. No doubt White did not mention the fact the door was locked, in the hope that the men would rush up and unlock it without thinking. But he had underestimated Paul's determination to kill him.

When the first man arrived at the door, he swore and then shouted, "It's locked, sir."

"That I had observed," White said, icily, adding, as though to a stupid child, "Turn the key."

"Ain't no key 'ere," a man by the first door called. "Is it up there?" The cursing from the man at the second door confirmed that it was not. A hasty conference among the would-be rescuers brought no solution.

"You better think of something fast," one man yelled, peering through the key-hole. "The fire's got 'old and no mistake. There ain't no one going to get out of there if something ain't done soon."

Impatiently, from inside the ward, White took control. "Don't trouble with a key. The window is the only means of escape. Take mattresses from the next ward. Place them under the window in the yard. The one I was just at," he added, not trusting their combined intelligence.

The men ran to obey, concerned now with Tom. As they did so, White, sheltering the child as best he could, walked back to the window and lifted him onto the sill. Having glimpsed down, the child clung to him sobbing, his arms tight around White's neck, his tears falling onto White's cheek and his pleas urging White not to leave him. At first roughly, and then more gently, White spoke to the child. He told him how the men wanted nothing but to save him and would surely catch him, him so small and the men so strong. "Have you not watched them," he asked, smiling, "throwing my sacks of corn about all day? Those sacks weigh far more than you do and they cannot reach out and grab at the men as you can." Taking the rusty tin Tom so treasured from the boy's hand, he added, "Let me have that and I shall throw it to you as soon as you are on your feet."

Observing that the men had brought only two mattresses and that this would allow no room for error, White told Tom to hang tightly to the window frame and hastily collected blankets from the nearest beds, stamping on them where they smouldered. Then he speedily tied them together, wrapped one end around Tom's waist and lowered the boy as far as the roughly made rope would allow. Alerting the men below as to his intention, he let the rope drop. As the child rolled onto the mattresses and scrambled to his feet, White watched anxiously. Those who then looked from the child back up to the man swore later that they saw him smile with joy, as no one had ever seen him do before.

"Here, my clever fellow," White called to Tom and threw down the tin. He cheered as the boy caught it in both hands and held it tight.

With Tom safe amongst them, the men moved away, some reluctantly, to allow White to jump.

"Your turn now," someone called, while others muttered angrily that they hoped he would break his neck.

But, instead of jumping, White moved away from the window and walked back into the room.

CHAPTER FIFTY NINE

All eyes remained on the window, waiting for White's return, except mine. All this time, I had been keeping an eye out for Jack, the one person I had always relied on to know what to do, but he had been no where to be seen. Now, I spotted him arriving on the edge of the crowd and beginning to make his way through, glancing up at the window as he went. Suddenly, he stopped and stood as though making up his mind on what action to take. As he stood there, he patted his jacket and seemed relieved that what he was feeling for was there in the inside pocket. Then, resolutely, he made his way inside the workhouse and disappeared from my view.

At the door of the boys' ward Jack took from his pocket a key. It was a key he should not have had, but was one he had had made secretly after we had been attacked. He had decided then that he would always possess the means of gaining access to the ward were we ever in trouble.

As Jack entered the ward, the draught fanned the flames within, making them flare like demons excited to learn there was a great world outside in which they could spread more destruction and harm. Quickly pulling the door to behind him, Jack stood, seized by panic. As the fumes burned his throat and nose and the heat scorched his face and hands, it was as though, amongst the falling sparks and debris, he were back on board a ship in the middle of battle, afraid to witness the men dying in agony around him.

"'Ere, sir," he called, pulling himself together and peering into the smoke and flames for a sight of White. "This way. The door's unlocked and we'll soon 'ave you out of 'ere."

There was no reply and Jack felt angry that White should make him stand there, where the fire reached out towards him and sparks were falling on his skin and clothes. His body was covered with sweat and tears filled his eyes without bringing any relief to the sting of the fumes and heat.

Tensed as he was, Jack jumped at a tiny sound to his right. Moving along the wall in that direction, he made out the form of William White suddenly emerging from the dark fog. The black smuts covering his face could not hide his expression of fear, but he showed no relief at the sight of his rescuer.

"Why are you here?" White demanded.

"To save you, sir," Jack answered. As he wondered why any explanation was necessary, he was suddenly struck by the madness of it all. Here was he, putting his life at risk, to save a man he would have killed earlier in the evening, had not fate intervened. What an ideal time to get rid of White without being blamed!

"My mind is made up," White said, his voice so hoarse that Jack was not sure whether he heard the man correctly. "Go away. I want no choice in case I weaken. Go out and lock the door again. I did not ask for help."

An anger as hot as the heat around them consumed Jack. "You're coming, like it or not," he croaked, grabbing at White and pulling him towards the door. "I ain't getting blamed for not saving you."

"No! No!" White was shouting, but the fumes took the strength from his utterance and made it sound as though he were whispering. "I have stared death in the face and felt less fear than staring at the rest of my life." Bitterly, he went on, "What has fired my ambition? Nothing more than fear. I have been running away from myself..."

Spitting out the black muck in his mouth, Jack said, "Let's talk outside."

For a moment, sufficient time for Jack to drag him out of the door, White gave in. Jack leaned against the wall, his lungs pulling in the fresh air, but White strained his voice to talk.

"Come? Why? To kill another child? To hear for more endless years the child who cries within me?"

"We all 'ave within us the child we once was, sir. You're no different from the rest of us," he added, losing his patience.

"Do you hear the weeping?" White asked, looking at Jack as though seeing him in a new light. "I think you do."

"I 'ear 'im alright. I 'ear the child 'oo was sent to sea at six years old. I 'ear 'im screaming as 'e feels the lash and the pain of it. And I 'ear the loneliness and the opelessness of it all." His anger at the memory turned on White. "But I 'ear the cries of other children, too. I come 'ere to protect 'em from all as makes them weep. Why did you come 'ere? To cause nothing but pain and grief?"

William White appeared to be searching his memory for the answer and, coughing, prepared to speak.

"They made me," he murmured half to himself, frightened at the recollection. Using the language of childhood he continued, "The big boys beat us. They were so much bigger than we new boys. Then they put the canes in our hands and made us beat each other. When younger boys came, they made us beat them." He took a deep breath and went on, "It gave me peace. Can you believe it, my cruelty brought me peace? How could I be beaten when I wielded the cane?"

It was beyond Jack's understanding and this was no place to waste time. Smoke had crept around the door and the noise above their heads told him the rafters were alight there, too. Again, he pulled at White's arm. "It was you as saved Tom," he urged. "Come on, Mr White, let's save ourselves now."

Somehow, White found the voice to rave at Jack. "Don't you listen?" His face was blackened and swollen from the fire, making his eyes extra bright and prominent. "I cannot help myself Don't you think that I have tried? Good God, do you think I want to do the Devil's work, but he lives in me and will never let me go."

Suddenly, his anger drained from White. "I am doing this for the innocent child I used to be, for the one I saw in the lad just now. Let me do this, I beg you." Mocking himself, he almost laughed, "Surely William John Bull White can act like a man."

"But, sir, your mother?"

"Tell her," White said, smiling weakly, "that I heard a child crying and went back to find him." Without another word, White walked to the door and, moaning quietly as he felt the burn from the door knob, went inside.

Knowing it was madness, but feeling that, after all, there was something in this man worth saving, Jack stepped up to the door. At that second, someone grabbed his arm and spun him round.

"Get out of the way," Paul yelled, holding out the key in his hand. I got to let 'im out. I ain't a murderer," he sobbed, "even if 'e is."

Jack held him back. "The door's unlocked, has been for some time. Now get out of my way. There's a child crying in there. No, don't you go in. Get 'elp, that's the best thing you can do. We need more men. Water, gallons of water. Wet blankets." He snatched at Paul's hand. "Give me that key."

For once in his life, Paul did as he was told. Immediately, Jack checked that he had returned his own key to his pocket. Then he took the one which Paul had returned and put it in the lock. He walked back into the ward.

CHAPTER SIXTY

As consciousness returned, Jack became aware that he was moaning in pain. As his mind came once again to register the messages from his senses one part of it told him to return to sleep, away from the burning sensation on his skin and the dry, aching soreness which filled his throat and chest. Another part, and this he obeyed, told him to try and make sense of his surroundings and that it was important to recall what had happened to him. He realised that he was soaking wet and stifled his moans to listen to what was happening around him. Had the enemy boarded and fired his ship? Had he jumped into the ocean to try and save himself?

As though fighting his way back to the surface, Jack thrashed about and felt restraining, but gentle hands holding him down. Through swollen eyelids he saw people leaning over him. They paused in applying salve to his face and bandaging his arms to smile at him and make jokes about its taking more than the burning down of a ward in the workhouse to kill Jack Star. Wanting to question them, Jack tried to open his mouth, but his swollen lips seemed to have melted together.

"Don't try to talk," Campion advised him. "Sip a little of this ice cold water and let it trickle down your throat"

"'E'd be better off with a lump of butter. That'll sooth his throat," a woman said. She went to fetch some.

Now Jack knew where he was, he struggled to recall how he had got there. Somehow, he knew that he had an important message to pass on, but that he must not just blurt it out. Every single word of it must be exactly right. As events came back to him, he realised that, if he got the message wrong, he could implicate Paul in a crime or even make people think that he, himself, had killed White. The right words kept escaping or becoming jumbled, but at last he felt ready to speak. He must keep it brief and simple. Least said, soonest mended. And he could always add to it later, if he wished. First, he must give the impression that he thought White could still be alive.

"Did White escape, too? Is he alive?"

As Jack had struggled to speak, Campion had leaned down over him. Now he answered, "There's a body in there. We're sure that it's him, but it was right in the eye of the fire. They've stopped the fire spreading, now, but it's still too hot to get the body out. Now, you rest." It was clear that Campion was afraid Jack had prevented White from escaping and was anxious that he should say nothing to incriminate himself.

"And the child," Jack asked, "is he safe?"

"We found no child," Campion answered in a puzzled tone. "They're all accounted for."

"White was sure 'e 'eard a child crying for 'elp. I could 'ear no one, but the noise from the fire were so great I couldn't be certain."

The relief Campion felt was obvious. "That explains why he was in the burning ward," he commented. "We had all been asking ourselves that question."

"Tell his mother," Jack murmured. He added, "White was a very brave man," and fell asleep.

It was a week or more before Jack arose from his sick bed. His reluctance to leave it reflected the seriousness of his wounds and his wish to avoid close questioning. Only he knew the full truth of what had happened and it was only years later that he told me and a few others the facts as I have related them here. At the time, rumour added to rumour, centering on the key found in the lock. The would-be rescuers of Tom swore the doors had been locked with no key in sight, but it was decided, just as Jack had planned, that the key must have dropped out in White's efforts to open the door and had then been kicked aside accidentally by the men. Both White and the men had assumed, in their anxiety and struggle to open it, that the door was locked, when it was, in fact, distorted by the heat and difficult to open at the best of times.

Knowing rumours and inquiries would persist until Mrs White accepted his account of her son's death, Jack at length agreed to her request to visit her, taking Tom with him. Tom, having been scrubbed and attired in clothes given by the townspeople to replace the stock destroyed in the fire, looked quite the little gentleman.

Convinced there was more to the matter than she had so far heard and uncertain what questions to ask, Mrs White asked Tom and Jack to relate the events in their own words. Tom did so eagerly, standing at Mrs White's knee and, as he told how Mr White had saved him and his tin, his eyes were fixed on her face and he put his hand trustingly on hers as they lay on her lap. Listening, Mrs White gazed at the child's face and, after a while, took his hand in hers.

"I see, Mr Star," she observed when Tom had finished speaking, "that I am to learn more about my son than I expected."

"Yes, ma'am," Jack replied, knowing her meaning.

"But, first, Mr Star, tell me how my son came to die in that ward."

Not wishing to become entangled in lies, Jack kept his story simple. "When I see the boy were safely down and realised that Mr White could see that it was not safe for him to jump, I ran upstairs and, after a struggle, opened the ward door to direct him to it through the smoke by my voice. 'E reached me and rested outside for a moment. Then 'e were certain that 'e 'eard a child crying and 'e returned to search for 'im. 'E were buried, I understand, with falling debris. 'E couldn't 'ave been able to get out again. I 'ad followed 'im in, but recall nothing of my time in the ward. They tell me that I must have been knocked out by something falling before I had gone far into the room."

Clearly, Mrs White suspected that this was not the whole truth. "And that is all you can tell me? That is all you will tell me?"

"Yes, ma'am," Jack answered, finding it difficult to look her in the face.

"It seems that I am never to know the whole truth, but I must know that no one else was involved in my son's death. I must have an honest answer to my next question, Mr Star. Did anyone murder my son?"

"No, ma'am," Jack replied without hesitation, relieved to be able to look her in the eye and tell the whole truth.

"Was he in that room of his own free will and able to leave had he wanted?"

"Most certainly ma'am, as God is my witness."

"What were my son's last words?"

"That he could hear a child crying and 'ad to return to find 'im."

Seeing that Mrs White saw these words as confirming her worst fears and not wishing her to think that her son had ended his own life in a cowardly fashion, Jack told her, "I can tell you in all truth that your son was one of the bravest men I have ever known."

With quiet dignity, Mrs White said, "I have no doubt of that, Mr Star." Then she was silent, nestling Tom to her. It was a while before she kissed his head and asked, "And are my suspicions true on this matter?"

"The boy, ma'am? 'E is, indeed, your grandson."

Holding the boy even more tightly and making it clear that she would fight to keep him, Mrs White asked, "Does anyone else have a claim upon him?"

"No, ma'am. Whenever a child is left at the work'ouse, I make it my business to find out all I can about 'im. You might not believe it, ma'am, but there are those 'oo ain't the parents 'oo will claim a child for all sorts of reasons."

"And my grandson? What do you know about him?"

"'Is mother was a respectable young shop girl, who died giving 'im birth. She and the child 'ad been disowned by 'er family." Unable to think of another way of saying that no one wanted to care for a bastard child, he went on, "Rumour 'ad it that the baby was your son's. 'Is mother was not the kind of girl to go with more than one man and she 'ad been seen several times with your son. As Tom's grown, ma'am, 'is looks 'ave confirmed the rumours."

"Did my son know there was a child?"

"Avoiding the fact that White had known since before the child was born and had done nothing to help mother or child, Jack answered, "The child touched 'is 'eart in the end, ma'am. I am quite sure 'e saw 'imself when young in the boy."

"And the child has touched mine already. Where else should my grandson live, but with me?" Smiling at him, she told Tom, "You shall have the room your father had before he went away to school."

"Am I to go away to school?" Tom asked nervously. "1 can read and write hundreds of words."

"No, my child, I shall not make that mistake again."

Realising grandmother and grandson were barely aware of his presence, Jack took his leave. Mrs White had rediscovered her young son in Tom's innocent smile. He was showing her the tin "kind Mr White" had saved from the fire for him.

CHAPTER SIXTY ONE

While Mrs White accepted that no one was to blame for her son's death, except, perhaps, her husband and herself, the authorities were determined that the arsonist responsible for the destruction of the workhouse should be brought to justice. Gideon pleaded innocence, declaring that there were those who had seen him trying to hold the crowd back, but his sons, to save their own skins, were quick to tell everything. The sons were transported and Gideon hoped to join them, but, with all the unrest about the New Poor Law, it was decided that an example must be set for those who might wish to follow Gideon's example. Gideon was duly hanged.

Paul was left to carry the guilt that he had played a part in revealing his father's plans, but I felt and feel no guilt. He deserved to be punished for abandoning Paul, trying to kill me and for bringing down my mother to his own level. As to my mother, she spent a few weeks weeping and pleading with me to look after her, a poor, wronged and weak woman. For a while, Jack and Mary were afraid I might be softhearted and take responsibility for her, as she had never done for me. Then the matter was suddenly taken out of my hands. She took off with a boatman and we heard later that she had deserted him for the lure of London.

And my father? I could not rest until I knew the answer to one question. Did my father really know that he had a son? Had he really washed his hands of me, even before I was born? I discussed the matter with Mary, or, rather, I told her what I planned to do. Mary recommended that I let sleeping dogs lie, but I had to tie up this last end before I could get on living my life. Wisely, Mary did not try to dissuade me.

"When will you go, then?" she asked.

"It's Sunday tomorrow, so I'll set off then. Mr Campion has given me a day off work on Monday. I'll lose a day's pay, Mary, but I have a bit put by and I'll see you're not short when I pay for the week's keep."

"If you're not here for two days, I shall see you pay two days less for your keep, young man," Mary told me in a voice which said she was not having any nonsense from me. "But," she added, "you know travelling on a Sunday isn't as easy as other days. Hemsbridge is a good twenty miles away and you'll not get there and back in two days on foot."

"I'll manage," I replied, "even if I have to limp every time someone comes in sight. And I've got a plan all worked out for when I get there. I'll just look around and find out what I can about my pa .....about Edward Kilsby, without letting on 'oo I am."

"Whatever you think best, Nat," Mary said, clearly deciding my mind was made up and that I would not listen even if she pointed out that that was no plan at all.

The next morning, while it was still dark, I set out to face my father. As it grew light, I managed to find a ride here and there on a boat, a waggon and even on horseback and, for the rest, I cut across fields and footpaths, where I could, and saved myself the odd mile or two. By evening I was walking along the main street through Hemsbridge, a large village, which some might even have called a town. It was only then, tired and weary, that I realised I had no real idea what I would do next.

At that point, as it so often does, Fate took a hand.

"Why are you still hanging about, my lad? I thought you left here long ago." The voice was angry and so was the face of the man who approached me.

I looked behind me to see to whom he was speaking and, finding no one there, looked back at the man.

He was staring at me and then his expression relaxed, "Sorry, lad. You must wonder why I'm shouting at you, when you're a stranger. Or are you?" he asked, gazing at me again. "You're the splitting image of my son. What's your name, lad?"

"'Oo's asking?" I demanded aggressively, not wanting to reveal who I was. Looking at me again, the smile vanished from his face. "Now I know who you are. Just as friendly as him, are you?"

"I am to me friends," I answered.

"Well, that's one difference. He never had any friends."

"'Oo are you talking about?" I wanted to know, having decided, for the moment, to deny all knowledge of my father.

"I bet a tanner you're Edward Kilsby's son, ain't you?"

"My name's Nathaniel Swubble," I said with as much dignity as I could muster, "And I'd be obliged if you'd tell me 'oo you are."

"I'm Jonathon Kilsby and I'd have sworn you were a Kilsby, too. Are you sure you ain't?"

Suddenly, I was blubbering like a child. "I ain't never been sure 'oo I was." I had never spoken a truer word in my whole life.

"There, lad, none of that. Perhaps you don't know the whole truth, any more than we did. He never spoke to me no more than to any of his relations, but we were always given to understand by your mother that you'd died at birth."

"Honest?" I asked, longing for him to answer that this was the Gospel truth. He did and put his hand on my arm.

"Now, come with me and meet me wife and children. As they're my children, that makes 'em your cousins, don't it?" He smiled at me like a man who had just completed a trick of producing a dozen rabbits from a hat.

"Cousins," I repeated, as impressed as if he had. "'Ow many, uncle?"

"That's more like it, nephew. There's six of 'em, as you'll soon see."

We hurried along. I felt as proud as punch to be walking side by side with a relation of mine. "So you're speaking to me father now, are you, uncle?"

Jonathon Kilsby halted and gazed at me.

"What, uncle?" I asked, uncomfortable under his stare.

"He died last week. Your Pa died last week. Didn't you have no idea?"

What could I say? I felt disappointment, anger and sorrow in equal proportions. I would never know whether he would, in spite of himself, have come to love me like a son. And I had been deserted once more.

"So I'll never get to know 'im," I said, at last.

"You wouldn't have got to know him, had he lived. He never acknowledged he had a son. Ain't spoken to me for years, nor any of his relations, even his own mother. We're all too sinful, though we're no better nor worse than anyone else."

By this time, we had arrived at his house and he quickly explained to his wife, without any great fuss, who this blubbering child was. She gave me one big hug and then left my uncle and me to eat the meal, which had appeared as though by magic, while she sat silently in the corner.

We had passed the meal talking of this and that before I could bring myself to ask, "'Ow long did my father know I were still alive?"

Without beating about the bush, my uncle answered, "He saw you at a Sunday school service. You being the image of my boy, he recognised you and learnt you was at the workhouse and the right age to be his son."

"And 'e didn't tell you till a week or so ago?" I asked, wanting confirmation that they had not ignored my existence.

"Just as I said, Nat. He told me on his death bed. You see," he added

324

kindly, "he was thinking about you in the end."

So much did I need to believe that, I accepted it as the truth. Then I felt Jonathon glance towards his wife and she silently gave him permission to introduce another matter.

"Your father left £200 and he asked me to see that you got it."

"I don't want 'is money," I spat out, without a moment's thought.

"That's no way for a sensible young man to talk," my aunt said disapprovingly, "and I'm sure you're a sensible boy being your uncle's nephew. It'll buy you a good apprenticeship in any trade you fancy and keep you 'til you earn your own money."

"I'm a clerk," I said, with pride.

"Know where you get your reading and writing from, then," she said and asked me about my work.

I told her with pride that I was also going into business with Paul, who had inherited the family boat. He would work the boat up and down the canal, while I kept the books and looked out in the Yard for word of loads he could take.

"And who's going to work the boat with him?" my uncle asked.

"We're looking for a good, reliable and honest feller," I told him.

"Look no further," my uncle announced. "Your eldest cousin, a steady feller, has saved up ever since he started work on the boats. He's looking out for a small business to invest his money and himself in."

Once again, my aunt gave my uncle a look and he knew what it meant. He might like the look of me, his new relation, but she wanted to know more about Paul and me before her son joined us in business.

"We'll have to see how things go along," she said. "Is there someone older you know who can look after your interests?"

"Yes, aunt," I answered with pride. "There's Jack Star 'oo 'as always been like a father to me." I told them all about Jack and, if they thought he sounded too good to be true, they came to change their minds when they met him.

As we had talked, my youngest cousins had come quietly into the room and, having stared at me from afar, had gradually gathered around me. When they had reached the stage of familiarity of pushing and shoving to establish who should stand closest to me, my aunt introduced them one by one and I smiled at the shy, but smiling faces looking back at me.

Suddenly, my uncle stood up. "Let's get it over with, then, Nat." It was time for us to go to the churchyard to see my father's grave. Without another word, we walked to the grave yard and I fell in behind my uncle as he led me along the narrow path to the newest grave, marked by a pile of freshly turned earth.

"There," Jonathon murmured, "is the last earthly resting place of your father, Edward Kilsby."

Not knowing what else to do, I looked solemn, removed my cap and bowed my head, but there was a dark, empty place within me where love and respect for my father should have dwelt. Aware that I had no tears to shed, I filled the silence by bending down and gathering up a handful of soil to scatter on the grave.

As though reading my thoughts, my uncle said, "I'll tell you stories of when we were children and never had a care in the world." Then, putting his arm around my shoulder, he went on, "Don't be bitter, Nat. Let his life teach you that, if nothing else, bitterness destroys you from the inside, like an apple rotting from the core."

I stayed with my uncle and aunt until it was time to return to my own home. Paul was full of tales of my cousin, who had been sent to tell me of my father's death, but had missed me as I travelled in the opposite direction. At first, I was jealous that they had become such friends in my absence, but it was soon clear that they had included me in all their plans for the future. I did not think my aunt would have much luck in preventing my cousin, Bob, coming into business with us.

So my childhood drew to a close, with great plans being made for my future. Perhaps, some day, I shall tell you whether these plans worked out for me and for Paul and relate to you what happened next to Tom and to Virtue, who was also adopted by Mrs White, to Felicity and Martin and to Jack and Mary and all the other people of Myddlington. Perhaps, some day, I shall tell you whether I returned in poverty to the workhouse, or moved into the house at the end of the lane.